Sabbat Gigante

NÉSTOR DÍAZ DE VILLEGAS
Sabbat Gigante

LIBRO PRIMERO
Hojas de Rábano

bokeh

© Néstor Díaz de Villegas, 2017

© Fotografía de cubierta: W Pérez Cino, 2017

© Bokeh, 2017

Leiden, NEDERLAND
www.bokehpress.com

ISBN 978-94-91515-73-6

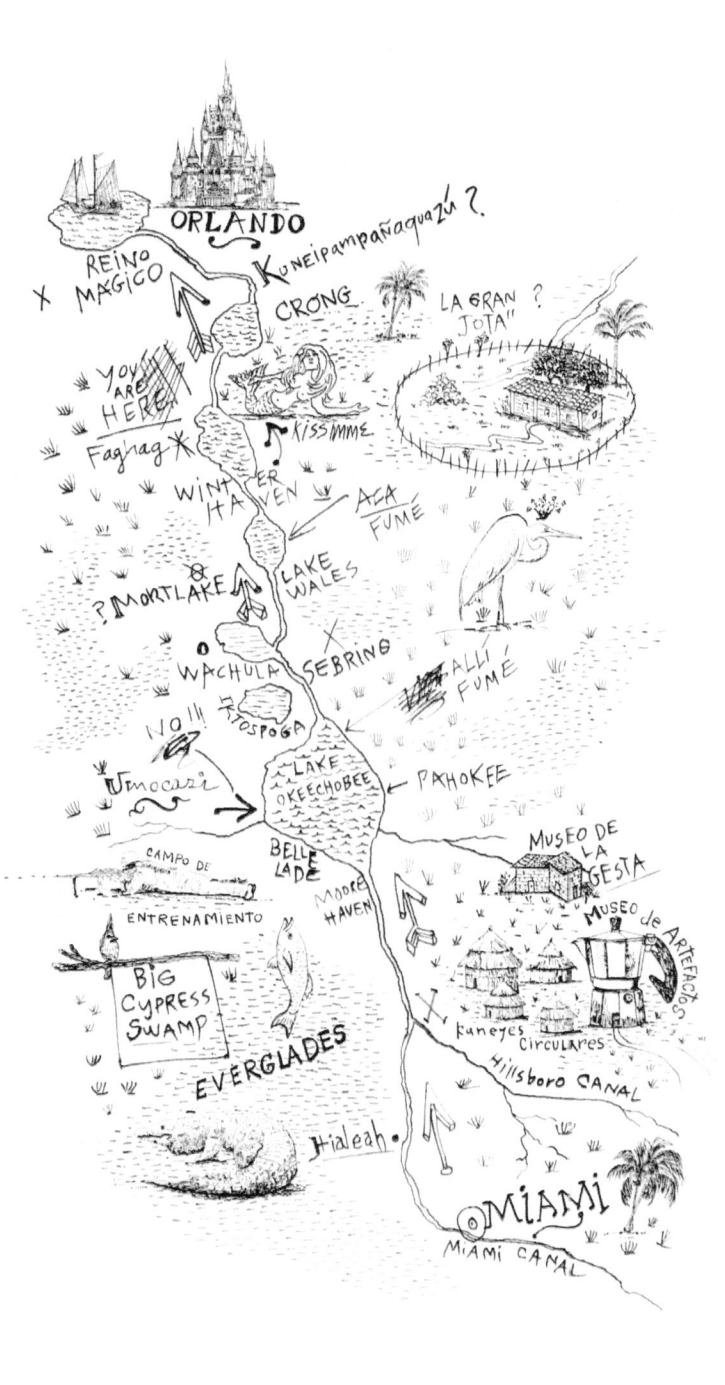

Si deshecha en menudos pedazos…

Bonifacio Byrne

Ecce libro

Aquel que conozca el *Régimen* será honrado por los príncipes y los grandes de la Tierra.

Ireneo Filaleteo

I.

Mis amigos me oyen desbarrar y me piden que escriba un libro; pero, ¿qué libro puedo escribir yo? La idea de la escritura como artimaña y anacronismo de un orden superado se instaló en mi conciencia desde la primera infancia. Si el ateísmo revolucionario me impidió creer en dios, la educación compulsiva consiguió desengañarme de lo libresco. Entonces, ¿para qué escribir?

Fidel Castro hizo su primera aparición en las portadas de las revistas[1], era la creación de una novela por entregas – Herbert Matthews fue su Delia Fiallo[2]. Pertenezco a la edad del libelo y el melodrama. Mi mundo estaba preordinado por la mala escritura.

Los libros que se publicaron en la Cuba de mi juventud eran «los clásicos»; crecí entre tomos muertos que se desho-

---

[1] *Bohemia*, enero 11, 1959; *Life*, enero 19, 1959; *Time*, enero 26, 1959.

[2] Herbert Matthews (New York, 1900-1977), reportero de *The New York Times* que entrevistó a Fidel Castro en la Sierra Maestra, en 1957. Delia Fiallo (La Habana, 1924), célebre telenovelista cubana, autora de *Lucecita* (1967) y *La heredera* (1982), entre otras.

jaban de solo tocarlos. Incapaz de creer en la actualidad, ni en la posibilidad, y mucho menos en la posteridad de los libros, estos nunca se me presentaron como alternativa. Soy el hijo de la analfabetización revolucionaria.

Sucede, además, que resido en el primer mundo y que escribo de una revolución en el tercero, quizás en el cuarto, pues el proceso cubano rebasa los límites del tercermundismo. Privado de un territorio nacional, hablo desde un gueto transnacional. Soy un librepensador esposado a la idea de la dictadura[3].

2.

Mis hábitos de lectura son, como he explicado, los de la analfabetización socialista. El Líder nos impuso su manera de leer, después una cartilla y más tarde un Instituto del Libro. Esto se consideró una conquista social, aunque a la larga resultara ser otra servidumbre. Se ha dicho que nada subyuga como un libro, pero se olvida decir que el más subyugante es aquel que un dictador nos endilga.

«Primero iba al final, después leía un poco en el medio, y solo cuando tenía una idea precisa del contenido comenzaba a devorarlo metódicamente», dice Hugh Trevor-Roper de los hábitos de lectura del *Führer*, en *Hitler's Table Talk*[4].

Fidel y Lezama eran ratones de biblioteca, y Martí llevó a la muerte un tomito de la vida de Cicerón. La lectura

---

3 «Ustedes son libres porque son servidores...» (1 Pedro 2:16, Biblia TLA).

4 *Hitler's Table Talk* (1953). Traducción y notas de H. R. Trevor-Roper. London: Widenfeld & Nicolson.

fanática, propia de próceres, es comunicada al aula, donde se inculcan temas escogidos[5].

Tenía razón Nietzsche en considerar *El Quijote* una desgracia nacional para España: pero no fue en la península sino en «la más española de las colonias ultramarinas» donde el quijotismo llegó a convertirse en instrumento del Terror. Todo ideal fascista tiene su origen en lecturas quijotescas.

En mi caso, sería un abuelo postizo quién me iniciara en la literatura[6], aunque más que de simple lectura se trató de *enseñanza*, en el sentido de revelar o mostrar el libro. Su rica biblioteca ocupaba un oscuro librero en el centro de la casa donde transcurrió lo mejor de mi niñez. Cada tomo estaba forrado en papel de cera y atado con un bramante.

Primero, mi abuelo me hacía lavar las manos con agua y jabón, después colocaba el petate sobre pliegos de periódicos abiertos encima de una mesa. Desataba las soguillas y me dejaba mirar. Así llegué a ver los cuatro antiguos volúmenes de *Los miserables* de Víctor Hugo; los seis tomos encuadernados en piel de becerro de la *Historia de los Girondinos,* de Lamartine; el *Emilio,* de Rousseau; *Cándido,* de Voltaire;

---

5   «I can't quite put my finger on, but I can just imagine some beautiful SS man loving *The Little Prince*». Andre Gregory y Wallace Shawn (1981): *My Dinner with Andre*. Por lo que a mí respecta, pido disculpas de antemano por no haber resistido la tentación de las notas al pie [contra J. D. Salinger, que las consideraba un «crimen estético», *an aesthetic evil*]. En cambio, aquí las notas aparecen como *evidencias*, son parte de una *estética del crimen*.

6   José Pedro López López, y su esposa, Concepción Rabassa Rabassa, la comadrona que me «recibió». Si bien no llegué a ser el ahijado de esta singular pareja de ocultistas —algo que ellos le reprocharon siempre a mis padres— fui en cambio el elegido de entre todos los recibidos, el bienamado, el discípulo y el vástago espiritual.

Ramuntcho, de Pierre Loti; *Urania* y *La pluralidad de los mundos habitados*, de Camille Flammarion.

Cada tarde, a la hora de la siesta, mi abuela se tumbaba en el cuarto del fondo y yo me acurrucaba contra su espalda entalcada, encarando el sillón de respaldar alto desde donde el amado anciano, que me había adoptado como discípulo, descubría para mí el misterio de los libros.

3.

¿Cómo pasar por alto el hecho de que mi prometedora carrera de pintor moderno fuera promovida y, a la vez, abortada, por el mismo sistema docente del nuevo orden nacionalsocialista? Considerando el entorno del último medio siglo en Cuba tampoco es casual que mi biografía presente más de una grotesca coincidencia con la del joven Adolfo Hitler[7].

También yo arribé a las puertas de la Academia con el firme propósito de presentarme a los exámenes de ingreso: mi traslado a la capital, a los quince años, por medios e iniciativa propios, no solo revela el tamaño de mis ambiciones juveniles, sino la afinidad esencial de ambos períodos.

Sufrir que otros más talentosos o afortunados dieran el salto hacia la inalcanzable Escuela Nacional de Arte de La Habana mientras yo quedaba rezagado en la Escuela Provincial de Arte de Las Villas fue una de las experiencias más amargas de mi vida. Adelantándome a la conclusión del curso escolar exigí tomar allí las pruebas de admisión,

---

[7] «Mi más caro deseo es poder deambular por Italia como un pintor desconocido». Trevor-Roper 1953: 11.

y fui rechazado. Un año más tarde me expulsaban también de San Alejandro, la academia de segunda por la que tuve que transarme. De pronto me vi solo en la ciudad más hostil al forastero que pueda imaginarse, sin otro refugio que la casa de mis parientes en la calle San Lázaro (¡*entre Genios y Cárcel!*). Fue entonces que, al estilo de los despechados, busqué consuelo en la poesía[8].

4.

¿Dónde se encuentra el puente [*Brücke*] avizorado por mí que conecta el expresionismo y el fascismo[9]? Peter Selz lo señala en su célebre estudio sobre el tema: «Al expresionista

---

[8] «La inclinación consciente hacia las artes plásticas fue tan fuerte en Goethe que en un período trascendental de su vida llegó a considerarse destinado, efectivamente, a la práctica de esa forma de arte y, de algún modo, entendió su labor poética como una manera de compensación por la frustrada carrera de pintor». Richard Wagner, *Beethoven*, traducción al inglés de Albert R. Parsons, Indianapolis: Benham Brothers, 1873.

[9] «Ahora él vaga por las calles, muerto de hambre; a veces empeña y vende sus últimas posesiones; su ropa está cada vez más sucia; y así se hunde en su entorno, que, sumándose a las degracias materiales, también le emponzoña el alma. Si lo desalojan, o si (como pasa a menudo), el desahucio ocurre en invierno, su miseria es grande. A veces encuentra algún tipo de empleo, pero la misma historia se repite. Y vuelve a repetirse una segunda vez, y la tercera es aún peor, y poco a poco aprende a soportar la eterna inseguridad, cada vez con mayor indiferencia. Por fin, la repetición se vuelve hábito». Adolfo Hitler, «El destino del trabajador», *Mein Kampf*, 1927. Traducción al inglés de Ralph Manheim. Boston: Houghton Mifflin, 1943. A propósito de este nuevo estilo de escritura, Bertolt Brecht exclama: «¡El expresionismo es espantoso!».

le preocupa la proyección visual de su experiencia emotiva. En general, lo impulsa la necesidad de expresar conflictos irresueltos, con la sociedad y con sus propias ansiedades. Lo cual resulta, frecuentemente, en afiebradas acusaciones y afirmaciones urgentes del yo, expresadas con extrema agitación formal. El dramatismo casi nunca está ausente de la pintura expresionista y el artista es más dado a atacar el lienzo que a acariciarlo»[10].

Una de las grandes ironías de la Historia del Arte, según se desprende del párrafo anterior, es que el *Führer* llegara a insertarse en el mismo movimiento artístico que condenó por degenerado. La degeneración vendría a ser, entonces, una función estética recursiva. Es lo que parece sugerir Ralph Manheim en el prólogo a la traducción inglesa de *Mi lucha*, cuando escribe que Hitler «arremetió contra el crisol multicultural vienés, aunque estaba inconscientemente influido por su estilo literario»[11].

El interés de los expresionistas por el arte medieval, el grabado gótico y la escultura primitiva, encuentra un complemento en el gusto hitleriano por el cine, la historieta, la ópera wagneriana, la arquitectura clásica y la metafísica popular. En el caso de Fidel Castro, se alaba su inmensa capacidad para el ensamblaje de datos, la viñeta histórica y la dialéctica fácil. Se trata, en ambos casos, de eclecticismos: como agregado de lecturas dispersas, el fascismo es la fuente de todo multiculturalismo.

---

[10]   Peter Selz (1957): *German Expressionist Painting*. Berkeley: University of California Press.

[11]   «Hitler inveighed against the Vienesse melting pot, but was unconsciously influenced by its literary style». Manheim (1943), «Introduction». En *Mein Kampf*, xvii.

Se cuenta que a la sola mención de la palabra «cultura», Goebbels solía llevarse la mano a la pistola[2], y en la medida en que el vanguardismo fue un automatismo, esa reacción maquinal define la moderna praxis artística. ¿Olvidamos acaso que el objetivo último de la vanguardia era la muerte de la cultura, su *solución final*?

Pero mi verdadero propósito es mostrar aquí cómo el artista, herido en su amor propio, impugna el veredicto del destino, sin entender que precisamente a causa del fracaso se le abren las puertas de la gloria, pues la expulsión, el ridículo y la emblemática patada en el culo son las constancias de su lucha y del triunfo ineluctable de su voluntad.

5.

El hecho de que mi carrera fuera interrumpida por la cárcel (1974-79) significa que no llegué a ingresar en la universidad, ni a realizar estudios superiores. La interrupción provocó un estado permanente de creación, pues embarqué en un programa autodidacta que no culminaría nunca.

Los cincuenta son el momento propicio, el tiempo justo que me confiere la perspectiva correcta. He dejado pasar

---

12   «Wenn ich Kultur höre... entsichere ich meinen Browning!». «Cuando oigo hablar de cultura... le quito el seguro a mi Browning!», la célebre frase aparece en la obra teatral *Schlageter* (acto I, escena I), del dramaturgo expresionista Hanns Johst (1890-1978), dicha por el personaje de Thiemann, en diálogo con el protagonista: «Conozco toda esa basura desde el año dieciocho... fraternidad, igualdad... libertad... belleza y dignidad. ¡Se necesita una buena carnada para pescarlas! Tienes la palabra en la boca y de pronto te dicen: "¡Manos arriba! ¿Andas desarmado, cerdo votante republicano?" No, no, lejos de mí con todo ese ajiaco ideológico...».

medio siglo para acercarme a mi objetivo: estoy hecho con los materiales de mi propio proceso cincuentenario. Tal vez fuera preciso esperar tras las alambradas: esa fue mi formación. Lo que aprendí en las canteras no lo anticiparon los constructores de socialismos.

Últimamente, debido al deterioro y la corrupción, han salido a la luz las interioridades del régimen, pero yo vi sus sellos en las puertas, sufrí en sus internados, conocí sus hábitos y tendencias, padecí la promiscuidad de la carne y la confusión de las clases, dormí debajo de un puente, comí de basureros, robé en los supermercados, descendí a mazmorras cada vez más estrechas hasta llegar a residir en un armario, esperando en cualquier momento la llegada de la policía.

6.

«Viena, la ciudad que para muchos es el epítome del placer inocente, ese hermoso parque de los enamorados, para mí, lamento decirlo, representa apenas un lacerante recuerdo del período más triste de mi vida... La sola mención de *la ciudad fenicia* evoca cinco años de vicisitudes y miseria».

[Nota del traductor Ralph Manheim: «La alusión a la isla feliz de los fenicios es común en Alemania, aunque no tanto en los países de habla inglesa. Que Hitler la mencione no quiere decir que haya leído La Odisea»].

Observar cómo para Carleton Beals, Ernest Hemingway y Francis Ford Coppola, La Habana es la ciudad fenicia precisamente a causa de su libertinaje; en cambio, para Meyer Lansky, Libertad Lamarque y Lucho Gatica, es el lugar de los placeres inocentes. También los cubanos somos fenicios y con frecuencia nos cita alguien que no leyó el libro: *¡Los* *fenicios!* Tampoco esa interjección cubana tendría sentido en los países de habla inglesa[13].

«No fue por su propio esfuerzo que el conejillo de Indias pudo salir sano y salvo de la mala experiencia», lamenta el Franz Biberkopf que llegaría a ser Canciller[14]. De modo que también mi tarea era denunciar el error expresionista, ir más allá del adorno, la bagatela y el detalle sórdido. Más allá de la Cultura.

He aquí que nuestro demagogo se agencia una barba, un bigote y un traje verdeolivo, el disfraz «tipo C» de Jeremiah Peachum[15], y sale a explotar la riqueza que la ciudad ofrece, el oro del sentimentalismo, el filón inagotable de mala conciencia. Los imponderables –penuria, fatalidad, indigencia– entran con él en el mercado de la susceptibilidad socialista.

7.

Advertid cómo el Líder reclama los temas sagrados (el Apóstol, la Sierra, los Doce, la Epifanía, etc.) Debemos construir mitologías personales, mitologizar enérgicamente con el material de nuestras propias biografías (Kurt Gödel:

---

13   Lo de *Five Years* parece coincidir con el *lustrum* de la canción homónima de David Bowie (1972). Cfr. Manuel de la Caridad Mitre (2001): *Repertorio musical estéreo como acompañamiento del Sabbat*.

14   Ralph Manheim (1943): «Introduction». En *Mein Kampf*, xviii.

15   «Mire, señor Peachum, desde pequeño he sido un desgraciado. Mi mamá era una borracha y mi padre un jugador. Abandonado a mi suerte desde muy temprano, sin la amorosa guía de una madre, me fui hundiendo cada vez más en el cieno de la gran ciudad. Nunca he conocido los cuidados paternales ni la bendición de un hogar acogedor». Bertolt Brecht (1928): *La ópera de los tres centavos*.

«¡Generalicemos categóricamente en el sentido del mínimo común!»). Por mi parte, puedo añadir que el camino de este libro, su recorrido, comienza en un autobús de la Grayhound, el lobo gris que me conduce de este a oeste en el territorio norteamericano. Mi trayecto es el tránsito que *El libro de Lambspring* ilustra con el doble emblema del perro corasceno y la perra de Armenia: un salto mortal, una traslación metafísica, el viaje de Santiago el Mayor y el de Cristóforo cargando al Niño.

Así como el difunto es transportado de Menfis a Tebas, mi pasaje dobló la ruta de la columna fidelista, el trayecto de Anubis, la travesía de Abram, de Harán a Betel[16]. Se trataba de un *espín*, o gambito cuántico, y de una bifurcación (*Entzweiung*). Parto del Atlántico y llego al Pacífico; arranco del pantano y arribo a la montaña. Pero, antes, referiré mi expulsión, o mi «salida» de Miami, que se debió enteramente a circunstancias ocultas, pues el 22 de diciembre de 1999 había tropezado con un tal Lázarus a la entrada de la casa de Haydee la santera. Lázarus llevaba puesto un bonete rojo de Santa Claus y, enseguida, apenas nos conocimos, partimos ladinamente hacia mi apartamento[17]. Ese apartamento, en los altos de una vieja mansión dividida en un piso alto y otro bajo, había sido, durante veinte años, la residencia de los esposos Fernando y Miñuca Villaverde [cineastas], por lo que yo lo bauticé con el nombre de Villa Verde, morada filosofal y antro de Mercurio donde escribí algunos de mis

---

16   «Vuestros padres habitaron antiguamente de esotra parte del río… y servían a dioses extraños». Josué, 24:2, Reina-Valera, 1909.

17   Lazarus, del hebreo *Eleazar* (El'azar), hijo de Aaron, gran sacerdote, significa «Dios ayuda». La fiesta de Lázaro de Betania, el santo mendigo, se celebra en Cuba el 17 de diciembre.

tratados secretos[18]. Allí entramos y allí se entabló una breve *liaison dangereuse* que desembocaría en la debacle. Lázarus era un santero que montaba los espíritus de varios esclavos muertos, entre ellos, el de una virgen negra. Esa virgencita, de aretes de oro y vestidos prestados, merodeaba la Villa mientras yo escribía los sonetos de *Por el camino de Sade*[19].

Ahora debo decir que fui dedicado a San Lázaro, el Babalú Ayé yoruba, a causa de una dolencia infantil. En 1958, a los dos años de edad, enfermé de polineuritis, un caso grave que requirió hospitalización. [No valdría la pena mencionar aquí mi ingreso en la Clínica Moderna de Cienfuegos si no fuera porque el doctor Carlos Dorticós Torrado, hermano del futuro Presidente de la República, fue mi médico de cabecera]. Mi madre recurrió entonces a la santería, acudió a los brujos, a alguna negra vieja del Escombray que probablemente había consultado antes por otros motivos, y por consejo de esa santera se vistió de saco y pidió limosnas durante un año[20]. Con el dinero de las dádivas mandó a hacer unas piernitas de plata que deben colgar todavía en los muros del templo de El Rincón. Mi recuperación milagrosa, luego de varios meses de invalidez, resultó en la promesa de vestirme de rojo por un período de *cinco años*. La promesa nunca fue cumplida, al menos exteriormente: en lo oculto llevo vestido de rojo toda la vida; es decir, de Azufre, variante tonal del cárdeno, el color del

---

18   Miñuca Villaverde (1984): *Ciudad de las carpas*, documental; Fernando Villaverde (1964): *El mar*, cortometraje, La Habana.

19   *In nothing art thou black save in thy deeds, / And thence this slander, as I think, proceeds.* W. Shakespeare, Sonnet CXXXI; *Por el camino de Sade / Sade's Way*. San Francisco: Pureplay Press, 2003.

20   «Pero yo, cuando ellos enfermaron, me vestí de saco». Tehillim, 35:13.

Mercurio filosófico. Desde un principio pasé a formar parte de una arlequinada alquímica: llevo un traje *interiorizado* color fuego.

A la familia de mi madre se le conocía en el pueblo con el nombre de Los Colorados, y es probable que los Machado [*maqqaba*, macabeos], gente pecosa de ojos pardos y cabellera bermeja, fueran judíos portugueses[21]. San Lázaro, Saturno, o el Perro, es, desde entonces, mi lazarillo y tutor, y sus muletas de plata me llevan por el camino oculto que va del levante al poniente, de Miami a La Meca. Pero nada de eso Lázarus lo veía. Mi huída, como siervo fugitivo que abandona la Villa Verde y viaja en un *barco de piedra* —el sarcófago de la Grayhound— hacia la ciudad de Los Ángeles, era un evento que no entregaba su símbolo indiscriminadamente.

8.

Este libro no quiere parecerse a ninguna de nuestras disquisiciones platónicas: es la biografía no autorizada de la Cuba nacionalsocialista. La novelística no tiene cabida aquí, ni la poética, y mucho menos el fraude del barroco,

---

21 «Otra característica del Judas de los autos sacramentales es el color rojo del cabello… y es posible que el rojo, que es el color de la sangre, estuviera reservado para aquellos personajes protagónicos que encarnaban a asesinos: Judas, por haber aceptado el dinero sangriento y por su conexión con el Campo de Sangre, y Herodes a causa de la Masacre de los Inocentes». Hyam Maccoby (1992): *Judas Iscariot and the Myth of the Jewish Evil*. Así, en 1 Samuel, 17:42, encontramos la siguiente descripción del rey David: «Y cuando el filisteo miró y vió a David lo tuvo en poco; porque era joven y rojo (*ish adomim*) y de hermoso parecer». *Sagradas Escrituras*, 1569. La designación davídica tiene la misma raíz de los vocablos «Edom» e «idumeo».

porque el barroquismo, en tiempos de Castro, deberá ser denunciado como degeneración.

Castro *imita* lo cubano (dato importante: ¡este extranjero no sabe bailar!). El castrismo es el doblaje del espectáculo musical batistiano y el efecto nefasto de lo foráneo en las *bellas formas* nacionales[22]. Castro es el cubano caído que parodia los ritmos y la pulsión de su entorno[23].

Castro es un inmigrante español en La Habana; al Moncada regresa con un pelotón de voluntarios. El movimiento inverso aparece en la Avellaneda, insertada diacrónicamente en el panteón ibérico: transmigraciones de lo cubanœspañol[24]. La avellanedización del estro nativo y su peregrinaje de vuelta a la Madre Patria, los años perdidos de Martí en Valencia, su bachillerato en Zaragoza, etc., son los antecedentes históricos que facilitarán, llegado el momento, la adopción del tirano por la Comunidad [espiritual] Autónoma de Galicia.

Los Castro son cubanos conversos. Los criollos los tratan de *sâle mètèque* y ven en su gesta el doblaje de la Guerra Civil española –la gran guerra sucia– ahora corregida y reimaginada, pues entre nosotros la facción republicana resultó

---

[22]   «Los extranjeros son admitidos solo como un favor, y únicamente a condición de que no violen la bella forma». Immanuel Kant (1790): *Crítica del juicio estético.*

[23]   «Imitation is the activity of an incomplete being in search of completeness [...] Orgasmic pleasure is the feeling of achievement experienced by an incomplete being». Branko Bokun (1977): *Man: The Fallen Ape.* New York: Doubleday.

[24]   «El fogoso orador Alfredo Zayas... llegó a afirmar que la Avellaneda había venido a *tomar posesión de España en nombre de las letras y de la poesía cubanas*...» Lorenzo Cruz-Fuentes (1996): *Gertrudis Gómez de Avellaneda, Autobiografía y cartas.* Huelva: Diputación Provincial de Huelva.

victoriosa. Es esa la seudorepública que triunfa el primero de enero de 1959[25]. El castrismo nos entrega atados de pies y manos a la iberización escatológica y la transliteración jacobea.

Si los españoles pudieron entender la revolución cubana como doblaje, como culminación de un proceso histórico pendiente, es porque el quijotismo se las hizo inteligible. [La revolución es un juguete. Solo es cuestión de atizar el principio lúdico presente en el manejo de la acción heroica y todo el mundo jugará al castrismo].

Esta sencilla adaptación debería ser considerada una buena nueva, pues los contenidos de la gnosis fascista presentes en la administración del Estado cubano, y de las entidades políticas que se desprenden de ellos, son renormalizados: con el castrismo, los símbolos del autoritarismo hispánico quedan insertos en un programa moderno.

9.

De modo que la escritura –o su simulacro– aparece en mí automáticamente como consecuencia de leer veinte, treinta y hasta cuarenta libros al mismo tiempo. Los libros procrean literatura, sobre todo si no se los termina, si se les frecuenta como meras fuentes de información y saqueo, como trozos selectos, arbitrariamente escogidos.

---

[25] «Also he [Guevara] had several friends who were children of Spaniards exiled by or killed in the Spanish Civil War. The role of such political aware children of Spain cannot be overestimated in discussing the Latin-American revolutionary experience». Hugh Thomas (1971): *Cuba: The Pursuit of Freedom.* New York: Harper & Row.

Si tenemos en cuenta que en el estado de ansiedad «la información del medio ambiente exterior es rápida y selectivamente procesada en base a consideraciones esquemáticas internas»[26], entonces, en un estado de «angustia ética» (Carlos González Palacios, *Valoración de José Martí*, 1953[27]), nos sentiremos sensorialmente prostituidos, como si nos entregáramos a mil autores al mismo tiempo.

Finalmente tenía asegurada la indispensable angustia. La amargura acumulada produjo ansiedad, y la ansiedad parió, a su vez, una mala conciencia. La congoja anticastrista era mi imperativo y el nudo argumental de mi «novela». Pero (dudé entonces), ¿acaso no era el conocimiento bíblico, libresco, el principio corruptor? El conocimiento prostituye, pues al saber demasiadas cosas, al concebir ideas disímiles en promiscuidad con múltiples autores, quedamos preñados de íncubos.

Si traducir es traicionar, me dije, leer es concebir criaturas de las traiciones, ya que la lectura comporta la traslación desde el nivel P1 de percepción semiautomática al R1-R2 de registro e incorporación en la memoria. El fenómeno de *rapid sampling* descrito por Bonanno y Singer, en *Bipolar modes of subjective regulation*, equivale a un «probarlo todo» y a un *se vale todo*[28].

La red mundial de comunicaciones viabiliza esta actividad básica del espíritu humano: la conexión simultánea

---

[26]   George A. Bonanno & Jerome L. Singer (1990): *Repressive Personality Style: Theoretical and Methodolical Implications for Health and Pathology*, Chicago: University of Chicago Press.

[27]   «Limpia congoja», dice Fryda Schultz de Mantovani, en *Genio y figura de José Martí*, 1970.

[28]   Bonanno & Singer 1990: 181.

de todas las cosas (mi Sabbat requiere la lectura *ipso facto* de unos comentarios producidos *super tempus*). Existe un número finito de contenidos en la memoria que compite de acuerdo a las leyes del movimiento browniano: mi pensamiento, o su manifestación fenomenológica, ocurre por superposición probabilística de estados particulares (Pascal; *Pensées*, 372). Admito que llegado a este punto me resultó imposible detener la avalancha de asociaciones.

Habiendo manoseado y peinado, en fin, todas las bibliotecas disponibles en mi nuevo entorno, me disponía a dar inicio a mi historia. El vocablo «exhaustivo» viene a la mente al hablar del forrajeo metódico. Empatando y zurciendo *exhaustivamente* –la Física, la Cábala, la Lógica y la Mayéutica– arribé a la conclusión de que *El Monte*[29] de Lydia Cabrera debía ser mi modelo; un libro al parecer confuso y carente de estructura, pero que en realidad consigue la formulación de una superestructura caótica y la fundación de una nueva normativa estocástica: Lydia no solo «habla como los negros» (en los *Cuentos negros de Cuba*[30]) sino que razona con las categorías contraculturales del esclavo (en *El Monte*). ¡Precisamente lo que necesitaba!

En el registro del análisis literario cubano falta un estudio de la organización secreta de *El Monte*. Recordemos que *La jungla*, de Wifredo Lam, presenta el mismo corte ortogonal al rebanamiento de lo real[31]. Lydia crea un nuevo orden

---

[29]   Lydia Cabrera (1954): *El Monte: igbo, finda, ewe orisha, vititi nfinda (Notas sobre las religiones, la magia, las supersticiones y el folklore de los negros criollos y el pueblo de Cuba)*. La Habana: ediciones CR.

[30]   Lydia Cabrera (1936): *Contes nègres de Cuba*. Paris: Gallimard.

[31]   «El rebanamiento ortogonal es como un destorcimiento de la fibra», explica David Malament en su *Introduction to Gödel*, 1995.

iterativo: sus cuentos negros carecen de sentido direccional. Tampoco puede decirse que exista direccionalidad en la cosmogonía de *La jungla*: la sabiduría afrocubana radica más bien en la manera de «ver las cosas», en la práctica de generalizaciones[32].

La aparición de Fidel Castro, como cualquier evento sincrético, es, vista desde esta perspectiva, el cumplimiento de una profecía que abarca la totalidad de la *Weltanschauung* yoruba: el advenimiento del «ngánda» o destino [santo] encarnado. El Monte dotado de ánima es Eggüe, nuestro bosque de Birnam, allí donde los negros brujos anunciaron a uno «no nacido de vientre de mujer», un «desmadrado» al que habían robado el alma en la cuna [*Prolem sine matre creatam*. Ovidio, *Metamorfosis*, II, 553].

10.

Pero he aquí que mi Nueva Ciencia, mi reflexión política, se presenta como una disciplina del olvido. Reclamar el olvido que nos hizo perder la memoria de la existencia

---

32   María Hortensia de Rioja (en su *Enseñanza de Sabbat Gigante*, suplemento literario del *Heraldo Cubano-Americano* correpondiente a la edición del 8 de septiembre de 2005) comenta lo siguiente: «Lo que Lam pintó en *La jungla* es lo que [Herbert] Matthews vió en la Sierra. El castrismo es la nueva brujería: su revelación depende del mismo macabro, del mismo ímpetu superticioso y el mismo sincretismo jesuita-karabalí. Me explico: en el cuadro de Lam aparece la "sacra milicia", unos fantasmas que nos pasan por delante en una columna infinita cuya superposición de estados solo existe en lo oculto. El castrismo depende de esas presencias, de esas prendas situadas en el más allá. El *deceso*, más que el deseo, lo carga de fuerza. Al conjunto de apariciones esotéricas (entidades espagíricas) llamamos "los guerreros"; su materialización histórica, de acuerdo a Isaac Kámara, es el castrismo».

previa —aunque, por esta única vez, de manera auténticamente contrarrevolucionaria.

El acto de recordar, en el universo castrista, estaba condicionado por la creencia, pero a partir de ahora, rememorar ha de ser lo contrario de todo creer. Provocar el olvido del olvido: es a un *ars oblivionalis* a lo que aspiramos. Una vuelta en redondo a fin de revivir la realidad que cayó en la conmemoración y que encontró allí su muerte prematura.

Sabbat Gigante

Seré un Don Francisco. Los escritores que interprete serán mis celebridades. Es como *re*-animador, como conductor, que entiendo mi tarea, circunscrita a las exigencias del puro entretenimiento. Un oportunista que se vale de la fama ajena para conseguir lo que quiere[33]. Mi libro será, entonces, un programa, en el sentido político del término y también en el sentido computacional: es decir, una máquina universal, una *máquina gigante*.

Dante, Milton, Blake, Martí, Fidel, Cervantes: nigromantes, empresarios, productores de escenas, interrogadores de celebridades, famosos antes que otra cosa, creadores de espectáculo, que es el producto universal neto. Nabokov concluyó, en su novela póstuma[34], que éramos arlequines. Poner a un arlequín a hablar, a matar, a tomar jugo de tomate, a comer un sándwich, a asaltar un cuartel y una

---

[33] «El científico debe aparecer a los ojos del epistemólogo sistemático como un oportunista inescrupuloso». Albert Einstein, *Albert Einstein: Philosopher-Scientist. Reply to Criticisms*, 1949. «Lo mismo podría decirse del novelista», acota Kámara. [N. de la E.]

[34] Vladimir Nabokov (1974): *Look at the Harlequins!* New York: McGraw Hill. El tema del arlequín, examinado extensamente en este libro, aparece en una escena clave de la *La muerte y la brújula* (1942), fantasía política del argentino Jorge Luis Borges.

nación; crear un Robin Hood, una selva y un molino de viento: Don Quijote como Don Francisco[35].

12.

Medallones para Sabbat: «...volver al aquelarre de brujas de Guamuhaya, el Monte Hermón de los rebeldes, los *comedores de vacas*. La naturaleza sensual del bosque consiguió que los hombres del Segundo Frente descuidaran la revolución y que solo se ocuparan de hacer el amor a las terneras; dedicados a la comida y la bebida, al sacrificio de reses y el corte de carne: un *carnaval* en sentido estricto. "Mientras haya carne hay esperanza", sentencia Dalia Pérez en *La carne de René*[36]. Los comevacas eran cofrades de la carne, y vivían en la cueva de La Vieja. Vuelan brujas que expulsan pedos por los traseros. Transvección sobre escobas de palmiche. Aparece la Niña de Placetas. Allí hubo una carnicería...»

13.

Medallones para Sabbat: «¡Por fin entro en materia! Poco a poco vislumbro el propósito de un libro que se presenta como pieza totalitaria. Que nada falte; después, vaciar, estro-

---

35   «Someone brought tomato juice, ham sandwiches made with crackers and tins of coffee. In honor of the occasion, Senor Castro broke open a box of good Havana cigars and for the next three hours we sat there while he talked». Herbert L. Matthews (1957): «Cuban Rebel is Visited in Hideout». *The New York Times*, febrero 24.

36   Virgilio Piñera (1952): *La carne de René*. Buenos Aires: Siglo XX.

pear y dejar muerta la letra. Concebir el castrismo como el más grande fiasco literario jamás acaecido. La espectacularidad del desastre creó las condiciones de su serialización, de manera que los extremos se tocan: si el poeta, llámese Isaac Kámara o Fernando de Call, ha fracasado vergonzosamente en producir escritura, escogerá entonces el camino del castrismo. "Había una vez una república…", escribe el tirano, y será él quien nos haga el cuento de la República[37]. Y también: "Os voy a contar una *historia*", donde el ambiguo vocablo toma una segunda acepción política. *¡Incipit Cuba Nuova!* Aquí me engancho, viajo en la barba, en el lomo, en los hombros, en la lengua de ese gigante. Hacer historia es terminar por el principio…»

14.

La malhadada excursión de Herbert L. Matthews y su esposa

Esposa

Llevé a mi esposa en el carro como camuflaje. Cuba está en el tope de la estación turística y nada podía lucir más inocente que una parejita de viajeros americanos mediotiempo.

Paño

Me puse la ropa que había comprado en La Habana para una excursión de pesquería, suficientemente gruesa para el aire frío de las noches en la sierra y suficientemente encubridora para servir de camuflaje.

---

[37] Fidel Castro Ruz (1953): *La Historia me absolverá.*

MUSICALIZACIÓN

Los hombres del señor Castro tienen una señal característica que llegué a escuchar insistentemente: dos chiflidos bajos, suaves, atonales.

ESCENOGRAFÍA

a) La luz de la luna era intensa.

b) Matojos y arboledas tupidas, chorreando agua de lluvia, el suelo fangoso y enchumbado cubierto de una gruesa capa de hojas.

c) Finalmente salimos del camino y nos deslizamos por la cuesta de una loma hasta un arroyo oscuro que corría, fangoso, bajo la luna.

d) Sabíamos que había tropas rodeándonos.

SONIDO

Por fin oímos un cauteloso chiflido de bienvenida, un chiflido doble, al que uno de los nuestros respondió con otro chiflido.

BOSQUE

Hubo un breve cuchicheo, nos hicieron señas, nos deslizamos por una cuesta hasta una arboleda. Las hojas y las ramas chorreando, la densa vegetación, el fango bajo las suelas, el claro de luna, todo daba la impresión de una jungla tropical, más parecido a Brasil que a Cuba. La oscuridad del bosque no permitía distinguir nada.

PIROTECNIA

Hablaron en susurros. Un hombre me contó como había visto a las tropas gubernamentales destrozar y dar candela a la tienda de víveres de un hermano suyo, y cómo lo arrastraban fuera de la tienda y lo mataban.

Luz
   Con la llegada de la luz pude ver cuán jóvenes eran.

Encuentro fortuito con los símbolos alquímicos

El Pulguero de la Cuarenta estaba situado en un antiguo autocine que todavía en 1985 conservaba los viejos altoparlantes dispersos por el estacionamiento y la gran pantalla encalada: detrás de la pantalla estaba la casa de los encargados. El *drive-in* abría los días de semana, y los sábados y domingos se transformaba en un rastro. Por aquel entonces yo frecuentaba el pulguero, allí tuve la primera revelación del fin del mundo. De pronto me vi metido en una muchedumbre, arrastrado por una turba que corría sin dirección fija por los callejones, entre abarrotes de géneros y pequeñas quincallas, y entendí que, aunque existía y probablemente seguiría existiendo, el mundo había tocado a su fin. Me acerqué temblando a una tienda donde un buhonero ofrecía una serie de objetos disímiles calzados con libros y colocados sobre una alfombra. Enciclopedias, muñequitos de porcelana, relojes de cuerda y tres escudos de madera tallada: uno, con los instrumentos de laboratorio, otro del que no recuerdo los detalles, y un tercero, rematado por una corona, que ostentaba, en abismo, una estrella bermeja de seis puntas entre ramas de roble[38]. Lo adquirí por cuatro

---

[38]   *La estrella de los magos.* Oro niño, oro rejuvenecido, reyezuelo.

dólares y le pedí al vendedor que me separara los otros. Así
me lo prometió. Regresé el sábado siguiente y pregunté por
él, pero se había marchado. Desapareció del rastro y nunca
más volví a verlo.

16.

Una De Call, diez de Arenas (construcción de un personaje)

Existe una sincronicidad de diversos factores (históricos,
éticos, etiológicos) en la Pasión de Fernando de Call[39] que
hace coincidir la plaga, los males del Mariel, el cáncer, la
escritura, el éxodo, el sexo, la pederastia, los humores, los
tumores, la travesía, el choteo, la fiebre y la mecanografía
en un solo proceso sinérgico-luciferino.

Consustanciación. También los elementos simples sucum-
ben: el pan y el vino son la carne y la sangre de la Bestia. El
mero hecho de existir, según Fernando, equivale a participar
involuntariamente de la eucaristía castrista. El sida, esa
enfermedad creada por «el hombre», es otro síndrome, otra
afección política. Reinaldo pronostica un mundo afligido
por los más graves padecimientos, una vía dolorosa que es
la Vía Seca[40].

---

[39] Pseudonombre novelístico asignado aquí arbitrariamente al escritor
cubano Reinaldo Arenas (1947-1990), en lo adelante llamado también De Call,
Call (*kahal*), o simplemente, *Fernando* (ABBA, 1976).

[40] «Esta Vía Seca, que te enseñaré y que describiré para ti, es bastante
peligrosa, pero si sigues mis enseñanzas, no te ocasionará daños». Rabí Abraham Eleazar (1760): *Antiguo tratado alquímico de Abraham el Judío*, Leipzig.
«Existen dos vías, la Seca y la Húmeda. Personalmente, sigo la primera, por
una cuestión de deber y predilección, aunque también conozco la segunda».
Cyliani (1832): *Hermes desvelado.*

La Vía Seca es el sello del estilo virgiliano y, en el sistema arenista, Virgilio es el santo patrón. Reinaldo cuelga una foto del santo en la pared de la buhardilla neoyorquina y le pide tres años de vida (Virgilio se los concede en un milagro secreto).

De Virgilio toma prestada la idea sacrílega del castrismo como experiencia mística, y del envilecimiento [*Rosa, la genuflexa*] como ascesis y praxis. Su éxtasis es de santón y linda en lo erótico. Para Reinaldo, como para Virgilio, pederastia significa, a un tiempo, parusía y postrimería; el santo le concede prolongar el éxtasis en tres años que equivalen a tres días («...yo debí morir en 1988»).

Reinaldo es René, el hijo de la cofradía de la carne, el retoño de una idea de 1956 («A la noche comen en casa... dos maricas cubanos...», Adolfo Bioy Casares , 2006: *Borges*) y la hipóstasis del hombre virgiliano. La profecía se cumple: René culmina en Reinaldo.

Virgilio fue «como un padre» para R, que no conoció al suyo. Si *La carne de René* es la novela patrística, *El asalto*, que cierra el ciclo cómico, será la epopeya de la madre. El arco que abre con *Celestino antes del alba* cierra en *Antes que anochezca* («Y fue la tarde y la mañana del *diem horribilem*...»).

La patria feliz, la isla bienaventurada, también llamada «urbe fenicia», el Paradiso donde nacer era una fiesta, contenía el germen de su propia disolución: ahora los demonios disponen de la isla, Próspero pierde el control de los libros, Calibán reina.

17.

En la obra de Reinaldo Arenas asistimos al sacrificio del estilo, que el artista arroja bajo las patas de Asmodeo; R repudia la pusilanimidad de la poesía, la cobardía de la literatura, transformándose así en héroe contraliterario. Su heroificación es la consecuencia imprevista del sacrificio del estilo: en R la revolución política se presenta –una vez más– como problema estético.

La imposibilidad de su situación –que demanda un sacrificio– lo convierte en personaje trágico, pues no hay que olvidar que la tragedia [en Piñera] es el teorema primitivo (*the play's the thing*); Reinaldo, como un Kurt Gödel de los últimos días, demuestra la recursividad del heroísmo para cualquier situación dada, siendo esta la prueba definitiva de su propia degradación.

La negación, sin embargo, no es deconstrucción: Reinaldo no deconstruye, no hay trazas en él de Lezama ni de Virgilio, debido a que ha descartado de plano la perspectiva histórica.

Reinaldo es el *Homo Revolutionibus*, aquel para quien la Historia dejó de *contar*. A los encantamientos heroicos sucumbe su Servando Teresa de Mier, pues el éxtasis historicista es el estigma de la vieja espiritualidad.

18.

Medallones para Sabbat: «Imaginar a Fidel en casa de María Antonia, narrándole sus hazañas políticas (1948-1953) a Ernesto Guevara, y concebir un sentimiento en el pecho del joven médico, un entendimiento en su frente de niño, el reconocimiento de la autoridad del narrador y de la inevitabilidad de la narrativa: la imitación de Castro nace allí como ejercicio espiritual…»

«La beatería origenista, también llamada textología, que deploramos en los escritores cubanos de la generación del noventa, está ausente de la obra de Reinaldo Arenas».

19.

La creación de nopersonas no es difícil, ocurre espontáneamente en las primeras horas del Triunfo: es entonces que T deja de significar «tiempo» para denotar el valor propio del Principio [Br'eshit][41].

Mucho más compleja es la creación de un «nobanco» en un «noparque», porque las cosas (*rerum*) se resisten a interceder por T, y más bien lo revierten. El pretérito, entendido como posteridad potencial, es el acicate de un Winston Smith (*1984*), pero hasta la ilusión cronológica le fue arrebatada al Contrasusurrador de *El asalto*[42].

Cada palabra de esta obra de 1988 está «maleada», y se adivina el casco que esgrime la pluma y garabatea sentencias torcidas. Hay algo caprino en el rostro que nos mide desde la solapa, algo de chivo degollado en la dulzura odiosa de los ojos.

[Además, estaba el sonido que emitía al hablar, un ceceo sibilante de guajiro taimado, la lengua interviniendo donde no la han llamado, ensalivando lo que sale del labio: más

---

41 Según reza el primer verso de Génesis: *Br'eshit bara Elohim et ha'shamaim v'et ha'aretz.*

42 Reinaldo Arenas (1990): *El asalto.* Miami: Universal.

que de un simple escape de aire, se trataba de un efecto neumático-neurasténico].

Cuando no hay Inquisición, cuando el hereje se ha instalado precariamente en el «mundo libre», parecería que dios mismo se encargara de fulminarlo. En el caso de Rey, será una plaga. Es evidente que el terreno calcinado por el herpes, el salpullido y el sarcoma donde se mueve nuestro antihéroe es un paisaje ascético, un paraje de santos. Lo vemos pujar el sudor agrio del esfuerzo plebeyo por producir sentido. El mundo es un desierto regado de bestias y homúnculos. Un «camello» es un grupo de seres agachados, enganchados por los antebrazos, que avanza en fila.

El asalto es apenas veladamente autobiográfico: Reinaldo, igual que el Contrasusurrador, «revienta» (es decir: destruye, pervierte, ensucia, mancilla) los grandes modelos modernos y antiguos de la literatura universal que le sirven de epígrafes a los capítulos de su noveleta. De alguna manera, el índex es mucho más novelístico que la novela misma, y nos enfrenta a su funesta bibliomanía.

No olvidemos que Reinaldo Arenas fue primero, y quizás exclusivamente, un bibliotecario, y que ese oficio, aparte de provocar desazón crónica y un acuciante complejo de inferioridad, ocasiona, como norma, deformaciones del gusto en el artista que lo ejerce temprano.

Reinaldo parece denunciar, en el índex, no tanto la escasez como la sobreabundancia editorial castrista, la plétora literaria a que es sometido el reo en la Colonia Penitenciaria. En el relato kafkiano, al que tanto debe *El asalto,* el condenado interpreta un dictamen escrito a cuchilla sobre el pergamino de su propio pellejo. Es de este *tipo* de literatura que trata la obra de Fernando.

Entre abril de 1984 y diciembre de 1986, el escritor, exiliado en Nueva York, había comenzado a perder la lengua, según queda consignado en las páginas iniciales de *El portero*[43] («¿*testimoniado*? ¿Existe esa palabra en nuestra lengua?»).

Vemos la lengua de San Antonio en un relicario, en la basílica del santo, en Padua, y comprendemos que cada libro de Arenas es una homilía a las transgresiones de ese órgano –la lengua como asiento de la espiritualidad–, ya que, para nuestro escritor, no puede haber *spiritu* si no viene asociado a una parte, a un miembro, o incluso, a un apéndice y un humor.

Así, la mujer se presenta en su escritura como el depósito de toda impureza: lo femenino supura, chorrea, se viene y excreta. Los fluidos se bambolean dentro de un vaso vaciado de *esencia*. Entre las muchas otras palabras campesinas que Reinaldo entrelaza en su «tapiz de pelos, latones y vidrios rotos», figuran reiteradamente «yegua» y «despotrica»: así el lenguaje [*cubano*] es forzado a «ponerse en cuatro».

El caballo no es más una bestia noble sino el signo de la necesidad ciega: *El asalto* puede leerse como una suerte de bestiario, y de breviario de funciones endocrinas. En la mujer, en la yegua, en sus funciones, períodos y reglas, en sus evacuaciones y vaivenes hormonales, en la ignominia de su materialidad (de su *maternidad*) va implícito el problema del Mal y la Caída. Ella es la Gran Prostituta que cabalga la Bestia, la ramera martiana, poluta con la semilla de mil

---

43 Reinaldo Arenas (1990): *El portero*. Miami: Universal.

usurpadores, pero sobre todo de uno, el gran desconocido: *el que concibió al Hijo.*

Quien escribe esta fábula equina ha vivido en el campo y ha visto cómo las jacas se someten a la posesión del labriego, cómo lo reciben y se vuelven sus cómplices (sus «queridas»), cómo aceptan calladas el estéril lechazo del hombre (del que están separadas por un abismo de especie): Hijo de Bestia, el artista cae en el mundo expulsado por el mismo hueco que puja y aprieta, incapaz de distinguirse del menstruo o del semen. El miasma es el Hijo[44].

21.

Cada página de Reinaldo Arenas es (y por siempre ha de ser) lo contrario de un saber. Sublime ignorancia empeñada en la más alta aspiración: el sacrificio del estilo en aras de la consustanciación en el Mal.

Antes de sucumbir al Mal, debemos encarnar lo malo —*die Böse* nietzscheano— en la literatura y el arte. Pero el arenismo es «lo malo» malogrado.

Cabe aquí una distinción axiológica entre los contenidos específicos de «lo malo» en la persona del artista, y las trazas del mal en la cultura de la época y su asimilación en el torrente espiritual del siglo, del que el escritor es tribu-

---

44 «Vulcanus Minervam adamavit, voluitque cum ea congredi; renuit illa, et virginitatem praeoptavit, et se occultavit quodam in loco Atticae, quem ab ipso Hephaestium appellarunt; is enim illi insidiatus, et sperans comprehendere, ejus hasta percussus est, atque adeo deposuit insequendi studium, et in pavimentum naturam effudit, unde natus est puer, quem Erichthounium vocavit». Pseudo-Erastóstenes (1795): *Catasterismi.* Gotinga: Vandenhoeck et Ruprecht.

tario. En otras palabras: ¿cuánto hay de malo específico en su arte, y cuánto pertenece a la radiación de fondo de una edad mediocre?

El mal gusto produce malestar. Por la vía del dolor, lo malogrado llega a erigirse en pilar de la nueva sociedad. La condena del placer oficial, y el reproche a la conformidad de los que se acoplan, emergen [en *El asalto*] como los nuevos mandamientos del gusto anticastrista.

22.

En literatura, tendemos a circunscribirnos a la época clásica y echar a un lado las leyendas de la edad media y oscura: pero es evidente que el machetazo en el cráneo de San Antonio vale por toda una Odisea, que el apedreamiento de Caribdis y Mosila da en el blanco perpetuamente.

A los huesos, la sangre y las piedras los recogen, primero, los relicarios, y después los museos y mausoleos. Quedan martirologios en cimborrios, sufrimientos en medallones. Una religión sin dolor, sin sudores y pujos, insiste Reinaldo, no merece el amor del pueblo.

Por eso hoy solo tenemos a Reinaldo, el Sacrificado, el santo que nos legó su lengua en un Pentateuco, cinco novelas malas con que calzar el altar cojo de nuestro martirio. Para eso, al menos, sirvió la letra, para acumular volumen, un grueso expediente contra el castrismo: página tras página, capítulo tras capítulo, su obra llena el hueco que media entre la epifanía y el aborto.

«Sólo hay un responsable: Fidel Castro. Los sufrimientos del exilio, las penas del destierro, la soledad y las enfermedades que haya podido contraer en el destierro seguramente

43

no las hubiera sufrido de haber vivido libre en mi país»
(Reinaldo Arenas, Epístola).

23.

Mi prosa púrpura, o el color oculto

De pequeño viví en la calle Nueva, también llamada
Menéndez Peláez, en el número 15, donde nací. Era una
casa de martillo con un solo cuarto; en la sala papá tenía
un chinchal con un solo empleado. Al fondo del patio había
un corral por donde pasaron varios cochinos de distintos
tamaños, que mi padre alimentaba con palmiche. Ese fue
mi corralito en los primeros años, creo que de los tres a los
ocho. Allí pasaba horas jugando. Una vez traje tizas de la
escuela, de distintos colores, las raspé y las fui echando en
un jarro que había puesto a calentar sobre una hornilla.
La hervidura arrojó un color púrpura que me llenó de alegría. Había descubierto un color alquímico: el color oculto.
Recuerdo la impresión que me causó la aparición del violeta
en mi Vaso. Luego mi abuelo libresco me proporcionaría
unas probetas y un pequeño equipo de laboratorio en el que
calciné diversas sustancias.

Miré a lo hondo de mi pensamiento y allí estaba aco-
rralada la novela. ¡Un conjunto de ensayos, de tientos, de
cuentos! Un pozo ciego que, en lo profundo, reflejaba mi
cara. Una cara, dicho sea en honor a la verdad, crispada por
la imbecilidad propia y ajena, por el dolor y el asco, marcada
por el impacto de mil aerolitos, palabras duras como huevos
lanzadas contra mí, una viruela, la facha de un apedreado,
¡y allí anidaba mi novela! Solo había que sacarla, acariciarla,

zarandearla, imprimirle forma. El problema de la forma apareció enseguida, como aparece siempre que una idea se insinúa a la mente del autor. R. L. Stevenson se quejaba: «Tal es la amargura del arte: encuentro un buen efecto y algún capricho del sentido viene a interponerse...»; pero la forma –la *bella forma* nacional– había sido sometida en Cuba a los rigores del esclavismo, y los efectos de ese calamitoso experimento quedaron plasmados en textos canónicos.

La cultura cubana, enfrentada al oscurantismo de la esclavitud, terminó por interiorizar las aporías y patakíes de unos pueblos extraños arrastrados en cadenas hasta nuestras playas. El modelo del saber como contrasentido está en *La jungla* y en *El Monte*, es decir, en nuestro *pensamiento salvaje*.

[El Poeta enmarca un eslabón de su grillete: aparece el primer *readymade* neoyorquino. Hace un anillo con el eslabón, y el círculo se cierra[45]].

En el círculo me miraba como quien se encorva y mete la cabeza por entre las piernas: un nudo. Si tuviera que describir el efecto que produjo en mí el descubrimiento tardío de la novela, de los personajes que merodeaban en el fondo de mi confusión, el asombro que me causó –¡y el desencanto!– descubrir un mundo dentro de mí. ¡De mí! ¡De pinga! ¡Del fetichista, del comunista, del pasionario, del equivocado, del hijo unigénito de la gran revolución fascista! Fue como el que sale de la morgue después de haber sido dado por muerto y aspira el aire puro del amanecer.

---

45   «Cuando fué Doña Leonor a Nueva York [...] le dio a su hijo, como regalo, al llegar, una sortija hecha con un eslabón de la cadena del grillete que llevó en presidio. Tenía la sortija como un centímetro de ancho con la palabra CUBA tallada en grandes letras». Blanca Z. de Balart (1945): *El Martí que yo conocí*. La Habana: Trópico.

24.

No olvidar que se trata, en mi caso, de un pintor [frustrado] convertido en literato (y, por ende, en demagogo). El efecto de mi literatura deriva de la inhabilidad para representar el mundo en los términos del medio artístico en que debí expresarme y de la necesidad de hacerlo en los de aquel que me fue meramente posible [y que aparece aquí como *accidente*], contaminado de pintura, de grabado, de garabato inacabado, pues conserva de la carrera trunca la marca de lo incompleto, de lo perpetuamente en ciernes, lo que quizás sea la seña de algo mayor, algo más general, de un carácter nacional, una tara de lo cubano y demasiado cubano, un rasgo de la susodicha situación política hecha estética. De lo cubano como idea incompleta arrancan sus contradicciones, sus inacabables «cien años de lucha», que podría igualmente llamar *mi* lucha, la conciencia de haber sido algo trunco y estanco, una idea perdida, como las que refiere Pascal (en 370), que escapan y quedan nulas[46]. El hecho de tener que expresarme en un medio distinto, y acaso inferior, al que me estaba deparado, es el verdadero problema de mi literatura.

25.

A cada cual le tocará vengarse de alguna vejación: a mí me tocó *El Niño*, quizás porque de niño a mí me vejaron. Entre cajones de muñequitos apilados en los talleres de una

---

46   Blaise Pascal, *Pensées,* 370: [El azar concede los pensamientos, y el azar los quita; no hay arte ninguno para conservarlos ni para adquirirlos. Pensamiento en fuga, yo lo quería escribir; en cambio, escribo que se me escapó].

fábrica clausurada después de la Revolución, ahora cuarto de desahogo, el azul agrio del traje de marinero del Pato Donald, el rojo cereza de los zapatos de Minnie, los veo en el piso, pliegos mojados, por entre las piernas de mi abusador.

Luego –quiero creerlo así– él arrancó unas páginas de esos folletines, que la nueva situación política había convertido en textos heréticos, y se limpió, restregándose con la hoja, y yo atendía a esos caracteres ficticios, iluminados como vitrales por la luz clandestina de una zapatería sellada. Herméticos, el niño y su amante, entre las máquinas de lo intervenido, de lo inevitable, el primer aspirante a mi belleza, el primer suplicante, «¡No digas nada!», el primero seducido por mi estilo.

Porque el estilo es el hombre, y yo encarnaba ya un modo de ser que era pura seducción aún antes de reconocerse, de deslindarse y tomar el atajo de lo artístico. Allí mi abusador y yo éramos todo olores, emanaciones carnales y efluvios de cuero en una tenería a la que las telarañas habían comenzado a tejer una mortaja; esto, en 1962 o 1963; el joven empleado de la fábrica –que caía aún por debajo de la condición de mi padre– ostentaba el odioso detalle de un labio de conejo. Estábamos en la cocina de la tía Ada, que daba al pasillo: por detrás podía llegarse al taller, rodeando el patio, y forzar la puerta nacionalizada. Los cubanos toman café de tarde, y como me portara mal, iría castigado, de la mano de R, a ese cuarto oscuro cuyo espacio paralelo a la casa era el tiempo que duraba recorrerlo, salir por el frente y regresar a la compañía de los tíos, que mis pobres padres visitaban religiosamente, y reincorporarnos a la escena abandonada hacía un instante, como si nada, como dos astronautas que circularan el cosmos para reencontrarse a menudo entre bandejas y tazas humeantes, en el intervalo de un intercurso, de un trago amargo, de un acto [*sexual*] en un Acto, de una violación del espacio sideral, ya devuelto, apaciguado. Apaciguado, devuelto. Cada noche.

26.

En mi primer relato juvenil, *El santo grial,* una nave surcaba el espaciotiempo durante cien generaciones de cosmonautas inseminados y peripatéticos hasta chocar con un cristal [invisible] y romper la barrera del más acá: entonces veían los rostros gigantescos de los comensales de una Última Cena. Habían viajado dentro del copón divino. Arribaban al Año Cero. Unos barbudos, «y haced esto en conmemoración mía…», celebraban la eucaristía. Creo que luego leí el mismo cuento escrito por Lem o Calvino[47].

---

[47] «A poet once said, "The whole universe is in a glass of wine." We will probably never know in what sense he meant that, for poets do not write to be understood. But it is true that if we look at a glass of wine closely enough we see the entire universe». Richard Feynman (1994): *Six Easy Pieces.* Boulder: Perseus Books. Véase Lucas 22:42, «Padre, si quieres, pasa de mí esta copa». Reina-Valera (1909).

Hojas de Rábano

Tomar el arte por el lado de los efectos sociales se parece mucho a tomar el rábano por las hojas o a estudiar el hombre por su sombra.

José Ortega y Gasset,
La deshumanización del arte

471

EN EL PRINCIPIO se les prohibió a los cubanos ocuparse de Fidel, aunque no se pusieran reparos en ofrecerlo como objeto de estudio a los sabios extranjeros. Esto se debe a que Fidel ha sido «un extranjero y peregrino entre nosotros» [Br'echit 23:4], uno venido del Oriente, vestigio de Galicia, cubano *per accidens*[48].

470

El yate Granma es el sarcófago de piedra que lo trajo de México, que es nuestro Egipto. «Metieron su cuerpo en un sarcófago de mármol, y éste en una barca cuyo único timonel era Dios». Castro dobla el pasaje jacobeo: primero

---

48 «Por ejemplo, de la estatua es causa, de un modo, Policleto, y, de otro modo, un escultor, porque el escultor es *accidentalmente* Policleto». Aristóteles, *Metafísica*, libro V, cap. 2.

navegante, después peregrino; la Vía Húmeda, después la
Vía Seca.

469

La barba de Fidel es imitación de la de Cristo y le permi-
tió pasar por Redentor. Sin ella no hubiera podido seducir
al pueblo[49].

468

Fidel es la mujer barbuda de Jusepe de Ribera, el símbolo
de la histeria [colectiva] y el menstruo (sangramiento). Notar
que la mujer estuvo excluida de las representaciones oficiales
y que solo tardíamente se reveló la existencia de las esposas
reales, de Dalia Soto, de Nati Revuelta. Más que como
Padre, Fidel gobernó como mala Madre[50]. La mujer vino
a ser el emblema de la República (venal, traicionera, pros-
tituida). La barba fidelista encubre una barbilla femenina.
Celia, Cheché, María Antonia, Melba, Vilma: los alias de
Fidel, *das Ewig-Weibliche.*

---

[49]   «Enfantin se dejó crecer la barba a imitación de Jesús y exhibía el
título "Le Père" bordado en la pechera de la camisa». Edmund Wilson (1940):
To the Finland Station: A Study in the Writing and Acting of History. Considerar alternativamente el verso: «Com'st thou to beard me in Denmark?» W.
Shakespeare, *Hamlet,* Acto 2, Escena 2.

[50]   «¡La Historia es una madrastra cruel!». Vladimir Ilich Lenin, en conversación con Máximo Gorky, citado por Wilson 1940 [a partir de aquí las
notas son de la Editora, a menos que se indique lo contrario].

En México, «en casa de María Antonia», se inaugura la dimensión hispanoamericana del castrismo (o «nuestroamericana», si entendemos el panfleto epónimo como un programa de apropiación cubano). Así la guerrilla vino a ser la continuación de la Conquista y, en el marco de la revolución permanente, la persistencia del Imperio por otros medios.

«Nuestra América», en boca de Martí y Fidel, es el grito de guerra de la Ideología Española.

Martí y Fidel personifican, para los cubanos, el problema de la supremacía española. La división fidelista de gusanos y revolucionarios es un rezago de la limpieza de sangre.

«Solo los sucesos especialmente dramáticos, como un asesinato o un crimen, y los terrores más extremos, se me han quedado grabados textualmente en español». Elías Canetti (1983): *La lengua absuelta*.

El imperio español, más haragán o más desengañado que el anglosajón, no quiso, o no pudo, seguir adelante después de alcanzar la Edad de Oro. «En su lengua hablamos» quiere decir: en una lengua muerta.

462

El castrismo, en su decadencia, es quijotesco, y de un patetismo que ni el mismo Alonso Quijano llegó a conocer, porque la Ideología Española debió esperar por un Fidel que encarnara el derrumbe y la locura de lo hispano, uno que delegara en sus súbditos el papel de Sanchos, y en la Isla de Cuba el doble símbolo de Dulcinea y Barataria.

461

Con el castrismo retorna la figura del Capitán General que aísla a Cuba y se empeña en privarla de la influencia yanqui. Lo que entendemos por «castrismo» [en tanto oposición al norte] no es más que la reacción española antimoderna.

460

Al condenar lo cubanoamericano, Fidel rechaza un nuevo tipo de hispanidad reconciliado con su componente moderno. Por eso Martí, el primer modernista cubanoamericano, es también la primera víctima de los españoles.

459

El fidelismo, en tanto movimiento político, es un retroceso hacia el encastillamiento feudal y la ideología de molinos de viento.

458

Fidel Castro es un molino de viento.

Castro es la leyenda negra encarnada, el tenebrismo personificado. Cuba es Barataria, y Fidel, el Sancho sublimado, transplantado a un escenario tropical.

Fidel es Calibán. Próspero, en cambio, representa el principio de prosperidad anglosajón.

La guerra de El Salvador, o la gran masacre centroamericana, es la lección que Castro da a los indígenas faltos de fe que dos décadas antes habían rechazado el guevarismo en Bolivia. La intervención castrista los pone de rodillas; acatan por la fuerza lo que no les entró por la doctrina. Castro repite la hazaña de Cortés: con un puñado de hombres (los Doce) reconquistó el imperio aborigen.

Castro, o la Ideología Española.

No porque lo español asuma las peculiaridades o el temperamento de lo cubano, ni porque declare su soberanía en un paraje situado a muchas leguas de España, ni porque se apropie del paisaje, el carácter y los accidentes geográficos de ese territorio afín, deja de ser español. Evitar la tentación de la autonomía, de deslindar por la mera costumbre de rescindir y acotar, cuando el impulso contrario, hacia la subordinación y la coincidencia, resultaría, en nuestro caso, mucho más ventajoso y expeditivo.

452

El castrismo es una idea universal que acoge a extranjeros y apóstatas. La conversión del Che en México es el primer ejemplo de su versatilidad y universalidad. El castrismo no pertenece a los cubanos como pueblo elegido, sino que es ecuménico e inmediatamente adaptable a las circunstancias y características de *todos los pueblos*.

451

Que se niegue la dictadura castrista es un hecho tremendamente positivo para la moral de los cubanos, pues de otro modo estarían aferrados a «su» dictadura, como los argentinos, los chilenos o cualquier otro pueblo sudamericano, y no serían distintos de un pueblo sudamericano. La negación de la dictadura no hace más que confirmar la excepcionalidad de la experiencia cubana dentro de la moderna profusión de simulacros políticos. El rechazo les permite existir en el mundo a la manera de un auténtico pueblo elegido.

450

El nihilismo cubano no prendió en Latinoamérica; prosperaron, en cambio, las ideas erróneas salidas del Oriente, el tirabuzón dialéctico de nuestros marxistas, la catequesis amulatada del leninismo, una Vulgata lista para ser consumida por el actor, el escritor, el académico y el cantautor.

El símbolo castrista suplió la demanda pública de ideales en rebaja.

449

Los cubanos no creyeron en «Bolivia», se mofaron del Bolívar hipostasiado en una prole de repúblicas fallidas. Nuestra isla feliz tenía constancia del fracaso de las guerras independentistas y entendía que solo Cuba, españolísima y norteamericanizada, podía considerarse propiamente una civilización moderna. El desencanto del ideal separatista es el punto de arranque de nuestro jingoísmo.

448

«…que el ideal separatista era ya negocio pasado, cosa juzgada y abandonada, muy principalmente a causa del lastimoso estado de inestabilidad y desorden que brindaban las flamantes repúblicas americanas» (José M. Pérez Cabrera (1952): *Historia de la Nación Cubana*).

447

La guerra de «independencia» ocurre, entre nosotros, en los momentos en que el concepto decimonónico de separatismo ha caído en descrédito (como «cosa juzgada y abandonada») y ya solo puede degenerar en *bellum perpetuum*. Con la guerrilla, el conflicto irresuelto se propaga y se hace endémico.

446

«La generalizada inseguridad del país se hace patente en
el uso extendido de las armas. El vaquero en los campos,
el pastor en las llanuras, tienen su mosquete y su cuchillo a
mano. El granjero rara vez sale al mercado sin su trabuco»
(Washington Irving (1829): *The Alhambra*).

445

Con cuán poco se conformó el intelectual comprome-
tido, con qué poco se contentó el profesor entusiasta y cuán
sobornables resultaron ser las conciencias de los poetas, los
académicos y los novelistas, fueron factores determinantes
en la celeridad y la profundidad de la penetración castrista
en Latinoamérica. En cambio, en la Cuba profunda, los
carboneros, los zapateros, los choferes, y hasta las costure-
ras, entendieron el error castrista apriorísticamente, lo cual
demuestra qué poco cuenta la *intelligentsia* en tiempos de
crisis.

444

La posesión por España –también llamada «conquista»–
es el único momento de deseo y auténtica lujuria que expe-
rimentó nuestra América en toda su Historia.

443

«Cuando Cuba sea libre…», solemos decir, pero sin pre-
guntarnos a qué clase de mundo vendrá esa Cuba libre. ¿Y
acaso no fue mejor que feneciera en el 58, en el momento

de su esplendor cabrerainfantil, con su cine, su Orígenes, sus barbudos y su Tropicana?

442

Siempre habrá alguien que penetre en el templo y lea las Escrituras y sea sacado a patadas y perseguido hasta la salida del pueblo, solo por atreverse a interpretar los textos de una manera *sensacional*.

441

Los llamó y les pidió que volvieran a ser taxistas, locutores, vedettes, garroteros; que regresaran a sus hogares, a sus negocios. Que lo dejaran solo.

440

Renunciar a una creencia es mucho más apremiante que el abandono de «las cosas de este mundo».

439

En cuanto a lo espiritual, ¡qué vulgar es la liberación que llega de la mano de un profeta, de un redentor, de un creyente! ¡Qué falsas las promesas de los salvadores y qué claras las cuentas de los cobradores! ¡Y qué dudosas las pruebas de los que curan y alfabetizan!

438

Tribu perdida. Los decanos son los nuevos diáconos; los pedagogos, implacables guevaristas encargados de preservar la pureza del culto. Los exiliados son los «judíos del Caribe», expulsados del templo, postergados en las listas de aspirantes, saboteados en las candidaturas, vilipendiados y puestos en la picota pública, acusados de mafiosos y usureros. En otras palabras: no solo hemos perdido, sino que *estamos* perdidos.

437

Solo con el del judío podría equipararse el lugar que ocupa el gusano en el inconsciente colectivo. Cuando se le acusa de mafioso, se trata de la antigua usura elevada a la categoría de crimen organizado. Es en ese espacio simbólico donde el cubano del gueto tuvo que asentarse y recomenzar su vida: en las circunstancias del judío errante a quien los latinoamericanos rechazaron por el solo hecho de haber *errado*, de haber tomado el rumbo equivocado.

436

Parásitos.
Escorias.
Enfermos.
Larvas.
Lacras.
Delincuentes.
Ladrones.
Basura.

Reaccionarios.
Espías.
Traidores.
Bandidos.

Del judío al gusano no hay más que un asco, y mis personajes, mis avatares y zombis, terminaron por acatar el papel que les asignó la cultura dominante. Es decir: terminaron aceptando la metamorfosis y practicando voluntariamente el mimetismo.

Del ingrato, el escoria, el bandido, el traidor y el renegado se constituyó un pueblo condenado y, por eso mismo, *elegido*, al tiempo que se completaba un cuerpo [*corpus*] de escrituras, discursos, memorias, epístolas, lamentaciones y retractaciones donde la historia maldita quedó asentada en Libro, y la figura pública del gusano adscrita al canon de la sociopatología judaica.

Y ese Judas creado por las circunstancias mesiánicas que aparece en el panorama mito-histórico como consecuencia del advenimiento de un nuevo credo, es el Traidor del auto sacramental castrista.

431

Fidel Castro describe la ciudad fenicia en un hermoso pasaje de sus Escrituras: «Os voy a referir una historia. Había una vez una república. Tenía su Constitución, sus leyes, sus libertades, Presidente, Congreso, tribunales; todo el mundo podría reunirse, asociarse, hablar y escribir con entera libertad. El gobierno no satisfacía al pueblo, pero el pueblo podía cambiarlo y ya solo faltaban unos días para hacerlo. Existía una opinión pública respetada y acatada y todos los problemas de interés colectivo eran discutidos libremente. Había partidos políticos, horas doctrinales de radio, programas polémicos de televisión, actos públicos, y el pueblo palpitaba de entusiasmo».

430

Es en razón de esas condiciones óptimas que aparece el Mesías: él es el síntoma y el producto de una edad de iluminismo y libertinaje, de decadencia e incertidumbre. Si Fulgencio Batista es el «hombre plausible en grado superlativo» [Ruby Hart Phillips (1959): *Cuba, Island of Paradox*], entonces Fidel Castro es el *Homo Batistianus*, pues en él se realiza superlativamente «todo aquello que el Sistema fue capaz de concebir y de lograr» [Guy Debord (1967): *La Societé du Spectacle*].

429

Fidel es un Hamlet [su lema es «Patria o Muerte»] que se absuelve a sí mismo y condena a la patria que lo parió.

Y ese hombre último –importa anotarlo– creará, a su vez, al gusano. El gusano es su creación suprema, como mismo él había sido la más perfecta creación del batistato. Nuestra relación con Castro es la de la criatura con el Creador.

Hay una suerte de reivindicación tardía en el hecho de que el mosntruoso gusano (*ungeheuren Ungeziefer*[51]) regresa a Cuba convertido en «mariposa»: una metamorfosis (*Verwandelt*). De la transformación, sin embargo, también es responsable el Líder que le convoca y le asigna el papel de usurero. Es como mercaderes y marchantes que los gusanos regresan cargados de gusanos[52], de fetiches y vitualla. Se les impone una vez más la función de mulas, de viajantes de lo degenerado.

Nueva Ciencia. Hay dos sistemas de conocimiento: el sistema castrista y el anticastrista; es decir, la Ciencia oficial y la secreta, la enseñanza oral que permaneció oculta y fue transmitida clandestinamente.

---

[51]   *Ungeziefer* (*vermin*, gusano) es la palabra que Franz Kafka usa para describir a Gregor Samsa en *La metamorfosis* (1915).

[52]   Nombre genérico de las valijas que lleva el exiliado cubano de visita a su país natal.

425

No se ha comprendido el verdadero alcance de la revolución castrista si no se la entiende como un evento universal que relativizó la totalidad de la existencia.

424

Diseño: «...un complejo de interacomodación, y de interacomodación ordenada, cuya omnintegridad de orden interacomodaticio solo podría ser descrito como intelectualmente inmaculado» (Buckminster Fuller, 1975: *Synergetics*).

423

El conocimiento moderno (en el sentido de *corriente*) del castrismo solo puede alcanzarse mediante la sinergia de todas las partes interacomodadas, para lo cual se requiere una multiplicidad de estilos en omnintegridad.

422

Fulcanelli enseña que la Ciencia oculta es una ciencia positiva. Pero nuestra ciencia positiva deberá ser, por fuerza, una Ciencia *oculta*.

421

El sustrato formal de la Nueva Ciencia es el «método Virgilio». En Virgilio Piñera, en el universo cerrado de sus novelas, aparece el tema de la conspiración; y, como trasfondo de la conjura, un sistema político [un orden implicado] que solo se hará patente cuando la realidad revolucionaria lo actualice.

420

Sincretismo. Una dosis de absurdo, y de absurdismo virgiliano, del tipo de sinsentido que practican los cofrades de la carne, dota al castrismo de su atractivo universal: el vulgo necesita una sinrazón.

419

Continuación del machadato, continuación del batistato, continuación de la tradición caudillista latinoamericana, continuación de la línea sucesoria de los Capitanes Generales, continuación del orden jesuita y de su jerarquía militar-espiritual, continuación del revolucionarismo martiano, continuación del gorilismo: el fidelismo como continuismo.

418

Extra Ecclesiam nulla salus: ¡Fuera de la Revolución nada!

417

Castro con alma de Cristo. El castrismo es la nueva alianza de lo humano y lo divino, o la manera en que el hombre se diviniza en sus «acciones», lo que es decir: en sus *hechos de sangre*. Así quedó oficialmente superada la antigua clave: privada, pagana y republicana.

416

Porque el nuevo mesianismo suponía el desarrollo monstruoso de un solo aspecto, de un único principio y de un
vínculo exclusivo dentro de la plétora de tendencias y propensiones del Antiguo Régimen. Quizás la cuerda más floja
y la más baja por ser la más apegada a la muerte y al martirio.
Sobre todo, el nuevo culto no daba señales de vida: nacía
muerto, era un aborto y una mimesis.

415

En *El martirio de San Vitale*, de Federico Barocci, en la
Pinacoteca de Brera (también en el cuarto de desahogo de
Magali Perdomo, en Princeton, recostado a la lavadora de
ropa), vemos cómo entierran vivo al santo. Un «entierro en
vida», es decir: un *des*-tierro. Hay picos y palas alrededor
del hueco, atributos del trabajo manual que preconiza la
dictadura del proletariado. Es el mismo estado de cosas
(*rerum*) que representan la hoz y el martillo.

414

Que Cristo *se muestre* es la precondición de su martirio.
«¿Por qué no te manifiestas?» [Juan 14:22]; los discípulos conciben la muerte del Líder como exhibicionismo.
Su vida no había sido más que un proceso de revelado:
queda fija en la tela del tiempo. La doctrina aparece en
una serie de parábolas, es decir, de arcos de sentido contra
el telón del firmamento. Manifestarse y correr el riesgo
de ser atacado, como en 1972, por mano del orate Laszlo

Toth, en el Vaticano. Cristianismo significa «ponerse al alcance del vulgo».

413

Desfacer entuertos, desenredar el embrollo de la revolución, parecía ser mi tarea. Pero, ¿acaso no era el cristianismo el modelo de decepción como conocimiento, de *agnosis* como sistema del mundo? Desenmarañar la madeja de lo real maravilloso, de la pobreza de espíritu, de lo «latino» americano, de la indigencia irradiante, de los sermones montañosos, de lo arcádico revolucionario, era proponer una manera nueva de conocer, pero, sobre todo, ¡de descreer!

412

El castrismo conserva, como material hereditario, las características de todos los regímenes que lo precedieron. El batistato sobrevive en él como gen egoísta.

411

Toda revolución política está determinada tanto por los valores de su momento inercial como por las condiciones de su entorno natural.

410

Fidel nacionalizó las grandes empresas norteamericanas, pero la Historia, la misma que lo absolverá, continúa en manos yanquis. También la Revolución (que es nuestro inconfesable *bellum civile*) fue rebajada a la categoría de «diferendo» con los Estados Unidos. No es posible estudiar un proceso de apropiación colonial más claramente que en el caso de nuestros conflictos: los desmanes de la United Fruit Co. fueron nada comparados con el robo de toda una Historia.

409

La profecía de William Randolph Hearst se ha cumplido. Los cubanos proveen los «poemas-en-prosa» [revoluciones] mientras que los norteamericanos continúan suministrando la crítica y las interpretaciones. Si los cubanos quedan como exponentes líricos de su Historia, mientras los norteamericanos aportan los *hard facts*, es decir, la realidad constante y sonante, entonces los americanos están en todo el derecho de considerarse amos de nuestra *story*, en el sentido periodístico de *scoop* que Herbert Matthews da al término al apropiarse del evento de la Sierra.

408

Negarse una Historia completa, inteligible, es el deber de todo contrarrevolucionario.

407

«Las publico, no es necesario subrayarlo, sin asomo de pretensión científica…», advierte Lydia Cabrera, al inicio de las notas dispersas que integran *El Monte*. «El método seguido, ¡si de método aún vagamente, pudiera hablarse en el caso de este libro!, lo han impuesto con sus explicaciones y digresiones, inseparables unas de otras, mis informantes, incapaces de ajustarse a ningún plan…»

406

De ser una ciencia inexacta nuestra Historia pasó a ser una religión universal.

405

Entender que el castrismo es refutable, pero, sobre todo, decidible, formalizable, es ya un gran paso de avance.

404

Mientras que en lo tocante a la economía interna el castrismo es unidimensional, en cuestiones de política exterior es polimorfo y polifacético, de modo que el efecto propagandístico sea absoluto. El castrismo busca consumidores, no sufragantes: tal es su gran aporte a la economía política.

403

El castrismo es la etapa superior del capitalismo espectacular. Los mismos mecanismos propagandísticos que disparan la adquisición impulsiva de un producto, hacen que el consumidor se *convierta* al castrismo.

402

«La mercancía es, en primer lugar, un objeto que existe fuera de nosotros, una cosa que, por sus mismas propiedades, satisface algún deseo humano. La naturaleza de ese deseo, o si, por ejemplo, se origina en el estómago o en la imaginación, no cambia nada». Karl Marx (1867): *Das Kapital.*

401

También el castrismo se origina en la imaginación.

400

El castrismo es la aberración terminal del consumismo. Con el castrismo, el capitalismo se realiza plenamente en sus contradicciones.

399

Maquiavelo enseña que «con la longevidad y la persistencia del gobierno, el recuerdo de las innovaciones y las razones para realizarlas, desaparecen». Es por eso que llegó a haber un solo periódico, un solo dentífrico, un sola marca de cigarrillos y un solo Partido.

398

Filosofía barata. El castrismo debe ser, en principio, económicamente inviable. No es el paradigma marxista lo que lleva al desastre en el modelo económico cubano, sino la necesidad doctrinal de miseria.

397

Los exiliados cubanos, víctimas de la más larga dictadura hemisférica, fueron repudiados en Latinoamérica por una cuestión eminentemente racial: eran demasiado españoles para ser indígenas y demasiado oscuros (viz: *complicados*) para pasar por blancos.

396

Únicamente la burguesía es capaz de fanatizarse y contagiar de su fanatismo a la plebe. Lo que transmite es un *ideal*, es decir, la creencia en una idea falsa. Solo la burguesía siente cargos de conciencia y desesperación de clase: la angustia facilita el contagio.

395

¿Por qué el castrismo no se refleja en los espejos? Porque carece de teoría. Los intelectuales cubanos se cohibieron de explicarlo y evitaron meterse en el terreno pantanoso del castrismo por temor a ser identificados con los atributos negativos del fenómeno en cuestión. Dedicarse al castrismo era una mancha en el expediente, una medalla de deshonra. El castrismo fue abandonado a los diletantes, los extranjeros y los judíos del pensamiento y de la crítica. El castrismo era el fruto maldito que sólo se consumía en el gueto. «Castrismo» era la mala palabra que se profiere en la barbería y en la funeraria, lanzada desde la tribuna por agoreros y locutores. El castrismo era un mal de ojo: había que colgarse del cuello un ramo de mastuerzo antes de aproximársele. Es por eso que faltó una ciencia del castrismo, porque esa nueva *scienza* debía ser necesariamente ocultista e internarse en el campo de las supercherías, del vampirismo y el espiritismo. Falta *El Monte* del castrismo, el tratado que revele sus prácticas secretas. Falta una teratología castrista, una etiología castrista, una virología castrista, un *Tristes Trópicos* castrista. El castrismo vuela invisible en la noche y enferma la rosa blanca de la expresión poética: bañado de menstruo y de mierda, embarrado de tierra de cementerio y pelos de mártires, hecho con bilongos y sortilegios, el castrismo llegó al mundo.

394

El castrismo es nuestro Talmud o Enseñanza. Aprendimos de él más que de cualquier otro evento: la explosión de una supernova no tendría la misma importancia para nosotros. El castrismo es una lección de gastronomía, ginecología, agricultura, estética, elocuencia, etc. El castrismo es *sefer*, pero no en el sentido pedagógico, sino en el estrictamente jaláquico. Y aunque suplantó *El Capital* y los *Ejercicios espirituales*, carece de Libro. Su libro no ha sido escrito: permanece abierto, como enseñanza oral, dentro de quienes lo vivimos. Somos los autores del castrismo, su tradición.

393

En las matemáticas se intentó la purificación de cualquier traza de lo intuitivo y lo temporal. Este proceso alcanzó el clímax con Hilbert, que formalizó la geometría, con Frege, que reconstruyó la aritmética con base lógica, y con Cantor, que sentó la jerarquía de infinitos. Sin embargo, mientras que los matemáticos (siguiendo a Platón) hacían todo lo posible por expulsar el tiempo del reino de las matemáticas, los físicos se esforzaban por reintroducirlo en esas mismas matemáticas purificadas de cualquier vestigio temporal.

En otras palabras, «los que se ocupaban», según explica Palle Yourgrau, «de las teorías del Tiempo, empleaban un instrumento expresamente diseñado para ser indiferente a lo temporal[53]». Otro tanto podría decirse de quienes se ocupan del castrismo.

392

Es a las generaciones de gusanos por venir, que inevitablemente nos sucederán y que heredarán nuestro papel en el espectáculo castrista, a quienes me dirijo. Quiero dejarles dicho cómo vivimos, cómo escapamos, cómo sufrimos, cómo luchamos, cómo mutamos y en qué dialecto nos escribimos.

391

La abolición del castrismo es la abolición de una esclavitud.

390

Carleton Beals, Ángel Castro, Menoyo, Herbert Matthews, Che Guevara: «extranjeros y peregrinos entre nosotros». Solo a los ojos de los extraños La Habana clásica es Sodoma, aunque en sí misma, en sus estadísticas y porcentajes (de televisores, periódicos, carros, teléfonos, clínicas, cines, abortos y aparatos de radio), fuera Atenas.

---

[53] Cfr. Palle Yourgrau (1999): «Temporal Mathematics», *Gödel Meets Einstein*.

389

El tono origenista era de desengañada devoción, de jubiloso fatalismo, paradojas y oxímoros que lograron confundirse con las virtudes eclesiásticas y ser tomados por la expectativa fúnebre de la parusía, pero que prefiguraban, en cambio, una «situación política hecha estética».

388

«Inspirada en la de Cristo, el escultor había introducido una modificación capital: en vez de la patética y angustiada faz de Jesús, la cara de René en yeso se ofrecía, no caída sobre el pecho, sino erguida, y la boca mostraba la risa de una persona satisfecha. Podría afirmarse que acababa de oír un chiste» Virgilio Piñera (1952): *La carne de René*.

387

In hoc signo vinces. El chiste consistía en que un intelectual latinoamericano (lo que Julio Cortázar llamó «típico autodidacto de país subdesarrollado») llegara a instalarse en el Palacio y a gobernar desde el Castillo, y que su silueta, «inspirada en la de Cristo», adornara la Plaza.

386

El Che era proclamado senador y Poeta Máximo. El politiquero imponía una estética. Si el poeta había sido desterrado de la República era, precisamente, para evitar un caso como el de Cuba, y ahora Latinoamérica debía evitar ser «otra Cuba» como mismo Cuba había evitado, en el XIX, convertirse en «otro Saint-Domingue».

385

El hecho de que el nuevo fanatismo llegara de la mano de Virgilio, con el Cristo «que acababa de oír un chiste», y que su libro profético viera la luz en Buenos Aires, no es el aspecto menos significativo de la llamada «metafísica origenista».

384

Guevara es el *descubridor* de Cuba en el mismo sentido en que Colón enfrentó lo desconocido y creyó haber llegado a Cipango cuando ancló en Baracoa. Antes de enero de 1959, Guevara desconoce la existencia de nuestra capital, de la misma manera que las tropas de Cortés ignoran la existencia de Tenochtitlán, aunque ganen batallas en la periferia y avancen hacia la ciudad dorada. También para el Che estuvo claro que con La Habana caía una cultura, que en La Habana terminaba el mundo.

383

Martí, el Oscuro: «Que no hay inmigración buena cuando, aunque traiga mano briosa, trae corazón hostil o frío. Es estéril el consorcio de dos razas opuestas».

382

Manolito habló dándonos la espalda, ocupado en mangonear la quilla del yate Efemérides a través de los preocupantes canales del lago Kuneipampañaguazú. Entretanto el fuego forestal arrasaba el bosque de malaleucas.

—Igual que el Che, Hatuey fue un forastero entre nosotros. Su muerte en Cuba es muerte en Bolivia. Dice en la hoguera: «La Historia me absolverá». Pero su destino está ahora en nuestras manos...

El sol brilló en el cielo como un proyector de cine.

—Su destino no está en nuestras manos —protestó Isaac, sudando.

—No veo... cómo... —insistió la Gorda, abanicante.

Se miró las manos, llevadas en su Nombre a la frente desde niña.

—Depende de nosotros condenarlo otra vez a la pira, al muy sedicioso. ¿Por qué perpetuar el error? Las compañías cerveceras fueron responsables... Volvieron potable la revolución. Comercializaron la imagen de un taíno fascista explotador de naboríes.

—¡Basta de historicismos! —explotó Isaac, desde su palo mayor.

—¡En escala de tiempo y espacio, la dictadura taína fue mucho más espectacular y mucho más criminal que la de los propios españoles! —insistió Manolo.

—¡Pero qué decís! —chilló la Gorda, con acento argentino.

381

El batistato, que es la Edad de Oro de Cuba, hizo lucir bien al castrismo naciente. La ciudad hermosa, con grandes avenidas y carros de último modelo [todavía hasta bien entrados los años sesenta] fue el telón de fondo del castrismo. La elegancia batistiana, el vestuario de época, le sirvieron de camuflaje, pero el castrismo estaba debajo, y una vez que la ciudad envejeció y cayeron los afeites de la Gran Ramera, cuando se rompieron los remiendos y se desportilló el muro, apareció el castrismo. Los primeros turistas vieron un castrismo que se había metido dentro del cuerpo del batistato como un *bodysnatcher*. Por eso René Ariza dijo que había que «vigilarse al Castro que cada uno tiene dentro[54]».

380

Batista huye, hace mutis, sale de escena. Su fuga es heroica; su renuncia, superior a la epifanía castrista. Escapar como acto de magia, el «saber desaparecer» martiano elevado a una ciencia del existir. Pirándose, Batista obra irreprochablemente y, tal vez, hasta *patrióticamente*.

379

El abandono batistiano es lo opuesto de la Voluntad: es un desertar hacia lo involuntario. Por eso no debería hablarse de «triunfo» castrista (lo cual implica una victoria de la voluntad en sentido estricto), pues la llegada al poder del castrismo es el producto del abandono y la huída. El hecho capital de nuestra historia moderna, en tanto historia posmoderna, es la fuga.

378

Se nos enseñó que la Pasión del Batista repudiado era crística, que su caída era la consecuencia del rechazo popular.

---

54   En *Conducta impropia* (1984), el documental de Néstor Almendros y Orlando Jiménez Leal.

Aparece entre nosotros el procurador romano (Matthews) que consulta al populacho y pone a decidir a los doctores de la Ley, a los altos magistrados de la cultura, a los mandarines de la prensa y el espectáculo. La respuesta es unánime: ¡Dennos a Fidel! Así, Matthews proclama: *Ecce Homo*.

377

Batista es nuestro Mediodía (*zohar*), y el batistato, la Edad de Oro, una época límite más allá de la cual tenía que comenzar necesariamente el ocaso.

376

El castrismo es una bifurcación (*Entzweiung*) de lo cubano; es por ello que, en nuestro caso, deberá hablarse de evolución unitaria lineal y no de revolución; o de evolución unitaria lineal *dentro* del batistato, y circunscribir el castrismo a su función de onda.

375

La consecuencia de haber nacido escritor en Cuba es aborrecer a los escritores, porque fueron necesarias incontables reescrituras y una trama, para dar forma al Terror.

374

¿Acaso no hay columnas helénicas en las iglesias cristianas? Los artistas hacen el cuento con lo que tienen a mano. El arte, como la política, se vale de cualquier cosa con tal de hacerse *creer*.

De la iglesia de Santo Domingo de Guzmán, en Oaxaca, a La Habana victoriosa del castrismo, el espectáculo barroco gana brillantez en proporción directa al grado de desesperanza de los espectadores. Concebir el barroco como secuela y acompañamiento de la Conquista, como la celebración artística de un poder absoluto; los retablos de oro de esa alegría imperialista cantan un hosanna a la fuerza bruta que hizo posible sojuzgar un territorio tan enorme, un territorio mágico (Jauja, La Habana, el Potosí), vastísimas culturas. Porque el tamaño de una iglesia, y su riqueza, dependen de la capacidad del derrotado para entender, y padecer, el Triunfo.

A la entrada del batistato hay un ángel que empuña una espada flamígera. Es un ángel español. El Padre corrió las cercas hasta adueñarse de todo el Jardín. Tras la Caída, resulta inimaginable el antiguo estado de cosas: el Paraíso como reminiscencia.

El Hijo dispone de los enormes recursos que el Padre [mercenario] ha robado. Las cercas caminan de noche. La movilidad de las cercas impone al Hijo la dinámica de un poder nocturno e ilegítimo.

370

Lo que comenzó tímidamente como liberación de la Ciudad, como conquista del Cuartel, como toma del Palacio; lo que fingió modestia, evitó el culto de la personalidad, renunció al sueldo histórico y se avergonzó de ocupar las mansiones de la plutocracia, va apropiándose, poco a poco, de parcelas cada vez más amplias de la realidad, de zonas nunca antes reclamadas por la política, de trozos cada vez más extensos de la cultura, la agricultura, la geografía, la metafísica, el deporte, la medicina y el arte, hasta llegar a abarcar la «totalidad de lo que es el caso».

369

La relativización castrista de la Historia es otra consecuencia de la relativización de la existencia, que Gödel deploraba[55].

368

También el Universo Castro es un universo cerrado: UC.

---

[55] «A relative lapse of time, however, if any meaning at all can be given to this phrase, would certainly be something entirely different from the lapse of time in the ordinary sense, which means change in the existing. The concept of existence, however, cannot be relativized without destroying its meaning completely». Kurt Gödel (1949): *A remark about the relationship between relativity theory and idealistic philosophy.* Collected Works, Vol. II. Según Isaac Kámara, el castrismo es ese «lapso de tiempo» en sentido relativista.

Superhombre. Castro nació en la estrella de cuarzo de la hispanidad en quiebra.

CASTROLEO. Los cubanos veníamos de un Paraíso donde los automóviles del año rodaban por las Vías Blancas. La anualidad (o actualidad) radical de lo cubano y su velocidad, representada por el Impala y el «último modelo», desaparecen súbitamente para dar paso al año gallego, el año de Castro, que dura un jubileo.

¡Cuántos infartos de personas despojadas de sus posesiones, puestas de rodillas, fulminadas por el decomiso, el gran golpe que las priva de todo, pero sobre todo de *argumentos*, les roba la razón! La mentira es el demonio que se las lleva, azules y estrambóticas, aferradas a sus herramientas, abrazadas a sus medios de producción, a sus yunques y sus bigornias, todavía con las bocas llenas de puntillas y el martillo en el aire, agarradas a su verdad. Una embolia era la única respuesta posible al advenimiento del castrismo.

Notar cómo su posibilidad arranca de un atentado en un callejón oscuro de la urbe, con la muerte del doble, Manolo de Castro[56], y cómo continúa en la carnicería de Bogotá y en el sangramiento del Moncada. Advertir cómo esa idea cubana reclama hoy un lugar exaltado entre las nociones de nuestro tiempo, y cómo consiguió desbancar al leninismo, al maoísmo, al fascismo y al marxismo y llegar a proclamarse cosmogonía, etiología, metafísica, farmacopea, agronomía, poética, ecología y semiótica.

363

La irrupción del comisario argentino en nuestro medio queda plasmada en un rosario de discursos y declaraciones (reunidos y prologados por el intelectual converso Roberto Fernández Retamar, Ediciones Era, México, 1967), unos textos sagrados que, décadas más tarde, aún nos producen estupor, indignación, bochorno y total incredulidad por haber sido precisamente nuestra sociedad alegre, irresponsable y perdida la que cayera víctima del pesimismo lunfardo.

362

Considerar el hecho de que también yo podría caer luchando por Cuba antes de terminar este libro, y ser *uno de ellos.*

---

[56] «After Manolo de Castro left the university, he was appointed director general of national sports in the Ministry of Education [...] Manolo de Castro and a friend were killed by two masked men on the night of February 22, 1948». Antonio de la Cova (2006): *The Moncada Attack, Birth of the Cuban Revolution.* Columbia: The University of South Caroline Press.

El guevarismo se confundió entre las mercancías y ahora es cosa entre las cosas. Porque la «cosa» –que continúa siendo el vehículo de transmisión indispensable– asegura el comercio aun después que las ideas han desaparecido.

Si Martí es el autor intelectual del Moncada, Batista es su genitor por la imago, el creador de la polis que dio sentido y trasfondo a la Revolución. El castrismo tiene, así, dos autores.

Las obras de Fulgencio Batista, en Ediciones Botas de Ciudad México, pertenecen al canon literario. Batista se adelanta a la muerte del autor: *Piedras y leyes* es el grado cero de nuestras Escrituras.

Cuba esperaba a un líder espiritual, a un mesías, a un Cristo origenista, y apareció un Jefe militar: José Eugenio, no José Cemí.

Ecclesia. Una pequeña mutación lezamiana produjo a Armando Álvarez Bravo; otra, a Severo Sarduy; aún otra, a Lorenzo García Vega; de un costado de *Orígenes* nacieron

Baquero, Fina, Gaztelu, los Diego, Retamar y hasta Fidel Castro.

356

Construcciones del tipo «confitados mirabeles» son irremediablemente pedestres. La iteración de «nieve», «nevado» y «nevaban» (diez veces en *Muerte de Narciso*) es un error garrafal al que nos hemos acostumbrado. La versificación lezamiana es corriente; su imaginería, plebeya; sus poemas están hechos de parodias, tropiezos y ripios. Pero, aún así, es una poesía peligrosa. Ensalzarla o salvarla no consigue nada. Solo cuando uno se da cuenta –y da cuenta– de su bajeza y vulgaridad, comienza el verdadero proceso de interpretación.

355

Lezama se vuelve una vieja costumbre (como cualquier otro costumbrismo).

354

La cadena sintáctica de equivocaciones en el cuento del bastón, de Guillermo Cabrera Infante, es el equivalente novelístico de la excursión de Herbert Matthews a la Sierra. La torpeza verbal, el error semántico, lo que se «pierde en la traducción», la construcción bombástica, el embrollo estilístico, son los elementos de los que está constituido también el hecho histórico.

En la narrativa de Matthews, Fidel reaparece, mientras que en la versión oficial del gobierno batistiano, desaparece («…the interview and the adventures described by Correspondent Matthews can be considered as a chapter in a fantastic novel», declara el Ministro de Defensa, Santiago Verdeja Neyra). Hay dos Fideles[57], hay dos bastones. La realidad del castrismo, y sus usos, dependerán, en lo adelante, de las creencias del narrador.

Hasta unos hombres sin importancia pueden desestabilizar una ciudad, pero volver a ponerla sobre los pies es difícil, a no ser que, súbitamente, un dios diga cómo. (Píndaro, «IV Oda Pítica»).

La preeminencia habanera con respecto a Matanzas y al resto de Cuba se extiende a toda la América «latina». En vez de tratarlos simplemente de «bárbaros», preferíamos hablar de «los países de allá abajo» (los países «bajos») a fin de denotar la distancia geográfica y espiritual que nos separaba de las regiones australes[58].

---

[57]   Cfr. Libro segundo, *Tria Juncta in Uno*, sobre «Los dos Fideles».

[58]   «El razonable temor de ver reproducirse en Cuba los alternados episodios de despotismo y anarquía que venían ofreciendo por entonces las nuevas nacionalidades hispanoamericanas, constituía para los partidarios del intermedio autonómico el mejor argumento que oponer al radicalismo predominante». Guillermo de Zéndegui (1991): *Todos somos culpables*. Miami: Universal.

350

La Habana, no Matanzas, es nuestra Atenas, y aunque aquella le cediera el título a su hermana, se sobrentendía que ella era la auténtica Ciudad Estado. Dejar que Matanzas fuera «falsa» Atenas (como falsa es la Grecia de Virgilio: falsa alarma y falsa tragedia) no hizo más que confirmar su posición primada.

349

Gerardo Machado es el fundador de la Atenas del Caribe. «Como un reemplazo del Mediterráneo por las aguas que circundan nuestra isla…», extrapola Lezama, en el prólogo de su *Antología,* 1965.

348

Lezama y Virgilio son los poetas del machadato, y hablan «en griego»: en el lenguaje de la tragedia.

347

«…y de esta manera estalla siempre una rabia íntima contra aquel presuntuoso pueblecillo que se atrevió a calificar para siempre de "bárbaro" a todo aquello no nativo de su patria: ¿quiénes son esos, nos preguntamos, que, aunque solo puedan mostrar un esplendor histórico efímero, unas instituciones ridículamente limitadas y estrechas, un dudoso vigor en su moralidad, y que incluso están señalados con feos vicios, pretenden tener entre los pueblos la dignidad y la posición especial que al genio corresponde entre la masa? Por desgracia, nadie ha tenido hasta ahora la suerte de encontrar la copa de cicuta con que semejante ser pudiera quedar sencillamente eliminado: pues todo el veneno producido por la envidia, la calumnia, la rabia, no ha bastado para aniquilar aquella magnificencia contenida en sí misma». Friedrich Nietzsche (1872): *El nacimiento de la tragedia.*

346

En Lezama y Machado, la fuente es griega. La tragedia machadista determina la forma en que se representa el mito en nuestras bellas letras. La poesía cubana es griega por influencia de El Egregio, que, actuando desde un Olimpo de obras públicas, levanta templos, palacios y un Capitolio.

345

Los grandes poetas de la ciudad machadista son Lezama y Virgilio. La aparición del Capitolio propicia el motivo oriental de *Muerte de Narciso* y el falso helenismo de *Electra Garrigó.*

344

En *Electra Garrigó*, la sencillez griega apela al sentido común mediante una economía de medios intrínsecamente plebeya. El clasicismo virgiliano deberá entenderse, entre nosotros, como la expresión de un mínimo común denominador, o como la formulación estética de un lagrangeano «principio del menor esfuerzo».

343

«En Grecia la larga esclavitud, y en Cuba el largo coloniaje, trajeron hábitos de ligereza, movilidad, horror al esfuerzo constante, propensión a la pereza bullanguera que hace más ruidosa la obra de verdad que realiza». *Capacidad masónica de los pueblos hispano-americanos*, Francisco de Paula Rodríguez. *Símbolo*, No. 30, Tomo V.

342

Lo que sucumbe hoy a la indigencia socialista es el constructivismo basado en aquel sentido común. Las demoliciones comenzaron entonces, en el apogeo de la revolución de 1933, y aunque el desplome de la urbe no ocurriría hasta veinte años más tarde, ya el petardo había sido plantado en sus cimientos. Hay un oráculo, en la verja de un palacio en ruinas, que aparece en *El acoso*, de Alejo Carpentier: «Se venden escombros».

341

«No debimos haber derrumbado todo si no teníamos la intención de derribar también las ruinas», lo dice Jarry, en *Ubú encadenado*.

340

Si la voladura de la ciudad es deconstructivista, el vandalismo comienza con Lezama y *Narciso*. Que Lezama llegara a integrar un modelo canónico es inconcebible, pues su programa pretendía acabar con la poesía, hacer volar el sentido (*logos*), para lo cual debió fragmentar primero las raíces griegas.

339

El machadato culmina con la rampante aparición del nihilismo lezamiano y del poema-manifiesto que anuncia el fin de la Primera República, *Muerte de Narciso,* cuya composición data, probablemente, de 1932. Todo lo que antecede a ese soliloquio platónico podría considerarse, entre nosotros, presocrático, pues solo en *Narciso* se consuma la experiencia cubana de la autorreflexión: *Nosce te Ipsum.*

338

Narciso es bifurcación: marca el instante trágico en que la unidad nacional se quiebra, la corriente se parte y el cubano enfrenta al cubano en *bellum civile.*

337

Todo Lezama –y Orígenes, por la vía del dadá– está escrito «en griego».

336

Quizás, a primera vista, no parezca que el idioma cubano cambiara mucho en el último siglo [como cambió, por ejemplo, el dialecto de los *Versos sencillos* con respecto al de *Dador*], aunque una segunda mirada nos revele que el lenguaje lezamiano nos resulta hoy tan incomprensible precisamente por ser anticuado; y no porque los «lezamanismos» envejecieran prematuramente, sino porque nuestra lengua es mucho más moderna de lo que suponíamos. Es decir: nos alejamos de Lezama y, simultáneamente, Lezama se aleja de nosotros debido a un proceso de recesión.

335

Los cubanos no acaban de entender que lo que ocurrió en agosto de 1933 fue la revolución dadaísta: «No más pintores, no más literatos, no más músicos, no más escritores, religiones, imperialistas, anarquistas, socialistas, bolcheviques, proletarios, demócratas, burgueses, aristócratas, ejército, policía, patria: en fin, basta de todas esas imbecilidades. No más nada, nada, nada… ¡Todos los miembros de dadá son presidentes!»[59].

334

El golpe de estado de un sargento oriental perfectamente desconocido y el subsiguiente vacío de poder; las intrigas de Sumner Wells; el chantaje de los estudiantes; el sepelio de Martínez Villena; la intervención de los artistas; la aclamación del galeno Grau San Martín; la traición de Mañach; la muerte de Mella, pero más que todo, la caída del gran proveedor de sentido, el generador de legitimidad, el constructor egregio, Gerardo Machado y Morales, inauguró una era en la que todos los miembros de la sociedad en desbandada fueron presidentes.

---

[59]   Tristan Tzara (1920): *Manifiesto Dada #5*.

¡Qué moderado nos parece hoy, por comparación, el programa dadaísta! Sin embargo, podría tomarse, sin temor a exagerar, como el verdadero origen del castrismo. El dadaísmo cubano creó las condiciones subjetivas para el derrumbe de la Primera República. Lo que quiere decir: para el desmontaje de la ilusión artística machadista.

La perreta de Machado provoca la famosa respuesta de Martínez Villena. El enfermo enmudece, tose, se atora y finalmente encuentra las palabras. Salen de su boca y caen como un esputo en el piso del despacho: *asno con garras*. Animal mitológico, suerte de grifo o quimera, criatura doble encerrada en su palacio de mármol, en su templo griego. La frase conserva aún el sabor clásico: *asno de oro*.

Lezama y Virgilio crean la revolución estéticamente, la procuran metafísicamente, son los genitores de la crisis. La República cae en escena debido a una «falsa alarma», de la misma manera que el ser (la imagen nacional, la célebre *imago* lezamiana) caerá en el vacío de su reflejo e itera-ción *ad hominem*. La nación da muestras de decadencia, señas inequívocas de enfermedad [en Lezama y Virgilio], y también de una propensión mecánica a la imitación, la recursividad y la simetría.

Lo que triunfa en 1959 es la tendencia comunista del programa batistiano. El comunismo –que es solo otro aspecto del batistato, otro elemento de su construcción, que Batista potenció y trajo al poder durante la campaña de 1938– ya estaba presente en la amalgama antimachadista antes de ser legitimizado. A partir de ese impulso inicial comienza su ascenso imparable: Batista, el epistemólogo oportunista, debe ser visto como nuestro primer socialista.

Antonio Guiteras Holmes pasa a engrosar las filas de los *Cuban Americans*: era pelirrojo, pecoso, taciturno, alto, maletudo, ascético y tenía un solo traje.

Sumner Welles, octubre 4, 1933, a Leslie Buell, Director de la Asociación para la Política Exterior Norteamericana: «Grau cree que gobernar consiste en la promulgación de decretos, no importa cuán mal concebidos o imposibles de cumplir, y al parecer su mente padece los efectos de una dieta de literatura mal digerida, del tipo *El Capital* de Carlos Marx, un libro que cita con harta frecuencia».

Sumner Welles a Buell, octubre 24, 1933: «Los puestos en cada departamento han sido cubiertos con miembros de los llamados comités de jóvenes y estudiantes, que despiden a los antiguos empleados y designan a otros nuevos, efectuando los cambios frecuentemente a punta de pistola, con el natural resultado de que la administración del poder ha caído en el caos total».

326

El automóvil, que es el clásico *prop* batistiano, deviene objeto de museo en la era castrista. El asalto al Cuartel se lleva a cabo en autos, uno de los cuales queda perennemente atascado a las puertas de la Historia.

325

PATAS

Patas cónicas,
como los conos de luz
de una saleta nuclear.

Patas canónicas,
pilares de la sociedad.
En el cincuentinueve ustedes
estaban firmemente plantadas
en el Einstein-Minkovski.

324

El efecto de renormalización castrista hace que el observador contemporáneo acepte la ruina como un hecho natural —o acaso como un hecho estético; vale decir: *infuso*—, cuando debería considerar también la presencia de ciertos elementos destructivos, ya que de lo contrario la decadencia podría ser tomada por un derrumbe *clásico* [abstracto], lo cual requiere la proyección del estado ruinoso hacia un plano ideal; pero lo cierto es que la ciudad fue destruida por una serie de golpes calculados; se trata de una ciudad deshauciada, más que arruinada, se decretó su desalojo: Camarioca, Varadero, el Mariel, etc. Hay un Ministerio de Recuperación de Bienes Malversados que contabiliza el patrimonio de los que se fueron. Se descabeza la estatua, mas no por un acto de violencia anárquica, sino por un programa socialista de obras públicas.

323

Cometo los mismos errores que denuncio en los otros: pero mis defectos saltan a la vista.

322

¡Recuérdalo, no hay escritura en tus Escrituras! No hay libro. El ensayo debe ser visto aquí como una forma de desahogo, muela de alienados, de perpetuos principiantes, frecuentadores de salones adonde nadie los invitó, en Brickell o en Kendall, gente desahuciada que había dejado de interesarse en la literatura décadas atrás, y cuyo ímpetu artístico (entre comillas) emanaba de una única experiencia seminal, algo no poco común en la vida diaria, sobre todo en la sexual, cuando la libido se desarrolla a partir de una inmadurez, de un error, de una eyaculación incompleta, de un coito infinitamente corrupto. La interrupción prematura del placer es la fuente de la ansiedad que pasa por poesía entre los diletantes congregados en las tertulias del gueto. Los escritores auténticos estaban en otra parte, recluidos en sus manicomios, empeñados en empuñar el bolígrafo con manos lisiadas: para ellos la cháchara hueca de los cenáculos resultaba intolerable. Por eso, las citas, cuando ocurren entre charlatanes, recaen invariablemente en unos conceptos que han permanecido encerrados todo un quinquenio en el corralito de la emotividad.

321

Deploraba la tendencia a ponerse viejo que venía camuflada en las ansias de claridad. «¡Adiós al ordencito!», exclamó un día, y ya desde entonces abrigaba la esperanza de acabar con todo. Le tomó algún tiempo identificar ese *todo*. «¡Una teoría negativa de todas las cosas!», anunció un mañana, convencido de haberla descubierto. Después se metió en el camarote y pasó encerrado siete días con sus noches, fumando sin parar, espantando fantasmas y maldiciendo al demonio de la continuidad. Que Isaac Kámara solo podía ser Isaac Kámara le mortificaba, cuando por todas partes veía una nube de posibilidades, un temblor, un mariposeo, una serie de estados superpuestos... La sombra de su mano en las paredes del camarote, llevándose la pipa a la boca, el pelo desgreñado saliendo por debajo de la boina roja, el uniforme amarillo con una *P* desteñida en la espalda (*pfi*, como solía pronunciar él esa letra, que denotaba su función de onda[60]), todo envuelto en las tinieblas que lanzaba la lámpara china sobre las planchas laminadas de un yate de recreo, al que íbamos acostumbrándonos poco a poco después de diez años de travesía, era como la proyección de una película soviética, bastante mala.

---

60   Isaac Kámara y los Compañeros hacen su aparición aquí como *p-zombis*, los «zombis filosóficos» descritos por David Chalmers en *The Conscious Mind* (1996), Oxford University Press.

Mientras que el término «fascista» goza de cada vez mayor oportunidad indéxica, el epíteto «comunista» ha experimentado una singular sufragación y transvaloración: de lo peyorativo, alrededor de 1848, a lo elogioso, entre intelectuales, desde 1900. Marx le dio rango filosófico y Engels una historia natural. En cualquier época «lo comunista» ha asumido un doble valor. La dualidad valorativa reside tanto en su recto sentido como en el aspecto modal de sus *usos*, aun cuando no llegue a consignarse su importe haeccéitico. «Comunista, esgrimido contra un enemigo ideológico, es sinónimo de antiestético», nos aclaró Isaac.

319

La manera en que Fidel esquivó (o negoció) la dialéctica de su ser-o-no-ser, el carácter indefinible de sus creencias, lo equívoco de sus propensiones y principios, sirve para ilustrar la vieja categoría filosófica de la negación de la negación. Batista habla de la caída del valor relativo del término «comunista», que llegó a considerarse entonces una acusación gratuita. Se lo tildó de melodramático, de rocambolesco, e incluso, de negroide.

318

Igual que el dios de Maimónides, el comunismo solo admite predicados negativos que afirmen su existencia[61].

---

[61]   «Todo aquello que implique corporealidad o pasividad en referencia a Dios deberá ser negativizado». Moisés Maimónides, *Guía del perplejo*, Primera parte, capítulo LV. The Chicago University Press, 1963.

Como la mentira avanza por la uña, así transcurren los días y los años en el yate Efemérides. Con el ritmo de lo malhadado. Como una mácula.

El origenismo nació negado. Como Narciso —su santo patrón–, era un aborto (botan al feto junto con el agua: es decir, a la criatura en lo líquido). El narcisismo acarrea su propio *contrarium*. El acto (primer Acto) de precipitarse en el reflejo, es ya un límite: el origen abocado inmediatamente a la capitulación. *Nosce te Ipsum* (Lezama es nuestro Sócrates). Porque el ser elevado al absurdo recursivo cae interminablemente en el error del sí mismo.

¿A qué se refiere Lezama cuando habla de «Jardines invisibles» si no a las Islas Afortunadas, esas que habitábamos ya sin pasar por la muerte?

ÁLBUM DE MADRES CUBANAS

Espejo de justicia: Olga Guillot
Trono de sabiduría: Lydia Cabrera
Causa de nuestra alegría: Celia Cruz
Vaso espiritual: Selma Sánchez
Vaso digno de honor: Haydee Santamaría

Vaso de insigne devoción: La Lupe
Rosa mística: Fe del Valle
Torre de David: Pura del Prado
Torre de marfil: Uma Clavija
Casa de oro: Marta Estrada
Arca de la Alianza: Mariana Grajales
Puerta del cielo: Cecilia Valdés
Estrella de la mañana: Zoé Valdés
Salud de los enfermos: Ana Mendieta
Refugio de los pecadores: Marta Abreu
Consoladora de los afligidos: Mirta de Perales
Auxilio de los cristianos: Yezabel Bottom

313

Un viejo amigo. Lo encontré frente al Payless Shoes de la Doce Avenida, carcomido de sarcoma de Kaposi, si en un tiempo apuesto y bien dotado, ahora un paria en la Calcuta que es Miami. El ángulo de los escalones parecía estar hecho para admitirlo, cabía allí encorvado, como un anacoreta. Hablamos de los buenos tiempos idos, de algunos episodios de nuestras vidas que nos comprometían para la eternidad. Me pidió que le trajera comida y hasta me dio las gracias por haberlo reconocido.

312

El hereje no lo es para un tiempo y un lugar específicos sino para todos los tiempos y todas las circunstancias. Por eso se ha dicho que las opiniones peligrosas lo acechan «en cualquier sitio y época en que haga y en que sufra la Historia».

«Dar la cara», es lo que hace un hereje, mientras que un simple autor se esconde tras la máscara de la escritura.

Hurgar en los puntos de contacto entre el Hitler de los *advertisements*, el Warhol ilustrador y el Duchamp de los cuadros de segunda. Conectar al *Führer* de los paisajes en formato toalla –el creador de la pintura mala, el escritor expresionista, el lector de novelitas de indios y vaqueros, el admirador de Ramón Díaz de la Escosura, el fanático de la ópera, el doble de Charlot– con los modelos de la transvanguardia y el posmodernismo. Comprobar que del esteticismo no hay escapatoria posible.

El problema de los múltiples universos aparece enunciado en una carta de Kurt Gödel a su madre: «De otra manera, por ejemplo, no podríamos saber si no moriremos también en el más allá»[62]. Uno imagina la muerte y crea escenarios lógicos que vienen a ser mundos coposibles. El gato encerrado está vivo y muerto, de la misma manera que vida y muerte se igualan como potencialidades de la evolución del sistema. Somos observadores de una y otra

---

[62] «Sonst könnten wir ja z. B. gar nicht wissen, ob wir in der ändern Welt nicht auch sterben werden». Carta de Kurt Gödel a su madre Marianne, Princeton, septiembre 12, 1961. Collected Works, Vol. IV, 2003.

posibilidad, pues, mientras haya vida, contemplaremos la muerte.

308

MEMENTO MORI. Comprometemos la dualidad vida-muerte al contemplarla: epistemológicamente, somos muertos-vivos.

307

Un personaje de novela: Eloísa Álvarez Gödel.

306

Examen de una reproducción ricamente enmarcada, en la casa de campo de Redlands, de la escritora y periodista Selma O'Flatter:

Quizás en España, en 1939, el mundo [el viejo mundo] llegó a su fin. Antonio López García representa el apocalipsis de lo real, el envejecimiento de la objetividad, el opacamiento (apocamiento) de Europa, un mundo en vías de volverse moho y sombra. La decadencia de lo representable coincide con la muerte de la democracia, que perece a manos de un pintor malo que pinta un aparador, una buhardilla y una percha en el sur de Madrid.

En las dos máscaras de *La cena* (1971-1980), y a pesar de la cuadratura cubista, no hay nada africano, sino madrileño. No es que irrumpa allí el espaciotiempo, sino que el cuadro no consigue completarse. La sopa y la papilla que las mujeres ingieren no pueden menos que desorganizarlas; la alcachofa es un objeto monstruoso, ajeno a esta o a cualquier otra mesa; y la carne, de un realismo fotográfico, es pecado, es canibalismo de última cena donde los alimentos pierden (junto al agua bendita embotellada) su capacidad redentora o gastronómica, y quedan como detrito, escombro en el mantel, evidencia de un crimen inconfesable.

305

Escena en que Adán Rueda de Morloc lo lleva de mañana a los baños. Antes de llegar se detienen en una construcción abandonada (un condo cualquiera). Encuentran un sapo negro encima de una tabla salpicada de cemento. Cae llovizna menuda en el callejón. Adán le dice al sapo: *Take me to your leader!* Están ahítos de ácido. Todo esto anticipa el mismo evento en el Efemérides, cuando Isaac pasa por las fiebres de la desintoxicación y ve aparecer al manatí y cree que es un mutante. Delira. El Manatí habla: «¡Querido amigo! La juventud añora juntarse en un haz. Solo la vejez nos permite individualizarnos, separarnos por fin de la gentuza. ¡Hazte viejo! Fíjate en el hippismo, que produjo los crímenes más horripilantes de la era de Acuario. Familias de fanáticos incestuosamente emparentadas en el crimen. Fue un fascismo en busca de un jefe: Charles Manson es Picatrix, un diablo bien conocido alrededor de 1514; Rabelais lo llama *le révérend père en diable Picatris, recteur de la faculté diabolologique.* ¿Sabes de quién te hablo? ¡De quien tú sabes!» *Take me to your leader...* repitió Adán. «Sabio y filósofo», cró el sapo, «muy versado en matemáticas y en el arte de la necromancia, *Scientia... semper acquirit et numquam diminuit, semper elevat et numquam degenerat, semper apparet et numquam se abscondit*». ¿Por qué les digo que Fernando de Call es nuestro pensador más profundo?, nos preguntó Isaac, asfixiado. Pues porque encarnó lo malo en los tiempos del Mal, y la enfermedad en la edad de la pestilencia. *A imitatio Picatrix*. ¿Y cómo responde Fernando a las críticas de Selma? Se le arroja al cuello, la golpea, quiere estrangularla. Magali contraataca; lo patea, lo saca de su casa a escobazos, como a un sapo, cuando Fernando se le aparece en New Jersey.

304

Dos cuadros enmarcados adornan el comedor formal de la empresaria: *Tempo verrà ancor*, un dibujo de Buonarroti, y la *Naturaleza muerta con piezas de caza, vegetales, frutas y cacatúa*, de Adrian van Utrecht.

303

La experiencia del exilio produce excitación [sexual]. Hablo del exilio como imitación y duplicado de la vida que conocimos en las condiciones naturales de la existencia previa. Perder el Paraíso y ser arrojados a la planicie ardiente, a las ciudades de la llanura: Miami, Sweetwater, Hialeah, Homestead, Westchester, Opa-locka, Overtown... Allí imitamos los municipios cubanos, las cliniquitas, los partidos, los sindicatos, las fechas y las ceremonias, así como los cumpleaños, los bautizos, los aniversarios, las jaboneras, el talco, los refrescos, etc. [Concebir la experiencia del destierro como una pequeña muerte en la Pequeña Habana].

Interesarse en el batistato requiere el ejercicio de una heurística que marche a contrapelo de las normas académicas aceptadas. El investigador del batistato deberá, incluso, avanzar a contracorriente del *instinto de conservación*. La industria del conocimiento castrista y el circuito de subvenciones y publicaciones académicas producen estipendios a los que deberá renunciar de antemano cualquier aproximación crítica.

Hablando del estado de las creencias positivistas previas al relativismo, Milic Čapek explica que «un animal cuya conducta ignore explícitamente el teorema de Euclides (según el cual, el camino más corto entre dos puntos es la línea recta) estaría en desventaja en sus esfuerzos por alcanzar su objetivo (en caso de huir de un enemigo) y sería irremediablemente alcanzado por sus competidores euclidianos»[63]. Este razonamiento compete hoy al problema del castrismo. En el medio ambiente académico, alguien que rechace la doctrina positivista de lo políticamente correcto –el guevarismo renormalizado– y la escala de valores neocastrista, se encontrará en desventaja con respecto a sus rivales en la feroz competencia por los puestos, los recursos y la atención del público. El guevarismo, como sistema dinámico en constante reajuste que abarca tanto las ciencias sociales como la estética, la ecología y la escolástica, es un *a priori*. La victoria final del guevarismo, como principio

---

[63]   Milic Čapek (1961): *The Philosophical Impact of Contemporary Physics*.

de causalidad, es un caso especial del principio darwinista de la supervivencia del más apto.

300

El poeta jurará mil veces que no sabía, se declarará inocente, dirá que vio en el Terror una poética y hasta una especie de justicia, y el público le creerá. Todo poeta se burla en secreto de su público.

299

Porque el poeta nunca está equivocado. Cuando afirma que el Terror es poesía sufre de un ataque momentáneo de lucidez. Se arrepentirá de lo dicho, pero el arrepentimiento es una emoción inferior, indigna de poetas.

298

«De los cobardes no se ha escrito nada» significa que los cobardes son incapaces de escribirse.

297

L'IMAGINATION AU POUVOIR. Imaginar a un cantautor que componga una balada en honor de Stroessner; pensar en un teatro donde se estrene una ópera dedicada a la memoria de Batista: ese anfiteatro y ese estadio estarían situados en un universo paralelo donde los hombres son verdaderamente libres. Pero a los hombres de la conciencia castrista nos está vedado imaginarlo.

Toda mente cerrada es castrista: también la abierta.

La Torre de Pei en llamas, agosto de 1984

La aparición de la Torre de Pei en el área de los antiguos asentamientos calusa, sobre el moderno gueto cubano, trajo a Miami la idea de la pirámide, el zigurat y la torre de Babel. Cierto atardecer de agosto de 1984, mientras caminaba por Flagra, a la altura del Federal Discount (frente al mercadito donde Minín Bujones era cajera, en la vecindad del antiguo *Burdines*) miré al cielo y vi la torre en llamas. Sus tres cuerpos retractables ascendían hacia el firmamento como un falo llameante que emergiera de sí mismo por partes, todavía no recubierto de espejos, cuando el hormigón armado era todo esqueleto. De los últimos pisos salían chispas y una columna de humo antiguo. Grandes llamaradas, las mangueras izadas, el cielo de añil y el sol escarlata declinando hacia el poniente, por detrás de la Torre, sobre el pantano. En la calle nos apretujábamos los curiosos bajo la pertinaz llovizna de cenizas. Miré en derredor y vi un mar de cabezas levantadas, de ojos intransigentes, fijos en la candela. Resplandores de oro en las caras de los que atendían al desastre. De mañana, la luz cayó como un reflector sobre la frialdad de lo real, que entregaba su arcano a los barrenderos.

En las rosas de Hitler confluyen dos corrientes estéticas: la noción clásica del arte («es más importante ver que pensar») y la idea expresionista de la pintura como «música para los ojos», donde el pensamiento toma precedencia sobre lo visto. Esas rosas maltrechas son afines a las de Kokoschka: la misma violencia de la pincelada, el mismo tono sucio, la misma mueca barroca [el esputo en el clavel], la grosería sublime y la neurosis del *art brut* están ahí también. «El espectáculo hereda las debilidades del proyecto filosófico occidental, que se propuso entender toda "actividad" en los términos de las categorías del "ver"», avisa Guy Debord en *La société du spectacle*.

293

«La Pintura predica lo que el hombre *quiere* ver y lo que *debe* ver, nunca lo que comúnmente ve», advierte Goethe. Y es en este sentido [romántico] que el castrismo llegó a ser una práctica artística y una nueva manera de ver.

292

La Revolución vino a liberarnos de nuestro éxito, a arrebatárnoslo y a robarnos algo precioso. Si los españoles despojaron de oro a los incas, entre nosotros no encontraron nada: solo con el tiempo Cuba llegaría a ser un Potosí, enriquecida a posteriori, una riqueza cifrada en imponderables. La verdadera conquista de Cuba debió esperar por la segunda mitad del siglo XX, cuando una cábala de anarquistas, linotipistas, panfleteros, nihilistas y mercenarios republicanos, de politicastros y truhanes ibéricos, ingresa a nuestro país y lo somete. Son mercenarios que escapan de otra guerra civil, nuestros conquistadores. La revolución comunista no tuvo éxito en el 33; pero a partir de 1939 las fuerzas antinacionales que salen de España se dispersan por el mundo. Podría trazarse el curso de esa ofensiva como la flecha roja de una invasión bárbara[64].

291

Gödel, en una carta a su madre: «El secreto (y el sentido) de un fraude no [...] es que *simula,* sino que *enmascara,* el verdadero fenómeno».

290

Vio la realidad través de las ranuras. Su respiración quedó atrapada en el interior de la máscara y le bañó la cara de un vapor hediondo.

289

El ensimismamiento produjo una imagen distorsionada del libro que tenía en las manos; las líneas se separaron y luego se penetraron, interpretadas unas en las otras. La forma del libro también cambió, debido a la bizquera que produce ese peculiar estado de conciencia. Pero, ¿cuál era el libro falso y cuál el verdadero?

---

[64] «*In Spain we lost a battle but in Cuba we won the war,* says [María Rosa] Almendros, whose father fought in the Spanish Civil War against Franco» [sic]. Olga R. Rodríguez (2001): *Revolution is a moment.* UC Berkeley School of Journalism.

288

La gente no entendía que la casa de crack era el laboratorio donde Kámara ponía a prueba sus teorías.

287

«Ese escalofrío de Casal, por ejemplo, siempre hemos sospechado que está dando testimonio del frío interior que hay en nuestro país, que empieza con él a sentirse». Cintio Vitier (1958): *Lo cubano en la poesía*. Lo cita Selma O'Flatter para refutar la idea del «barroco flamígero» de Fernando de Call.

286

Solo una figura como la de Castro podía provocar veneración y miedo, repugnancia y deseo. El diente negro, que centelleaba cada vez que sonreía, mantuvo al pueblo pendiente de cada una de sus palabras. Si es verdad que, como afirmó Robespierre, «no hay virtud sin terror», ahora los artistas cubanos entendían que tampoco podía haber una *estética* sin una cierta inclinación canallesca provocada por circunstancias extremas, y que Castro [o más bien, *lo castrista*] era el terreno epistemológico contra el que sus creaciones cobrarían sentido en lo adelante.

285

Quiero dejar sentado que ninguno de los Compañeros supo nunca quién era Kámara, porque Isaac Kámara fue él mismo exclusivamente en su escritura. Se trata de una voz que dice una cosa distinta cuando habla que cuando canta, o que no reconocemos como propia al escucharla en una grabación. Sabían, eso sí, que Isaac era al autor de unos poemas concretos, pero no conocían su pensamiento [la manera en que hablaba a solas]. Tampoco K reconoció a Guillermo Rosales entre los asistentes al maleficio, aunque tuviera una idea lejana de su rabia, de su sombra, y pudiera recordarlo en un gesto brusco en los escalones de la Biblioteca, en un sueño o en un conciliábulo. *El Negro* le decía: «¡Claro que lo conociste!» Pero Isaac lo desconoció.

284

No hay diferencias en el discurso de los pequeñoburgueses, todos se expresan en el dialecto de la revolución [que es la anomalía del lenguaje burgués, una manera errónea de designar las cosas]. Una buena mañana un ama de casa se levanta y llama al televisor «ornitorrinco», y el marido la sigue y le dice «resplandor» a la puerta. El mundo los oye expresarse y sabe que se trata de un error, pero no se atreve a contradecirlos. En algún momento, alguien, envalentonado por el (dis)curso que han tomado las cosas, llamará «ángel» al revólver, y más adelante «absolución» al crimen y «líder» al carnicero. Este desplazamiento del sentido se advierte primero en Virgilio, en su drama, que es el teatro del idioma. Por eso, cuando dice «frío» es caliente, dentro del mismo conflicto semiótico. Las clases bajas toman la palabra y se expresan en clichés. Mientras tanto, al otro lado de la ciudad, Lezama se dirige a un grupo de discípulos en un idioma indescifrable, una lengua en clave donde se toma una cosa por otra («nieve, frío, fría, nevados»). Ya el joyero, la maestra, el acomodador y el notario, el poeta, el actor y la baladista hablan ese dialecto. Se tratan de «compañeros».

283

Fidel Castro en la Biblioteca Nacional: «A nosotros nos interesa que no vaya a terminar esto en una cámara húngara». Expresiones que cayeron en desuso. Allí Fidel es Virgilio.

282

La revolución, que es el lenguaje de la burguesía, sirve de punto de contacto con las clases bajas. Así el burgués, el aristócrata, el mierda, el oligarca, el buscavidas y el artista se tocan, sus intereses coinciden: Martí, Fidel, Batista, Franqui, Virgilio, Vitier, Guillén, Melba, Retamar, Feijóo y Baragaño invocan la revolución. Virgilio tiene sus razones (nobleza, indigencia, indiferencia) para abrazarla, y Lezama, simplemente, por haber sido declarado «víctima de las circunstancias». No debió ser pobre y, si lo era, había llegado el momento de subsanar el error, la hora de la rectificación. Lezama *debía* ser rico, pero en expresiones, en reconocimientos, en publicaciones y encargos. Virgilio no tendría que sufrir más de pobreza abyecta: la revolución lo convertiría en su príncipe mendigo.

281

El problema del lenguaje politécnico marxista antecede a la revolución, lo traen con ellos los viejos ideólogos («proletariado», «dialéctica», «vanguardia», «planteamiento», «contradicción», «cantera», etc.) como rezago de una época histórica superada. De esa época que pretendió superarse por el marxismo sobrevive el lenguaje especializado, enrarecido, sectario e ideologizante, el lenguaje partidista que nació y se concretó en la etapa previa, pero que todavía hoy constituye el verdadero problema. En la literatura de Virgilio el lenguaje viciado se instaura como dispositivo dramático. Los burgueses se tratan, conversan y materializan en lugares comunes [lo pequeñoburgués es, por definición, el *mínimo común*]. Ningún otro orden social había conseguido establecerse antes como aspiración de todos. Así surge el principio totalitario: lo burgués, y especialmente el *gusto* burgués, tiende a lo absoluto.

280

Lo burgués consuma y subsume la totalidad de la experiencia humana y se declara Fin de la Historia. Solo que, para llegar a establecerse, un orden inmutable debe pasar primero por la revolución, expresarse en la revolución y negarse a sí mismo. Solo entonces se darán las condiciones objetivas de su establecimiento perpetuo. La perpetuidad de un orden reaccionario es revolucionaria.

279

Si [según Stuart Mill] la supresión de la individualidad es despotismo, el batistato no lo fue. No suprimió, sino que exacerbó la individualidad. La aparición de una individualidad límite marca el apogeo del batistato. El destino trágico de la República estuvo signado por la incapacidad batistiana para suprimir esa individualidad hipertrofiada.

Nos aguarda, al doblar de la esquina, el engendro del castrismo, su Ismaelillo: lo políticamente correcto, que tira el traje de Comandante y se viste de facilitador y de activista. El castrismo como especialista en sexualidad, el castrismo multicultural que ejerce su dictadura desde el hogar, la cátedra y la prensa, desde el laboratorio, la escuela, el mercado, el huerto y la cocina. El castrismo como diversionismo, entretenimiento y lugar común. Hoy, más que nunca, una oposición sana y auténticamente contrarrevolucionaria debe oponerse a esa influencia foránea y luchar contra la tiranía que viene disfrazada de optimismo.

277

Notas para posible novela:

−cogiendo un profundo resuello
−exhalando un hondo suspiro
−hablando entrecortadamente por entre volutas de humo
−soltando un largo chillido
−hablando precipitadamente
−mirando el reloj de muñeca
−mirando el reloj de pared
−levantándose el cuello del abrigo
−dándole vueltas al anillo de compromiso
−sí, él es mi compromiso
−¡sin compromisos!
−no, no tienes por qué
−abrió la boca
−el dedo siguió la línea del horizonte

—se sacudió una migaja
—habló despacio, con la boca llena
—masticó y habló al mismo tiempo
—tragó, tomó un sorbo de Cisco
—se mojó los labios con la lengua

276

No estaba claro si sabían lo que vendría después, pero la tarde comenzó como comienzan todas las tardes de piedra: alegres, contentos, rebosantes de felicidad, *rozagantes*, diríamos. Se habían bañado, se habían limpiado. Habían hecho abluciones y enjuagues: Kolonia, Violetas Imperiales, Agua de Florida, todo mezclado con talco funguicida. El manatí se deslizó por el agua, su cuerpo de torpedo, ancho y vacío, navegando de espaldas en el canal, estilo mariposa, las cerdas húmedas, impregnadas de óleo, fango, heces, residuos de lanchas rápidas y bicicletas acuáticas; se confundió entre los pedales, continuó su avance por el arroyo, agitando las pequeñas aletas, pellizcándose las tetas, conduciéndonos hacia las profundidades akásicas, hacia el laberinto acanalado, hacia los primeros remolinos. Expresó sus ideas, las cantó, las rimó, las escupió en hilillos de agua, hizo gárgaras con ellas, vació la uretra.

275

Van de *holiday*. El anuncio decía: «¡Todos tus sueños hechos realidad», y «Vacaciones de ensueño». La revolución se presenta como ese destino para los buenos burgueses de

Presiones y diamantes[65], un «viaje al imposible», de duración ilimitada. Y aunque la vacación presupone el retorno, las cosas se complican, las maletas se pierden, los vuelos se retrasan. En la cabaña de troncos junto al lago encuentran a un muerto debajo del entarimado. Algo horrible merodea en la oscuridad. En el bosque aúllan lobos. Las vacaciones se extienden indefinidamente. El hotel es una trampa. Los caminos están empantanados. Cae nieve. No hay salida. Han entrado en el período virgiliano glacial. De vacaciones a la glaciación.

274

¿Por qué me interesa la ciencia? Porque me ayuda a entender los sucesos políticos. Un hecho de sangre es solo un *evento*, y, por tanto, susceptible de ser analizado con las herramientas de la mecánica y la geometría. Bohr dijo: «Nuestra interpretación del material experimental descansa esencialmente sobre conceptos clásicos». Lo mismo podría decirse de la interpretación de la era republicana, si consideramos «clásicas» las nociones castristas recibidas. Esas nociones afectaron el lenguaje común y definieron el modelo de interpretación estándar. Son conceptos erróneos, distorsionados por una perspectiva falsa, cuya escala de valores se ha vuelto la norma.

273

Mi método es la nueva *scienza* −Bruno, Vico, Gödel, Bohr, Bokun, Fuller, Feyerabend: «nueva» por estar siempre en ciernes, perpetuamente en vías de establecerse. Cada

---

65   Virgilio Piñera (1967): *Presiones y diamantes*. La Habana: Unión.

problema exige recomenzar de cero, reinventar el aparataje científico completo. Completamente virgen porque «no ha conocido», lo que quiere decir también que es una *ignorancia*. [Bohr a Abraham Pais: «¡Sepa que soy un diletante!»].

272

Esa *scienza* permanece oculta y nunca deja de ser nueva, el estado de perpetua novedad es su estrategia y su peculiar manera de conocer. El ocultismo le permite sustraerse de la vista de los intrusos. Para llegar a ella, el investigador deberá abjurar de sus más queridas nociones, y hasta de su inteligencia.

271

Foucault, Derrida, Lyotard: el público se resiste a aceptar, a interiorizar, la última revolución epistemológica, de la misma manera que se resistió a pensar en términos relativistas. El Poder, consciente del alcance de la nueva revolución francesa, tomó la academia y la convirtió en su cuartel. El Poder se apropia de los koanes y las aporías de Guattari, Deleuze y Lévinas, y habla ahora desde la oposición, desde la episteme de la diferencia —pretende erigirse en *diferencia*. Eso es la «Izquierda». Pero la Izquierda no es más que docta ignorancia. La Izquierda es el Poder centralizado, el Partido único, el Estado policíaco, el intelectual como colaboracionista, el demagogo como proveedor de máximas, el tirano como procurador de objetividad[66].

---

[66] «Foucault es Robespierre; Deleuze es Danton; Derrida es Marat; Barthes es Bailly; etc...». Isaac Kámara (1989): *El espejo pendiente*. Omaha: Horca editores.

¿Por qué es importante considerar el pasado? Porque en ese pasado habíamos alcanzado el estado ideal que Francis Fukuyama llama «Fin de la Historia». El parlamentarismo, el sufragio, la liberalidad, la integración, el confort no son los únicos factores que permiten medir el grado de realización alcanzado por la Cuba clásica. Hay un parámetro acaso más importante: nuestro Estado de Derecho logró coexistir con un cierto *brutalismo policíaco*, cuya medida viene dada por un índice B (batistiano) que denota unos niveles saludables de censura de los elementos antisociales, anárquicos o disruptivos, por debajo del cual la sociedad cae en C (castrismo), que es el Estado policíaco irracional.

¡Ay, la propela del yate Efemérides! ¡Cuantos mediodías no dormitó bajo las ramas de las guásimas, enorme y frígido! Otros manatíes venían a admirarlo, a él, en su exilio, sorbiendo un daiquirí hecho de yerbas, lodo y rocío. Su lomo cobrizo a lo lejos, ¿no era el mojón en alta mar? ¡También una butifarra, una morcilla heroica! Del peludo hociquito salían canciones antiguas, de la época juvenil y mundial de Manatí. ¡Qué indigente y qué indígena le parecía todo ahora! El viento era limpio; el agua, corriente; la luz eléctrica brillaba en los fresnos decorados; las barriguitas de mil luciérnagas despedían un resplandor noctámbulo. Las jóvenes ondinas nadaban en los remansos, se volvían señoritas, maestras normalistas, tomaban clases de Cívica y de Economía del Hogar; fumaban cigarrillos rubios, cual murciélagos iniciáticos. Manatíes color fucsia, coral y verde champú;

manatíes de plástico, de juguete, de yarey trenzado, teñidos de magenta, de azul patrio, de amarillo pollito. Artesanías del pantano. Manatí es el último de los micosukees. Le dio dos mordidas a un sándwich de pechuga, se atarugó con un pastelillo de guayaba, encendió un mocho de tabaco arrojado a las aguas. Se zambulló: Buckminster Fuller y Disney, metidos hasta los ojos en el fango, lo vigilaban. Un flamenco posado en una pata deletreó con la otra la palabra «Materva». Manatí dormido, arrorró Manatí. La propela del yate Efemérides le abrió diez tajazos en el lomo. Lo dejaron por muerto, en los manglares.

268

Un idioma se ceba en otro. Los nombres de animales, árboles, flores, sensaciones y padecimientos, y los altos conceptos que aprendimos de niños, se corroen, se descomponen y se pudren. Una palabra lleva en el vientre el detrito de muchas otras.

267

Llegan, a través del Gran Canal, a un lago de fuego. Ven un groto de adelfas y, más allá, por entre las ramas, la esfera geodésica. Atracan en Epcot.

266

¡Que encojonada la conversación después del pipazo! ¡Qué calentura! ¡Hablar y despotricar y explayarse y esperar por lo que nunca llega! ¡Qué ganas de desnudarse, y qué revelación de que vamos desnudos, que bastó un trastazo para desavillarnos en cuerpo y alma! ¡Y qué miedo, qué terror tan puro! ¡Vacuidad aterradora! Como si nos cogieran por los pies y nos sacudieran y el espíritu cayera al suelo en seborucos, su peso en oro, más precioso que la pimienta, boronilla rastreada y llevada a la boca, degustada con malicia. ¡Transmutación del oro en plomo, del humo en miedo! ¡El paniqueo[67]! ¿Quiénes son los ricos y quiénes los pobres en una urbe poblada de zombis, cuando alguien decide levantarse a medianoche y salir a coronar?

265

DESARREGLO DE TODOS LOS SENTIDOS. «Terminé por considerar sagrado el desorden de mi mente». Isabel Rimbaud describe la agonía de su hermano: «Deliraba, y lo mezclaba todo, pero con arte».

264

La Funeraria Ravelo, donde velan a Blanca Rosa, está situada entre un lote de carros usados y un solar yermo. Hileras de banderitas cubanas ondean contra el cielo empedrado formando un paralelepípedo.

263

Un puntazo casual de la pluma en la página: un rayón. Cada vez que abro esa página creo que es un cabello y lo

---

67   Arthur Koestler, en *Scum of the Earth*, 1941, hace mención de los *paniquards* («During the first days of the war, people fled fearing the worst...»), un término afín a los vocablos *paniqueo* y *paniqueado*, provenientes del argot de la piedra.

soplo. Luego recuerdo el engaño, pero el efecto ya es parte del texto.

262

Los antiguos patriarcas no descartaban la muerte («Hasta en la muerte serás mi Guía», Tehillim 48:14), ni esperaban vida eterna, pues estaban satisfechos con lo que tenían: «A ti clamé, y Tú me respondiste». Solo la chusma pretende no morir nunca. A ella van dirigidas las falsas promesas de eternidad.

261

¿Quién dijo que la vida eterna es negocio? Los mercaderes en el Poder.

260

El «otro» está en la punta del tabaco fumado al revés. El tizón en la boca del brujo y la perilla en la boca del Santo. Le dan de fumar. Aspira. Una penetración en el otro mundo: una *intromisión*.

259

Todavía está por decidirse si JC era realmente el hijo de dios, y tal vez se trate de una proposición indecidible. El castrismo padece el mismo tipo de indecibilidad, que le sirve de fundamento doctrinal: nunca sabremos si fue un error o un milagro. Considerad la ambigüedad de Guevara, a quien Sartre declara «un modelo de humanidad» y que los cubanos vemos como «un zarrapastroso asesino»[68].

258

El que fuma le mama el rabo al dios del tabaco, un dios primitivo, arahuaco, venido del fondo del Orinoco, de un pasado sangriento, pestilente, contagioso. El gargajo en la espalda: Colba nació de un esputo.

257

«Consta que ciertos indios antillanos creían que los muertos en su viaje de ultratumba iban hacia el oeste, o sea hacia donde muere el sol, hacia la región de las tinieblas nocturnas. Esta creencia, muy extendida en muchos pueblos, era la que hacía decir a los taínos de Haití que sus muertos iban a Coaibai, vocablo que indicando un país montañoso del Occidente, parece ser el mismo vocablo *Cuba*». Fernando Ortiz (1943): *Las cuatro culturas indias de Cuba*. La Habana: Arellano y Cía.

256

Coaibai: el enterrorio donde el Imperio español vino a morir.

---

68 La figura byroniana del Che, queda plasmada, *avant la lettre*, en la célebre glosa de Lady Caroline Lamb: «He left a name to all succeeding times / Linked to one virtue and a thousand crimes». *Glenarvon*, 1816.

Las páginas de Talmud, aposentos del palacio de Jokmá, celdas y salones interconectados por corredores y pasadizos: Rashi a la derecha, el Rábano a la izquierda, Guemará en el centro. La celosía de signos deja entrar la luz de los ojos. Una voz fuerte llega de los claustros vecinos. Estatuas y mascarones filtran el eco de lo que se dice en las salas contiguas: *glory, glory, glory hole*. Hay conversaciones sobre temas políticos, médicos, astrológicos, sexuales, triviales… De un lado a otro [van y vienen] como jayots, los relampagueos: *Aún cuando salgan de Él y vuelen hacia Él, permanecerán firmemente anclados a Él.*

La clave no está en el deseo de regresar al pasado para resucitar a Lois Lane, como hace Superman, sino en el mismo *acto* de mover la Tierra (la rueda) en contrasentido. El rebobinado deshace las «formaciones» (*yetzirah*) de la Historia.

Sitra Ahra, la ribera satánica, sucia y sagrada, del río Yabbok, el arroyo de la Muerte. También el brazalete del M-26-7 está partido en dos campos: Mercurio y Azufre, las dos Naturalezas, las mitades del Hermafrodita, las dos Cubas, los Dos Ríos.

Alejandro de Humboldt descubrió que los indios otomacos tomaban unos polvos de semilla de niopo mezclados con harina de casabe y cal obtenida de cierta concha y tostados en un *burén* (voz arahuaca) con cuya pasta hacen bolas. *El tubo era un hueso bifurco de aura tiñosa.* Desde el Amazonas, bajando por el Orinoco, viene la costumbre de arrebatarnos.

En un cuarto de Overtown, una negra joven sale del baño envuelta en una toalla. Se tira en la cama y enrollamos un tabaco de pintintín, o ella lo enrolla con pericia. Saca la lengua y moja el papel de lado a lado como si cerrara un sobre. Después de fumar partimos en barca por el Nilo de humo, bogamos entre paredes de seda. Una luz milagrosa nos baña, los viejos ventiladores nos abanican. Ella canta un guaguancó, o alguna otra melodía que encaja como un remo en el paisaje drogado. Sabe de qué hablo, y me sorprende con salidas políticamente incorrectas... «¡Eun crime mandarul niñu paeste paí...!», dice, saltando desnuda de la cama, «¡Tilal-lo nuna canata! ¡Eun crime!»[69].

«En marzo de 1940 comienza un tranquilo capítulo de su vida. En Princeton, Gödel es elegido anualmente, desde 1940 hasta 1946, miembro del Instituto de Estudios Avan-

---

[69]   Félix Lira de Arruabarrena, en sus *Comentarios marginales a las «Hojas de Rábano»* (1999), acusa a Kámara de ser un *Male sifrei tenáh*: una «canasta llena de libros».

zados […] Al principio Adela y él vivieron en apartamentos alquilados. En abril de 1948 se hacen ciudadanos de Estados Unidos y en agosto de 1949 compran la casa de Linden Lane donde pasan el resto de sus días». Hao Wang (1996): *A Logical Journey: from Gödel to Philosophy*.

249

Martí y nosotros [los gusanos] tuvimos la misma experiencia de arrobo ante el paisaje de otras latitudes, el mismo deseo de absorción de lo ajeno, el mismo sentimiento de vacío y, simultáneamente, de comunión, de identificación y deslumbramiento. Éramos exiliados, no había regreso posible, y las nuevas circunstancias estaban obligadas a hablarnos.

248

Un libro obliga; la estructura del objeto impone un orden. Confiar la idea a la página conlleva un formalismo. La teoría demanda el *theatros* de su representación.

247

Un *efficiency* consiste en un único ambiente que resume en un cuadrilátero la experiencia de la vivienda (ver *Tawaraya boxing ring-cum-conversation pit*, del diseñador Masanori Umeda). Es el *abode* reducido a su mínima expresión: las cuatro paredes. En propiedad, todo lo que extienda esas paredes (extensiones: también llamadas en Miami *adicciones*) resulta superfluo. El *efficiency* es, por lo regular, una habitación que los dueños de la casa han cercenado, violenta e ilegalmente, al cuerpo principal de la vivienda: a un dormitorio simple se le añaden un baño minúsculo y una cocinita (se trata a veces de un par de resistencias).

246

Los invasores del Mariel tomaron los apartamentos abandonados, el Miami River Inn, El Transilvania, El Borinquen, La Paloma, provocando una reforma urbana local, una revolución cubana de bienes raíces. La ola migratoria tuvo el efecto de un desalojo y los hermosos edificios fueron rebajados a la condición de cuarterías, que los marielitas bautizaron con el nombre de *maleficios* (el título de una telenovela mexicana de 1983, con Ernesto Alonso y Jaqueline Andere en los papeles protagónicos).

245

LAS RUINAS FILOSOFALES. Privados de sus legítimos dueños los edificios pierden el *spiritu*. Desparece lo «edificante», es decir, la razón que los mantuvo vivos: ahora son estructuras filosóficamente vacuas o evacuadas. Vienen a ocuparlos los expatriados, los parias, los gusanos y los zombis. Son edificios posesos, que antes del derrumbe, ya eran ruinas, debido a que sus inquilinos habían huido. La aceleración de la Historia (no el paso del tiempo) produce el efecto de abandono.

244

«Están también sus discursos filosóficos, un amasijo compuesto a la carrera y organizado pobremente, hechos con máximas y símbolos calcados de las enseñanzas neoplatónicas. Esos discursos, lo mismo que los *Panegíricos*, son gárrulos y artificiales, y tienen muy poco valor como ejercicios filosóficos y literarios». Gaetano Negri (1905): *Juliano el Apóstata*. New York: Charles Scribner's Sons.

243

«Escuchad este sabio consejo político: "Vended lo que poseéis y dad limosna; haceos de bolsas que no se envejezcan" (Lucas 12:33). ¿Podría concebirse algo más sagaz? Pues, cuando la humanidad obedezca tu orden, no quedará nadie que pueda comprar; y si este laudable precepto fuese implementado, ¿qué ciudad, qué nación, qué familia sobreviviría? Cuando los bienes hayan sido repartidos no habrá casa ni familia que tenga con qué comerciar, lo que significa que donde se entregue todo a los pobres, los mercaderes serán mendigos». Juliano el Apóstata, *Contra Galileos*. Fragmento IX. Reconstrucción de Newmann, Leipzig, 1880.

242

Isaac Kámara es el *Pissed Christ*.

241

Ocultos para ser libres es la serpiente escondida entre las *Hojas de Rábano*.

240

Biblioteca pública. Lengua de extraterrestres. Escritura en clave en las márgenes de los libros. Formulaciones de orates; versos de analfabetos; axiomas de vagabundos. Un personaje con barba mugrosa, estupa de cabellos, sotana harapienta. Garabateos. Garrapateos. El discurso del alienado que mueve el lápiz entre las hojas. Ciudad escrita, cloaca de signos. Huellas de kétchup.

239

En 1980, Miami era una ciudad enferma. El tirano había conseguido transmitir el virus por larga distancia. «Sin Mariel no hay pestilencia», sentenció Fernando de Call. Las Marías, Fernando, Selma, Victrola, Magali y Humberto Perdomo, crean el teatro de la crisis. Un frenesí recorría la urbe, un deseo y una esperanza (falsa) la corrompían. Marchas y contramarchas, huelgas de hambre, ríos de carros, paros inútiles, mítines en los portales, protestas y concentraciones multitudinarias, y todo porque Castro nos hizo creer que había llegado la hora.

238

Si es verdad que la Revolución fracasó en apropiarse de territorios, no es menos cierto que, de alguna manera, fuimos amos y señores, que campeamos por nuestro respeto, que exigimos derechos divinos, que chantajeamos, asesinamos, invadimos, violamos, sojuzgamos... ¡y que después lo perdimos todo! Otra vez la mayor pérdida será Cuba, que se perderá a sí misma.

Y, a pesar de las derrotas, hay un lugar donde conquistamos una cabeza de playa: *Miami*.

Trágico destino el de un pueblo llamado a realizar grandes conquistas, para las que requería toda la crueldad, el desprecio y la codicia del mundo, ¡y que encontrara en sí mismo nada más que *choteo*!

Según Fernando de Call, todos llevamos a un Castro escondido bajo la piel; Castro existe bajo la guisa de todos los vivos y de todos los muertos: Martí, Batista, Sakuntala, Cucalambé, Villaverde, la Avellaneda y Bonifacio Byrne. Castro procrea a sus precursores.

Après moi, Fidel!

Kaneyes de cristal. Los egipcios de la tercera dinastía, que comenzaron a utilizar la piedra en lugar del ladrillo de barro, esculpían hojas de palmera en los bloques de cantera, a imitación de los antiguos techos de guano. Esto sucedió también en Tropicana.

232

En Tropicana, las sociedades secretas de negros brujos y la Cosa Nostra concertan un sincretismo; Renato Carosone pone de moda un híbrido: el *mambo italiano*. Mientras tanto sube a escena la encarnación definitiva de cierto personaje dramático que había permanecido en las sombras, y que el año 1952 toca con un haz luminoso: *El Indio*.

231

Cruce de Indio y Karabalí: aparición del Modernismo.

230

El *Modern* cubano reinterpreta lo paleolítico en clave atómica. El chic habanero se apropia los «palos y piedras» guanajatabeyes. El sincretismo de Tropicana toma en vano el nombre de Babalú.

229

Se levantan unos arcos de cristal —nuestros arcos de Triunfo— que conmemoran los años de vacas gordas, a los que sucederán ineluctablemente otros de vacas flacas. Sobreviene la Plaga, la era del sarmentoso Rodney. La misa negra ha comenzado. Se contagia la urbe. La rumba es el baile de San Vito. Cuba monta el Santo, celebra el aquelarre.

228

Las musas danzan en la fuente donde vive Babalú. En el jardín reina el fauno tocado por la lepra, Pan de extremidades deformes, supremo bailarín y coreógrafo *assoluto* de una danza nacional en la que lo primitivo es catapultado al centro mismo de la escena mundial. La deidad de la Plaga, nuestra divinidad sarmentosa, emigra a Hollywood, ya es un nombre de pila en los hogares del Imperio. La gente olvida el significado y consume el significante: la brujería viaja oculta en el fetiche.

227

Brujería

El edificio del Arte
de cristal y acero
se levanta sobre un omiero.

Sobre bases primitivas
todo lo *Modern*
y lo habanero.

226

Un insecto en forma de hoja se ceba en su presa.

225

Caes, hacha o cuchillo amolado
Sobre el triste prepucio asustado
Corta el taburete, ruedo al cuadrado
Que con tachuelas define el espacio
Peludito, ancho, el pellejo escrito
Donde carenan las posaderas

Recostado contra el marco de la casa
Coloca la palangana entre las piernas
Y afina la puntería antes de bajar
La mano empuñada. Descarga
En ese pánico palmo cárnico
Con dobladuras y repujados de piel
El estilete definitorio de lujo
Aquella daga que quita, exacta
El último grito del mármol seminal
Órbita de un pretendiente al trono
Lo que queda es muñón, tronco
Si es que después de todo era
Esto lo que llamamos «renacimiento».
Baja la mano, okey, pide la palabra:
eunuco.

224

Una serie de mártires, vírgenes, santones y otros inter-
mediarios sirven de agentes de cambio en el relevo de para-
digmas, pues, a fin de establecerse, el Sistema requiere de
corredores de sensiblerías, de mercaderes de lágrimas.

223

Recobrar a Batista es reponer las vocales a una lengua
muerta.

Boarding Home[70]: la Madre de las casas

La locura (forma extrema de espiritualización) presupone un proceso de desenganche y desmaterialización, lo que para nosotros implica también una *descubanización*. Lo cubano pierde el sustrato material (los cubiches roen la plataforma insular y desprenden la Isla de su base, en las postrimerías de Fernando de Call: la locura como desprendimiento de la base existencial). Si los triunfadores son aquellos que se anclan a sus posesiones (casa, carro y yate), el loco, en cambio, está *poseído*, es un *poseso*.

Lo cual explica la frase de Selma O'Flater en el banquete de cumpleaños de Isaac: «Poseída de posesión», con la que pretende describir el doble misterio de la propiedad privada, una propiedad cuyo valor consiste, básicamente, en la acumulación [de posesión]; poseer acumulado y destilado en el acto puro de «tener». O'Flatter dice también: «Tener o no tener», que es, en último análisis, la prueba de la existencia: «Tanto tienes, *tanto vales*». En efecto, ese valor supremo, del

---

70 José Martí, el precursor de Guillermo Rosales, entra a New York por un «boardinghouse», el de Carmita Miyares de Mantilla, localizado en 51 East 29 Street. «These were the modern problems that boarders and flâneurs alike confronted in real metropolitan life much as they did in complicatedly "realistic" boardinghouse literature». Thomas Butler Gunn (2009): *The Physiology of New York Boarding-Houses*. Introducción de David Faflik, p. xxviii. Rutgers Press. Publicado originalmente por Mason Brothers, 1857.

que hasta un apóstol o un loco de remate rehúsan prescindir, es lo que aquí llamamos *home*.

220

El perdedor vive en la estrechez del cuarto, del *efficiency*, del maleficio y eventualmente de la calle, del banco del parque, debajo de un puente o dentro de una caja de cartón. La anchura callejera es limitadora a causa justamente de su falta de límites. No existen coordenadas, y las que existen, por ser demasiado vastas, definen un territorio suprapersonal. Así, el perdedor termina cayendo fuera de los confines familiares, más allá de lo humano, internándose en la pura vastedad ontológica.

El triunfador, en cambio, se encuentra a sus anchas en el ámbito de lo posible (la tía *dentro* del carro[71]), que es el perímetro óntico de la cordura. Al triunfador le están vedados tanto el conocimiento de la desproporción como la experiencia del despropósito, mientras que el loco pagará con la derrota por su conocimiento *ilimitado*.

219

Las excursiones de Guillermo Rosales culminan en la última salida (desde el apartamento de *El Negro*), de la que nunca regresará, pues es sabido que en medio de la calle Flagra se disparó al corazón. Podemos desandar sus pasos en la novela y ver por los ojos del loco la imagen de la ciudad maldita.

---

71   «Aquí estarás bien. Comprenderás que ya nada más se puede hacer». Guillermo Rosales (1987): *Boarding Home*. Barcelona: Salvat.

Rosales es un alienado en el sentido clínico (el «hombre contra sí mismo» de Menninger, y el *extranjero* de sí); en cambio, su novela alude a una alienación geográfica: «A veces pienso que si hubiera nacido en Brasil, España, Venezuela o Escandinavia hubiera salido huyendo también de sus calles, puertos y praderas». Ahora sabemos que no es de un país de donde huye el exiliado total, sino del ser, del «sí mismo».

Todo suicida mata a la patria en la infancia.

William Figueras no es un loco «libre» (en el sentido de serlo en sí y para sí): es un *yuródivi*, un «loco de Castro», creado por decreto, por una orden ejecutiva que emana de la instancia más alta. Su exilio fue decidido por otro. Rosales quiere ignorar este hecho y continuar creyéndose un exiliado por cuenta propia, lo cual no es más que es otro *efecto* castrista.

William Figueras es un «loco» en la acepción legal que dio a ese término el gobierno revolucionario: es decir, otro de los tantos expulsados, deportados, o simplemente lanzados como proyectiles contra la salud mental del Imperio.

214

Politización del sueño. En las pesadillas del loco tiene lugar la batalla de ideas: Castro aparece allí como *phantasmagon.* En las pesadillas del cubano (es decir: del gusano), Castro es omnipotente y omnisciente: es Castro Pantocrator.

213

A Rosales no le queda nada por conocer, excepto la muerte. Es un conocedor de sistemas o, al decir de Wallace Stevens, un *conocedor del caos.* La revolución, con sus campañas masivas de alfabetización, su propaganda permanente y la perversión unilateral de la función intelectiva, produce omnisciencia. También el suicidio supone una liberación por el conocimiento, y por un *exceso* de conocimiento.

212

La muerte de Rosales expresa el *telos* revolucionario a manera de conclusión literaria o *denouement.* Cierra con broche de oro la narrativa nacional: la bala en el pecho tiene la robustez de un último argumento. Que el autor muera para que su obra viva toma allí la escenificación más patética.

211

La locura es la claridad que permite a Rosales ver un lugar justo en el mundo. Pero el loco también ve diablos en las paredes y dictadores en los sueños. Es un vidente en ambos sentidos.

En el libro de Rosales ocurre la transfiguración de Castro en personaje novelístico: al espiritualizarlo, al hacerlo objeto de sus obsesiones literarias, el narrador lo *absuelve*. La absolución de Castro ocurre siempre que se lo narra.

Existe una instalación de Kienholz titulada *Ward 9* que ilustra el problema de *Boarding Home*. Hay un loco desnudo maniatado a una columbina, la cabeza es una pecera llena de agua rosada donde nada un pez peleador. Hay otra columbina, con otro loco idéntico dentro de un globo de cómic festoneado de neón. El loco del sueño, como una oveja negra, se «cuenta» a sí mismo.

Boarding Home es el alma del hombre bajo el castrismo.

En la escritura de *El Negro*, la influencia de los poetas ingleses se expresa como una melancolía que no proviene de ningún sentimiento propio: más bien es la consecuencia no anticipada de la traducción. Quizás ese efecto automático sea lo que se entendió por «poesía» entre los exiliados cubanos de un cierto momento histórico.

La impresión que deja la lectura de Coleridge en español deberá ser entendida en su relación diferencial [con el original]. Así, el Coleridge de Rosales es el resultado de una operación secundaria:

¡Ay!, de esos diablos que así te persiguen
Viejo Marino, te proteja Dios.
¿Por qué me miras así? Con mi ballesta.
Yo di muerte a Albatros... [sic].

Lo que transmiten en sus obras los poetas del gueto como consecuencia de recibir emociones por trasmano, es inauténtico; la inautenticidad es transmutada en efecto poético, en un modelo cubano de autenticidad. Rosales confunde la poética «inglesa» con la «miamense», y llega a creer que en 1817 John Keats sentía lo mismo que él siente (...*una pobre cosa ya al borde de la tumba, endeble y paralítica...*) en Miami.

Observar que *El Negro* dice: «Tengo miedo de que te haga daño», refiriéndose al libro de Henry Miller [que le entrega a Rosales]; a lo que William responde: «¡No jodas!». Así confiamos que el libro no le hará daño (a William), aunque no estemos seguros de que no matará a Guillermo. Para averiguar el desenlace se requiere salir del texto. *Boarding Home* es una trampa: imposible saber cuándo estamos dentro o fuera (de la vida, de la muerte, del *home*, de Miami, de la locura) de Cuba.

«Solo la experiencia de la Nada constituye un conti-
nuo. "Dentro" es temporal, "fuera" es eterno». Buckminster
Fuller (1975): *Synergetics*.

Desconocemos si el libro de Henry Miller le hizo daño
a William, pero sabemos el efecto que tuvo en Guillermo:
lo trastornó hasta el punto de llevarlo al suicidio. El libro
de Miller provoca una crisis: su efecto diferido es la lectura
del libro que tenemos en las manos. Guillermo se apunta al
pecho con la pistola que (en la novela) es un arma libresca.
Su locura es quijotesca: la pistola novelada lo lleva a matar
en la realidad. William dispara, Guillermo cae.

El Negro denuncia el carácter letal del libro. Lo que le
entrega es el arma que lo matará, y William lo reconoce,
aunque finge no saberlo. *El Negro* tuvo que haber percibido,
en el momento en que se lo puse en las manos, lo dañino
del artefacto. La influencia del libro es patente: aparece en
los exergos de los dos únicos cuadernos que *El Negro* dio
a la luz.

La muerte de Rosales es necesaria: que muera por culpa
de *El Negro* es un golpe metafísico.

200

Es un escándalo que le cambiaran el título en la edición Siruela: las palabras inglesas de la edición príncipe (Salvat, 1987) ya desde la portada trababan la lengua, metían un corrientazo: *Boarding Home* (pronúnciense *Bordinjón*), electrochoque y retortijón. Hay una chicharra escondida en la mano que Rosales nos extiende a las puertas del Exilio.

199

La edición Siruela debe ser tomada como la traducción exitosa de un libro destinado al fracaso; o como la traducción del fracaso (literario) al idioma del éxito (editorial). Este es otro libro, no aquel que cayó en el olvido y aún más profundamente en la indiferencia. Es un libro bowdlerizado, hipócritamente expurgado de su *error*. Pero el acierto de *Boarding Home* consistía, justamente, en haber corrido la misma suerte de su autor.

198

Tras un viaje nostálgico, el gusano regresa aliviado al aeropuerto de Miami. Se abraza a los suyos, y grita: *Is gú tu-bi jon!* Miami es un manicomio y un *jon*. El reo retorna gozoso a la cárcel. El loco vuelve a su encierro y tranca las rejas tras de sí. El Gran Carcelero creó en la Pequeña Habana una prisión modelo.

197

El *Jon* es su obra maestra, su Escorial.

Rosales escribió una novela gótica en la que el loquero habita los sueños del loco.

El Doctor Castro es Doctor Ktzob, por transliteración kafkiana: castración.

Entonces el gusano puso un *Jon Sweet Jon* sobre la puerta de su celda...

Mientras que los personajes de *Boarding Home* poseen una historia personal, Castro aparece allí como el ente literario puro [el *phantasmagon* que habita las pesadillas del autor]. Cada cubano *cuenta* a Castro, concibe una nueva escena para él. Castro es, literalmente, el-que-vive-del-cuento.

La ciencia tradicional evitó tratar a Castro. Pero en Rosales, Castro se presenta por fin como una constante: aquello que odiamos, soñamos y tumbamos *constantemente*.

191

Quizás la ausencia de gran literatura en ciertos períodos grises se deba a que los genios se confundieron entre los mierdas, reservándose para tiempos mejores.

190

ENVIDIA DEL LIBRO. Entregarte en un libro, que tu presencia se confunda con la portada y tu ausencia con la contraportada; que las hojas se encarguen de decirlo por ti; que el texto hable; que el papel deje un rastro tuyo. Así quedó grabado Isaac Kámara en *Boarding Home.* El traspaso exhibe las clásicas circunvoluciones de la Idea que migra a la página. Una sombra recorre las hojas y queda plasmada en libro. «Quizás fuera mi karma», dijo Kámara, pensando en voz alta, a la altura de Iksatabón, en el segundo muelle de Mortlake. El bote seguía las líneas curváceas de un canal invisible cuya corriente nos arrastraba (aunque pareciera mentira) hacia nuestro destino. Una corriente que arrastra… hacia un destino… Nos habíamos habituado al prodigio. Colonias de indios operaban ruletas en la costa de oro, sus lumínicos perturbaban la paz de la corriente. Rompíamos letras brillosas, avanzando en línea recta, bañados en fosforescencias, naipes iridiscentes y dados gigantes que rodaban por el tapete nublado del firmamento y caían como piedras de luz en las ondas, «…y digo mi karma», continuó Isaac, iluminado, «porque cuando pequeño sucedió un episodio que marcó para siempre mi relación con los libros». Papá dejó el timón y vino a sentarse con nosotros. «¿De qué se trata, Isaac? Habla…», lo conminó. Isaac Ka dudó, sonrió amargamente antes de dar inicio a su relato. Después habló como si no le importara: «Bueno, yo era pequeño, creo que estaba en tercer grado. Yo tenía una prima, mi prima Lídice. Sucedió que por esos tiempos se cumplía un aniversario más de la destrucción de un pueblo checoslovaco llamado Lídice. La embajada de la República Socialista Checa hizo llegar a la niña –en realidad, a todos los niños del mundo que ostentaban ese nombre– dos libros ilustrados, uno de Caperucita Roja, otro de Hansel y Gretel. Los libros se abrían y de sus páginas saltaban árboles, cabañas, una cama de hierro, la silueta de un lobo en cuatro patas que movía la cola: eran libros hechizados. Me enamoré de esos libros, me encapriché con ellos[72]. Exigí, rogué, demandé que me consiguieran unos idénticos, para mí solo. ¡Quería poseer-los! Los padres de Lídice consintieron en prestármelos por unos días; luego, por unas semanas. Cuando el préstamo se prolongó más de la cuenta, reclamaron su devolución inmediata. Yo armé un escándalo, di una perreta mayús-cula. Me sentía morir, separado de *mis* libros. Ya no concebía la vida si no era en posesión de aquellos libros en tercera dimensión, libros volubles, que «salían para afuera» (a partir de entonces sobrevaloré ciertos aspectos estructurales de la literatura en menoscabo de lo estrictamente textual: ¿qué importancia podía tener la letra muerta si era posible abrir una puerta en la página?). Sufrí la pérdida de los libros de Lídice. Infructuosas cartas a la embajada checa falla-ron en conseguirme lo que tanto añoraba. "Los tomos en cuestión fueron enviados a las niñas que llevan el nombre de *Lídice* como recordatorio de la masacre perpetrada, en 1942, por las tropas alemanas en la aldea del mismo nom-

---

[72] Probablemente se trate de los libros de Leporello Verlag que menciona Walter Benjamin su ensayo «Traumkitsch», 1927.

bre", argüían los cónsules, diplomáticamente. Entonces mi nombre comenzó a pesarme; quise iniciar los trámites para cambiarlo. Finalmente, acepté que la suerte no me acompañaría, ni entonces ni nunca. Que el milagro [de los libros] recaería siempre en otros más afortunados, o mejor dotados que yo. Lo que escribiera quedaría en mera tipografía. Un puñado de pliegos impresos en cajas de plomo no bastaba, yo quería algo más. Pero Lídice no se me entregó…».

189

TEXTUS RECEPTUS. «¡Qué triste!», dijo mi padre. Después Isaac dijo: «Vago como un judío expulsado del Libro. Ando buscando un volumen que me acoja. Por eso entregué *El tiempo de los asesinos*, de Henry Miller, anticipando lo que vendría. *El Negro* escribió *El guardián de la noche* y le puso el exergo de Miller, y aunque no me mentó, yo estaba allí, en cuatro patas, entre las páginas que no dejaban ver mi sombra. Pero solo yo sabía que el libro de *El Negro* era la culminación de un proceso que partía de mí». «Claro, esas son cosas difíciles de explicar», dijo mi padre. «Los perdedores escriben la historia», añadió. «Sí», respondió Isaac, «y por entonces apareció la novela de Rosales, con el personaje de *El Negro*. Cual no sería mi sorpresa al leer que ese personaje le entrega mi libro a William Figueras. Entonces me dije: *La cadena va de Rimbaud a Miller, de Kámara a El Negro, y de Rosales a William*…» «Sí», dijo mi padre, «la cadena de plata. Solo que Isaac Ka es el eslabón perdido». «Efectivamente», respondió Isaac, taciturno, «me muevo en un espacio imaginario». Y concluyó: «En realidad, me muevo en un espacio donde es inútil situar nada». A lo que mi padre objetó: «Bueno, resides, después de todo, en un Mutus Liber. El libro de Lídice es la caja de plomo y dentro hay un gato encerrado que podría saltar en cualquier momento». Isaac suspiró: «¡Un gato negro!» A lo que yo agregué: «A propósito, sepan que, en *Una temporada en el infierno*, Rimbaud se ve a sí mismo como un negro: *Oui, j'ai les yeux fermés à votre lumière. Je suis une bête, un nègre*»[73]. Me quedé callada, después dije: «No es de extrañar, entonces, que *El Negro* viniera a ser el trasunto, la tumba y el espejo de William, aquel que *cerró los ojos a la luz de...* Alégrate, Isaac Kámara: eres la sombra de una sombra». Y papá: «Sombra nada más...»

188

La organización de los eventos a que nos entregamos en la mañana del 25 de julio de 2020 (Santiago Apóstol) representa la culminación del genio creativo-político-espectacular de Isaac Kámara. El viernes 24 atracamos en la marina Faghage, donde, para nuestra gran sorpresa, nos esperaban los dos compañeros hindúes que habíamos conocido en el 7Eleven. Alquilaron un horrible Ford Escalade, en el que nos metieron por fin alrededor de la medianoche. Conduciríamos por carreteras oscuras, entre bosques de magnolias que en esa estación comenzaban a cubrirse de gruesos capullos. Una débil fragancia empapaba el ambiente. Las flores

---

[73] En la misma cuerda: «No miréis que soy negra: es que me ha quemado el sol. Los hijos de mi madre, airados contra mí, me pusieron a guardar viñas». *Shir Hashirim*, 1:6. Reina-Valera, 1909. Henry Miller dice: «When he was writing his "nigger book" (*Une Saison en Enfer*), Rimbaud is said to have declared: "My fate depends on this book!"». *El tiempo de los asesinos* (1983). Traducción Roberto Bixo, Alianza Editorial; *The Time of the Assassins* (1956). New Directions.

resplandecían en la oscuridad cual suaves espectros o como cosas espectrales, no poseo en estos momentos la capacidad de producir imágenes. Eran *flashazos*. Es todo lo que recuerdo. Más que flores blancas, eran floripondios, franchipanes, botones barruecos. Cualquier metáfora, cualquier simulacro, aun en su expresión más simple, se me antoja ahora un ejercicio de impiedad. Había, eso sí, armadillos muertos en el asfalto, gruesos, torpes, herrumbrosos. La carne roja y violácea, las vísceras bajo el farol, entre pétalos mustios, arrollados. Entramos a un terraplén, una especie de gleba a las afueras del retirado camino. Doblamos dos veces, una a la derecha y otra a la izquierda, rozando a nuestro paso las pencas de nerviosas palmeras. Topamos por fin con la barda de una cabaña malamente iluminada que ostentaba en el techo de cinc un cartel apuntalado con vigas que decía «La Gran Jota». Este era el lugar adonde arribábamos luego de veinte años de travesía. Por haber sido los hindúes quienes nos recogían, yo tenía preguntas, múltiples interrogantes exacerbadas por la extensión inhumana del viajecito, que parecía cubrir la distancia entre dos galaxias. Verdaderamente, ¿habíamos zarpado de Miami? ¡De Miami! ¡Por Jove, no podía creerlo! ¿Y cuál era la causa, el porqué del viaje? Los compañeros indios tampoco podían creer que se tratara del rapto de un Niño. ¿Qué niño? ¿Un niño *azul*? ¿Y cuál era la meta? La voz de Swami Prabhupada saltó desde las páginas de mi Guitá: *The idea that there is a goal… is wrong. We are the goal.* Arpegio de cítara. *We are the goal.* Okay, *the goool…*

www.ingramcontent.com/pod-product-compliance
Lightning Source LLC
Chambersburg PA
CBHW020405030726
47496CB00007B/2320

The Collected Shorter Supernatural & Weird Fiction of Algernon Blackwood Volume 7

ALGERNON BLACKWOOD

The Collected Shorter Supernatural & Weird Fiction of Algernon Blackwood Volume 7

One Short Story, Three Novelettes and One Novella of the Strange and Unusual Including 'The Man Whom the Trees Loved', 'The Regeneration of Lord Ernie' and 'The Wendigo'

Algernon Blackwood

LEONAUR

The Collected Shorter Supernatural & Weird Fiction of
Algernon Blackwood
Volume 7
One Short Story, Three Novelettes and One Novella of the Strange and Unusual
Including 'The Man Whom the Trees Loved', 'The Regeneration of Lord Ernie' and
'The Wendigo'
by Algernon Blackwood

Leonaur is an imprint of Oakpast Ltd

ISBN: 978-1-916535-50-3 (hardcover)
ISBN: 978-1-916535-51-0 (softcover)

http://www.leonaur.com

Publisher's Notes

The views expressed in this book are not necessarily
those of the publisher.

Contents

The Man from the 'Gods'

That there was something wrong with all his work Le Maistre well knew. Words and music, as the critics never failed to remind him, "just missed" that nameless "something" which would have made them good—perhaps great. Moreover, he was sane enough to realise that the blame lay not with an uncomprehending public, but simply with himself. The spark of inspiration that was beyond question in all his work never gathered to the flame stage. Thus, his productions warmed people, but did not light them. He understood well enough what was lacking—and that no amount of mere painstaking "work" could put it right.

But on one occasion Le Maistre achieved a singular and startling success. As a sober record of fact, concealed by initials, it was reported in the Proceedings of the French Psychological Society for that year; and people who believed in the Subliminal Self, the Higher Ego, and all that consoling teaching about an attainable God within, made great havoc with the facts.

The way it came about, moreover, probably has a profound psychical significance. In any case, the result remains as the very best kind of tangible proof; for it was the only great thing he ever really achieved—this Fairy Play (so called); and its beauty was absolutely arresting.

He was something over fifty when he wrote it in its original form. The central idea came to him with the quick flash of a genuine inspiration; so, did most of the music; but, in the working out of both, the fire had become smothered. The spark had never gathered into flame. The result was mediocrity. Yet, like so many artists, he confused what was in his mind and imagination with what he had actually set down upon paper; for, when he went over the score to himself, he heard the original beauty in his thoughts and believed he had transferred into his work his own memory of that beauty. The music and words

7

themselves, however, had *not* caught it. Thus, those who heard the preliminary recital in his rooms were more or less bored according to their powers of divination.

"It's fine; it's original," they remarked, shaking their heads as they went home after the performance; "but just misses it!"

The transformation that changed the common lead into gold as by some mysterious process of spiritual alchemy came about as follows:—

The little play was finished, and Le Maistre, having his eye upon a certain manager, went to that particular theatre one night in order to study the "feel" of it—to catch the flavour of the house, the size of the stage, and any other details he could. The management had given him a dress circle box, and he saw admirably. It was characteristic of the man, rather, that he put himself to this far-fetched kind of trouble. During the performance his mind was keenly at work. Yet he saw nothing of what was going on before his eyes; he had come with a definite purpose; he saw his own play all the time, heard his own music; watched his own creatures come on and go off among his own scenery.

At the same time the music, light and colour provided a stimulus that acted upon his own imagination, and set all the finer machinery of his own creative genius working. Sub-consciously he revised his own work, with the illuminating result that a white light shone through his mind and showed up all the flaws, all the places where he had "missed it"; all the passages where he had trailed off into banality. And a tremendous desire went crashing through his being to revise his work in the light of this knowledge. "I felt," he said, "as though a great prayer had gone out of me—a cry, as it were, to my higher self to come to my assistance. Never in my life have I wished anything so intensely before."

Then, in that curious fashion with which many artists must be familiar, it all faded again, and the reaction set in. The effort had no doubt exhausted him. He turned his attention to the actual performances on the stage before him, and lost the power to visualize his own piece. But the play—trivial, vulgar and untrue to life—wearied him; and he withdrew into the back of the box, and incontinently— fell asleep upon the little plush sofa

When a considerable time later he woke up, the entire theatre was dark and empty; the piece was over; the audience had gone home to a man; and the building was deserted.

8

Le Maistre at once realised what had happened, though he could not understand why the final applause had not waked him, and hurried into his overcoat. A faint glimmer pervaded the vast auditorium, for as he leaned over the edge, he could just make out the rows of empty stalls, the scattered white patches where the discarded programmes lay, the music-stands of the orchestra, and the exit doors of glass where the pit began. The air still smelt unpleasantly of a crowd—wraps, furs, stale scent and cigarettes.

Then he struck a match and saw by his watch that it was two o'clock in the morning. He had slept three hours!

He pushed open the door and passed out into the passage, his one idea being how he could get out into the street, or how he would spend the time if he did not get out. He felt hungry, stiff and a trifle chilly. Feeling his way along by the backs of the upper circle seats, he advanced slowly and carefully, his footsteps making no sound upon the soft carpet, and so came at last to the first exit door. It was locked and barred. He tried the next door with the same result. There was no other exit—nothing but that narrow semi-circular gangway between the wall and the seats, a box at either end, and pillars at intervals to mark the distance. "Like the exercise-walk in a prison-yard," he thought to himself, laughing.

No single light was left burning anywhere in the building. Even the hall was in darkness. He saw the gilt-framed pictures of actors and actresses on the walls; a faint rumble from the streets reached him too—voices, traffic, footsteps, wind. Then he turned back into the theatre and carefully made his way down the aisle to the front, feeling the steps first with his toe, and peered over into the body of the house. A sea of shadows swam to and fro below him. Here and there certain stalls picked themselves out of the general gloom almost as though they were occupied; he could easily imagine he saw figures still sitting in them. . . .

And it was here, just at this point, he said, that he began for the first time to feel a little uneasy. A slight tremor of the nerves passed over him, and sitting down in one of the front-row seats he considered the situation carefully and deliberately. There was not much to consider. He was shut in for the rest of the night; the dress circle seemed to be the limits of his prison; he could get neither up nor down; there was no escape till the morning. The prospect was not pleasant; still, it was not very terrible, and his sense of humour would easily have carried him through with credit, but for one thing—this curiously disturbing sense of something he could not quite define: of something that was *going to happen*, it seemed. . . .

It was too vague, too remote for him to deal with squarely. His mind, always keenly imaginative and pictorial, preferred to see it in the terms of a picture. He thought of the Thames as he had sometimes seen it from the Chelsea Embankment in the dusk when dark barges, too far for their outline to be defined, come looming up through the mist. In this way thoughts lie in the depths of the mind; in this way they rise gradually before the consciousness; in this way the cause of his present discomfort would presently reach the point where he would recognise it and understand. In similar fashion, he felt this "something" that moved at the back of his mind, coming slowly forward.

A sudden idea came to him—

"If I could climb down to the auditorium floor, I might find a door open somewhere, or escape by way of the orchestra, perhaps!"

And the idea of action was pleasant; though how he climbed over the edge of the box in the dark and swarmed down the slippery pillar, landing with a crash upon the rim of the stage box below, he never quite understood. With a plunge he dropped backwards into the dark space, kicking over as he did so a couple of chairs, which fell with a loud clatter and woke resounding echoes all through the empty building. That clatter seemed prodigious. He held his breath for several seconds to listen, standing motionless against the wall with the distinct idea that all this noise would attract attention to himself, and that if, after all, there was any one watching him—that if among those shadows someone—

"Ah!" he exclaimed quickly. "Now I've got it! There is someone watching me in another part of the building. That's why I felt uneasy—"

That tumble into the box had shaken the thought up to the surface of his mind. The picture had emerged from the mist, and he recognised the cause of his uneasiness. All this time, though none of his senses had yet proved it to him, the mind of another person, perhaps the eyes too, had been focused upon him. He was not alone.

Le Maistre felt no alarm, he said, but rather a definite thrill of exhilaration, as though the idea of this other person came to him with a sense of pleasurable excitement. His first instinct to sit concealed in the corner of the box and await events he dismissed almost at once in favour of some kind of prompt action. Stumbling in the gloom, he made his way down to the orchestra, and while groping cautiously among the crowded easels, his hand touched a tiny knob, and a dozen lights that bent over the music folios, like little heads screened under black bonnets, sprang into brilliance. The first thing he noticed was that the fire curtain was down, closing the cavernous mouth of the stage.

The shaded lights, however, were so carefully arranged that they fell only upon the music, and the main body of the theatre still yawned in comparative darkness behind him. Vast and unfriendly it seemed; charged to the brim with faint shufflings and whispers as though an audience sat there stealthily turning over programmes. The stalls faced him like fixed but living beings; the balconies frowned down upon him; the boxes—especially the upper ones—had an air of concealing people behind their curtains. Far overhead, glimmered a huge skylight; he heard the wind sighing across it like wind in the rigging of a ship. And, more than once, he fancied he caught the faint tread of footsteps moving about among the stalls and gangways.

Regretting that he had turned the lights up (they made himself so conspicuous, so easily visible!), he made an instinctive movement to turn them out again; but he touched the wrong knob, so that a row of lights flashed out up under the roof. In that topmost gallery of all, known as "the gods," a little line of starry lights leaped into being, and the first thing he noticed as he looked up was the figure of a man leaning over the edge of the railing—watching him.

The same moment he saw that this figure was making a movement of some kind—a gesture. It beckoned to him. So, his feeling that someone was in the theatre with him was justified. There had been a man in the gods all the time.

Le Maistre admitted frankly that, in his first surprise, he collapsed backwards upon the stool usually occupied by the second 'cello. But his alarm passed with a strange swiftness, and gave place almost immediately to a peculiar and deep-seated thrill. The instant he perceived this dim figure of a man up there under the roof his heart leaped with an emotion that was partly delight, partly pleasurable anticipation, and partly—most curious of all—*awe*. And in a voice that was unlike his own, and that carried across the intervening space, for all its faintness, with perfect ease, he heard the words driven out of him as if by command of some deeper instinct than he understood—yet the very last words that he could have imagined as appropriate—

"You're up there in the gods!" he called out. "Won't you come down to me here?"

And then the figure withdrew, and he heard the sound of the footsteps descending the winding passages and stairs behind, as their owner obeyed him and came.

Alarmed, yet curiously exultant, Le Maistre stood up among the music-easels to await his coming. He was extraordinarily alert, prepared. He fumbled again with the little switch-board under the conductor's desk, for he wished to see the man face to face in full light—not to be gradually approached in darkness. But the only thing that came of the button he pressed was a creaking noise behind him, and when he turned quickly to examine, lo and behold, he saw the huge fire-curtain rising slowly and majestically into the air. And, as it rose, revealing the stage beyond, he got the distinct impression that this very stage, now empty, had a moment before been crowded with a throng of living people, and that even now they were there concealed among the wings within a few feet of where he stood, waiting the summons to appear.

Moreover, this discovery, far from causing him the kind of amazement that might have been expected, only communicated, for the second time within the space of a few minutes, another thrill of delight. Again, this lightning sense of exhilaration swept him from head to foot.

The footsteps, meanwhile, came nearer; sometimes disappearing behind a thickness of walls that rendered them inaudible, and at other times starting suddenly into greater clearness as they came down from floor to floor. Le Maistre, unable to endure the suspense any longer, felt impelled to go forward and meet them half-way. An intense desire to see this stranger face to face came upon him. He climbed awkwardly over the orchestra railing and made his way past the first rows of the stalls. Already the steps sounded upon the same floor as himself. Hardly a dozen yards, to judge by the fall of these oddly cushioned footsteps, could now separate them. He moved more slowly, and the stranger moved more slowly too—entering at last the gangway in which he stood.

"And it is from this point," to use the words of the report he afterwards wrote for the society, "that my memory begins to fade somewhat, or rather, that the sense of bewilderment grew so astonishingly disturbing that I find it difficult to look back and recall with accuracy the true sequence of what followed. My normal measurement of the passage of time changed too, I think; all went so swiftly, almost as in a dream, though at the time it did not appear to me to be short or hurried. But—describe the sense of glory, wonder and happiness that enveloped me as in a cloud, I simply cannot. As well might a *hashish-eater* attempt during the dullness of next morning to reconstruct the phantasmal wonder of all he experienced the night before. Only, this was no phantasy; it was real and actual, and more palpitatingly vivid than any other experience of my life.

"I stood waiting in the gangway while this other person—the stranger—came towards me along the narrow space between the wall and the main body of seats. The footsteps were unhurried and regular. It was very dark; all I could see were two faint patches of light where the exit doors of the pit glimmered beyond. First one patch of light, then the other, was temporarily obscured as he passed in front of these doors. Down he moved steadily towards me through the gloom, and at the barrier of velvet rope that separated the stalls from the pit, he stopped—just near enough for me to distinguish the head and shoulders of a man about my own height and about my own size. He stood facing me there, some ten or twelve feet away.

"For a few seconds there was complete silence—like the silence in a mine, I remember thinking—and I instinctively clenched my fists, almost expecting something violent to happen. But the next instant the man spoke; and the moment I heard his voice all traces of fear left me, and I felt nothing but this peculiarly delightful sense of exhilaration I have already mentioned. It ran through me like the flush of a generous wine, rousing all my faculties, critical and imaginative, to their highest possible power, yet at the same time so bewildering me for the moment that I scarcely realised what I was saying, doing, or thinking. From this point I went through the whole scene without hesitation or dismay—certainly without a thought of disobeying. I mean, it was a pleasure to me to help it all forward, rather than to seek to prevent.

"'Here I am,' said the man in a voice wholly wonderful. 'You called me down, and I have come!'

"'You have come from up there—from the gods,' I heard myself reply.

"'I have come from up there—from the gods,' he answered; and his sentence seemed to mean so much more than mine did, although we used identical words.

"I held on to the back of the stall nearest to me. I could think for the moment of nothing further to say. The idea of what was coming thrilled me inexpressibly, though I could only hazard wild guesses as to its character.

"'Are you ready then?' he asked.

"'Ready? Ready for what?'

"'For the rehearsal,' he said, 'the secret rehearsal.'

"'The secret rehearsal?' I stammered, pretending, as a child pretends in order to heighten its joy, that I did not understand.

"'—of your play, you know; your fairy play,' he finished the sentence.

"Then he moved towards me a few steps, and, hardly knowing why, I retreated. It was still impossible to see his face. The curious idea came to me that there was something odd about the man that prevented, and that would always prevent, me getting closer to him, and that perhaps I should never see his face completely at all. I cannot point to anything definite that caused this impression; I can merely report that it was so.

"'Look!' he went on, 'everyone is ready and waiting. The moment the music starts we can begin. You will find a violin down there; the rehearsal can go on at once.'

"And although it struck me at the time as most curious, he should be aware of the fact, it seemed quite natural, because I do play the violin, and in fact compose all my melodies first on that instrument before I put a pen to paper. At the same time, I can remember faintly protesting—

"'I?' I remember asking; 'I'm to play?'

"'Certainly,' replied this soft-spoken figure among the shadows. 'You're to play. Who else, pray? And see! Everyone is ready and waiting.'

"I was far too happily bewildered to object further; there seemed, indeed, no time for reflection at all; I felt impelled, driven forward as it were, to go through with the adventure and to ask no questions. Besides, I wanted to go through with it. I felt the old power of the first inspiration upon me—only heightened; I felt in me the supreme and splendid confidence that I could do it all better than I had ever dreamed—do it perfectly as it should be done. I was borne forwards upon a wave of inspiration that nothing in the whole world could interfere with.

"And, as I turned to obey, I saw for the first time that the stage was brilliantly lighted; that the scenery was the scenery already chosen by my mind; that the performers thronged the wings, and the opening

14

characters were actually standing in their places waiting for the signal of the music to begin. The performers, moreover, I perceived, were identical in figure, feature and bearing with those ideal performers who had already enacted the play upon the inner stage of my imagination. It was all, in fact, precisely as the original inspiration had come to me weeks ago before the fires of beauty had faded during the wearisome toil of working it all out in limited terms upon the paper.

"The power that drove me forward, and at the same time filled me with this splendour of untrammelled creation, refused me, however, the least moment for consideration. I could only make my way into the orchestra and pick up the first violin-case that came to hand, belonging, doubtless, to some member of the band I had listened to earlier in the evening; and all eyes were fixed upon me from the stage as I clambered into the conductor's seat and drew the bow across the strings to tune the instrument.

"At the first sound I realised that my fingers, accustomed to the harsh tones of my own cheaper fiddle, were now feeling their way over the exquisite nervous system of a genuine Guarnierius that responded instantly to the lightest touch; and that the bow in my right hand was so perfectly balanced that even the best Tourte ever made could only seem like a strip of raw, unfinished wood by comparison.

"For the bow 'swam' over the strings, the sound streamed, smooth as honey, past my ears, and my fingers found the new intervals as easily as if they had never known any other key-board. Harmonics, double-stopping and *arpeggios* issued from my efforts as perfectly as trills from the throat of a bird.

"In that moment I *lived*; I understood much; I heard my soul singing within me. . . . I finished tuning, and tapped sharply on the back of the violin to indicate that I was ready, and in the slight pause that ensued before I actually played the opening bars, I became aware that the stalls behind me, the boxes, the dress circle, and the whole house in fact right up to the 'gods,' were crowded with eager listeners; and, further, that the stranger—that man among the shadows in the background—standing ever beyond the reach of the light, still remained in some mysterious and potent fashion intimately in touch with my inner self, directing, helping, inspiring the performance from beginning to end.

"And, in front of me, upon the conductor's desk, lay the score of my own music in clearest manuscript, no longer crossed out and corrected as it lay in my rooms after all the first passion of beauty had been ground out of it, but lovely and perfect as the original inspiration had rushed flame-like into my soul months before.

"The whole performance from that moment—'rehearsal' seems no adequate word to describe it—went with the smoothness of a dream from beginning to end. Just as the music was my own music made perfect, so the words and songs were the mature expression of the original conception before my blundering efforts had confined them, stammering and incomplete, in broken form. Moreover—more wonderful still—I noticed the very places in my score where I had floundered, and where, in the laborious process of composition, the first inspiration had failed me and I had filled in with what was mediocre and banal.

"It was as if a master pointed out to me with the simplicity of true power the passages where the commonplace might pass—could—did pass—by deft, inspired touches into what was fine, moving, noble. . ... The lesson was a sublime one; at the time, however, it all seemed so ridiculously simple and easy that I felt I could never again write anything that was not great and splendid.

"Moreover, the acting, speaking and dancing provided the perfect medium for my ideas; and the whole performance was the consummate representation of my first conception; even the scenery shifted swiftly and noiselessly, and the intervals between the acts were hardly noticeable. . . . .

"And the end came with a curious abruptness, bringing me to myself—my limited, stammering, caged little self, as, it seemed, after these moments of intoxicating expression—with a sharp sense of pain that all was over; and I became aware that, without hurry, without noise, the entire audience that filled the huge building had risen to their feet like one man, and that thousands of hands were clapping silently the measure of their intense appreciation. From floor to ceiling, and from wall to wall, flew a great wave of emotion that swept their praise into me, gathered and focused into a single mighty draught of applause.

"It was, I remember thinking, all their thoughts of joy, their feelings of gratitude, beating in upon my soul in that form of praise which is the artist's only adequate reward; and it reminded me of nothing so much as the whirring of innumerable soft wings all rising through the air at the same moment. Pictorially, in this fashion, it came before my mind.

"Violin in hand, I rose too, and turned to face the auditorium, for I realised that they were calling for the author—for him who had

16

ministered so adequately to their pleasure—and that I must be prepared to say something in reply. I had, indeed, made my first bow, and
was already casting about in my mind for suitable words, when, for
the first time during the whole adventure—something in me *hesitated*.
Either it was that the sea of glimmering faces frightened me, or that
I was obeying instinctively some faint warning that it was not myself,
but some other, who was the true author of the play, and that it was
for him these thousands before me clamoured and called.

"But when, still hesitating in confusion, I turned again towards
the stage, I saw that the great fire curtain had meanwhile descended
and that a footstep, regular and unhurried, was at that very moment
coming forward towards the footlights. I heard the tread. I knew at
once who it was. The stranger from the shadows behind me who had
directed the entire performance was now moving to the front. It was
he for whom the audience clamoured; it was he who was the true
author of the play!

"And instantly I clamoured with them, forgetting my own small
pain in a kind of delightful exultation that I, too, owed this man everything, and that I should at last see him face to face and join my thanks
and gratitude to theirs.

"Almost that same instant he appeared and stood before the centre of the curtains, the glare of the footlights casting upwards into his
face. And he looked, not at the great throng behind and beyond me,
but down into *my own* face, into *my own* eyes, smiling, approving, his
expression radiant with a glory I have never seen before or since upon
any human countenance.

"And the stranger, I then realised—*was myself!*

"What happened next is so difficult to describe—though I scarcely
know why it should be so—that I cannot hope to convey the reality
of it properly, or paint the instantaneous manner in which he vanished and was gone. He neither faded nor moved. But in a second
that seemed to have no perceptible duration he was beside me—with
me—in me; and this swift way he became suddenly merged into myself has always seemed to me the most amazing thing I have ever
witnessed. The wave of delight and exultation swept into me anew. I
felt for one brief moment that I was as a god—with a god's power of
perfect expression.

"But for one second only; for, at once, a new sound, terrible and
overwhelming, rose in a flood and tore me away from all that I had
ever known. And the sound was ugly and distressing . . . and darkness

17

followed it. . .

"It was real clapping this time, the clapping of human hands . . . and an indifferent orchestra was playing a noisy march just below me with a great blare of brass out of tune. The lights were up all over the theatre; the audience, busy with wraps and overcoats and applause, were hurrying out. I saw the actors and actresses of the play bowing and scraping before the curtain; and the sight of the perspiration trickling down over the grease-paint of the leading man directly beneath my box struck me like a blow in the face.

"Then came the frantic whistling for broughams and taxicabs and the hoarse shouting from the street where men cried the evening papers in the roar of the outer world. I picked up my opera-hat, which had rolled into the middle of the floor while I had slept upon the sofa, scrambled into my overcoat, rushed out into the street, and told the driver of the first taxicab I found to drive for his life at double rates. . . .

"And all that night, before the memory of the wonder and the glory faded, I worked upon my score of words and music, striving to get down on the paper something at least of what had been shown to me. How much, or how little I succeeded it is now impossible to say. As I have already explained in this report, the memory faded with distressing swiftness. But I did my best. I hope—I believe—I am told, at least—that there is something in the work that people like. . . ."

The Damned

"I'm over forty, Frances, and rather set in my ways," I said good-naturedly, ready to yield if she insisted that our going together on the visit involved her happiness. "My work is rather heavy just now too, as you know. The question is, *could* I work there—with a lot of unassorted people in the house?"

"Mabel doesn't mention any other people, Bill," was my sister's rejoinder. "I gather she's alone—as well as lonely."

By the way she looked sideways out of the window at nothing, it was obvious she was disappointed, but to my surprise she did not urge the point; and as I glanced at Mrs. Franklyn's invitation lying upon her sloping lap, the neat, childish handwriting conjured up a mental picture of the banker's widow, with her timid, insignificant personality, her pale grey eyes and her expression as of a backward child. I thought, too, of the roomy country mansion her late husband had altered to suit his particular needs, and of my visit to it a few years ago when its barren spaciousness suggested a wing of Kensington Museum fitted up temporarily as a place to eat and sleep in. Comparing it mentally with the poky Chelsea flat where I and my sister kept impecunious house, I realised other points as well. Unworthy details flashed across me to entice: the fine library, the organ, the quiet work-room I should have, perfect service, the delicious cup of early tea, and hot baths at any moment of the day—without a geyser!

"It's a longish visit, a month—isn't it?" I hedged, smiling at the details that seduced me, and ashamed of my man's selfishness, yet knowing that Frances expected it of me. "There are points about it, I admit. If you're set on my going with you, I could manage it all right."

I spoke at length in this way because my sister made no answer. I saw her tired eyes gazing into the dreariness of Oakley Street and felt a pang strike through me. After a pause, in which again she said no word, I added: "So, when you write the letter, you might hint, perhaps, that I usually work all the morning, and—er—am not a very lively visitor! Then she'll understand, you see." And I half-rose to return to my diminutive study, where I was slaving, just then, at an absorbing article on Comparative Aesthetic Values in the Blind and Deaf.

But Frances did not move. She kept her grey eyes upon Oakley Street where the evening mist from the river drew mournful perspectives into view. It was late October. We heard the omnibuses thundering across the bridge. The monotony of that broad, characterless street seemed more than usually depressing. Even in June sunshine it was dead, but with autumn its melancholy soaked into every house between King's Road and the Embankment. It washed thought into the past, instead of inviting it hopefully towards the future. For me, its easy width was an avenue through which nameless slums across the river sent creeping messages of depression, and I always regarded it as Winter's main entrance into London—fog, slush, gloom trooped down it every November, waving their forbidding banners till March came to rout them.

Its one claim upon my love was that the south wind swept sometimes unobstructed up it, soft with suggestions of the sea. These lugubrious thoughts I naturally kept to myself, though I never ceased to regret the little flat whose cheapness had seduced us. Now, as I watched my sister's impassive face, I realised that perhaps she, too, felt as I felt, yet, brave woman, without betraying it.

"And, look here, Fanny," I said, putting a hand upon her shoulder as I crossed the room, "it would be the very thing for you. You're worn out with catering and housekeeping. Mabel is your oldest friend, besides, and you've hardly seen her since he died—"

"She's been abroad for a year, Bill, and only just came back," my sister interposed. "She came back rather unexpectedly, though I never thought she would go there to live—" She stopped abruptly. Clearly, she was only speaking half her mind. "Probably," she went on, "Mabel wants to pick up old links again."

"Naturally," I put in, "yourself chief among them." The veiled reference to the house I let pass.

It involved discussing the dead man for one thing.

"I feel *I* ought to go anyhow," she resumed, "and of course it would be jollier if you came too. You'd get in such a muddle here by yourself, and eat wrong things, and forget to air the rooms, and—oh, everything!" She looked up laughing. "Only," she added, "there's the

British Museum—?"

"But there's a big library there," I answered, "and all the books of reference I could possibly want. It was of you I was thinking. You could take up your painting again; you always sell half of what you paint. It would be a splendid rest too, and Sussex is a jolly country to walk in. By all means, Fanny, I advise—"

Our eyes met, as I stammered in my attempts to avoid expressing the thought that hid in both our minds. My sister had a weakness for dabbling in the various "new" theories of the day and Mabel, who before her marriage had belonged to foolish societies for investigating the future life to the neglect of the present one, had fostered this undesirable tendency. Her amiable, impressionable temperament was open to every psychic wind that blew. I deplored, detested the whole business. But even more than this I abhorred the later influence that Mr. Franklyn had steeped his wife in, capturing her body and soul in his sombre doctrines. I had dreaded lest my sister also might be caught.

"Now that she is alone again—"

I stopped short. Our eyes now made pretence impossible, for the truth had slipped out inevitably, stupidly, although unexpressed in definite language. We laughed, turning our faces a moment to look at other things in the room. Frances picked up a book and examined its cover as though she had made an important discovery, while I took my case out and lit a cigarette I did not want to smoke. We left the matter there. I went out of the room before further explanation could cause tension. Disagreements grow into discord from such tiny things—wrong adjectives, or a chance inflection of the voice. Frances had a right to her views of life as much as I had. At least, I reflected comfortably, we had separated upon an agreement this time, recognised mutually, though not actually stated.

And this point of meeting was, oddly enough, our way of regarding someone who was dead.

For we had both disliked the husband with a great dislike, and during his three years' married life had only been to the house once—for a weekend visit; arriving late on Saturday we had left after an early breakfast on Monday morning. Ascribing my sister's dislike to a natural jealousy at losing her old friend, I said merely that he displeased me. Yet we both knew that the real emotion lay much deeper. Frances, loyal, honourable creature, had kept silence; and beyond saying that house and grounds—he altered one and laid out the other—distressed her as an expression of his personality somehow ('distressed' was the

21

word she used), no further explanation had passed her lips.

Our dislike of his personality was easily accounted for—up to a point, since both of us shared the artist's point of view that a creed, cut to measure and carefully dried, was an ugly thing, and that a dogma to which believers must subscribe or perish everlastingly was a barbarism resting upon cruelty. But while my own dislike was purely due to an abstract worship of Beauty, my sister's had another twist in it, for with her "new" tendencies, she believed that all religions were an aspect of truth and that no one, even the lowest wretch, could escape "heaven" in the long run.

Samuel Franklyn, the rich banker, was a man universally respected and admired, and the marriage, though Mabel was fifteen years his junior, won general applause; his bride was an heiress in her own right—breweries—and the story of her conversion at a revivalist meeting where Samuel Franklyn had spoken fervidly of heaven, and terrifyingly of sin, hell and damnation, even contained a touch of genuine romance. She was a brand snatched from the burning; his detailed eloquence had frightened her into heaven; salvation came in the nick of time; his words had plucked her from the edge of that lake of fire and brimstone where their worm dieth not and the fire is not quenched. She regarded him as a hero, sighed her relief upon his saintly shoulder, and accepted the peace he offered her with a grateful resignation.

For her husband was a "religious man" who successfully combined great riches with the glamour of winning souls. He was a portly figure, though tall, with masterful, big hands, his fingers rather thick and red; and his dignity, that just escaped being pompous, held in it something that was implacable. A convinced assurance, almost remorseless, gleamed in his eyes when he preached especially, and his threats of hell fire must have scared souls stronger than the timid, receptive Mabel whom he married.

He clad himself in long frock-coats hat buttoned unevenly, big square boots, and trousers that invariably bagged at the knee and were a little short; he wore low collars, spats occasionally, and a tall black hat that was not of silk. His voice was alternately hard and unctuous; and he regarded theatres, ballrooms, and racecourses as the vestibule of that brimstone lake of whose geography he was as positive as of his great banking offices in the City. A philanthropist up to the hilt, however, no one ever doubted his complete sincerity; his convictions were ingrained, his faith borne out by his life—as witness his name

22

upon so many admirable Societies, as treasurer, patron, or heading the donation list. He bulked large in the world of doing good, a broad and stately stone in the rampart against evil. And his heart was genuinely kind and soft for others—who believed as he did.

Yet, in spite of this true sympathy with suffering and his desire to help, he was narrow as a telegraph wire and unbending as a church pillar; he was intensely selfish; intolerant as an officer of the Inquisition, his *bourgeois* soul constructed a revolting scheme of heaven that was reproduced in miniature in all he did and planned. Faith was the *sine qua non* of salvation, and by "faith" he meant belief in his own particular view of things—"which faith, except everyone do keep whole and undefiled, without doubt he shall perish everlastingly." All the world but his own small, exclusive sect must be damned eternally—a pity, but alas, inevitable. *He* was right.

Yet he prayed without ceasing, and gave heavily to the poor—the only thing he could not give being big ideas to his provincial and suburban deity. Pettier than an insect, and more obstinate than a mule, he had also the superior, sleek humility of a "chosen one." He was churchwarden too. He read the lesson in a "place of worship," either chilly or overheated, where neither organ, vestments, nor lighted candles were permitted, but where the odour of hair-wash on the boys' heads in the back rows pervaded the entire building.

This portrait of the banker, who accumulated riches both on earth and in heaven, may possibly be overdrawn, however, because Frances and I were "artistic temperaments" that viewed the type with a dislike and distrust amounting to contempt. The majority considered Samuel Franklyn a worthy man and a good citizen. The majority, doubtless, held the saner view. A few years more, and he certainly would have been made a baronet. He relieved much suffering in the world, as assuredly as he caused many souls the agonies of torturing fear by his emphasis upon damnation.

Had there been one point of beauty in him, we might have been more lenient; only we found it not, and, I admit, took little pains to search. I shall never forget the look of dour forgiveness with which he heard our excuses for missing Morning Prayers that Sunday morning of our single visit to The Towers. My sister learned that a change was made soon afterwards, prayers being "conducted" after breakfast instead of before.

The Towers stood solemnly upon a Sussex hill amid park-like modern grounds, but the house cannot better be described—it would be so wearisome for one thing—than by saying that it was a cross between an overgrown, pretentious Norwood villa and one of those saturnine Institutes for cripples the train passes as it slinks ashamed through South London into Surrey. It was "wealthily" furnished and at first sight imposing, but on closer acquaintance revealed a meagre personality, barren and austere. One looked for Rules and Regulations on the walls, all signed By Order. The place was a prison that shut out "the world." There was, of course, no billiard-room, no smoking-room, no room for play of any kind, and the great hall at the back, once a chapel, which might have been used for dancing, theatricals, or other innocent amusements, was consecrated in his day to meetings of various kinds, chiefly brigades, temperance or missionary societies.

There was a harmonium at one end—on the level floor—a raised dais or platform at the other, and a gallery above for the servants, gardeners, and coachmen. It was heated with hot-water pipes, and hung with Doré's pictures, though these latter were soon removed and stored out of sight in the attics as being too unspiritual. In polished, shiny wood, it was a representation in miniature of that poky exclusive Heaven he took about with him, externalizing it in all he did and planned, even in the grounds about the house.

Changes in The Towers, Frances told me, had been made during Mabel's year of widowhood abroad—an organ put into the big hall, the library made liveable and re-catalogued—when it was permissible to suppose she had found her soul again and returned to her normal, healthy views of life, which included enjoyment and play, literature, music and the arts, without, however, a touch of that trivial thoughtlessness usually termed worldliness. Mrs. Franklyn, as I remembered her, was a quiet little woman, shallow, perhaps, and easily influenced, but sincere as a dog and thorough in her faithful Friendship.

Her tastes at heart were Catholic, and that heart was simple and unimaginative. That she took up with the various movements of the day was sign merely that she was searching in her limited way for a belief that should bring her peace. She was, in fact, a very ordinary woman, her calibre a little less than that of Frances. I knew they used to discuss all kinds of theories together, but as these discussions never resulted in action, I had come to regard her as harmless. Still, I was not sorry when she married, and I did not welcome now a renewal of the former intimacy. The philanthropist she had given no children, or she would have made a good and sensible mother. No doubt she would marry again.

24

"Mabel mentions that she's been alone at The Towers since the end of August," Frances told me at teatime; "and I'm sure she feels out of it and lonely. It would be a kindness to go. Besides, I always liked her."

I agreed. I had recovered from my attack of selfishness. I expressed my pleasure.

"You've written to accept," I said, half statement and half question.

Frances nodded. "I thanked for you," she added quietly, "explaining that you were not free at the moment, but that later, if not inconvenient, you might come down for a bit and join me."

I stared. Frances sometimes had this independent way of deciding things. I was convicted, and punished into the bargain.

Of course, there followed argument and explanation, as between brother and sister who were affectionate, but the recording of our talk could be of little interest. It was arranged thus, Frances and I both satisfied. Two days later she departed for The Towers, leaving me alone in the flat with everything planned for my comfort and good behaviour—she was rather a tyrant in her quiet way—and her last words as I saw her off from Charing Cross rang in my head for a long time after she was gone:

"I'll write and let you know, Bill. Eat properly, mind, and let me know if anything goes wrong."

She waved her small gloved hand, nodded her head till the feather brushed the window, and was gone.

CHAPTER 2

After the note announcing her safe arrival a week of silence passed, and then a letter came; there were various suggestions for my welfare, and the rest was the usual rambling information and description Frances loved, generously italicised.

" . . .and we are quite alone," she went on in her enormous handwriting that seemed such a waste of space and labour, "though some others are coming presently, I believe. You could work here to your heart's content. Mabel *quite* understands, and says she would love to have you when you feel free to come. She has changed a bit—back to her old natural self: she never mentions *him*. The place has changed too in certain ways: it has more cheerfulness, I think. *She* has put it in, this cheerfulness, spaded it in, if you know what I mean; but it lies about uneasily and is not natural—quite. The organ is a beauty. She must be very rich now, but she's as gentle and sweet as ever. Do you know, Bill, I think he must have *frightened* her into marrying him? I get

25

the impression she was afraid of him." This last sentence was inked out, but I read it through the scratching; the letters being too big to hide.

"He had an inflexible will beneath all that oily kindness which passed for spiritual. He was a real personality, I mean. I'm sure he'd have sent you and me cheerfully to the stake in another century—*for our own good.* Isn't it odd she never speaks of him, even to me?" This, again, was stroked through, though without the intention to obliterate—merely because it was repetition, probably. "The only reminder of him in the house now is a big copy of the presentation portrait that stands on the stairs of the Multitechnic Institute at Peckham—you know—that life-size one with his fat hand sprinkled with rings resting on a thick Bible and the other slipped between the buttons of a tight frock-coat.

"It hangs in the dining room and rather dominates our meals. I wish Mabel would take it down. I think she'd like to, if she *dared.* There's not a single photograph of him anywhere, even in her own room. Mrs. Marsh is here—you remember her, *his* housekeeper, the wife of the man who got penal servitude for killing a baby or something—you said she robbed him and justified her stealing because the story of the unjust steward was in the Bible! How we laughed over that! *She's* just the same too, gliding about all over the house and turning up when least expected."

Other reminiscences filled the next two sides of the letter, and ran, without a trace of punctuation, into instructions about a Salamander stove for heating my work-room in the flat; these were followed by things I was to tell the cook, and by requests for several articles she had forgotten and would like sent after her, two of them blouses, with descriptions so lengthy and contradictory that I sighed as I read them—"unless you come down soon, in which case perhaps you wouldn't mind bringing them; not the mauve one I wear in the evening sometimes, but the pale blue one with lace round the collar and the crinkly front. They're in the cupboard—or the drawer, I'm not sure which—of my bedroom. *Ask Annie* if you're in doubt. Thanks most *awfully.* Send a telegram, remember, and we'll meet you in the motor any time. I don't quite know if I shall stay the whole month—*alone.* It all depends. . . ."

And she closed the letter, the italicised words increasing recklessly towards the end, with a repetition that Mabel would love to have me "for myself," as also to have a "man in the house," and that I only had to telegraph the day and the train. . . . This letter, coming by the second post, interrupted me in a moment of absorbing work, and, having read it through to make sure there was nothing requiring instant attention, I threw it aside and went on with my notes and reading. Within five minutes, however, it was back at me again. That restless thing called "between the lines" fluttered about my mind. My interest in the Balkan States—political article that had been "ordered"—faded.

Somewhere, somehow, I felt disquieted, disturbed. At first, I persisted in my work, forcing myself to concentrate, but soon found that a layer of new impressions floated between the article and my attention. It was like a shadow, though a shadow that dissolved upon inspection. Once or twice, I glanced up, expecting to find someone in the room, that the door had opened unobserved and Annie was waiting for instructions. I heard the buses thundering across the bridge. I was aware of Oakley Street.

Montenegro and the blue Adriatic melted into the October haze along that depressing Embankment that aped a riverbank, and sentences from the letter flashed before my eyes and stung me. Picking it up and reading it through more carefully, I rang the bell and told Annie to find the blouses and pack them for the post, showing her finally the written description, and resenting the superior smile with which she at once interrupted. "*I* know them, sir," and disappeared.

But it was not the blouses: it was that exasperating thing "between the lines" that put an end to my work with its elusive teasing nuisance. The first sharp impression is alone of value in such a case, for once analysis begins the imagination constructs all kinds of false interpretation. The more I thought, the more I grew fuddled. The letter, it seemed to me, wanted to say another thing; instead, the eight sheets conveyed it merely. It came to the edge of disclosure, then halted.

There was something on the writer's mind, and I felt uneasy. Studying the sentences brought, however, no revelation, but increased confusion only; for while the uneasiness remained, the first clear hint had vanished. In the end I closed my books and went out to look up another matter at the British Museum library. Perhaps I should discover it that way—by turning the mind in a totally new direction. I lunched at the Express Dairy in Oxford Street close by, and telephoned to Annie that I would be home to tea at five.

And at tea, tired physically and mentally after breathing the exhausted air of the Rotunda for five hours, my mind suddenly delivered up its original impression, vivid and clear-cut; no proof accompanied the revelation; it was mere presentiment, but convincing. Frances was

27

disturbed in her mind, her orderly, sensible, housekeeping mind; she was uneasy, even perhaps afraid; something in the house distressed her, and she had need of me. Unless I went down, her time of rest and change, her quite necessary holiday, in fact, would be spoilt. She was too unselfish to say this, but it ran everywhere between the lines. I saw it clearly now. Mrs. Franklyn, moreover—and that meant Frances too—would like a "man in the house." It was a disagreeable phrase, a suggestive way of hinting something she dared not state definitely. The two women in that great, lonely barrack of a house were afraid.

My sense of duty, affection, unselfishness, whatever the composite emotion may be termed, was stirred; also, my vanity. I acted quickly, lest reflection should warp clear, decent judgment.

"Annie," I said, when she answered the bell, "you need not send those blouses by the post. I'll take them down tomorrow when I go. I shall be away a week or two, possibly longer." And, having looked up a train, I hastened out to telegraph before I could change my fickle mind.

But no desire came that night to change my mind. I was doing the right, the necessary thing. I was even in something of a hurry to get down to The Towers as soon as possible. I chose an early afternoon train.

CHAPTER 3

A telegram had told me to come to a town ten miles from the house, so I was saved the crawling train to the local station, and travelled down by an express. As soon as we left London the fog cleared off, and an autumn sun, though without heat in it, painted the landscape with golden browns and yellows. My spirits rose as I lay back in the luxurious motor and sped between the woods and hedges. Oddly enough, my anxiety of overnight had disappeared. It was due, no doubt, to that exaggeration of detail which reflection in loneliness brings. Frances and I had not been separated for over a year, and her letters from The Towers told so little. It had seemed unnatural to be deprived of those intimate particulars of mood and feeling I was accustomed to. We had such confidence in one another, and our affection was so deep. Though she was but five years younger than myself, I regarded her as a child. My attitude was fatherly.

In return, she certainly mothered me with a solicitude that never cloyed. I felt no desire to marry while she was still alive. She painted in watercolours with a reasonable success, and kept house for me; I wrote, reviewed books and lectured on aesthetics; we were a humdrum couple of quasi-artists, well satisfied with life, and all I feared for her was that she might become a suffragette or be taken captive by one of these wild theories that caught her imagination sometimes, and that Mabel, for one, had fostered. As for myself, no doubt she deemed me a trifle solid or stolid—I forget which word she preferred—but on the whole there was just sufficient difference of opinion to make intercourse suggestive without monotony, and certainly without quarrelling.

Drawing in deep draughts of the stinging autumn air, I felt happy and exhilarated. It was like going for a holiday, with comfort at the end of the journey instead of bargaining for centimes.

But my heart sank noticeably the moment the house came into view. The long drive, lined with hostile monkey trees and formal wellingtonias that were solemn and sedate, was mere extension of the miniature approach to a thousand semidetached suburban "residences"; and the appearance of The Towers, as we turned the corner with a rush, suggested a commonplace climax to a story that had begun interestingly, almost thrillingly. A villa had escaped from the shadow of the Crystal Palace, thumped its way down by night, grown suddenly monstrous in a shower of rich rain, and settled itself insolently to stay.

Ivy climbed about the opulent red-brick walls, but climbed neatly and with disfiguring effect, sham as on a prison or—the simile made me smile—an orphan asylum. There was no hint of the comely roughness of untidy ivy on a ruin. Clipped, trained, and precise it was, as on a brand-new protestant church. I swear there was not a bird's nest nor a single earwig in it anywhere. About the porch it was particularly thick, smothering a seventeenth-century lamp with a contrast that was quite horrible. Extensive glass-houses spread away on the farther side of the house; the numerous towers to which the building owed its name seemed made to hold school bells; and the windowsills, thick with potted flowers, made me think of the desolate suburbs of Brighton or Bexhill.

In a commanding position upon the crest of a hill, it overlooked miles of undulating, wooded country southwards to the Downs, but behind it, to the north, thick banks of ilex, holly, and privet protected it from the cleaner and more stimulating winds. Hence, though highly placed, it was shut in. Three years had passed since I last set eyes upon, it, but the unsightly memory I had retained was justified by the reality. The place was deplorable.

It is my habit to express my opinions audibly sometimes, when impressions are strong enough to warrant it; but now I only sighed "Oh, dear," as I extricated my legs from many rugs and went into the house. A tall parlour-maid, with the bearing of a grenadier, received me, and standing behind her was Mrs. Marsh, the housekeeper, whom I remembered because her untidy back hair had suggested to me that it had been burnt. I went at once to my room, my hostess already dressing for dinner, but Frances came in to see me just as I was struggling with my black tie that had got tangled like a bootlace.

She fastened it for me in a neat, effective bow, and while I held my chin up for the operation, staring blankly at the ceiling, the impression came—I wondered, was it her touch that caused it?—that something in her trembled. Shrinking perhaps is the truer word. Nothing in her face or manner betrayed it, nor in her pleasant, easy talk while she tidied my things and scolded my slovenly packing, as her habit was, questioning me about the servants at the flat. The blouses, though right, were crumpled, and my scolding was deserved. There was no impatience even. Yet somehow or other the suggestion of a shrinking reserve and holding back reached my mind. She had been lonely, of course, but it was more than that; she was glad that I had come, yet for some reason unstated she could have wished that I had stayed away. We discussed the news that had accumulated during our brief separation, and in doing so the impression, at best exceedingly slight, was forgotten.

My chamber was large and beautifully furnished; the hall and dining room of our flat would have gone into it with a good remainder; yet it was not a place I could settle down in for work. It conveyed the idea of impermanence, making me feel transient as in a hotel bedroom. This, of course, was the fact. But some rooms convey a settled, lasting hospitality even in a hotel; this one did not; and as I was accustomed to work in the room I slept in, at least when visiting, a slight frown must have crept between my eyes.

"Mabel has fitted a work-room for you just out of the library," said the clairvoyant Frances.

"No one will disturb you there, and you'll have fifteen thousand books all catalogued within easy reach. There's a private staircase too. You can breakfast in your room and slip down in your dressing gown if you want to." She laughed. My spirits took a turn upwards as absurdly as they had gone down.

"And, how are *you*?" I asked, giving her a belated kiss. "It's jolly to be together again. I did feel rather lost without you, I'll admit."

"That's natural," she laughed. "I'm so glad."

She looked well and had country colour in her cheeks. She informed me that she was eating and sleeping well, going out for little walks with Mabel, painting bits of scenery again, and enjoying a complete change and rest; and yet, for all her brave description, the word somehow did not quite ring true. Those last words in particular did not ring true. There lay in her manner, just out of sight, I felt, this suggestion of the exact reverse—of unrest, shrinking, almost of anxiety. Certain small strings in her seemed over-tight. "Keyed-up" was the slang expression that crossed my mind. I looked rather searchingly into her face as she was telling me this.

"Only—the evenings," she added, noticing my query, yet rather avoiding my eyes, "the evenings are—well, rather heavy sometimes, and I find it difficult to keep awake."

"The strong air after London makes you drowsy," I suggested, "and you like to get early to bed."

Frances turned and looked at me for a moment steadily. "On the contrary, Bill, I dislike going to bed—here. And Mabel goes so early." She said it lightly enough, fingering the disorder upon my dressing table in such a stupid way that I saw her mind was working in another direction altogether. She looked up suddenly with a kind of nervousness from the brush and scissors.

"Billy," she said abruptly, lowering her voice, "isn't it odd, but I *hate* sleeping alone here? I can't make it out quite; I've never felt such a thing before in my life. Do you—think it's all nonsense?"

And she laughed, with her lips but not with her eyes; there was a note of defiance in her I failed to understand.

"Nothing a nature like yours feels strongly is nonsense, Frances," I replied soothingly.

But I, too, answered with my lips only, for another part of my mind was working elsewhere, and among uncomfortable things. A touch of bewilderment passed over me. I was not certain how best to continue. If I laughed, she would tell me no more, yet if I took her too seriously the strings would tighten further. Instinctively, then, this flashed rapidly across me: that something of what she felt, I had also felt, though interpreting it differently. Vague it was, as the coming of rain or storm that announce themselves hours in advance with their hint of faint, unsettling excitement in the air.

I had been but a short hour in the house—big, comfortable, luxurious house—but had experienced this sense of being unsettled, unfixed, fluctuating—a kind of impermanence that transient lodgers in hotels must feel, but that a guest in a friend's home ought not to feel, be the visit short or long. To Frances, an impressionable woman, the feeling had come in the terms of alarm. She disliked sleeping alone, while yet she longed to sleep. The precise idea in my mind evaded capture, merely brushing through me, three-quarters out of sight; I realised only that we both felt the same thing, and that neither of us could get at it clearly.

Degrees of unrest we felt, but the actual thing did not disclose itself. It did not happen.

I felt strangely at sea for a moment. Frances would interpret hesitation as endorsement, and encouragement might be the last thing that could help her.

"Sleeping in a strange house," I answered at length, "is often difficult at first, and one feels lonely. After fifteen months in our tiny flat one feels lost and uncared-for in a big house. It's an uncomfortable feeling—I know it well. And this is a barrack, isn't it? The masses of furniture only make it worse. One feels in storage somewhere underground—the furniture doesn't furnish. One must never yield to fancies, though—"

Frances looked away towards the windows; she seemed disappointed a little.

"After our thickly-populated Chelsea," I went on quickly, "it seems isolated here."

But she did not turn back, and clearly, I was saying the wrong thing. A wave of pity rushed suddenly over me. Was she really frightened, perhaps? She was imaginative, I knew, but never moody; common sense was strong in her, though she had her times of hypersensitiveness. I caught the echo of some unreasoning, big alarm in her. She stood there, gazing across my balcony towards the sea of wooded country that spread dim and vague in the obscurity of the dusk. The deepening shadows entered the room, I fancied, from the grounds below. Following her abstracted gaze a moment, I experienced a curious sharp desire to leave, to escape. Out yonder was wind and space and freedom. This enormous building was oppressive, silent, still.

Great catacombs occurred to me, things beneath the ground, imprisonment and capture. I believe I even shuddered a little.

I touched her shoulder. She turned round slowly, and we looked with a certain deliberation into each other's eyes.

32

"Fanny," I asked, more gravely than I intended, "you are not frightened, are you? Nothing has happened, has it?"

She replied with emphasis, "Of course not! How could it—I mean, why should I?" She stammered, as though the wrong sentence flustered her a second. "It's simply—that I have this ter—this dislike of sleeping alone."

Naturally, my first thought was how easy it would be to cut our visit short. But I did not say this. Had it been a true solution, Frances would have said it for me long ago.

"Wouldn't Mabel double-up with you?" I said instead, "or give you an adjoining room, so that you could leave the door between you open? There's space enough, heaven knows."

And then, as the gong sounded in the hall below for dinner, she said, as with an effort, this thing:

"Mabel did ask me—on the third night—after I had told her. But I declined."

"You'd rather be alone than with her?" I asked, with a certain relief.

Her reply was so gravely given, a child would have known there was more behind it: "Not that; but that she did not really want it."

I had a moment's intuition and acted on it impulsively. "She feels it too, perhaps, but wishes to face it by herself—and get over it?"

My sister bowed her head, and the gesture made me realise of a sudden how grave and solemn our talk had grown, as though some portentous thing were under discussion. It had come of itself—indefinite as a gradual change of temperature. Yet neither of us knew its nature, for apparently neither of us could state it plainly. Nothing happened, even in our words.

"That was my impression," she said, "—that if she yields to it, she encourages it. And a habit forms so easily. Just think," she added with a faint smile that was the first sign of lightness she had yet betrayed, "what a nuisance it would be—everywhere—if everybody was afraid of being alone—like that."

I snatched readily at the chance. We laughed a little, though it was a quiet kind of laughter that seemed wrong. I took her arm and led her towards the door.

"Disastrous, in fact," I agreed.

She raised her voice to its normal pitch again, as I had done. "No doubt it will pass," she said, "now that you have come. Of course, it's chiefly my imagination." Her tone was lighter, though nothing could convince me that the matter itself was light—just then. "And in any

33

case," tightening her grip on my arm as we passed into the bright enormous corridor and caught sight of Mrs. Franklyn waiting in the cheerless hall below, "I'm very glad you're here, Bill, and Mabel, I know, is too."

"If it doesn't pass," I just had time to whisper with a feeble attempt at jollity, "I'll come at night and snore outside your door. After that you'll be so glad to get rid of me that you won't mind being alone."

"That's a bargain," said Frances.

I shook my hostess by the hand, made a banal remark about the long interval since last we met, and walked behind them into the great dining room, dimly lit by candles, wondering in my heart how long my sister and I should stay, and why in the world we had ever left our cosy little flat to enter this desolation of riches and false luxury at all. The unsightly picture of the late Samuel Franklyn, Esq., stared down upon me from the farther end of the room above the mighty mantelpiece.

He looked, I thought, like some pompous Heavenly Butler who denied to all the world, and to us in particular, the right of entry without presentation cards signed by his hand as proof that we belonged to his own exclusive set. The majority, to his deep grief, and in spite of all his prayers on their behalf, must burn and "perish everlastingly."

CHAPTER 4

With the instinct of the healthy bachelor, I always try to make myself a nest in the place I live in, be it for long or short. Whether visiting, in lodging-house, or in hotel, the first essential is this nest—one's own things built into the walls as a bird builds in its feathers. It may look desolate and uncomfortable enough to others, because the central detail is neither bed nor wardrobe, sofa nor armchair, but a good solid writing-table that does not wriggle, and that has wide elbowroom.

And The Towers is vividly described for me by the single fact that I could not "nest" there.

I took several days to discover this, but the first impression of impermanence was truer than I knew. The feathers of the mind refused here to lie one way. They ruffled, pointed, and grew wild.

Luxurious furniture does not mean comfort; I might as well have tried to settle down in the sofa and armchair department of a big shop. My bedroom was easily managed; it was the private workroom, prepared especially for my reception, that made me feel alien and outcast.

Externally, it was all one could desire: an antechamber to the great library, with not one, but two generous oak tables, to say nothing of smaller ones against the walls with capacious drawers.

There were reading desks, mechanical devices for holding books, perfect light, quiet as in a church, and no approach but across the huge adjoining room. Yet it did not invite.

"I hope you'll be able to work here," said my little hostess the next morning, as she took me in—her only visit to it while I stayed in the house—and showed me the ten-volume catalogue.

"It's absolutely quiet and no one will disturb you."

"If you can't, Bill, you're not much good," laughed Frances, who was on her arm. "Even I could write in a study like this!"

I glanced with pleasure at the ample tables, the sheets of thick blotting paper, the rulers, sealing wax, paper knives, and all the other immaculate paraphernalia. "It's perfect," I answered with a secret thrill, yet feeling a little foolish. This was for Gibbon or Carlyle, rather than for my pot-boiling insignificancies. "If I can't write masterpieces here, it's certainly not *your* fault," and I turned with gratitude to Mrs. Franklyn. She was looking straight at me, and there was a question in her small pale eyes I did not understand. Was she noting the effect upon me, I wondered?

"You'll write here—perhaps a story about the house," she said, "Thompson will bring you anything you want; you only have to ring." She pointed to the electric bell on the central table, the wire running neatly down the leg. "No one has ever worked here before, and the library has been hardly used since it was put in. So, there's no previous atmosphere to affect your imagination—er—adversely."

We laughed. "Bill isn't that sort," said my sister; while I wished they would go out and leave me to arrange my little nest and set to work.

I thought, of course, it was the huge listening library that made me feel so inconsiderable—the fifteen thousand silent, staring books, the solemn aisles, the deep, eloquent shelves. But when the women had gone and I was alone, the beginning of the truth crept over me, and I felt that first hint of disconsolateness which later became an imperative No. The mind shut down, images ceased to rise and flow. I read, made copious notes, but I wrote no single line at The Towers.

Nothing completed itself there. Nothing happened.

The morning sunshine poured into the library through ten long narrow windows; birds were singing; the autumn air, rich with a faint aroma of November melancholy that stung the imagination pleasantly, filled my antechamber. I looked out upon the undulating wooded

35

landscape, hemmed in by the sweep of distant Downs, and I tasted a whiff of the sea. Rooks cawed as they floated above the elms, and there were lazy cows in the nearer meadows. A dozen times I tried to make my nest and settle down to work, and a dozen times, like a turning fastidious dog upon a hearth rug, I rearranged my chair and books and papers. The temptation of the catalogue and shelves, of course, was accountable for much, yet not, I felt, for all. That was a manageable seduction.

My work, moreover, was not of the creative kind that requires absolute absorption; it was the mere readable presentation of data I had accumulated. My notebooks were charged with facts ready to tabulate—facts, too, that interested me keenly. A mere effort of the will was necessary, and concentration of no difficult kind. Yet, somehow, it seemed beyond me: something forever pushed the facts into disorder .... and in the end I sat in the sunshine, dipping into a dozen books selected from the shelves outside, vexed with myself and only half-enjoying it. I felt restless. I wanted to be elsewhere.

And even while I read, attention wandered. Frances, Mabel, her late husband, the house and grounds, each in turn and sometimes all together, rose uninvited into the stream of thought, hindering any consecutive flow of work. In disconnected fashion came these pictures that interrupted concentration, yet presenting themselves as broken fragments of a bigger thing my mind already groped for unconsciously. They fluttered round this hidden thing of which they were aspects, fugitive interpretations, no one of them bringing complete revelation. There was no adjective, such as pleasant or unpleasant, that I could attach to what I felt, beyond that the result was unsettling. Vague as the atmosphere of a dream, it yet persisted, and I could not dissipate it.

Isolated words or phrases in the lines I read sent questions scouring across my mind, sure sign that the deeper part of me was restless and ill at ease.

Rather trivial questions too—half-foolish interrogations, as of a puzzled or curious child: Why was my sister afraid to sleep alone, and why did her friend feel a similar repugnance, yet seek to conquer it? Why was the solid luxury of the house without comfort, its shelter without the sense of permanence? Why had Mrs. Franklyn asked us to come, artists, unbelieving vagabonds, types at the farthest possible remove from the saved sheep of her husband's household? Had a reaction set in against the hysteria of her conversion? I had seen no signs of religious fervour in her; her atmosphere was that of an ordinary, high-minded woman, yet a woman of the world. Lifeless, though, a little, perhaps, now that I came to think about it: she had made no definite impression upon me of any kind. And my thoughts ran vaguely after this fragile clue.

Closing my book, I let them run. For, with this chance reflection came the discovery that I could not see her clearly—could not feel her soul, her personality. Her face, her small pale eyes, her dress and body and walk, all these stood before me like a photograph; but her Self evaded me. She seemed not there, lifeless, empty, a shadow— nothing. The picture was disagreeable, and I put it by. Instantly she melted out, as though light thought had conjured up a phantom that had no real existence. And at that very moment, singularly enough, my eye caught sight of her moving past the window, going silently along the gravel path. I watched her, a sudden new sensation gripping me. "There goes a prisoner," my thought instantly ran, "one who wishes to escape, but cannot."

What brought the outlandish notion, heaven only knows. The house was of her own choice, she was twice an heiress, and the world lay open at her feet. Yet she stayed—unhappy, frightened, caught. All this flashed over me, and made a sharp impression even before I had time to dismiss it as absurd. But a moment later explanation offered itself, though it seemed as far-fetched as the original impression. My mind, being logical, was obliged to provide something, apparently. For Mrs. Franklyn, while dressed to go out, with thick walking-boots, a pointed stick, and a motor-cap tied on with a veil as for the windy lanes, was obviously content to go no farther than the little garden paths. The costume was a sham and a pretence. It was this, and her lithe, quick movements that suggested a caged creature—a creature tamed by fear and cruelty that cloaked themselves in kindness—pacing up and down, unable to realise why it got no farther, but always met the same bars in exactly the same place. The mind in her was barred.

I watched her go along the paths and down the steps from one terrace to another, until the laurels hid her altogether; and into this mere imagining of a moment came a hint of something slightly disagreeable, for which my mind, search as it would, found no explanation at all. I remembered then certain other little things. They dropped into the picture of their own accord. In a mind not deliberately hunting for clues, pieces of a puzzle sometimes come together in this way, bringing revelation, so that for a second there flashed across me, vanishing instantly again before I could consider it, a large, distressing thought. I can only describe vaguely as a Shadow.

Dark and ugly, oppressive certainly it might be described, with something torn and dreadful about the edges that suggested pain and strife and terror. The interior of a prison with two rows of occupied condemned cells, seen years ago in New York, sprang to memory after it— the connection between the two impossible to surmise even. But the "certain other little things" mentioned above were these: that Mrs. Franklyn, in last night's dinner talk, had always referred to "this house," but never called it "home"; and had emphasised unnecessarily, for a well-bred woman, our "great kindness" in coming down to stay so long with her.

Another time, in answer to my futile compliment about the "stately rooms," she said quietly, "It is an enormous house for so small a party; but I stay here very little, and only till I get it straight again." The three of us were going up the great staircase to bed as this was said, and, not knowing quite her meaning, I dropped the subject. It edged delicate ground, I felt. Frances added no word of her own. It now occurred to me abruptly that "stay" was the word made use of, when "live" would have been more natural. How insignificant to recall! Yet why did they suggest themselves just at this moment . . .?

And, on going to Frances's room to make sure she was not nervous or lonely, I realised abruptly, that Mrs. Franklyn, of course, had talked with her in a confidential sense that I, as a mere visiting brother, could not share. Frances had told me nothing. I might easily have wormed it out of her, had I not felt that for us to discuss further our hostess and her house merely because we were under the roof together, was not quite nice or loyal.

"I'll call you, Bill, if I'm scared," she had laughed as we parted, my room being just across the big corridor from her own. I had fallen asleep, thinking what in the world was meant by "getting it straight again."

And now in my antechamber to the library, on the second morning, sitting among piles of foolscap and sheets of spotless blotting-paper, all useless to me, these slight hints came back and helped to frame the big, vague Shadow I have mentioned. Up to the neck in this Shadow, almost drowned, yet just treading water, stood the figure of my hostess in her walking costume. Frances and I seemed swimming to her aid. The Shadow was large enough to include both house and grounds, but farther than that I could not see. . . . Dismissing it, I fell to reading my purloined book again. Before I turned another page,

38

however, another startling detail leaped out at me: the figure of Mrs. Franklyn in the Shadow was not living. It floated helplessly, like a doll or puppet that has no life in it. It was both pathetic and dreadful.

Anyone who sits in reverie thus, of course, may see similar ridiculous pictures when the will no longer guides construction. The incongruities of dreams are thus explained. I merely record the picture as it came. That it remained by me for several days, just as vivid dreams do, is neither here nor there. I did not allow myself to dwell upon it. The curious thing, perhaps, is that from this moment I date my inclination, though not yet my desire, to leave. I purposely say "to leave."

I cannot quite remember when the word changed to that aggressive, frantic thing which is escape.

Chapter 5

We were left delightfully to ourselves in this pretentious country mansion with the soul of a villa. Frances took up her painting again, and, the weather being propitious, spent hours out of doors, sketching flowers, trees and nooks of woodland, garden, even the house itself where bits of it peered suggestively across the orchards. Mrs. Franklyn seemed always busy about something or other, and never interfered with us except to propose motoring, tea in another part of the lawn, and so forth. She flitted everywhere, preoccupied, yet apparently doing nothing. The house engulfed her rather. No visitor called. For one thing, she was not supposed to be back from abroad yet; and for another, I think, the neighbourhood—her husband's neighbourhood—was puzzled by her sudden cessation from good works. Brigades and temperance societies did not ask to hold their meetings in the big hall, and the vicar arranged the school-treats in another's field without explanation.

The full-length portrait in the dining room, and the presence of the housekeeper with the "burnt" back hair, indeed, were the only reminders of the man who once had lived here. Mrs. Marsh retained her place in silence, well-paid sinecure as it doubtless was, yet with no hint of that suppressed disapproval one might have expected from her. Indeed, there was nothing positive to disapprove, since nothing "worldly" entered grounds or building. In her master's lifetime she had been another "brand snatched from the burning," and it had then been her custom to give vociferous "testimony" at the revival meetings where he adorned the platform and led in streams of prayer. I saw her sometimes on the stairs, hovering, wandering, half-watching and half-listening, and the idea came to me once that this woman somehow formed a link with the departed influence of her bigoted employer. She, alone among us, *belonged* to the house, and looked at home there.

When I saw her talking—oh, with such correct and respectful mien—to Mrs. Franklyn, I had the feeling that for all her unaggressive attitude, she yet exerted some influence that sought to make her mistress stay in the building forever —live there. She would prevent her escape, prevent "getting it straight again," thwart somehow her will to freedom, if she could. The idea in me was of the most fleeting kind. But another time, when I came down late at night to get a book from the library antechamber, and found her sitting in the hall—alone—the impression left upon me was the reverse of fleeting.

I can never forget the vivid, disagreeable effect it produced upon me. What was she doing there at half-past eleven at night, all alone in the darkness? She was sitting upright, stiff, in a big chair below the clock. It gave me a turn. It was so incongruous and odd. She rose quietly as I turned the corner of the stairs, and asked me respectfully, her eyes cast down as usual, whether I had finished with the library, so that she might lock up. There was no more to it than that; but the picture stayed with me—unpleasantly.

These various impressions came to me at odd moments, of course, and not in a single sequence as I now relate them. I was hard at work before three days were past, not writing, as explained, but reading, making notes, and gathering material from the library for future use. It was in chance moments that these curious flashes came, catching me unawares with a touch of surprise that sometimes made me start. For they proved that my under-mind was still conscious of the Shadow, and that far away out of sight lay the cause of it that left me with a vague unrest, unsettled, seeking to "nest" in a place that did not want me. Only when this deeper part knows harmony, perhaps, can good brainwork result, and my inability to write was thus explained.

Certainly, I was always seeking for something here I could not find—an explanation that continually evaded me. Nothing but these trivial hints offered themselves. Lumped together, however, they had the effect of defining the Shadow a little. I became more and more aware of its very real existence. And, if I have made little mention of Frances and my hostess in this connection, it is because they contributed at first little or nothing towards the discovery of what this story tries to tell. Our life was wholly external, normal, quiet, and uneventful; conversation banal—Mrs. Franklyn's conversation in particular. They said nothing that suggested revelation.

Both were in this Shadow, and both knew that they were in it, but neither betrayed by word or act a hint of interpretation. They talked privately, no doubt, but of that I can report no details.

And so, it was that, after ten days of a very commonplace visit, I found myself looking straight into the face of a Strangeness that defied capture at close quarters. "There's something here that never happens," were the words that rose in my mind, "and that's why none of us can speak of it."

And as I looked out of the window and watched the vulgar blackbirds, with toes turned in, boring out their worms, I realised sharply that even they, as indeed everything large and small in the house and grounds, shared this strangeness, and were twisted out of normal appearance because of it. Life, as expressed in the entire place, was crumpled, dwarfed, emasculated. God's meanings here were crippled, His love of joy was stunted. Nothing in the garden danced or sang.

There was hate in it. "The Shadow," my thought hurried on to completion, "is a manifestation of hate; and hate is the Devil." And then I sat back frightened in my chair, for I knew that I had partly found the truth.

Leaving my books, I went out into the open. The sky was overcast, yet the day by no means gloomy, for a soft, diffused light oozed through the clouds and turned all things warm and almost summery. But I saw the grounds now in their nakedness because I understood. Hate means strife, and the two together weave the robe that terror wears. Having no so-called religious beliefs, myself, nor belonging to any set of dogmas called a creed, I could stand outside these feelings and observe. Yet they soaked into me sufficiently for me to grasp sympathetically what others, with more cabined souls (I flattered myself), might feel. That picture in the dining room stalked everywhere, hid behind every tree, peered down upon me from the peaked ugliness of the *bourgeois* towers, and left the impress of its powerful hand upon every bed of flowers.

"You must not do this, you must not do that," went past me through the air. "You must not leave these narrow paths," said the rigid iron railings of black. "You shall not walk here," was written on the lawns.

"Keep to the steps," "Don't pick the flowers; make no noise of laughter, singing, dancing," was placarded all over the rose-garden, and "Trespassers will be—not prosecuted but—*destroyed*" hung from the crest of monkey tree and holly. Guarding the ends of each artificial terrace stood gaunt, implacable policemen, warders, jailers. "Come with us," they chanted, "or be damned eternally."

I remember feeling quite pleased with myself that I had discovered this obvious explanation of the prison feeling the place breathed out. That the posthumous influence of heavy old Samuel Franklyn might be an inadequate solution did not occur to me. By "getting the place straight again," his widow, of course, meant forgetting the glamour of fear and foreboding his depressing creed had temporarily forced upon her; and Frances, delicately minded being, did not speak of it because it was the influence of the man her friend had loved. I felt lighter; a load was lifted from me. "To trace the unfamiliar to the familiar," came back a sentence I had read somewhere, "is to understand." It was a real relief. I could talk with Frances now, even with my hostess, no danger of treading clumsily. For the key was in my hands. I might even help to dissipate the Shadow, "to get it straight again." It seemed, perhaps, our long invitation was explained!

I went into the house laughing—at myself a little. "Perhaps after all the artist's outlook, with no hard and fast dogmas, is as narrow as the others! How small humanity is! And why is there no possible and true combination of *all* outlooks?"

The feeling of "unsettling" was very strong in me just then, in spite of my big discovery which was to clear everything up. And at the moment I ran into Frances on the stairs, with a portfolio of sketches under her arm.

It came across me then abruptly that, although she had worked a great deal since we came, she had shown me nothing. It struck me suddenly as odd, unnatural. The way she tried to pass me now confirmed my newborn suspicion that—well, that her results were hardly what they ought to be.

"Stand and deliver!" I laughed, stepping in front of her. "I've seen nothing you've done since you've been here, and as a rule you show me all your things. I believe they are atrocious and degrading!" Then my laughter froze.

She made a sly gesture to slip past me, and I almost decided to let her go, for the expression that flashed across her face shocked me. She looked uncomfortable and ashamed; the colour came and went a moment in her cheeks, making me think of a child detected in some secret naughtiness.

It was almost fear.

"It's because they're not finished then?" I said, dropping the tone of banter, "or because they're too good for me to understand?" For my criticism of painting, she told me, was crude and ignorant sometimes.

"But you'll let me see them later, won't you?"

Frances, however, did not take the way of escape I offered. She changed her mind. She drew the portfolio from beneath her arm instead. "You can see them if you *really* want to, Bill," she said quietly, and her tone reminded me of a nurse who says to a boy just grown out of childhood, "you are old enough now to look upon horror and ugliness—only I don't advise it."

"I do want to," I said, and made to go downstairs with her. But, instead, she said in the same low voice as before, "Come up to my room, we shall be undisturbed there." So, I guessed that she had been on her way to show the paintings to our hostess, but did not care for us all three to see them together. My mind worked furiously.

"Mabel asked me to do them," she explained in a tone of submissive horror, once the door was shut, "in fact, she begged it of me. You know how persistent she is in her quiet way. I—er—had to."

She flushed and opened the portfolio on the little table by the window, standing behind me as I turned the sketches over—sketches of the grounds and trees and garden. In the first moment of inspection, however, I did not take in clearly why my sister's sense of modesty had been offended. For my attention flashed a second elsewhere. Another bit of the puzzle had dropped into place, defining still further the nature of what I called "the Shadow." Mrs. Franklyn, I now remembered, had suggested to me in the library that I might perhaps write something about the place, and I had taken it for one of her banal sentences and paid no further attention. I realised now that it was said in earnest.

She wanted our interpretations, as expressed in our respective "talents," painting and writing. Her invitation was explained. She left us to ourselves on purpose.

"I should like to tear them up," Frances was whispering behind me with a shudder, "only I promised—" She hesitated a moment.

"Promised not to?" I asked with a queer feeling of distress, my eyes glued to the papers.

"Promised always to show them to her first," she finished so low I barely caught it.

I have no intuitive, immediate grasp of the value of paintings; results come to me slowly, and though everyone believes his own judgment to be good, I dare not claim that mine is worth more than that of any other layman, Frances had too often convicted me of gross ignorance and error.

I can only say that I examined these sketches with a feeling of amazement that contained revulsion, if not actually horror and disgust.

They were outrageous. I felt hot for my sister, and it was a relief to know she had moved across the room on some pretence or other, and did not examine them with me. Her talent, of course, is mediocre, yet she has her moments of inspiration—moments, that is to say, when a view of Beauty not normally her own flames divinely through her. And these interpretations struck me forcibly as being thus "inspired"—not her own.

They were uncommonly well done; they were also atrocious. The meaning in them, however, was never more than hinted. There the unholy skill and power came in: they suggested so abominably, leaving most to the imagination. To find such significance in a *bourgeois* villa garden, and to interpret it with such delicate yet legible certainty, was a kind of symbolism that was sinister, even diabolical. The delicacy was her own, but the point of view was another's.

And the word that rose in my mind was not the gross description of "impure," but the more fundamental qualification—"un-pure."

In silence I turned the sketches over one by one, as a boy hurries through the pages of an evil book lest he be caught.

"What does Mabel do with them?" I asked presently in a low tone, as I neared the end. "Does she keep them?"

"She makes notes about them in a book and then destroys them," was the reply from the end of the room. I heard a sigh of relief. "I'm glad you've seen them, Bill. I wanted you to—but was afraid to show them. You understand?"

"I understand," was my reply, though it was not a question intended to be answered. All I understood really was that Mabel's mind was as sweet and pure as my sister's, and that she had some good reason for what she did. She destroyed the sketches, but first made notes! It was an interpretation of the place she sought. Brother-like, I felt resentment, though, that Frances should waste her time and talent, when she might be doing work that she could sell. Naturally, I felt other things as well. . . .

"Mabel pays me five guineas for each one," I heard. "Absolutely insists."

I stared at her stupidly a moment, bereft of speech or wit. "I must either accept, or go away," she went on calmly, but a little white.

44

"I've tried everything. There was a scene the third day I was here—when I showed her my first result. I wanted to write to you, but hesitated—"

"It's unintentional, then, on your part—forgive my asking it, Frances, dear?" I blundered, hardly knowing what to think or say. "Between the lines" of her letter came back to me. "I mean, you make the sketches in your ordinary way and—the result comes out of itself, so to speak?"

She nodded, throwing her hands out like a Frenchman. "We needn't keep the money for ourselves, Bill. We can give it away, but—I must either accept or leave," and she repeated the shrugging gesture. She sat down on the chair facing me, staring helplessly at the carpet.

"You say there was a scene?" I went on presently, "She insisted?"

"She begged me to continue," my sister replied very quietly. "She thinks—that is, she has an idea or theory that there's something about the place—something she can't get at quite." Frances stammered badly.

She knew I did not encourage her wild theories.

"Something she feels—yes," I helped her, more than curious.

"Oh, you know what I mean, Bill," she said desperately. "That the place is saturated with some influence that she is herself too positive or too stupid to interpret. She's trying to make herself negative and receptive, as she calls it, but can't, of course, succeed. Haven't you noticed how dull and impersonal and insipid she seems, as though she had no personality? She thinks impressions will come to her that way. But they don't—"

"Naturally."

"So, she's trying me—us—what she calls the sensitive and impressionable artistic temperament. She says that until she is sure exactly what this influence is, she can't fight it, turn it out, 'get the house straight', as she phrases it."

Remembering my own singular impressions, I felt more lenient than I might otherwise have done. I tried to keep impatience out of my voice.

"And this influence, what—whose is it?"

We used the pronoun that followed in the same breath, for I answered my own question at the same moment as she did:

"*His*." Our heads nodded involuntarily towards the floor, the dining room being directly underneath.

And my heart sank, my curiosity died away on the instant; I felt bored.

A commonplace haunted house was the last thing in the world to amuse or interest me. The mere thought exasperated, with its suggestions of imagination, overwrought nerves, hysteria, and the rest.

Mingled with my other feelings was certainly disappointment. To see a figure or feel a "presence," and report from day to day strange incidents to each other would be a form of weariness I could never tolerate.

"But really, Frances," I said firmly, after a moment's pause, "it's too far-fetched, this explanation. A curse, you know, belongs to the ghost stories of early Victorian days." And only my positive conviction that there was something after all worth discovering, and that it most certainly was not this, prevented my suggesting that we terminate our visit forthwith, or as soon as we decently could. "This is not a haunted house, whatever it is," I concluded somewhat vehemently, bringing my hand down upon her odious portfolio.

My sister's reply revived my curiosity sharply.

"I was waiting for you to say that. Mabel says exactly the same. *He* is in it—but it's something more than that alone, something far bigger and more complicated." Her sentence seemed to indicate the sketches, and though I caught the inference I did not take it up, having no desire to discuss them with her just them indeed, if ever.

I merely stared at her and listened. Questions, I felt sure, would be of little use. It was better she should say her thought in her own way.

"He is one influence, the most recent," she went on slowly, and always very calmly, "but there are others—deeper layers, as it were—underneath. If his were the only one, something would happen. But nothing ever does happen. The others hinder and prevent—as though each were struggling to predominate."

I had felt it already myself. The idea was rather horrible. I shivered.

"That's what is so ugly about it—that nothing ever happens," she said.

"There is this endless anticipation—always on the dry edge of a result that never materializes. It is torture. Mabel is at her wits' end, you see. And when she begged me—what I felt about my sketches—I mean—"

She stammered badly as before.

I stopped her. I had judged too hastily. That queer symbolism in her paintings, pagan and yet not innocent, was, I understood, the result of mixture. I did not pretend to understand, but at least I could be patient. I consequently held my peace. We did talk on a little longer,

46

but it was more general talk that avoided successfully our hostess, the paintings, wild theories, and *him*—until at length the emotion Frances had hitherto so successfully kept under burst vehemently forth again.

It had hidden between her calm sentences, as it had hidden between the lines of her letter. It swept her now from head to foot, packed tight in the thing she then said.

"Then, Bill, if it is not an ordinary haunted house," she asked, "what is it?"

The words were commonplace enough. The emotion was in the tone of her voice that trembled; in the gesture she made, leaning forward and clasping both hands upon her knees, and in the slight blanching of her cheeks as her brave eyes asked the question and searched my own with anxiety that bordered upon panic. In that moment she put herself under my protection. I winced.

"And why," she added, lowering her voice to a still and furtive whisper, "does nothing ever happen? If only,"—this with great emphasis—"something *would* happen—break this awful tension—bring relief. It's the waiting I cannot stand." And she shivered all over as she said it, a touch of wildness in her eyes.

I would have given much to have made a true and satisfactory answer. My mind searched frantically for a moment, but in vain. There lay no sufficient answer in me. I felt what she felt, though with differences.

No conclusive explanation lay within reach. Nothing happened. Eager as I was to shoot the entire business into the rubbish heap where ignorance and superstition discharge their poisonous weeds, I could not honestly accomplish this. To treat Frances as a child, and merely "explain away" would be to strain her confidence in my protection, so affectionately claimed. It would further be dishonest to myself—weak, besides—to deny that I had also felt the strain and tension even as she did. While my mind continued searching, I returned her stare in silence; and Frances then, with more honesty and insight than my own, gave suddenly the answer herself—an answer whose truth and adequacy, so far as they went, I could not readily gainsay:

"I think, Bill, because it is too big to happen here—to happen anywhere, indeed, all at once—and too awful!"

To have tossed the sentence aside as nonsense, argued it away, proved that it was really meaningless, would have been easy—at any other time or in any other place; and, had the past week brought me none of the vivid impressions it had brought me, this is doubtless what

47

I should have done. My narrowness again was proved. We understand in others only what we have in ourselves. But her explanation, in a measure, I knew was true. It hinted at the strife and struggle that my notion of a Shadow had seemed to cover thinly.

"Perhaps," I murmured lamely, waiting in vain for her to say more. "But you said just now that you felt the thing was 'in layers', as it were. Do you mean each one—each influence—fighting for the upper hand?"

I used her phraseology to conceal my own poverty. Terminology, after all, was nothing, provided we could reach the idea itself.

Her eyes said yes. She had her clear conception, arrived at independently, as was her way.

And, unlike her sex, she kept it clear, unsmothered by too many words.

"One set of influences gets at me, another gets at you. It's according to our temperaments, I think." She glanced significantly at the vile portfolio. "Sometimes they are mixed—and therefore false. There has always been in me, more than in you, the pagan thing, perhaps, though never, thank God, like that."

The frank confession of course invited my own, as it was meant to do.

Yet it was difficult to find the words.

"What I have felt in this place, Frances, I honestly can hardly tell you, because—er—my impressions have not arranged themselves in any definite form I can describe. The strife, the agony of vainly-sought escape, and the unrest—a sort of prison atmosphere—this I have felt at different times and with varying degrees of strength. But I find, as yet, no final label to attach. I couldn't say pagan, Christian, or anything like that, I mean, as you do. As with the blind and deaf, you may have an intensification of certain senses denied to me, or even another sense altogether in embryo—"

"Perhaps," she stopped me, anxious to keep to the point, "you feel it as Mabel does. She feels the whole thing complete."

"That also is possible," I said very slowly. I was thinking behind my words. Her odd remark that it was "big and awful" came back upon me as true. A vast sensation of distress and discomfort swept me suddenly.

Pity was in it, and a fierce contempt, a savage, bitter anger as well. Fury against some sham authority was part of it.

"Frances," I said, caught unawares, and dropping all pretence, "what in the world can it be?" I looked hard at her. For some minutes neither of us spoke.

"Have *you* felt no desire to interpret it?" she asked presently, "Mabel did suggest my writing something about the house," was my reply, "but I've felt nothing imperative. That sort of writing is not my line, you know. My only feeling," I added, noticing that she waited for more, "is the impulse to explain, discover, get it out of me somehow, and so get rid of it. Not by writing, though—as yet." And again, I repeated my former question:

"What in the world do you think it is?" My voice had become involuntarily hushed. There was awe in it. Her answer, given with slow emphasis, brought back all my reserve: the phraseology provoked me rather:—"Whatever it is, Bill, it is not of God."

I got up to go downstairs. I believe I shrugged my shoulders. "Would you like to leave, Frances? Shall we go back to town?" I suggested this at the door, and hearing no immediate reply, I turned back to look. Frances was sitting with her head bowed over and buried in her hands. The attitude horribly suggested tears. No woman, I realised, can keep back the pressure of strong emotion as long as Frances had done, without ending in a fluid collapse. I waited a moment uneasily, longing to comfort, yet afraid to act—and in this way discovered the existence of the appalling emotion in myself, hitherto but half guessed.

At all costs a scene must be prevented: it would involve such exaggeration and overstatement. Brutally, such is the weakness of the ordinary man, I turned the handle to go out, but my sister then raised her head. The sunlight caught her face, framed untidily in its auburn hair, and I saw her wonderful expression with a start. Pity, tenderness, and sympathy shone in it like a flame. It was undeniable. There shone through all her features the imperishable love and yearning to sacrifice self for others which I have seen in only one type of human being. It was the great mother look.

"We must stay by Mabel and help her get it straight," she whispered, making the decision for us both.

I murmured agreement. Abashed and half ashamed, I stole softly from the room and went out into the grounds. And the first thing clearly realised when alone was this: that the long scene between us was without definite result. The exchange of confidence was really nothing but hints and vague suggestion. We had decided to stay, but it was a negative decision not to leave rather than a positive action. All our words and questions, our guesses, inferences, explanations, our most subtle allusions and insinuations, even the odious paintings themselves, were without definite result. Nothing had happened.

CHAPTER 6

And instinctively, once alone, I made for the places where she had painted her extraordinary pictures; I tried to see what she had seen. Perhaps, now that she had opened my mind to another view, I should be sensitive to some similar interpretation—and possibly by way of literary expression. If I were to write about the place, I asked myself, how should I treat it? I deliberately invited an interpretation in the way that came easiest to me—writing.

But in this case, there came no such revelation. Looking closely at the trees and flowers, the bits of lawn and terrace, the rose-garden and corner of the house where the flaming creeper hung so thickly, I discovered nothing of the odious, unpure thing her colour and grouping had unconsciously revealed.

At first, that is, I discovered nothing. The reality stood there, commonplace and ugly, side by side with her distorted version of it that lay in my mind. It seemed incredible. I tried to force it, but in vain. My imagination, ploughed less deeply than hers, or to another pattern, grew different seed. Where I saw the gross soul of an overgrown suburban garden, inspired by the spirit of a vulgar, rich revivalist who loved to preach damnation, she saw this rush of pagan liberty and joy, this strange license of primitive flesh which, tainted by the other, produced the adulterated, vile result.

Certain things, however, gradually then became apparent, forcing themselves upon me, willy-nilly. They came slowly, but overwhelmingly. Not that facts had changed, or natural details altered in the grounds— this was impossible—but that I noticed for the first time, various aspects I had not noticed before—trivial enough, yet for me, just then, significant. Some I remembered from previous days; others I saw now as I wandered to and fro, uneasy, uncomfortable—almost, it seemed, watched by someone who took note of my impressions. The details were so foolish, the total result so formidable. I was half aware that others tried hard to make me see. It was deliberate.

My sister's phrase, "one layer got at me, another gets at you," flashed, undesired, upon me.

For I saw, as with the eyes of a child, what I can only call a goblin garden—house, grounds, trees, and flowers belonged to a goblin world that children enter through the pages of their fairy tales. And what made me first aware of it was the whisper of the wind behind me, so that I turned with a sudden start, feeling that something had moved closer.

An old ash tree, ugly and ungainly, had been artificially trained to form an arbour at one end of the terrace that was a tennis lawn, and the leaves of it now went rustling together, swishing as they rose and fell. I looked at the ash tree, and felt as though I had passed that moment between doors into this goblin garden that crouched behind the real one.

Below, at a deeper layer perhaps, lay hidden the one my sister had entered.

To deal with my own, however, I call it goblin, because an odd aspect of the quaint in it yet never quite achieved the picturesque. Grotesque, probably, is the truer word, for everywhere I noticed, and for the first time, this slight alteration of the natural due either to the exaggeration of some detail, or to its suppression, generally, I think, to the latter. Life everywhere appeared to me as blocked from the full delivery of its sweet and lovely message. Some counter influence stopped it—suppression; or sent it awry—exaggeration.

The house itself, mere expression, of course, of a narrow, limited mind, was sheer ugliness; it required no further explanation. With the grounds and garden, so far as shape and general plan were concerned, this was also true; but that trees and flowers and other natural details should share the same deficiency perplexed my logical soul, and even dismayed it. I stood and stared, then moved about, and stood and stared again. Everywhere was this mockery of a sinister, unfinished aspect. I sought in vain to recover my normal point of view. My mind had found this goblin garden and wandered to and fro in it, unable to escape.

The change was in myself, of course, and so trivial were the details which illustrated it, that they sound absurd, thus mentioned one by one.

For me, they proved it, is all I can affirm. The goblin touch lay plainly everywhere: in the forms of the trees, planted at neat intervals along the lawns; in this twisted ash that rustled just behind me; in the shadow of the gloomy wellingtonias, whose sweeping skirts obscured the grass; but especially, I noticed, in the tops and crests of them. For here, the delicate, graceful curves of last year's growth seemed to shrink back into themselves. None of them pointed upwards. Their life had failed and turned aside just when it should have become triumphant.

The character of a tree reveals itself chiefly at the extremities, and it was precisely here that they all drooped and achieved this hint of goblin distortion—in the growth, that is, of the last few years. What ought to have been fairy, joyful, natural, was instead uncomely to the verge of the grotesque. Spontaneous expression was arrested. My mind perceived a goblin garden, and was caught in it. The place grimaced at me.

With the flowers it was similar, though far more difficult to detect in detail for description. I saw the smaller vegetable growth as impish, half-malicious. Even the terraces sloped ill, as though their ends had sagged since they had been so lavishly constructed; their varying angles gave a queerly bewildering aspect to their sequence that was unpleasant to the eye. One might wander among their deceptive lengths and get lost—lost among open terraces!—with the house quite close at hand. Unhomely seemed the entire garden, unable to give repose, restlessness in it everywhere, almost strife, and discord certainly.

Moreover, the garden grew into the house, the house into the garden, and in both was this idea of resistance to the natural—the spirit that says No to joy. All over it I was aware of the effort to achieve another end, the struggle to burst forth and escape into free, spontaneous expression that should be happy and natural, yet the effort forever frustrated by the weight of this dark shadow that rendered it abortive. Life crawled aside into a channel that was a cul-de-sac, then turned horribly upon itself. Instead of blossom and fruit, there were weeds. This approach of life I was conscious of—then dismal failure. There was no fulfilment.

Nothing happened.

And so, through this singular mood, I came a little nearer to understand the unpure thing that had stammered out into expression through my sister's talent. For the unpure is merely negative; it has no existence; it is but the cramped expression of what is true, stammering its way brokenly over false boundaries that seek to limit and confine. Great, full expression of anything is pure, whereas here was only the incomplete, unfinished, and therefore ugly. There was a strife and pain and desire to escape. I found myself shrinking from house and grounds as one shrinks from the touch of the mentally arrested, those in whom life has turned awry. There was almost mutilation in it.

Past items, too, now flocked to confirm this feeling that I walked, liberty captured and half-maimed, in a monstrous garden. I remembered days of rain that refreshed the countryside, but left these grounds, cracked with the summer heat, unsatisfied and thirsty; and how the big winds, that cleaned the woods and fields elsewhere, crawled here with difficulty through the dense foliage that protected The Towers from the North and West and East. They were ineffective, sluggish currents. There was no real wind. Nothing happened. I began to realise—far more clearly than in my sister's fanciful explanation about "layers"—that here were many contrary influences at work, mutually destructive of one another.

House and grounds were not haunted merely; they were the arena of past thinking and feeling, perhaps of terrible, impure beliefs, each striving to suppress the others, yet no one of them achieving supremacy because no one of them was strong enough, no one of them was true. Each, moreover, tried to win me over, though only one was able to reach my mind at all. For some obscure reason—possibly because my temperament had a natural bias towards the grotesque—it was the goblin layer. With me, it was the line of least resistance. . . .

In my own thoughts this "goblin garden" revealed, of course, merely my personal interpretation. I felt now objectively what long ago my mind had felt subjectively. My work, essential sign of spontaneous life with me, had stopped dead; production had become impossible.

I stood now considerably closer to the cause of this sterility. The Cause, rather, turned bolder, had stepped insolently nearer. Nothing happened anywhere; house, garden, mind alike were barren, abortive, torn by the strife of frustrate impulse, ugly, hateful, sinful. Yet behind it all was still the desire of life—desire to escape—accomplish. Hope—an intolerable hope—I became startlingly aware—crowned torture.

And, realising this, though in some part of me where Reason lost her hold, there rose upon me then another and a darker thing that caught me by the throat and made me shrink with a sense of revulsion that touched actual loathing. I knew instantly whence it came, this wave of abhorrence and disgust, for even while I saw red and felt revolt rise in me, it seemed that I grew partially aware of the layer next below the goblin. I perceived the existence of this deeper stratum. One opened the way for the other, as it were. There were so many, yet all inter-related; to admit one was to clear the way for all.

If I lingered, I should be caught—horribly. They struggled with such violence for supremacy among themselves, however, that this latest uprising was instantly smothered and crushed back, though not before a glimpse had been revealed to me, and the redness in my thoughts transferred itself to colour my surroundings thickly and appallingly—with blood. This lurid aspect drenched the garden, smeared the terraces, lent to the very soil a tinge as of sacrificial rites, that choked the breath in me, while it seemed to fix me to the earth my feet so longed to leave. It was so revolting that at the same time I felt a dreadful curiosity as of fascination—I wished to stay. Between these contrary impulses I think I actually reeled a moment, transfixed by a fascination of the Awful.

Through the lighter goblin veil, I felt myself sinking down, down, down into this turgid layer that was so much more violent and so much more ancient. The upper layer, indeed, seemed fairy by comparison with this terror born of the lust for blood, thick with the anguish of human sacrificial victims.

Upper! Then I was already sinking; my feet were caught; I was actually in it! What atavistic strain, hidden deep within me, had been touched into vile response, giving this flash of intuitive comprehension, I cannot say. The coatings laid on by civilization are probably thin enough in all of us. I made a supreme effort. The sun and wind came back. I could almost swear I opened my eyes. Something very atrocious surged back into the depths, carrying with it a thought of tangled woods, of big stones standing in a circle, motionless, white figures, the one form bound with ropes, and the ghastly gleam of the knife. Like smoke upon a battlefield, it rolled away. . . .

I was standing on the gravel path below the second terrace when the familiar goblin garden danced back again, doubly grotesque now, doubly mocking, yet, by way of contrast, almost welcome. My glimpse into the depths was momentary, it seems, and had passed utterly away.

The common world rushed back with a sense of glad relief, yet ominous now forever, I felt, for the knowledge of what its past had built upon.

In street, in theatre, in the festivities of friends, in music-room or playing field, even indeed in church—how could the memory of what I had seen and felt leave its hideous trace? The very structure of my Thought, it seemed to me, was stained.

What has been thought by others can never be obliterated until. . . .

With a start my reverie broke and fled, scattered by a violent sound that I recognised for the first time in my life as wholly desirable. The returning motor meant that my hostess was back.

Yet, so urgent had been my temporary obsession, that my first presentation of her was—well, not as I knew her now. Floating along with a face of anguished torture I saw Mabel, a mere effigy captured by others' thinking, pass down into those depths of fire and blood that only just had closed beneath my feet. She dipped away. She vanished, her fading eyes turned to the last towards some saviour who had failed her.

And that strange intolerable hope was in her face.

The mystery of the place was pretty thick about me just then. It was the fall of dusk, and the ghost of slanting sunshine was as unreal as though badly painted. The garden stood at attention all about me. I cannot explain it, but I can tell it, I think, exactly as it happened, for it remains vivid in me forever—that, for the first time, something *almost happened*, myself apparently the combining link through which it pressed towards delivery:

I had already turned towards the house. In my mind were pictures—not actual thoughts—of the motor, tea on the verandah, my sister, Mabel— when there came behind me this tumultuous, awful rush—as I left the garden. The ugliness, the pain, the striving to escape, the whole negative and suppressed agony that was the Place, focused that second into a concentrated effort to produce a result. It was a blinding tempest of long-frustrate desire that heaved at me, surging appallingly behind me like an anguished mob.

I was in the act of crossing the frontier into my normal self again, when it came, catching fearfully at my skirts. I might use an entire dictionary of descriptive adjectives yet come no nearer to it than this— the conception of a huge assemblage determined to escape with me, or to snatch me back among themselves. My legs trembled for an instant, and I caught my breath—then turned and ran as fast as possible up the ugly terraces.

At the same instant, as though the clanging of an iron gate cut short the unfinished phrase, I *thought* the beginning of an awful thing:

"The Damned ..."

Like this it rushed after me from that goblin garden that had sought to keep me:

"The Damned!"

For there was sound in it. I know full well it was subjective, not actually heard at all; yet somehow sound was in it—a great volume, roaring and booming thunderously, far away, and below me. The sentence dipped back into the depths that gave it birth, unfinished. Its completion was prevented. As usual, nothing happened. But it drove behind me like a hurricane as I ran towards the house, and the sound of it I can only liken to those terrible undertones you may hear standing beside Niagara. They lie behind the mere crash of the falling flood,

55

within it somehow, not audible to all—felt rather than definitely heard.

It seemed to echo back from the surface of those sagging terraces as I flew across their sloping ends, for it was somehow underneath them. It was in the rustle of the wind that stirred the skirts of the drooping wellingtonias. The beds of formal flowers passed it on to the creepers, red as blood, that crept over the unsightly building. Into the structure of the vulgar and forbidding house it sank away; The Towers took it home. The uncomely doors and windows seemed almost like mouths that had uttered the words themselves, and on the upper floors at that very moment I saw two maids in the act of closing them again.

And on the verandah, as I arrived breathless, and shaken in my soul, Frances and Mabel, standing by the tea table, looked up to greet me. In the faces of both were clearly legible the signs of shock. They watched me coming, yet so full of their own distress that they hardly noticed the state in which I came. In the face of my hostess, however, I read another and a bigger thing than in the face of Frances. Mabel knew. She had experienced what I had experienced. She had heard that awful sentence I had heard but heard it not for the first time; heard it, moreover, I verily believe, complete and to its dreadful end.

"Bill, did you hear that curious noise just now?" Frances asked it sharply before I could say a word. Her manner was confused; she looked straight at me; and there was a tremor in her voice she could not hide.

"There's wind about," I said, "wind in the trees and sweeping round the walls. It's risen rather suddenly." My voice faltered rather.

"No. It wasn't wind," she insisted, with a significance meant for me alone, but badly hidden. "It was more like distant thunder, we thought. How you ran too!" she added. "What a pace you came across the terraces!"

I knew instantly from the way she said it that they both had already heard the sound before and were anxious to know if I had heard it, and how. My interpretation was what they sought.

"It was a curiously deep sound, I admit. It may have been big guns at sea," I suggested, "forts or cruisers practicing. The coast isn't so very far, and with the wind in the right direction—"

The expression on Mabel's face stopped me dead.

"Like huge doors closing," she said softly in her colourless voice, "enormous metal doors shutting against a mass of people clamouring to get out." The gravity, the note of hopelessness in her tones, was shocking.

Frances had gone into the house the instant Mabel began to speak. "I'm cold," she had said; "I think I'll get a shawl." Mabel and I were alone.

I believe it was the first time we had been really alone since I arrived. She looked up from the teacups, fixing her pallid eyes on mine.

She had made a question of the sentence.

"You hear it like that?" I asked innocently. I purposely used the present tense.

She changed her stare from one eye to the other; it was absolutely expressionless. My sister's step sounded on the floor of the room behind us.

"If only—" Mabel began, then stopped, and my own feelings leaping out instinctively completed the sentence I felt was in her mind:

"—something would happen."

She instantly corrected me. I had caught her thought, yet somehow phrased it wrongly.

"We could escape!" She lowered her tone a little, saying it hurriedly.

The "we" amazed and horrified me; but something in her voice and manner struck me utterly dumb. There was ice and terror in it. It was a dying woman speaking—a lost and hopeless soul.

In that atrocious moment I hardly noticed what was said exactly, but I remember that my sister returned with a grey shawl about her shoulders, and that Mabel said, in her ordinary voice again, "It is chilly, yes; let's have tea inside," and that two maids, one of them the grenadier, speedily carried the loaded trays into the morning-room and put a match to the logs in the great open fireplace. It was, after all, foolish to risk the sharp evening air, for dusk was falling steadily, and even the sunshine of the day just fading could not turn autumn into summer. I was the last to come in.

Just as I left the verandah a large black bird swooped down in front of me past the pillars; it dropped from overhead, swerved abruptly to one side as it caught sight of me, and flapped heavily towards the shrubberies on the left of the terraces, where it disappeared into the gloom. It flew very low, very close. And it startled me, I think because in some way it seemed like my Shadow materialised—as though the dark horror that was rising everywhere from house and garden, then settling back so thickly yet so imperceptibly upon us all, were incarnated in that whirring creature that passed between the daylight and the coming night.

I stood a moment, wondering if it would appear again, before I followed the others indoors, and as I was in the act of closing the windows after me, I caught a glimpse of a figure on the lawn. It was some distance away, on the other side of the shrubberies, in fact where the bird had vanished. But in spite of the twilight that half magnified, half obscured it, the identity was unmistakable. I knew the housekeeper's stiff walk too well to be deceived. "Mrs. Marsh taking the air," I said to myself. I felt the necessity of saying it, and I wondered why she was doing so at this particular hour. If I had other thoughts, they were so vague, and so quickly and utterly suppressed, that I cannot recall them sufficiently to relate them here.

And, once indoors, it was to be expected that there would come explanation, discussion, conversation, at any rate, regarding the singular noise and its cause, some uttered evidence of the mood that had been strong enough to drive us all inside. Yet there was none. Each of us purposely, and with various skill, ignored it. We talked little, and when we did it was of anything in the world but that.

Personally, I experienced a touch of that same bewilderment which had come over me during my first talk with Frances on the evening of my arrival, for I recall now the acute tension, and the hope, yet dread, that one or other of us must sooner or later introduce the subject. It did not happen, however; no reference was made to it even remotely. It was the presence of Mabel, I felt positive, that prohibited. As soon might we have discussed Death in the bedroom of a dying woman.

The only scrap of conversation I remember, where all was ordinary and commonplace, was when Mabel spoke casually to the grenadier asking why Mrs. Marsh had omitted to do something or other—what it was I forget— and that the maid replied respectfully that "Mrs. Marsh was very sorry, but her 'and still pained her." I enquired, though so casually that I scarcely know what prompted the words, whether she had injured herself severely, and the reply, "She upset a lamp and burnt herself," was said in a tone that made me feel my curiosity was indiscreet, "but she always has an excuse for not doing things she ought to do."

The little bit of conversation remained with me, and I remember particularly the quick way Frances interrupted and turned the talk upon the delinquencies of servants in general, telling incidents of her own at our flat with a volubility that perhaps seemed forced, and that certainly did not encourage general talk as it may have been intended to do. We lapsed into silence immediately she finished.

But for all our care and all our calculated silence, each knew that something had, in these last moments, come very close; it had brushed us in passing; it had retired; and I am inclined to think now that the large dark thing I saw, riding the dusk, probably bird of prey, was in some sense a symbol of it in my mind—that actually there had been no bird at all, I mean, but that my mood of apprehension and dismay had formed the vivid picture in my thoughts. It had swept past us, it had retreated, but it was now, at this moment, in hiding very close. And it was watching us.

★★★★★★★★★★★★★★★★

Perhaps, too, it was mere coincidence that I encountered Mrs. Marsh, *his* housekeeper, several times that evening in the short interval between tea and dinner, and that on each occasion the sight of this gaunt, half-saturnine woman fed my prejudice against her. Once, on my way to the telephone, I ran into her just where the passage is somewhat jammed by a square table carrying the Chinese gong, a grandfather's clock and a box of croquet mallets. We both gave way, then both advanced, then again gave way—simultaneously. It seemed, impossible to pass. We stepped with decision to the same side, finally colliding in the middle, while saying those futile little things, half apology, half excuse, that are inevitable at such times. In the end she stood upright against the wall for me to pass, taking her place against the very door I wished to open.

It was ludicrous.

"Excuse me—I was just going in—to telephone," I explained. And she sidled off, murmuring apologies, but opening the door for me while she did so. Our hands met a moment on the handle.

There was a second's awkwardness—it was too stupid. I remembered her injury, and by way of something to say, I enquired after it. She thanked me; it was entirely healed now, but it might have been much worse; and there was something about the "mercy of the Lord" that I didn't quite catch. While telephoning, however—London call, and my attention focused on it—realised sharply that this was the first time I had spoken with her; also, that I had—touched her.

It happened to be a Sunday, and the lines were clear. I got my connection quickly, and the incident was forgotten while my thoughts went up to London. On my way upstairs, then, the woman came back into my mind, so that I recalled other things about her—how she seemed all over the house, in unlikely places often; how I had caught her sitting in the hall alone that night; how she was forever coming and going with her lugubrious visage and that untidy hair at the back that had made me laugh three years ago with the idea that it looked singed or burnt; and how the impression on my first arrival at The Towers was that this woman somehow kept alive, though its evidence was outwardly suppressed, the influence of her late employer and of his sombre teachings.

Somewhere with her was associated the idea of punishment, vindictiveness, revenge. I remembered again suddenly my odd notion that she sought to keep her present mistress here, a prisoner in this bleak and comfortless house, and that really, in spite of her obsequious silence, she was intensely opposed to the change of thought that had reclaimed Mabel to a happier view of life.

All this in a passing second flashed in review before me, and I discovered, or at any rate reconstructed, the real Mrs. Marsh. She was decidedly in the Shadow. More, she stood in the forefront of it, stealthily leading an assault, as it were, against The Towers and its occupants, as though, consciously or unconsciously, she laboured incessantly to this hateful end.

I can only judge that some state of nervousness in me permitted the series of insignificant thoughts to assume this dramatic shape, and that what had gone before prepared the way and led her up at the head of so formidable a procession. I relate it exactly as it came to me. My nerves were doubtless somewhat on edge by now. Otherwise, I should hardly have been a prey to the exaggeration at all. I seemed open to so many strange, impressions.

Nothing else, perhaps, can explain my ridiculous conversation with her, when, for the third time that evening, I came suddenly upon the woman half-way down the stairs, standing by an open window as if in the act of listening. She was dressed in black, a black shawl over her square shoulders and black gloves on her big, broad hands. Two black objects, prayer books apparently, she clasped, and on her head, she wore a bonnet with shaking beads of jet.

At first, I did not know her, as I came running down upon her from the landing; it was only when she stood aside to let me pass that I saw her profile against the tapestry and recognised Mrs. Marsh. And to catch her on the front stairs, dressed like this, struck me as incongruous—impertinent. I paused in my dangerous descent. Through the opened window came the sound of bells— church bells—a sound more depressing to me than superstition, and as nauseating. Though the action was ill judged, I obeyed the sudden prompting—was it a secret desire to attack, perhaps?—and spoke to her.

"Been to church, I suppose, Mrs. Marsh?" I said. "Or just going, perhaps?"

Her face, as she looked up a second to reply, was like an iron doll that moved its lips and turned its eyes, but made no other imitation of life at all.

"Some of us still goes, sir," she said unctuously.

It was respectful enough, yet the implied judgment of the rest of the world made me almost angry. A deferential insolence lay behind the affected meekness.

"For those who believe no doubt it is helpful," I smiled. "True religion brings peace and happiness, I'm sure—joy, Mrs. Marsh, joy!" I found keen satisfaction in the emphasis.

She looked at me like a knife. I cannot describe the implacable thing that shone in her fixed, stern eyes, nor the shadow of felt darkness that stole across her face. She glittered. I felt hate in her. I knew—she knew too—who was in the thoughts of us both at that moment.

She replied softly, never forgetting her place for an instant:

"There is joy, sir—in 'eaven—over one sinner that repenteth, and in church there goes up prayer to Gawd for those 'oo—well, for the others, sir, 'oo—"

She cut short her sentence thus. The gloom about her as she said it was like the gloom about a hearse, a tomb, a darkness of great hopeless dungeons. My tongue ran on of itself with a kind of bitter satisfaction:

"We must believe there are no others, Mrs. Marsh. Salvation, you know, would be such a failure if there were. No merciful, all-foreseeing God could ever have devised such a fearful plan—"

Her voice, interrupting me, seemed to rise out of the bowels of the earth:

"They rejected the salvation when it was offered to them, sir, on earth."

"But you wouldn't have them tortured forever because of one mistake in ignorance," I said, fixing her with my eye. "Come now, would you, Mrs. Marsh? No God worth worshipping could permit such cruelty. Think a moment what it means."

She stared at me, a curious expression in her stupid eyes. It seemed to me as though the "woman" in her revolted, while yet she dared not suffer her grim belief to trip. That is, she would willingly have had it otherwise but for a terror that prevented.

"We may pray for them, sir, and we do—we *may* 'ope." She dropped her eyes to the carpet.

"Good, good!" I put in cheerfully, sorry now that I had spoken at all.

"That's more hopeful, at any rate isn't it?"

She murmured something about Abraham's bosom, and the "time of salvation not being forever," as I tried to pass her. Then a half gesture that she made stopped me. There was something more she wished to say—to ask. She looked up furtively. In her eyes I saw the "woman" peering out through fear.

"Per'aps, sir." she faltered, as though lightning must strike her dead, "per'aps, would you think, a drop of cold water, given in His name, might moisten—?"

But I stopped her, for the foolish talk had lasted long enough. "Of course," I exclaimed, "of course. For God is love, remember, and love means charity, tolerance, sympathy, and sparing others pain," and I hurried past her, determined to end the outrageous conversation for which yet I knew myself entirely to blame. Behind me, she stood stock-still for several minutes, half bewildered, half alarmed, as I suspected. I caught the fragment of another sentence, one word of it, rather—"punishment"—but the rest escaped me. Her arrogance and condescending tolerance exasperated me, while I was at the same time secretly pleased that I might have touched some string of remorse or sympathy in her after all. Her belief was iron; she dared not let it go; yet somewhere underneath there lurked the germ of a wholesome revulsion.

She would help "them"—if she dared. Her question proved it.

Half ashamed of myself, I turned and crossed the hall quickly lest I should be tempted to say more, and in me was a disagreeable sensation as though I had just left the Incurable Ward of some great hospital. A reaction caught me as of nausea. Ugh! I wanted such people cleansed by fire. They seemed to me as centres of contamination whose vicious thoughts flowed out to stain God's glorious world. I saw myself, Frances, Mabel too especially, on the rack, while that odious figure of cruelty and darkness stood over us and ordered the awful handles turned in order that we might be "saved"—forced, that is, to think and believe exactly as she thought and believed.

I found relief for my somewhat childish indignation by letting myself loose upon the organ then. The flood of Bach and Beethoven brought back the sense of proportion. It proved, however, at the same

62

time that there *had* been this growth of distortion in me, and that it had been provided apparently by my closer contact—for the first time—with that funereal personality, the woman who, like her master, believed that all holding views of God that differed from her own, must be damned eternally. It gave me, moreover, some faint clue perhaps, though a clue I was unequal of following up, to the nature of the strife and terror and frustrate influence in the house. That housekeeper had to do with it. She kept it alive. Her thought was like a spell she waved above her mistress's head.

CHAPTER 7

That night I was wakened by a hurried tapping at my door, and before I could answer, Frances stood beside my bed. She had switched on the light as she came in. Her hair fell straggling over her dressing gown. Her face was deathly pale, its expression so distraught it was almost haggard.

The eyes were very wide. She looked almost like another woman.

She was whispering at a great pace: "Bill, Bill, wake up, quick!"

"I am awake. What is it?" I whispered too. I was startled.

"Listen!" was all she said. Her eyes stared into vacancy.

There was not a sound in the great house. The wind had dropped, and all was still. Only the tapping seemed to continue endlessly in my brain.

The clock on the mantelpiece pointed to half-past two.

"I heard nothing, Frances. What is it?" I rubbed my eyes; I had been very deeply asleep.

"Listen!" she repeated very softly, holding up one finger and turning her eyes towards the door she had left ajar. Her usual calmness had deserted her. She was in the grip of some distressing terror.

For a full minute we held our breath and listened. Then her eyes rolled round again and met my own, and her skin went even whiter than before.

"It woke me," she said beneath her breath, and moving a step nearer to my bed. "It was the Noise." Even her whisper trembled.

"The Noise!" The word repeated itself dully of its own accord. I would rather it had been anything in the world but that—earthquake, foreign cannon, collapse of the house above our heads! "The Noise, Frances! Are you *sure?*" I was playing really for a little time.

"It was like thunder. At first, I thought it was thunder. But a minute later it came again—from underground. It's appalling." She muttered

63

the words, her voice not properly under control.

There was a pause of perhaps a minute, and then we both spoke at once.

We said foolish, obvious things that neither of us believed in for a second. The roof had fallen in, there were burglars downstairs, the safes had been blown open. It was to comfort each other as children do that, we said these things; also, it was to gain further time.

"There's someone in the house, of course," I heard my voice say finally, as I sprang out of bed and hurried into dressing gown and slippers. "Don't be alarmed. I'll go down and see," and from the drawer I took a pistol it was my habit to carry everywhere with me. I loaded it carefully while Frances stood stock-still beside the bed and watched. I moved towards the open door.

"You stay here, Frances," I whispered, the beating of my heart making the words uneven, "while I go down and make a search. Lock yourself in, girl. Nothing can happen to you. It was downstairs, you said?"

"Underneath," she answered faintly, pointing through the floor.

She moved suddenly between me and the door.

"Listen! Hark!" she said, the eyes in her face quite fixed; "it's coming again," and she turned her head to catch the slightest sound. I stood there watching her, and while I watched her, shook.

But nothing stirred. From the halls below rose only the whirr and quiet ticking of the numerous clocks. The blind by the open window behind us flapped out a little into the room as the draught caught it.

"I'll come with you, Bill—to the next floor," she broke the silence.

"Then I'll stay with Mabel—till you come up again." The blind sank down with a long sigh as she said it.

The question jumped to my lips before I could repress it:

"Mabel is awake. She heard it too?"

I hardly know why horror caught me at her answer. All was so vague and terrible as we stood there playing the great game of this sinister house where nothing ever happened.

"We met in the passage. She was on her way to me."

What shook in me, shook inwardly. Frances, I mean, did not see it. I had the feeling just that the Noise was upon us, that any second it would boom and roar about our ears. But the deep silence held. I only heard my sister's little whisper coming across the room in answer to my question:

"Then what is Mabel doing now?"

And her reply proved that she was yielding at last beneath the dreadful tension, for she spoke at once, unable longer to keep up the pretence.

With a kind of relief, as it were, she said it out, looking helplessly at me like a child:

"She is weeping and gna—"

My expression must have stopped her. I believe I clapped both hands upon her mouth, though when I realised things clearly again, I found they were covering my own ears instead. It was a moment of unutterable horror. The revulsion I felt was actually physical. It would have given me pleasure to fire off all the five chambers of my pistol into the air above my head; the sound—a definite, wholesome sound that explained itself—would have been a positive relief. Other feelings, though, were in me too, all over me, rushing to and fro. It was vain to seek their disentanglement; it was impossible.

I confess that I experienced, among them, a touch of paralyzing fear—though for a moment only; it passed as sharply as it came, leaving me with a violent flush of blood to the face such as bursts of anger bring, followed abruptly by an icy perspiration over the entire body. Yet I may honestly avow that it was not ordinary personal fear I felt, nor any common dread of physical injury. It was, rather, a vast, impersonal shrinking—a sympathetic shrinking—from the agony and terror that countless others, somewhere, somehow, felt for themselves. The first sensation of a prison overwhelmed me in that instant, of bitter strife and frenzied suffering, and the fiery torture of the yearning to escape that was yet hopelessly uttered . . . . It was of incredible power. It was real. The vain, intolerable hope swept over me.

I mastered myself, though hardly knowing how, and took my sister's hand.

It was as cold as ice, as I led her firmly to the door and out into the passage. Apparently, she noticed nothing of my so near collapse, for I caught her whisper as we went. "You *are* brave, Bill; splendidly brave."

The upper corridors of the great sleeping house were brightly lit; on her way to me she had turned on every electric switch her hand could reach; and as we passed the final flight of stairs to the floor below, I heard a door shut softly and knew that Mabel had been listening—waiting for us. I led my sister up to it. She knocked, and the door was opened cautiously an inch or so. The room was pitch black. I caught no glimpse of Mabel standing there. Frances turned to me with a hurried whisper, "Billy, you *will* be careful, won't you?" and went in. I just had time to answer that I would not be long, and Frances to reply, "You'll find us here" when the door closed and cut her sentence short before its end.

★★★★★★★★★★★★★★★★

But it was not alone the closing door that took the final words. Frances—by the way she disappeared I knew it—had made a swift and violent movement into the darkness that was as though she sprang. She leaped upon that other woman who stood back among the shadows, for, simultaneously with the clipping of the sentence, another sound was also stopped—stifled, smothered, choked back lest I should also hear it. Yet not in time. I heard it—a hard and horrible sound that explained both the leap and the abrupt cessation of the whispered words.

I stood irresolute a moment. It was as though all the bones had been withdrawn from my body, so that I must sink and fall. That sound plucked them out, and plucked out my self-possession with them. I am not sure that it was a sound I had ever heard before, though children, I half remembered, made it sometimes in blind rages when they knew not what they did. In a grown-up person certainly, I had never known it. I associated it with animals rather—horribly. In the history of the world, no doubt, it has been common enough, alas, but fortunately today there can be but few who know it, or would recognize it even when heard.

The bones shot back into my body the same instant, but red-hot and burning; the brief instant of irresolution passed; I was torn between the desire to break down the door and enter, and to run—run for my life from a thing I dared not face.

Out of the horrid tumult, then, I adopted neither course. Without reflection, certainly without analysis of what was best to do for my sister, myself or Mabel, I took up my action where it had been interrupted. I turned from the awful door and moved slowly towards the head of the stairs.

But that dreadful little sound came with me. I believe my own teeth chattered. It seemed all over the house—in the empty halls that opened into the long passages towards the music-room, and even in the grounds outside the building. From the lawns and barren garden, from the ugly terraces themselves, it rose into the night, and behind it came a curious driving sound, incomplete, unfinished, as of wailing for deliverance, the wailing of desperate souls in anguish, the dull and dry beseeching of hopeless spirits in prison.

That I could have taken the little sound from the bedroom where I actually heard it, and spread it thus over the entire house and grounds, is evidence, perhaps, of the state my nerves were in.

The wailing assuredly was in my mind alone. But the longer I hesitated, the more difficult became my task, and, gathering up my dressing gown, lest I should trip in the darkness, I passed slowly down the staircase into the hail below. I carried neither candle nor matches; every switch in room and corridor was known to me. The covering of darkness was indeed rather comforting than otherwise, for if it prevented seeing, it also prevented being seen. The heavy pistol, knocking against my thigh as I moved, made me feel I was carrying a child's toy, foolishly. I experienced in every nerve that primitive vast dread which is the thrill of darkness. Merely the child in me was comforted by that pistol.

The night was not entirely black; the iron bars across the glass front door were visible, and, equally, I discerned the big, stiff wooden chairs in the hall, the gaping fireplace, the upright pillars supporting the staircase, the round table in the centre with its books and flower-vases, and the basket that held visitors' cards. There, too, was the stick and umbrella stand and the shelf with railway guides, directory, and telegraph forms. Clocks ticked everywhere with sounds like quiet footfalls. Light fell here and there in patches from the floor above.

I stood a moment in the hall, letting my eyes grow more accustomed to the gloom, while deciding on a plan of search. I made out the ivy trailing outside over one of the big windows . . . and then the tall clock by the front door made a grating noise deep down inside its body—it was the Presentation clock, large and hideous, given by the congregation of his church—and, dreading the booming strike it seemed to threaten, I made a quick decision. If others beside myself were about in the night, the sound of that striking might cover their approach.

So, I tiptoed to the right, where the passage led towards the dining room. In the other direction were the morning- and drawing- rooms, both little used, and various other rooms beyond that had been *his*, generally now kept locked. I thought of my sister, waiting upstairs with that frightened woman for my return. I went quickly, yet stealthily.

And, to my surprise, the door of the dining room was open. It had been opened. I paused on the threshold, staring about me. I think I fully expected to see a figure blocked in the shadows against the heavy sideboard, or looming on the other side beneath his portrait. But the room was empty; I *felt* it empty. Through the wide bow-windows that gave on to the verandah came an uncertain glimmer that even shone reflected in the polished surface of the dinner-table, and again I perceived the stiff outline of chairs, waiting tenantless all round it, two larger ones with high carved backs at either end.

The monkey trees on the upper terrace, too, were visible outside against the sky, and the solemn crests of the wellingtonias on the terraces below. The enormous clock on the mantelpiece ticked very slowly, as though its machinery were running down, and I made out the pale round patch that was its face. Resisting my first inclination to turn the lights up—my hand had gone so far as to finger the friendly knob—I crossed the room so carefully that no single board creaked, nor a single chair, as I rested a hand upon its back, moved on the parquet flooring. I turned neither to the right nor left, nor did I once look back.

I went towards the long corridor filled with priceless *objets d'art*, that led through various antechambers into the spacious music-room, and only at the mouth of this corridor did I next halt a moment in uncertainty. For this long corridor, lit faintly by high windows on the left from the verandah, was very narrow, owing to the mass of shelves and fancy tables it contained. It was not that I feared to knock over precious things as I went, but, that, because of its ungenerous width, there would be no room to pass another person—if I met one. And the certainty had suddenly come upon me that somewhere in this corridor another person at this actual moment stood.

Here, somehow, amid all this dead atmosphere of furniture and impersonal emptiness, lay the hint of a living human presence; and with such conviction did it come upon me, that my hand instinctively gripped the pistol in my pocket before I could even think. Either someone had passed along this corridor just before me, or someone lay waiting at its farther end—withdrawn or flattened into one of the little recesses, to let me pass. It was the person who had opened the door. And the blood ran from my heart as I realised it.

It was not courage that sent me on, but rather a strong impulsion from behind that made it impossible to retreat: the feeling that a throng pressed at my back, drawing nearer and nearer; that I was already half surrounded, swept, dragged, coaxed into a vast prison-house where there was wailing and gnashing of teeth, where their worm dieth not and their fire is not quenched. I can neither explain nor justify the storm of irrational emotion that swept me as I stood in that moment, staring down the length of the silent corridor towards the music-room at the far end, I can only repeat that no personal bravery sent me down it, but that the negative emotion of fear was swamped in this vast sea of pity and commiseration for others that surged upon me.

My senses, at least, were no whit confused; if anything, my brain registered impressions with keener accuracy than usual. I noticed, for instance, that the two swinging doors of baize that cut the corridor into definite lengths, making little rooms of the spaces between them, were both wide-open—in the dim light no mean achievement. Also, that the fronds of a palm plant, some ten feet in front of me, still stirred gently from the air of someone who had recently gone past them. The long green leaves waved to and fro like hands. Then I went stealthily forward down the narrow space, proud even that I had this command of myself, and so carefully that my feet made no sound upon the Japanese matting on the floor.

It was a journey that seemed timeless. I have no idea how fast or slow I went, but I remember that I deliberately examined articles on each side of me, peering with particular closeness into the recesses of wall and window. I passed the first baize doors, and the passage beyond them widened out to hold shelves of books; there were sofas and small reading-tables against the wall.

It narrowed again presently, as I entered the second stretch. The windows here were higher and smaller, and marble statuettes of classical subject lined the walls, watching me like figures of the dead. Their white and shining faces saw me, yet made no sign. I passed next between the second baize doors. They, too, had been fastened back with hooks against the wall. Thus, all doors were open—had been recently opened.

And so, at length, I found myself in the final widening of the corridor which formed an antechamber to the music-room itself. It had been used formerly to hold the overflow of meetings. No door separated it from the great hall beyond, but heavy curtains hung usually to close it off, and these curtains were invariably drawn. They now stood wide. And here—I can merely state the impression that came upon me—I knew myself at last surrounded. The throng that pressed behind me, also surged in front: facing me in the big room, and waiting for my entry, stood a multitude; on either side of me, in the very air above my head, the vast assemblage paused upon my coming.

The pause, however, was momentary, for instantly the deep, tumultuous movement was resumed that yet was silent as a cavern underground. I felt the agony that was in it, the passionate striving, the awful struggle to escape. The semi-darkness held beseeching faces that fought to press themselves upon my vision, yearning yet hopeless eyes, lips scorched and dry, mouths that opened to implore but found no craved delivery in actual words, and a fury of misery and hate that made the life in me stop dead, frozen by the horror of vain pity. That intolerable, vain Hope was everywhere.

And the multitude, it came to me, was not a single multitude, but many; for, as soon as one huge division pressed too close upon the edge of escape, it was dragged back by another and prevented. The wild host was divided against itself. Here dwelt the Shadow I had "imagined" weeks ago, and in it struggled armies of lost souls as in the depths of some bottomless pit whence there is no escape. The layers mingled, fighting against themselves in endless torture. It was in this great Shadow I had clairvoyantly seen Mabel, but about its fearful mouth, I now was certain, hovered another figure of darkness, a figure who sought to keep it in existence, since to her thought were due those lampless depths of woe without escape. . . . Towards me the multitudes now surged.

★★★★★★★★★★★★★★★

It was a sound and a movement that brought me back into myself. The great clock at the farther end of the room just then struck the hour of three. That was the sound. And the movement—? I was aware that a figure was passing across the distant centre of the floor. Instantly I dropped back into the arena of my little human terror. My hand again clutched stupidly at the pistol butt. I drew back into the folds of the heavy curtain. And the figure advanced.

I remember every detail. At first it seemed to me enormous—this advancing shadow—far beyond human scale; but as it came nearer, I measured it, though not consciously, by the organ pipes that gleamed in faint colours, just above its gradual soft approach. It passed them, already halfway across the great room. I saw then that its stature was that of ordinary men. The prolonged booming of the clock died away. I heard the footfall, shuffling upon the polished boards. I heard another sound—a voice, low and monotonous, droning as in prayer. The figure was speaking. It was a woman. And she carried in both hands before her a small object that faintly shimmered—a glass of water. And then I recognised her.

There was still an instant's time before she reached me, and I made use of it. I shrank back, flattening myself against the wall. Her voice ceased a moment, as she turned and carefully drew the curtains together behind her, closing them with one hand. Oblivious of my presence, though she actually touched my dressing gown with the hand that pulled the cords, she resumed her dreadful, solemn march, disappearing at length down the long *vista* of the corridor like a shadow.

But as she passed me, her voice began again, so that I heard each word distinctly as she uttered it, her head aloft, her figure upright, as though she moved at the head of a procession:

"A drop of cold water, given in His name, shall moisten their burning tongues."

It was repeated monotonously over and over again, droning down into the distance as she went, until at length both voice and figure faded into the shadows at the farther end.

For a time, I have no means of measuring precisely, I stood in that dark corner, pressing my back against the wall, and would have drawn the curtains down to hide me had I dared to stretch an arm out. The dread that presently the woman would return passed gradually away. I realised that the air had emptied, the crowd her presence had stirred into activity had retreated; I was alone in the gloomy under-space of the odious building. . . . Then I remembered suddenly again the terrified women waiting for me on that upper landing; and realised that my skin was wet and freezing cold after a profuse perspiration.

I prepared to retrace my steps. I remember the effort it cost me to leave the support of the wall and covering darkness of my corner, and step out into the grey light of the corridor. At first, I sidled, then, finding this mode of walking impossible, turned my face boldly and walked quickly, regardless that my dressing gown set the precious objects shaking as I passed. A wind that sighed mournfully against the high, small windows seemed to have got inside the corridor as well; it felt so cold; and every moment I dreaded to see the outline of the woman's figure as she waited in recess or angle against the wall for me to pass.

Was there another thing I dreaded even more? I cannot say. I only know that the first baize doors had swung to behind me, and the second ones were close at hand, when the great dim thunder caught me, pouring up with prodigious volume so that it, seemed to roll out from another world. It shook the very bowels of the building. I was closer to it than that other time, when it had followed me from the goblin garden.

There was strength and hardness in it, as of metal reverberation. Some touch of numbness, almost of paralysis, must surely have been upon me that I felt no actual terror, for I remember even turning and standing still to hear it better.

"That is the Noise," my thought ran stupidly, and I think I whispered it aloud; "the Doors are closing." The wind outside against the windows was audible, so it cannot have been really loud, yet to me it was the biggest, deepest sound I have ever heard, but so far away, with such awful remoteness in it, that I had to doubt my own ears at the same time. It seemed underground—the rumbling of earthquake gates that shut remorselessly within the rocky Earth—stupendous ultimate thunder. *They* were shut off from help again. The doors had closed.

I felt a storm of pity, an agony of bitter, futile hate sweep through me. My memory of the figure changed then. The Woman with the glass of cooling water had stepped down from Heaven; but the Man— or was it Men?—who smeared this terrible layer of belief and Thought upon the world! . . .

I crossed the dining room—it was fancy, of course, that held my eyes from glancing at the portrait for fear I should see it smiling approval —and so finally reached the hall, where the light from the floor above seemed now quite bright in comparison. All the doors I closed carefully behind me; but first I had to open them. The woman had closed every one.

Up the stairs, then, I actually ran, two steps at a time. My sister was standing outside Mabel's door. By her face I knew that she had also heard. There was no need to ask. I quickly made my mind up.

"There's nothing," I said, and detailed briefly my tour of search. "All is quiet and undisturbed downstairs." May God forgive me!

She beckoned to me, closing the door softly behind her. My heart beat violently a moment, then stood still.

"Mabel," she said aloud.

It was like the sentence of a judge, that one short word.

I tried to push past her and go in, but she stopped me with her arm. She was wholly mistress of herself, I saw.

"Hush!" she said in a lower voice. "I've got her round again with brandy. She's sleeping quietly now. We won't disturb her."

She drew me farther out into the landing, and as she did so, the clock in the hall below struck half-past three. I had stood, then, thirty minutes in the corridor below. "You've been such a long time." she said simply. "I feared for you," and she took my hand in her own that was cold and clammy.

CHAPTER 8

And then, while that dreadful house stood listening about us in the early hours of this chill morning upon the edge of winter, she told me, with laconic brevity, things about Mabel that I heard as from a distance. There was nothing so unusual or tremendous in the short recital, nothing indeed I might not have already guessed for myself. It was the time and scene, the inference, too, that made it so afflicting: the idea that Mabel believed herself so utterly and hopelessly lost—beyond recovery damned.

That she had loved him with so passionate a devotion that she had given her soul into his keeping, this certainly I had not divined—probably because I had never thought about it one way or the other. He had "converted" her, I knew, but that she had subscribed whole-heartedly to that most cruel and ugly of his dogmas—this was new to me, and came with a certain shock as I heard it. In love, of course, the weaker nature is receptive to all manner of suggestion.

This man had "suggested" his pet brimstone lake so vividly that she had listened and believed. He had frightened her into heaven; and his heaven, a definite locality in the skies, had its foretaste here on earth in miniature—The Towers, house, and garden. Into his *dolorous* scheme of a handful saved and millions damned, his enclosure, as it were, of sheep and goats, he had swept her before she was aware of it. Her mind no longer was her own. And it was Mrs. Marsh who kept the thought-stream open, though tempered, as she deemed, with that touch of craven, superstitious mercy.

But what I found it difficult to understand, and still more difficult to accept, was that, during her year abroad, she had been so haunted with a secret dread of that hideous after-death that she had finally revolted and tried to recover that clearer state of mind she had enjoyed before the religious bully had stunned her—yet had tried in vain. She had returned to The Towers to find her soul again, only to realise that it was lost eternally. The cleaner state of mind lay then beyond recovery.

In the reaction that followed the removal of his terrible "suggestion," she felt the crumbling of all that he had taught her, but searched in vain for the peace and beauty his teachings had destroyed. Nothing came to replace these. She was empty, desolate, hopeless; craving her former joy and carelessness, she found only hate and diabolical calculation.

This man, whom she had loved to the point of losing her soul for him, had bequeathed to her one black and fiery thing—the terror of the damned. His thinking wrapped her in this iron garment that held her fast.

All this Frances told me, far more briefly than I have here repeated it.

In her eyes and gestures and laconic sentences lay the conviction of great beating issues and of menacing drama my own description fails to recapture. It was all so incongruous and remote from the world I lived in that more than once a smile, though a smile of pity, fluttered to my lips; but a glimpse of my face in the mirror showed rather the leer of a grimace. There was no real laughter anywhere that night.

The entire adventure seemed so incredible, here, in this twentieth century—but yet delusion, that feeble word, did not occur once in the comments my mind suggested though did not utter. I remembered that forbidding Shadow too; my sister's watercolours; the vanished personality of our hostess; the inexplicable, thundering Noise, and the figure of Mrs. Marsh in her midnight ritual that was so childish yet so horrible.

I shivered in spite of my own "emancipated" cast of mind.

"There is no Mabel," were the words with which my sister sent another shower of ice down my spine. "He has killed her in his lake of fire and brimstone."

I stared at her blankly, as in a nightmare where nothing true or possible ever happened.

"He killed her in his lake of fire and brimstone," she repeated more faintly.

A desperate effort was in me to say the strong, sensible thing which should destroy the oppressive horror that grew so stiflingly about us both, but again the mirror drew the attempted smile into the merest grin, betraying the distortion that was everywhere in the place.

"You mean," I stammered beneath my breath, "that her faith has gone, but that the terror has remained?" I asked it, dully groping. I moved out of the line of the reflection in the glass.

She bowed her head as though beneath a weight; her skin was the pallor of grey ashes.

"You mean," I said louder, "that she has lost her—mind?"

"She is terror incarnate," was the whispered answer. "Mabel has lost her soul. Her soul is—there!" She pointed horribly below. "She is seeking it . . .?"

The word "soul" stung me into something of my normal self again.

74

"But her terror, poor thing, is not—cannot be—transferable to *us!*" I exclaimed more vehemently. "It certainly is not convertible into feelings, sights and—even sounds!"

She interrupted me quickly, almost impatiently, speaking with that conviction by which she conquered me so easily that night.

"It is her terror that revived 'the Others.' It has brought her into touch with them. They are loose and driving after her. Her efforts at resistance have given them also hope—that escape, after all, is possible. Day and night, they strive.

"Escape! Others!" The anger fast rising in me cropped of its own accord at the moment of birth. It shrank into a shuddering beyond my control.

In that moment, I think, I would have believed in the possibility of anything and everything she might tell me. To argue or contradict seemed equally futile.

"His strong belief, as also the beliefs of others who have preceded him," she replied, so sure of herself that I actually turned to look over my shoulder, "have left their shadow like a thick deposit over the house and grounds. To them, poor souls imprisoned by thought, it was hopeless as granite walls—until her resistance, her effort to dissipate it—let in light. Now, in their thousands, they are flocking to this little light, seeking escape. Her own escape, don't you see, may release them all!"

It took my breath away. Had his predecessors, former occupants of this house, also preached damnation of all the world but their own exclusive sect? Was this the explanation of her obscure talk of "layers," each striving against the other for domination? And if men are spirits, and these spirits survive, could strong Thought thus determine their condition even afterwards?

So many questions flooded into me that I selected no one of them, but stared in uncomfortable silence, bewildered, out of my depth, and acutely, painfully distressed. There was so odd a mixture of possible truth and incredible, unacceptable explanation in it all; so much confirmed, yet so much left darker than before. What she said did, indeed, offer a quasi-interpretation of my own series of abominable sensations—strife, agony, pity, hate, escape—but so far-fetched that only the deep conviction in her voice and attitude made it tolerable for a second even. I found myself in a curious state of mind.

I could neither think clearly nor say a word to refute her amazing statements, whispered there beside me in the shivering hours of the early morning with only a wall between ourselves and—Mabel. Close behind her words I remember this singular thing, however—that an atmosphere as of the Inquisition seemed to rise and stir about the room, beating awful wings of black above my head.

Abruptly, then, a moment's common sense returned to me. I faced her.

"And the Noise?" I said aloud, more firmly, "the roar of the closing doors? We have *all* heard that! Is that subjective too?"

Frances looked sideways about her in a queer fashion that made my flesh creep again. I spoke brusquely, almost angrily. I repeated the question, and waited with anxiety for her reply.

"What noise?" she asked, with the frank expression of an innocent child. "What closing doors?"

But her face turned from grey to white, and I saw that drops of perspiration glistened on her forehead. She caught at the back of a chair to steady herself, then glanced about her again with that side-long look that made my blood run cold. I understood suddenly then. She did not take in what I said. I knew now. She was listening—for something else.

And the discovery revived in me a far stronger emotion than any mere desire for immediate explanation. Not only did I not insist upon an answer, but I was actually terrified lest she would answer. More, I felt in me a terror lest I should be moved to describe my own experiences below-stairs, thus increasing their reality and so the reality of all.

She might even explain them too!

Still listening intently, she raised her head and looked me in the eyes.

Her lips opened to speak. The words came to me from a great distance, it seemed, and her voice had a sound like a stone that drops into a deep well, its fate though hidden, known.

"We are in it with her, too, Bill. We are in it with her. Our interpretations vary—because we are—in parts of it only. Mabel is in it—*all*."

The desire for violence came over me. If only she would say a definite thing in plain King's English! If only I could find it in me to give utterance to what shouted so loud within me! If only—the same old cry— something would happen! For all this elliptic talk that dazed my mind left obscurity everywhere. Her atrocious meaning, nonetheless, flashed through me, though vanishing before it wholly divulged itself.

It brought a certain reaction with it. I found my tongue. Whether I actually believed what I said is more than I can swear to; that it seemed to me wise at the moment is all I remember. My mind was in a state of obscure perception less than that of normal consciousness.

"Yes, Frances, I believe that what you say is the truth, and that we are in it with her"—I meant to say I with loud, hostile emphasis, but instead I whispered it lest she should hear the trembling of my voice—"and for that reason, my dear sister, we leave tomorrow, you and I— today, rather, since it is long past midnight—we leave this house of the damned. We go back to London."

Frances looked up, her face distraught almost beyond recognition. But it was not my words that caused the tumult in her heart. It was a sound—the sound she had been listening for—so faint I barely caught it myself, and had she not pointed I could never have known the direction whence it came. Small and terrible it rose again in the stillness of the night, the sound of gnashing teeth. And behind it came another—the tread of stealthy footsteps. Both were just outside the door.

The room swung round me for a second. My first instinct to prevent my sister going out—she had dashed past me frantically to the door—gave place to another when I saw the expression in her eyes. I followed her lead instead; it was surer than my own. The pistol in my pocket swung uselessly against my thigh. I was flustered beyond belief and ashamed that I was so.

"Keep close to me, Frances," I said huskily, as the door swung wide and a shaft of light fell upon a figure moving rapidly. Mabel was going down the corridor. Beyond her, in the shadows on the staircase, a second figure stood beckoning, scarcely visible.

"Before they get her! Quick!" was screamed into my ears, and our arms were about her in the same moment. It was a horrible scene. Not that Mabel struggled in the least, but that she collapsed as we caught her and fell with her dead weight, as of a corpse, limp, against us. And her teeth began again. They continued, even beneath the hand that Frances clapped upon her lips. . . .

We carried her back into her own bedroom, where she lay down peacefully enough. It was so soon over. . . . The rapidity of the whole thing robbed it of reality almost. It had the swiftness of something remembered rather than of something witnessed. She slept again so quickly that it was almost as if we had caught her sleepwalking. I cannot say. I asked no questions at the time; I have asked none since; and my help was needed as little as the protection of my pistol. Frances was strangely competent and collected. . . . I lingered for some time uselessly by the door, till at length, looking up with a sigh, she made a sign for me to go.

"I shall wait in your room next door," I whispered, "till you come." But, though going out, I waited in the corridor instead, so as to hear the faintest call for help. In that dark corridor upstairs I waited, but not long. It may have been fifteen minutes when Frances reappeared, locking the door softly behind her. Leaning over the banisters, I saw her.

"I'll go in again about six o'clock," she whispered, "as soon as it gets light. She is sound asleep now. Please don't wait. If anything happens, I'll call—you might leave your door ajar, perhaps."

And she came up, looking like a ghost.

But I saw her first safely into bed, and the rest of the night I spent in an armchair close to my opened door, listening for the slightest sound. Soon after five o'clock I heard Frances fumbling with the key, and, peering over the railing again, I waited till she reappeared and went back into her own room. She closed her door. Evidently, she was satisfied that all was well.

Then, and then only, did I go to bed myself, but not to sleep. I could not get the scene out of my mind, especially that odious detail of it which I hoped and believed my sister had not seen—the still, dark figure of the housekeeper waiting on the stairs below—waiting, of course, for Mabel.

CHAPTER 9

It seems I became a mere spectator after that; my sister's lead was so assured for one thing, and, for another, the responsibility of leaving Mabel alone—Frances laid it bodily upon my shoulders—was a little more than I cared about. Moreover, when we all three met later in the day, things went on so exactly as before, so absolutely without friction or distress, that to present a sudden, obvious excuse for cutting our visit short seemed ill-judged. And on the lowest grounds it would have been desertion.

At any rate, it was beyond my powers, and Frances was quite firm that she must stay. We therefore did stay. Things that happen in the night always seem exaggerated and distorted when the sun shines brightly next morning; no one can reconstruct the terror of a nightmare afterwards, nor comprehend why it seemed so overwhelming at the time.

I slept till ten o'clock, and when I rang for breakfast, a note from my sister lay upon the tray, its message of counsel couched in a calm and comforting strain. Mabel, she assured me, was herself again and remembered nothing of what had happened; there was no need of any violent measures; I was to treat her exactly as if I knew nothing.

"And, if you don't mind, Bill, let us leave the matter unmentioned between ourselves as well. Discussion exaggerates; such things are best not talked about. I'm sorry I disturbed you so unnecessarily; I was stupidly excited. Please forget all the things I said at the moment."

She had written "nonsense" first instead of "things," then scratched it out. She wished to convey that hysteria had been abroad in the night, and I readily gulped the explanation down, though it could not satisfy me in the smallest degree.

There was another week of our visit still, and we stayed it out to the end without disaster. My desire to leave at times became that frantic thing, desire to escape; but I controlled it, kept silent, watched and wondered. Nothing happened. As before, and everywhere, there was no sequence of development, no connection between cause and effect; and climax, none whatever. The thing swayed up and down, backwards and forwards like a great loose curtain in the wind, and I could only vaguely surmise what caused the draught or why there was a curtain at all. A novelist might mould the queer material into coherent sequence that would be interesting but could not be true.

It remains, therefore, not a story but a history. Nothing happened.

Perhaps my intense dislike of the fall of darkness was due wholly to my stirred imagination, and perhaps my anger when I learned that Frances now occupied a bed in our hostess's room was unreasonable. Nerves were unquestionably on edge. I was forever on the lookout for some event that should make escape imperative, but yet that never presented itself. I slept lightly, left my door ajar to catch the slightest sound, even made stealthy tours of the house below-stairs while everybody dreamed in their beds. But I discovered nothing; the doors were always locked; I neither saw the housekeeper again in unreasonable times and places, nor heard a footstep in the passages and halls.

The Noise was never once repeated. That horrible, ultimate thunder, my intensest dread of all, lay withdrawn into the abyss whence it had twice arisen. And though in my thoughts it was sternly denied existence, the great black reason for the fact afflicted me unbelievably. Since Mabel's fruitless effort to escape, the doors kept closed remorselessly. She had failed; *they* gave up hope. For this was the explanation that haunted the region of my mind where feelings stir and hint before they clothe themselves in actual language. Only I firmly kept it there; it never knew expression.

But, if my ears were open, my eyes were opened too, and it were idle to pretend that I did not notice a hundred details that were capable of sinister interpretation had I been weak enough to yield. Some protective barrier had fallen into ruins round me, so that Terror stalked behind the general collapse, feeling for me through all the gaping fissures.

Much of this, I admit, must have been merely the elaboration of those sensations I had first vaguely felt, before subsequent events and my talks with Frances had dramatised them into living thoughts. I therefore leave them unmentioned in this history, just as my mind left them unmentioned in that interminable final week. Our life went on precisely as before—Mabel unreal and outwardly so still; Frances, secretive, anxious, tactful to the point of slyness, and keen to save to the point of self-forgetfulness.

There were the same stupid meals, the same wearisome long evenings, the stifling ugliness of house and grounds, the Shadow settling in so thickly that it seemed almost a visible, tangible thing. I came to feel the only friendly things in all this hostile, cruel place were the robins that hopped boldly over the monstrous terraces and even up to the windows of the unsightly house itself. The robins alone knew joy; they danced, believing no evil thing was possible in all God's radiant world.

They believed in everybody; their god's plan of life had no room in it for hell, damnation, and lakes of brimstone. I came to love the little birds. Had Samuel Franklyn known them, he might have preached a different sermon, bequeathing love in place of terror!

Most of my time I spent writing; but it was a pretence at best, and rather a dangerous one besides. For it stirred the mind to production, with the result that other things came pouring in as well. With reading it was the same. In the end I found an aggressive, deliberate resistance to be the only way of feasible defence. To walk far afield was out of the question, for it meant leaving my sister too long alone, so that my exercise was confined to nearer home. My saunters in the grounds, however, never surprised the goblin garden again. It was close at hand, but I seemed unable to get wholly into it. Too many things assailed my mind for anyone to hold exclusive possession, perhaps.

Indeed, all the interpretations, all the "layers," to use my sister's phrase, slipped in by turns and lodged there for a time. They came day and night, and though my reason denied them entrance they held their own as by a kind of squatter's right. They stirred moods already in me, that is, and did not introduce entirely new ones; for every mind conceals ancestral deposits that have been cultivated in turn along the whole line of its descent. Any day a chance shower may cause this one or that to blossom. Thus, it came to me, at any rate. After darkness the Inquisition paced the empty corridors and set up ghastly apparatus in the dismal halls; and once, in the library, there swept over me that easy and delicious conviction that by confessing my wickedness I could resume it later, since Confession is expression, and expression brings relief and leaves one ready to accumulate again. And in such mood, I felt bitter and unforgiving towards all others who thought differently.

Another time it was a Pagan thing that assaulted me—so trivial yet oh, so significant at the time—when I dreamed that a herd of centaurs rolled up with a great stamping of hoofs round the house to destroy it, and then woke to hear the horses tramping across the field below the lawns; they neighed ominously and their noisy panting was audible as if it were just outside my windows.

But the tree episode, I think, was the most curious of all—except, perhaps, the incident with the children which I shall mention in a moment—for its closeness to reality was so unforgettable.

Outside the east window of my room stood a giant wellingtonia on the lawn, its head rising level with the upper sash. It grew some twenty feet away, planted on the highest terrace, and I often saw it when closing my curtains for the night, noticing how it drew its heavy skirts about it, and how the light from other windows threw glimmering streaks and patches that turned it into the semblance of a towering, solemn image. It stood there then so strikingly, somehow like a great old-world idol, that it claimed attention.

Its appearance was curiously formidable. Its branches rustled without visibly moving and it had a certain portentous, forbidding air, so grand and dark and monstrous in the night that I was always glad when my curtains shut it out. Yet, once in bed, I had never thought about it one way or the other, and by day had certainly never sought it out.

One night, then, as I went to bed and closed this window against a cutting easterly wind, I saw—that there were two of these trees. A brother wellingtonia rose mysteriously beside it, equally huge, equally towering, equally monstrous. The menacing pair of them faced me there upon the lawn. But in this new arrival lay a strange suggestion that frightened me before I could argue it away. Exact counterpart of its giant companion, it revealed also that gross, odious quality that all my sister's paintings held.

I got the odd impression that the rest of these trees, stretching away dimly in a troop over the farther lawns, were similar, and that, led by this enormous pair, they had all moved boldly closer to my windows. At the same moment a blind was drawn down over an upper room; the second tree disappeared into the surrounding darkness.

It was, of course, this chance light that had brought it into the field of vision, but when the black shutter dropped over it, hiding it from view, the manner of its vanishing produced the queer effect that it had slipped into its companion—almost that it had been an emanation of the one I so disliked, and not really a tree at all! In this way the garden turned vehicle for expressing what lay behind it all . . .!

The behaviour of the doors, the little, ordinary doors, seems scarcely worth mention at all, their queer way of opening and shutting of their own accord; for this was accountable in a hundred natural ways, and to tell the truth, I never caught one in the act of moving. Indeed, only after frequent repetitions did the detail force itself upon me, when, having noticed one, I noticed all. It produced, however, the unpleasant impression of a continual coming and going in the house, as though, screened cleverly and purposely from actual sight, someone in the building held constant invisible intercourse with—others.

Upon detailed descriptions of these uncertain incidents I do not venture, individually so trivial, but taken all together so impressive and so insolent. But the episode of the children, mentioned above, was different. And I give it because it showed how vividly the intuitive child-mind received the impression—one impression, at any rate—of what was in the air. It may be told in a very few words. I believe they were the coachman's children, and that the man had been in Mr. Franklyn's service; but of neither point am I quite positive.

I heard screaming in the rose-garden that runs along the stable walls—it was one afternoon not far from the tea-hour—and on hurrying up I found a little girl of nine or ten fastened with ropes to a rustic seat, and two other children—boys, one about twelve and one much younger— gathering sticks beneath the climbing rose trees. The girl was white and frightened, but the others were laughing and talking among themselves so busily while they picked that they did not notice my abrupt arrival.

Some game, I understood, was in progress, but a game that had become too serious for the happiness of the prisoner, for there was a fear in the girl's eyes that was a very genuine fear indeed. I unfastened her at once; the ropes were so loosely and clumsily knotted that they had not hurt her skin; it was not that which made her pale. She collapsed a moment upon the bench, then picked up her tiny skirts and dived away at full speed into the safety of the stable-yard.

There was no response to my brief comforting, but she ran as though for her life, and I divined that some horrid boys' cruelty had been afoot.

It was probably mere thoughtlessness, as cruelty with children usually is, but something in me decided to discover exactly what it was.

And the boys, not one whit alarmed at my intervention, merely laughed shyly when I explained that their prisoner had escaped, and told me frankly what their "gime" had been. There was no vestige of shame in them, nor any idea, of course, that they aped a monstrous reality.

That it was mere pretence was neither here nor there. To them, though make-believe, it was a make-believe of something that was right and natural and in no sense cruel. Grown-ups did it too. It was necessary for her good.

"We was going to burn her up, sir," the older one informed me, answering my "Why?" with the explanation, "Because she wouldn't believe what we wanted 'er to believe."

And, game though it was, the feeling of reality about the little episode was so arresting, so terrific in some way, that only with difficulty did I confine my admonitions on this occasion to mere words. The boys slunk off, frightened in their turn, yet not, I felt, convinced that they had erred in principle. It was their inheritance. They had breathed it in with the atmosphere of their bringing-up. They would renew the salutary torture when they could—till she "believed" as they did.

I went back into the house, afflicted with a passion of mingled pity and distress impossible to describe, yet on my short way across the garden was attacked by other moods in turn, each more real and bitter than its predecessor. I received the whole series, as it were, at once. I felt like a diver rising to the surface through layers of water at different temperatures, though here the natural order was reversed, and the cooler *strata* were uppermost, the heated ones below.

Thus, I was caught by the goblin touch of the willows that fringed the field; by the sensuous curving of the twisted ash that formed a gateway to the little grove of sapling oaks where fauns and satyrs lurked to play in the moonlight before Pagan altars; and by the cloaking darkness, next, of the copse of stunted pines, close gathered each to each, where hooded figures stalked behind an awful cross. The episode with the children seemed to have opened me like a knife. The whole place rushed at me.

I suspect this synthesis of many moods produced in me that climax of loathing and disgust which made me feel the limit of bearable emotion had been reached, so that I made straight to find Frances in order to convince her that at any rate I must leave. For, although this was our last day in the house, and we had arranged to go next day, the dread was in me that she would still find some persuasive reason for staying on.

And an unexpected incident then made my dread unnecessary. The front door was open and a cab stood in the drive; a tall, elderly man was gravely talking in the hall with the parlour maid we called the Grenadier. He held a piece of paper in his hand. "I have called to see the house," I heard him say, as I ran up the stairs to Frances, who was peering like an inquisitive child over the banisters. . . .

"Yes," she told me with a sigh, I know not whether of resignation or relief, "the house is to be let or sold. Mabel has decided. Some Society or other, I believe—"

I was overjoyed: this made our leaving right and possible. "You never told me, Frances!"

"Mabel only heard of it a few days ago. She told me herself this morning. It is a chance, she says. Alone she cannot get it 'straight'.

"Defeat?" I asked, watching her closely.

"She thinks she has found a way out. It's not a family, you see, it's a Society, a sort of Community—they go in for thought—"

"A Community!" I gasped. "You mean religious?"

She shook her head. "Not exactly," she said smiling, "but some kind of association of men and women who want a headquarters in the country—a place where they can write and meditate—*think*— mature their plans and all the rest—I don't know exactly what."

"Utopian dreamers?" I asked, yet feeling an immense relief come over me as I heard. But I asked in ignorance, not cynically. Frances would know.

She knew all this kind of thing.

"No, not that exactly," she smiled. "Their teachings are grand and simple—old as the world too, really—the basis of every religion before men's minds perverted them with their manufactured creeds—"

Footsteps on the stairs, and the sound of voices, interrupted our odd impromptu conversation, as the Grenadier came up, followed by the tall, grave gentleman who was being shown over the house. My sister drew me along the corridor towards her room, where she went in and closed the door behind me, yet not before I had stolen a good look at the caller— long enough, at least, for his face and general appearance to have made a definite impression on me. For something strong and peaceful emanated from his presence; he moved with such quiet dignity; the glance of his eyes was so steady and reassuring, that my mind labelled him instantly as a type of man one would turn to in an emergency and not be disappointed.

I had seen him but for a passing moment, but I had seen him twice, and the way he walked down the passage, looking competently about him, conveyed the same impression as when I saw him standing at the door—fearless, tolerant, wise. "A sincere and kindly character," I judged instantly, "a man whom some big kind of love has trained in sweetness towards the world; no hate in him anywhere." A great deal, no doubt, to read in so brief a glance! Yet his voice confirmed my intuition, a deep and very gentle voice, great firmness in it too.

"Have I become suddenly sensitive to people's atmospheres in this extraordinary fashion?" I asked myself, smiling, as I stood in the room and heard the door close behind me. "Have I developed some clairvoyant faculty here?" At any other time, I should have mocked.

And I sat down and faced my sister, feeling strangely comforted and at peace for the first time since I had stepped beneath The Towers' roof a month ago. Frances, I then saw, was smiling a little as she watched me.

"You know him?" I asked.

"You felt it too?" was her question in reply. "No," she added, "I don't know him—beyond the fact that he is a leader in the Movement and has devoted years and money to its objects. Mabel felt the same thing in him that you have felt—and jumped at it."

"But you've seen him before?" I urged, for the certainty was in me that he was no stranger to her.

She shook her head. "He called one day early this week, when you were out. Mabel saw him. I believe—" she hesitated a moment, as though expecting me to stop her with my usual impatience of such subjects—"I believe he has explained everything to her—the beliefs he embodies, she declares, are her salvation—might be, rather, if she could adopt them."

"Conversion again!" For I remembered her riches, and how gladly a Society would gobble them.

"The layers I told you about," she continued calmly, shrugging her shoulders slightly—"the deposits that are left behind by strong thinking and real belief—but especially by ugly, hateful belief, because, you see—unfortunately there's more vital passion in that sort—"

"Frances, I don't understand a bit," I said out loud, but said it a little humbly, for the impression the man had left was still strong upon me and I was grateful for the steady sense of peace and comfort he had somehow introduced. The horrors had been so dreadful. My nerves, doubtless, were more than a little overstrained. Absurd as it must sound, I classed him in my mind with the robins, the happy, confiding robins who believed in everybody and thought no evil! I laughed a moment at my ridiculous idea, and my sister, encouraged by this sign of patience in me, continued more fluently.

"Of course, you don't understand, Bill? Why should you? You've never thought about such things. Needing no creed, yourself, you think *all* creeds are rubbish."

"I'm open to conviction—I'm tolerant," I interrupted.

"You're as narrow as Sam Franklyn, and as crammed with prejudice," she answered, knowing that she had me at her mercy.

"Then, pray, what may be his, or his Society's beliefs?" I asked, feeling no desire to argue, "and how are they going to prove your Mabel's salvation? Can they bring beauty into all this aggressive hate and ugliness?"

"Certain hope and peace," she said, "that peace which is understanding, and that understanding which explains all creeds and therefore tolerates them."

"Toleration! The one word a religious man loathes above all others! His pet word is damnation—"

"Tolerates them," she repeated patiently, unperturbed by my explosion, "because it includes them all."

"Fine, if true" I admitted, "very fine. But how, pray, does it include them all?"

"Because the key-word, the motto, of their Society is, '*There is no religion higher than Truth*,' and it has no single dogma of any kind. Above all," she went on, "because it claims that no individual can be 'lost.' It teaches universal salvation. To damn outsiders is uncivilized, childish, impure. Some take longer than others—it's according to the way they think and live—but all find peace, through development, in the end. What the creeds call a hopeless soul, it regards as a soul having further to go. There is no damnation—"

86

"Well, well," I exclaimed, feeling that she rode her hobby horse too wildly, too roughly over me, "but what is the bearing of all this upon this dreadful place, and upon Mabel? I'll admit that there is this atmosphere—this—er—inexplicable horror in the house and grounds, and that if not of damnation exactly, it is certainly damnable. I'm not too prejudiced to deny *that*, for I've felt it myself."

To my relief she was brief. She made her statement, leaving me to take it or reject it as I would.

"The thought and belief its former occupants—have left behind. For there has been coincidence here, a coincidence that must be rare. The site on which this modern house now stands was Roman, before that Early Britain, with burial mounds, before that again, Druid—the Druid stones still lie in that copse below the field, the *Tumuli* among the *ilexes* behind the drive. The older building Sam Franklyn altered and practically pulled down was a monastery; he changed the chapel into a meeting hall, which is now the music room; but, before he came here, the house was occupied by Manetti, a violent Catholic without tolerance or vision; and in the interval between these two, Julius Weinbaum had it, Hebrew of most rigid orthodox type imaginable—so they all have left their—"

"Even so," I repeated, yet interested to hear the rest, "what of it?"

"Simply this," said Frances with conviction, "that each in turn has left his layer of concentrated thinking and belief behind him; because each believed intensely, absolutely, beyond the least weakening of any doubt —the kind of strong belief and thinking that is rare anywhere today, the kind that wills, impregnates objects, saturates the atmosphere, haunts, in a word. And each, believing he was utterly and finally right, damned with equally positive conviction the rest of the world. One and all preached that implicitly if not explicitly. It's the root of every creed. Last of the bigoted, grim series came Samuel Franklyn."

I listened in amazement that increased as she went on. Up to this point her explanation was so admirable. It was, indeed, a pretty study in psychology if it were true.

"Then why does nothing ever happen?" I enquired mildly. "A place so thickly haunted ought to produce a crop of no ordinary results!"

"There lies the proof," she went on in a lowered voice, "the proof of the horror and the ugly reality. The thought and belief of each occupant in turn kept all the others under. They gave no sign of life at the time. But the results of thinking never die. They crop out again the moment there's an opening. And, with the return of Mabel in her negative state, believing nothing positive herself the place for the first time found itself free to reproduce its buried stores.

"Damnation, hell-fire, and the rest—the most permanent and vital thought of all those creeds, since it was applied to the majority of the world—broke loose again, for there was no restraint to hold it back. Each sought to obtain its former supremacy. None conquered. There results a pandemonium of hate and fear, of striving to escape, of ago-nized, bitter warring to find safety, peace—salvation. The place is satu-rated by that appalling stream of thinking—the terror of the damned. It concentrated upon Mabel, whose negative attitude furnished the channel of deliverance. You and I, according to our sympathy with her, were similarly involved. Nothing happened, because no one layer could ever gain the supremacy."

I was so interested—I dare not say amused—that I stared in silence while she paused a moment, afraid that she would draw rein and end the fairy tale too soon.

"The beliefs of this man, of his Society rather, vigorously thought and therefore vigorously given out here, will put the whole place straight. It will act as a solvent. These vitriolic layers actively denied, will fuse and disappear in the stream of gentle, tolerant sympathy which is love. For each member, worthy of the name, loves the world, and all creeds go into the melting-pot; Mabel, too, if she joins them out of real conviction, will find salvation—"

"Thinking, I know, is of the first importance," I objected, "but don't you, perhaps, exaggerate the power of feeling and emotion which in religion are *au fond* always hysterical?"

"What is the world," she told me, "but thinking and feeling? An in-dividual's world is entirely what that individual thinks and believes—interpretation. There is no other. And unless he really thinks and really believes, he has no permanent world at all. I grant that few people think, and still fewer believe, and that most take ready-made suits and make them do. Only the strong make their own things; the lesser fry, Mabel among them, are merely swept up into what has been manu-factured for them. They get along somehow. You and I have made for ourselves, Mabel has not. She is a nonentity, and when her belief is taken from her, she goes with it."

It was not in me just then to criticize the evasion, or pick out the sophistry from the truth. I merely waited for her to continue.

"None of us have Truth, my dear Frances," I ventured presently, seeing that she kept silent.

"Precisely," she answered, "but most of us have beliefs. And what one believes and thinks affects the world at large. Consider the legacy of hatred and cruelty involved in the doctrines men have built into their creeds where the *sine qua non* of salvation is absolute acceptance of one particular set of views or else perishing everlastingly—for only by repudiating history can they disavow it—"

"You're not quite accurate," I put in. "Not all the creeds teach damnation, do they? Franklyn did, of course, but the others are a bit modernised now surely?"

"Trying to get out of it," she admitted, "perhaps they are, but damnation of unbelievers—of most of the world, that is—is their rather favourite idea if you talk with them."

"I never have."

She smiled. "But I have," she said significantly, "so, if you consider what the various occupants of this house have so strongly held and thought and believed, you need not be surprised that the influence they have left behind them should be a dark and dreadful legacy. For thought, you know, does leave—"

The opening of the door, to my great relief, interrupted her, as the Grenadier led in the visitor to see the room. He bowed to both of us with a brief word of apology, looked round him, and withdrew, and with his departure the conversation between us came naturally to an end. I followed him out. Neither of us in any case, I think, cared to argue further.

★★★★★★★★★★★★★★★★★★

And, so far as I am aware, the curious history of The Towers ends here too. There was no climax in the story sense. Nothing ever really happened. We left next morning for London. I only know that the Society in question took the house and have since occupied it to their entire satisfaction, and that Mabel, who became a member shortly afterwards, now stays there frequently when in need of repose from the arduous and unselfish labours she took upon herself under its aegis. She dined with us only the other night, here in our tiny Chelsea flat, and a jollier, saner, more interesting and happy guest I could hardly wish for. She was vital—in the best sense; the lay figure had come to life. I found it difficult to believe she was the same woman whose fearful effigy had floated down those dreary corridors and almost disappeared in the depths of that atrocious Shadow.

What her beliefs were now I was wise enough to leave unquestioned, and Frances, to my great relief, kept the conversation well away from such inappropriate topics. It was clear, however, that the woman had in herself some secret source of joy, that she was now an aggressive, positive force, sure of herself, and apparently afraid of nothing in heaven or hell. She radiated something very like hope and courage about her, and talked as though the world were a glorious place and everybody in it kind and beautiful. Her optimism was certainly infectious.

The Towers were mentioned only in passing. The name of Marsh came up—not *the* Marsh, it so happened, but a name in some book that was being discussed—and I was unable to restrain myself. Curiosity was too strong. I threw out a casual enquiry Mabel could leave unanswered if she wished. But there was no desire to avoid it. Her reply was frank and smiling.

"Would you believe it? She married," Mabel told me, though obviously surprised that I remembered the housekeeper at all; "and is happy as the day is long. She's found her right niche in life. A sergeant—"

"The army!" I ejaculated.

"Salvation Army," she explained merrily.

Frances exchanged a glance with me. I laughed too, for the information took me by surprise. I cannot say why exactly, but I expected at least to hear that the woman had met some dreadful end, not impossibly by burning.

"And The Towers, now called the Rest House," Mabel chattered on, "seems to me the most peaceful and delightful spot in England—"

"Really," I said politely.

"When I lived there in the old days—while you were there, perhaps, though I won't be sure."

Mabel went on, "the story got abroad that it was haunted. Wasn't it odd? A less likely place for a ghost I've never seen. Why, it had no atmosphere at all." She said this to Frances, glancing up at me with a smile that apparently had no hidden meaning. "Did *you* notice anything queer about it when you were there?"

This was plainly addressed to me.

"I found it—er—difficult to settle down to anything," I said, after an instant's hesitation. "I couldn't work there—"

"But I thought you wrote that wonderful book on the Deaf and Blind while you stayed with me," she asked innocently.

I stammered a little. "Oh no, not then. I only made a few notes—er—at The Towers. My mind, oddly enough, refused to produce at all down there. But—why do you ask? Did anything—was anything *supposed* to happen there?"

She looked searchingly into my eyes a moment before she answered:

"Not that I know of," she said simply.

The Man Whom the Trees Loved

1

He painted trees as by some special divining instinct of their essential qualities. He understood them. He knew why in an oak forest, for instance, each individual was utterly distinct from its fellows, and why no two beeches in the whole world were alike. People asked him down to paint a favourite lime or silver birch, for he caught the individuality of a tree as some catch the individuality of a horse. How he managed it was something of a puzzle, for he never had painting lessons, his drawing was often wildly inaccurate, and, while his perception of a Tree Personality was true and vivid, his rendering of it might almost approach the ludicrous. Yet the character and personality of that particular tree stood there alive beneath his brush—shining, frowning, dreaming, as the case might be, friendly or hostile, good or evil. It emerged.

There was nothing else in the wide world that he could paint; flowers and landscapes he only muddled away into a smudge; with people he was helpless and hopeless; also, with animals. Skies he could sometimes manage, or effects of wind in foliage, but as a rule he left these all severely alone. He kept to trees, wisely following an instinct that was guided by love. It was quite arresting, this way he had of making a tree look almost like a being—alive. It approached the uncanny.

"Yes, Sanderson knows what he's doing when he paints a tree!" thought old David Bittacy, C.B., late of the Woods and forests. "Why, you can almost hear it rustle. You can smell the thing. You can hear the rain drip through its leaves. You can almost see the branches move. It grows." For in this way somewhat he expressed his satisfaction, half to persuade himself that the twenty guineas were well spent (since his wife thought otherwise), and half to explain this uncanny reality of life that lay in the fine old cedar framed above his study table.

Yet in the general view the mind of Mr. Bittacy was held to be austere, not to say morose. Few divined in him the secretly tenacious love of nature that had been fostered by years spent in the forests and jungles of the eastern world. It was odd for an Englishman, due possibly to that Eurasian ancestor. Surreptitiously, as though half ashamed of it, he had kept alive a sense of beauty that hardly belonged to his type, and was unusual for its vitality. Trees, in particular, nourished it. He, also, understood trees, felt a subtle sense of communion with them, born perhaps of those years he had lived in caring for them, guarding, protecting, nursing, years of solitude among their great shadowy presences.

He kept it largely to himself, of course, because he knew the world, he lived in. He also kept it from his wife—to some extent. He knew it came between them, knew that she feared it, was opposed. But what he did not know, or realise at any rate, was the extent to which she grasped the power which they wielded over his life. Her fear, he judged, was simply due to those years in India, when for weeks at a time his calling took him away from her into the jungle forests, while she remained at home dreading all manner of evils that might befall him. This, of course, explained her instinctive opposition to the passion for woods that still influenced and clung to him. It was a natural survival of those anxious days of waiting in solitude for his safe return.

For Mrs. Bittacy, daughter of an evangelical clergyman, was a self-sacrificing woman, who in most things found a happy duty in sharing her husband's joys and sorrows to the point of self-obliteration. Only in this matter of the trees she was less successful than in others. It remained a problem difficult of compromise.

He knew, for instance, that what she objected to in this portrait of the cedar on their lawn was really not the price he had given for it, but the unpleasant way in which the transaction emphasised this breach between their common interests—the only one they had, but deep.

★★★★★★★★★★★★★

Sanderson, the artist, earned little enough money by his strange talent; such checks were few and far between. The owners of fine or interesting trees who cared to have them painted singly were rare indeed, and the "studies" that he made for his own delight he also kept for his own delight. Even were there buyers, he would not sell them. Only a few, and these peculiarly intimate friends, might even see them, for he disliked to hear the undiscerning criticisms of those who did not understand. Not that he minded laughter at his craftsmanship—he admitted it with scorn—but that remarks about the personality of

94

the tree itself could easily wound or anger him. He resented slighting observations concerning them, as though insults offered to personal friends who could not answer for themselves. He was instantly up in arms.

"It really *is* extraordinary," said a Woman who Understood, "that you can make that cypress seem an individual, when in reality all cypresses are so *exactly* alike."

And though the bit of calculated flattery had come so near to saying the right, true, thing, Sanderson flushed as though she had slighted a friend beneath his very nose. Abruptly he passed in front of her and turned the picture to the wall.

"Almost as queer," he answered rudely, copying her silly emphasis, "as that *you* should have imagined individuality in your husband, *Madame*, when in reality all men are so *exactly* alike!"

Since the only thing that differentiated her husband from the mob was the money for which she had married him, Sanderson's relations with that particular family terminated on the spot, chance of prospective orders with it. His sensitiveness, perhaps, was morbid. At any rate the way to reach his heart lay through his trees. He might be said to love trees. He certainly drew a splendid inspiration from them, and the source of a man's inspiration, be it music, religion, or a woman, is never a safe thing to criticise.

"I do think, perhaps, it was just a little extravagant, dear," said Mrs. Bittacy, referring to the cedar check, "when we want a lawnmower so badly too. But as it gives you such pleasure—"

"It reminds me of a certain day, Sophia," replied the old gentleman, looking first proudly at herself, then fondly at the picture, "now long gone by. It reminds me of another tree—that Kentish lawn in the spring, birds singing in the lilacs, and someone in a muslin frock waiting patiently beneath a certain cedar—not the one in the picture, I know, but—"

"I was not waiting," she said indignantly, "I was picking fir-cones for the schoolroom fire—"

"Fir-cones, my dear, do not grow on cedars, and schoolroom fires were not made in June in my young days."

"And anyhow it isn't the same cedar."

"It has made me fond of all cedars for its sake," he answered, "and it reminds me that you are the same young girl still—"

She crossed the room to his side, and together they looked out of the window where, upon the lawn of their Hampshire cottage, a ragged Lebanon stood in a solitary state.

"You're as full of dreams as ever," she said gently, "and I don't regret the check a bit—really. Only it would have been more real if it had been the original tree, wouldn't it?"

"That was blown down years ago. I passed the place last year, and there's not a sign of it left," he replied tenderly. And presently, when he released her from his side, she went up to the wall and carefully dusted the picture Sanderson had made of the cedar on their present lawn. She went all round the frame with her tiny handkerchief, standing on tiptoe to reach the top rim.

"What I like about it," said the old fellow to himself when his wife had left the room, "is the way he has made it live. All trees have it, of course, but a cedar taught it to me first—the 'something' trees possess that make them know I'm there when I stand close and watch. I suppose I felt it then because I was in love, and love reveals life everywhere." He glanced a moment at the Lebanon looming gaunt and sombre through the gathering dusk. A curious wistful expression danced a moment through his eyes.

"Yes, Sanderson has seen it as it is," he murmured, "solemnly dreaming there its dim hidden life against the forest edge, and as different from that other tree in Kent as I am from—from the vicar, say. It's quite a stranger, too. I don't know anything about it really. That other cedar I loved; this old fellow I respect. Friendly though—yes, on the whole quite friendly. He's painted the friendliness right enough. He saw that. I'd like to know that man better," he added. "I'd like to ask him how he saw so clearly that it stands there between this cottage and the forest—yet somehow more in sympathy with us than with the mass of woods behind—a sort of go-between. *That* I never noticed before. I see it now—through his eyes. It stands there like a sentinel—protective rather."

He turned away abruptly to look through the window. He saw the great encircling mass of gloom that was the forest, fringing their little lawn. It pressed up closer in the darkness. The prim garden with its formal beds of flowers seemed an impertinence almost—some little coloured insect that sought to settle on a sleeping monster—some gaudy fly that danced impudently down the edge of a great river that could engulf it with a toss of its smallest wave. That forest with its thousand years of growth and its deep spreading being was some such slumbering monster, yes. Their cottage and garden stood too near its running lip. When the winds were strong and lifted its shadowy skirts of black and purple .... He loved this feeling of the forest Personality; he had always loved it.

"Queer," he reflected, "awfully queer, that trees should bring me such a sense of dim, vast living! I used to feel it particularly, I remember, in India; in Canadian woods as well; but never in little English woods till here. And Sanderson's the only man I ever knew who felt it too. He's never said so, but there's the proof," and he turned again to the picture that he loved. A thrill of unaccustomed life ran through him as he looked. "I wonder; by Jove, I wonder," his thoughts ran on, "whether a tree—er—in any lawful meaning of the term can be—alive. I remember some writing fellow telling me long ago that trees had once been moving things, animal organisms of some sort, that had stood so long feeding, sleeping, dreaming, or something, in the same place, that they had lost the power to get away. ... !"

Fancies flew pell-mell about his mind, and, lighting a cheroot, he dropped into an armchair beside the open window and let them play. Outside the blackbirds whistled in the shrubberies across the lawn. He smelt the earth and trees and flowers, the perfume of mown grass, and the bits of open heath-land far away in the heart of the woods. The summer wind stirred very faintly through the leaves. But the great New Forest hardly raised her sweeping skirts of black and purple shadow.

Mr. Bittacy, however, knew intimately every detail of that wilderness of trees within. He knew all the purple coombs splashed with yellow waves of gorse; sweet with juniper and myrtle, and gleaming with clear and dark-eyed pools that watched the sky. There hawks hovered, circling hour by hour, and the flicker of the peewit's flight with its melancholy, petulant cry, deepened the sense of stillness.

He knew the solitary pines, dwarfed, tufted, vigorous, that sang to every lost wind, travellers like the gypsies who pitched their bush-like tents beneath them; he knew the shaggy ponies, with foals like baby centaurs; the chattering jays, the milky call of the cuckoos in the spring, and the boom of the bittern from the lonely marshes. The undergrowth of watching hollies, he knew too, strange and mysterious, with their dark, suggestive beauty, and the yellow shimmer of their pale dropped leaves.

Here all the forest lived and breathed in safety, secure from mutilation. No terror of the axe could haunt the peace of its vast subconscious life, no terror of devastating Man afflict it with the dread of premature death. It knew itself supreme; it spread and preened itself without concealment. It set no spires to carry warnings, for no wind brought messages of alarm as it bulged outwards to the sun and stars.

But, once its leafy portals left behind, the trees of the countryside were otherwise. The houses threatened them; they knew themselves in danger. The roads were no longer glades of silent turf, but noisy, cruel ways by which men came to attack them. They were civilized, cared for—but cared for in order that someday they might be put to death. Even in the villages, where the solemn and immemorial repose of giant chestnuts aped security, the tossing of a silver birch against their mass, impatient in the littlest wind, brought warning.

Dust clogged their leaves. The inner humming of their quiet life became inaudible beneath the scream and shriek of clattering traffic. They longed and prayed to enter the great peace of the forest yonder, but they could not move. They knew, moreover, that the forest with its august, deep splendour despised and pitied them. They were a thing of artificial gardens, and belonged to beds of flowers all forced to grow one way . . . .

"I'd like to know that artist fellow better," was the thought upon which he returned at length to the things of practical life. "I wonder if Sophia would mind him for a bit—?" He rose with the sound of the gong, brushing the ashes from his speckled waistcoat. He pulled the waistcoat down. He was slim and spare in figure, active in his movements. In the dim light, but for that silvery moustache, he might easily have passed for a man of forty. "I'll suggest it to her anyhow," he decided on his way upstairs to dress. His thought really was that Sanderson could probably explain his world of things he had always felt about—trees. A man who could paint the soul of a cedar in that way must know it all.

"Why not?" she gave her verdict later over the bread-and-butter pudding; "unless you think he'd find it dull without companions."

"He would paint all day in the forest, dear. I'd like to pick his brains a bit, too, if I could manage it."

"You can manage anything, David," was what she answered, for this elderly childless couple used an affectionate politeness long since deemed old-fashioned. The remark, however, displeased her, making her feel uneasy, and she did not notice his rejoinder, smiling his pleasure and content—"Except yourself and our bank account, my dear." This passion of his for trees was of old a bone of contention, though very mild contention. It frightened her. That was the truth. The Bible, her Baedeker for earth and heaven, did not mention it. Her husband, while humouring her, could never alter that instinctive dread she had. He soothed, but never changed her. She liked the woods, perhaps as spots for shade and picnics, but she could not, as he did, love them.

And after dinner, with a lamp beside the open window, he read aloud from *The Times* the evening post had brought, such fragments as he thought might interest her. The custom was invariable, except on Sundays, when, to please his wife, he dozed over Tennyson or Farrar as their mood might be. She knitted while he read, asked gentle questions, told him his voice was a "lovely reading voice," and enjoyed the little discussions that occasions prompted because he always let her with them with "Ah, Sophia, I had never thought of it quite in *that* way before; but now you mention it I must say I think there's something in it . . . ."

For David Bittacy was wise. It was long after marriage, during his months of loneliness spent with trees and forests in India, his wife waiting at home in the bungalow, that his other, deeper side had developed the strange passion that she could not understand. And after one or two serious attempts to let her share it with him, he had given up and learned to hide it from her. He learned, that is, to speak of it only casually, for since she knew it was there, to keep silence altogether would only increase her pain.

So, from time to time, he skimmed the surface just to let her show him where he was wrong and think she won the day. It remained a debatable land of compromise. He listened with patience to her criticisms, her excursions and alarms, knowing that while it gave her satisfaction, it could not change himself. The thing lay in him too deep and true for change. But, for peace's sake, some meeting-place was desirable, and he found it thus.

It was her one fault in his eyes, this religious mania carried over from her upbringing, and it did no serious harm. Great emotion could shake it sometimes out of her. She clung to it because her father taught it her and not because she had thought it out for herself. Indeed, like many women, she never really *thought* at all, but merely reflected the images of others' thinking which she had learned to see. So, wise in his knowledge of human nature, old David Bittacy accepted the pain of being obliged to keep a portion of his inner life shut off from the woman he deeply loved. He regarded her little biblical phrases as oddities that still clung to a rather fine, big soul—like horns and little useless things some animals have not yet lost in the course of evolution while they have outgrown their use.

"My dear, what is it? You frightened me!" She asked it suddenly, sitting up so abruptly that her cap dropped sideways almost to her ear. For David Bittacy behind his crackling paper had uttered a sharp exclamation of surprise. He had lowered the sheet and was staring at her over the tops of his gold glasses.

"Listen to this, if you please," he said, a note of eagerness in his voice, "listen to this, my dear Sophia. It's from an address by Francis Darwin before the Royal Society. He is president, you know, and son of the great Darwin. Listen carefully, I beg you. It is *most* significant."

"I *am* listening, David," she said with some astonishment, looking up. She stopped her knitting. For a second she glanced behind her. Something had suddenly changed in the room, and it made her feel wide awake, though before she had been almost dozing. Her husband's voice and manner had introduced this new thing. Her instincts rose in warning. "*Do* read it, dear." He took a deep breath, looking first again over the rims of his glasses to make quite sure of her attention. He had evidently come across something of genuine interest, although herself she often found the passages from these "Addresses" somewhat heavy.

In a deep, emphatic voice he read aloud:

"'It is impossible to know whether or not plants are conscious; but it is consistent with the doctrine of continuity that in all living things there is something psychic, and if we accept this point of view—'"

"*If*," she interrupted, scenting danger.

He ignored the interruption as a thing of slight value he was accustomed to.

"'If we accept this point of view,'" he continued, "'we must believe that in plants there exists a faint copy of *what we know as consciousness in ourselves.*'"

He laid the paper down and steadily stared at her. Their eyes met. He had italicised the last phrase.

For a minute or two his wife made no reply or comment. They stared at one another in silence. He waited for the meaning of the words to reach her understanding with full import. Then he turned and read them again in part, while she, released from that curious driving look in his eyes, instinctively again glanced over her shoulder round the room. It was almost as if she felt someone had come in to them unnoticed.

"We must believe that in plants there exists a faint copy of what we know as consciousness in ourselves."

"*If*," she repeated lamely, feeling before the stare of those questioning eyes she must say something, but not yet having gathered her wits together quite.

"*Consciousness*," he rejoined. And then he added gravely: "That, my dear, is the statement of a scientific man of the Twentieth Century."

Mrs. Bittacy sat forward in her chair so that her silk flounces crackled louder than the newspaper. She made a characteristic little sound between sniffling and snorting. She put her shoes closely together, with her hands upon her knees.

"David," she said quietly, "I think these scientific men are simply losing their heads. There is nothing in the Bible that I can remember about any such thing whatsoever."

"Nothing, Sophia, that I can remember either," he answered patiently. Then, after a pause, he added, half to himself perhaps more than to her: "And, now that I come to think about it, it seems that Sanderson once said something to me that was similar.

"Then Mr. Sanderson is a wise and thoughtful man, and a safe man," she quickly took up, "if he said that."

For she thought her husband referred to her remark about the Bible, and not to her judgment of the scientific men. And he did not correct her mistake.

"And plants, you see, dear, are not the same as trees," she drove her advantage home, "not quite, that is."

"I agree," said David quietly; "but both belong to the great vegetable kingdom."

There was a moment's pause before she answered.

"Pah! the vegetable kingdom, indeed!" She tossed her pretty old head. And into the words she put a degree of contempt that, could the vegetable kingdom have heard it, might have made it feel ashamed for covering a third of the world with its wonderful tangled network of roots and branches, delicate shaking leaves, and its millions of spires that caught the sun and wind and rain. Its very right to existence seemed in question.

2

Sanderson accordingly came down, and on the whole his short visit was a success. Why he came at all was a mystery to those who heard of it, for he never paid visits and was certainly not the kind of man to court a customer. There must have been something in Bittacy he liked.

Mrs. Bittacy was glad when he left. He brought no dress-suit for one thing, not even a dinner-jacket, and he wore very low collars with big balloon ties like a Frenchman, and let his hair grow longer than was nice, she felt. Not that these things were important, but that she considered them symptoms of something a little disordered. The ties were unnecessarily flowing.

For all that he was an interesting man, and, in spite of his eccentricities of dress and so forth, a gentleman. "Perhaps," she reflected in her genuinely charitable heart, "he had other uses for the twenty guineas, an invalid sister or an old mother to support!" She had no notion of the cost of brushes, frames, paints, and canvases. Also, she forgave him much for the sake of his beautiful eyes and his eager enthusiasm of manner. So many men of thirty were already *blasé*.

Still, when the visit was over, she felt relieved. She said nothing about his coming a second time, and her husband, she was glad to notice, had likewise made no suggestion. For, truth to tell, the way the younger man engrossed the older, keeping him out for hours in the forest, talking on the lawn in the blazing sun, and in the evenings when the damp of dusk came creeping out from the surrounding woods, all regardless of his age and usual habits, was not quite to her taste. Of course, Mr. Sanderson did not know how easily those attacks of Indian fever came back, but David surely might have told him.

They talked trees from morning to night. It stirred in her the old subconscious trail of dread, a trail that led ever into the darkness of big woods; and such feelings, as her early evangelical training taught her, were temptings. To regard them in any other way was to play with danger.

Her mind, as she watched these two, was charged with curious thoughts of dread she could not understand, yet feared the more on that account. The way they studied that old mangy cedar was a trifle unnecessary, unwise, she felt. It was disregarding the sense of proportion which deity had set upon the world for men's safe guidance.

Even after dinner they smoked their cigars upon the low branches that swept down and touched the lawn, until at length she insisted on their coming in. Cedars, she had somewhere heard, were not safe after sundown; it was not wholesome to be too near them; to sleep beneath them was even dangerous, though what the precise danger was she had forgotten. The *upas* was the tree she really meant.

At any rate she summoned David in, and Sanderson came presently after him.

For a long time, before deciding on this peremptory step, she had watched them surreptitiously from the drawing-room window—her husband and her guest. The dusk enveloped them with its damp veil of gauze. She saw the glowing tips of their cigars, and heard the drone of voices. Bats flitted overhead, and big, silent moths whirred softly over the rhododendron blossoms.

And it came suddenly to her, while she watched, that her husband had somehow altered these last few days—since Mr. Sanderson's arrival in fact. A change had come over him, though what it was she could not say. She hesitated, indeed, to search. That was the instinctive dread operating in her. Provided it passed she would rather not know. Small things, of course, she noticed; small outward signs. He had neglected *The Times* for one thing, left off his speckled waistcoats for another. He was absent-minded sometimes; showed vagueness in practical details where hitherto he showed decision. And—he had begun to talk in his sleep again.

These and a dozen other small peculiarities came suddenly upon her with the rush of a combined attack. They brought with them a faint distress that made her shiver. Momentarily her mind was startled, then confused, as her eyes picked out the shadowy figures in the dusk, the cedar covering them, the forest close at their backs. And then, before she could think, or seek internal guidance as her habit was, this whisper, muffled and very hurried, ran across her brain: "It's Mr. Sanderson. Call David in at once!"

And she had done so. Her shrill voice crossed the lawn and died away into the forest, quickly smothered. No echo followed it. The sound fell dead against the rampart of a thousand listening trees.

"The damp is so very penetrating, even in summer," she murmured when they came obediently. She was half surprised at her open audacity, half repentant. They came so meekly at her call. "And my husband is sensitive to fever from the East. No, *please do not throw away your cigars. We can sit by the open window and enjoy the evening while you smoke.*"

She was very talkative for a moment; subconscious excitement was the cause.

"It is so still—so wonderfully still," she went on, as no one spoke; "so peaceful, and the air so very sweet . . . .and God is always near to those who need His aid." The words slipped out before she realised quite what she was saying, yet fortunately, in time to lower her voice, for no one heard them. They were, perhaps, an instinctive expression of relief. It flustered her that she could have said the thing at all.

Sanderson brought her shawl and helped to arrange the chairs; she thanked him in her old-fashioned, gentle way, declining the lamps which he had offered to light. "They attract the moths and insects so, I think!"

The three of them sat there in the gloaming. Mr. Bittacy's white moustache and his wife's yellow shawl gleaming at either end of the little horseshoe, Sanderson with his wild black hair and shining eyes midway between them. The painter went on talking softly, continuing evidently the conversation begun with his host beneath the cedar. Mrs. Bittacy, on her guard, listened—uneasily.

"For trees, you see, rather conceal themselves in daylight. They reveal themselves fully only after sunset. I never *know* a tree," he bowed here slightly towards the lady as though to apologize for something he felt she would not quite understand or like, "until I've seen it in the night. Your cedar, for instance," looking towards her husband again so that Mrs. Bittacy caught the gleaming of his turned eyes, "I failed with badly at first, because I did it in the morning. You shall see to-morrow what I mean—that first sketch is upstairs in my portfolio; it's quite another tree to the one you bought. That view"—he leaned forward, lowering his voice—"I caught one morning about two o'clock in very faint moonlight and the stars. I saw the naked being of the thing—"

"You mean that you went out, Mr. Sanderson, at that hour?" the old lady asked with astonishment and mild rebuke. She did not care particularly for his choice of adjectives either.

"I fear it was rather a liberty to take in another's house, perhaps," he answered courteously. "But, having chanced to wake, I saw the tree from my window, and made my way downstairs."

"It's a wonder Boxer didn't bit you; he sleeps loose in the hall," she said.

"On the contrary. The dog came out with me. I hope," he added, "the noise didn't disturb you, though it's rather late to say so. I feel quite guilty." His white teeth showed in the dusk as he smiled. A smell of earth and flowers stole in through the window on a breath of wandering air.

Mrs. Bittacy said nothing at the moment. "We both sleep like tops," put in her husband, laughing. "You're a courageous man, though, Sanderson, and, by Jove, the picture justifies you. Few artists would have taken so much trouble, though I read once that Holman Hunt, Rossetti, or someone of that lot, painted all night in his orchard to get an effect of moonlight that he wanted."

He chattered on. His wife was glad to hear his voice; it made her feel more easy in her mind. But presently the other held the floor again, and her thoughts grew darkened and afraid Instinctively she feared the influence on her husband. The mystery and wonder that lie in woods, in forests, in great gatherings of trees everywhere, seemed so real and present while he talked.

"The Night transfigures all things in a way," he was saying; "but nothing so searchingly as trees. From behind a veil that sunlight hangs before them in the day they emerge and show themselves. Even buildings do that—in a measure—but trees particularly. In the daytime they sleep; at night they wake, they manifest, turn active—live. You remember," turning politely again in the direction of his hostess, "how clearly Henley understood that?"

"That socialist person, you mean?" asked the lady. Her tone and accent made the substantive sound criminal. It almost hissed, the way she uttered it.

"The poet, yes," replied the artist tactfully, "the friend of Stevenson, you remember, Stevenson who wrote those charming children's verses."

He quoted in a low voice the lines he meant. It was, for once, the time, the place, and the setting all together. The words floated out across the lawn towards the wall of blue darkness where the big forest swept the little garden with its league-long curve that was like the shore-line of a sea. A wave of distant sound that was like surf accompanied his voice, as though the wind was fain to listen too:

Not to the staring Day,
For all the importunate questionings he pursues
In his big, violent voice,
Shall those mild things of bulk and multitude,
The trees—God's sentinels ...
Yield of their huge, unutterable selves

But at the word
Of the ancient, sacerdotal Night,
Night of many secrets, whose effect—
Transfiguring, hierophantic, dread—
Themselves alone may fully apprehend,
They tremble and are changed:
In each the uncouth, individual soul
Looms forth and glooms

Essential, and, their bodily presences
Touched with inordinate significance,
Wearing the darkness like a livery
Of some mysterious and tremendous guild,
They brood—they menace—they appal.

The voice of Mrs. Bittacy presently broke the silence that followed.

"I like that part about God's sentinels," she murmured. There was no sharpness in her tone; it was hushed and quiet. The truth, so musically uttered, muted her shrill objections though it had not lessened her alarm. Her husband made no comment; his cigar, she noticed, had gone out.

"And old trees in particular," continued the artist, as though to himself, "have very definite personalities. You can offend, wound, please them; the moment you stand within their shade you feel whether they come out to you, or whether they withdraw." He turned abruptly towards his host. "You know that singular essay of Prentice Mulford's, no doubt 'God in the Trees'—extravagant perhaps, but yet with a fine true beauty in it? You've never read it, no?" he asked.

But it was Mrs. Bittacy who answered; her husband keeping his curious deep silence.

"I never did!" It fell like a drip of cold water from the face muffled in the yellow shawl; even a child could have supplied the remainder of the unspoken thought.

"Ah," said Sanderson gently, "but there *is* 'God' in the trees. God in a very subtle aspect and sometimes—I have known the trees express it too—that which is *not* God—dark and terrible. Have you ever noticed, too, how clearly trees show what they want—choose their companions, at least? How beeches, for instance, allow no life too near them—birds or squirrels in their boughs, nor any growth beneath? The silence in the beech wood is quite terrifying often! And how pines like bilberry bushes at their feet and sometimes little oaks—all trees making a clear, deliberate choice, and holding firmly to it? Some trees obviously—it's very strange and marked—seem to prefer the human."

The old lady sat up crackling, for this was more than she could permit. Her stiff silk dress emitted little sharp reports.

"We know," she answered, "that He was said to have walked in the garden in the cool of the evening"—the gulp betrayed the effort that it cost her—"but we are nowhere told that He hid in the trees, or anything like that. Trees, after all, we must remember, are only large vegetables."

"True," was the soft answer, "but in everything that grows, has life, that is, there's mystery past all finding out. The wonder that lies hidden in our own souls lies also hidden, I venture to assert, in the stupidity and silence of a mere potato."

The observation was not meant to be amusing. It was *not* amusing. No one laughed. On the contrary, the words conveyed in too literal a sense the feeling that haunted all that conversation. Each one in his own way realised—with beauty, with wonder, with alarm—that the talk had somehow brought the whole vegetable kingdom nearer to that of man. Some link had been established between the two. It was not wise, with that great forest listening at their very doors, to speak so plainly. The forest edged up closer while they did so.

And Mrs. Bittacy, anxious to interrupt the horrid spell, broke suddenly in upon it with a matter-of-fact suggestion. She did not like her husband's prolonged silence, stillness. He seemed so negative—so changed.

"David," she said, raising her voice, "I think you're feeling the dampness. It's grown chilly. The fever comes so suddenly, you know, and it might be wide to take the tincture. I'll go and get it, dear, at once. It's better." And before he could object, she had left the room to bring the homeopathic dose that she believed in, and that, to please her, he swallowed by the tumbler-full from week to week.

And the moment the door closed behind her, Sanderson began again, though now in quite a different tone. Mr. Bittacy sat up in his chair. The two men obviously resumed the conversation—the real conversation interrupted beneath the cedar—and left aside the sham one which was so much dust merely thrown in the old lady's eyes.

"Trees love you, that's the fact," he said earnestly. "Your service to them all these years abroad has made them know you."

"Know me?"

"Made them, yes,"—he paused a moment, then added—"made them *aware of your presence*; aware of a force outside themselves that deliberately seeks their welfare, don't you see?"

"By Jove, Sanderson—!" This put into plain language actual sensations he had felt, yet had never dared to phrase in words before. "They get into touch with me, as it were?" he ventured, laughing at his own sentence, yet laughing only with his lips.

"Exactly," was the quick, emphatic reply. "They seek to blend with something they feel instinctively to be good for them, helpful to their essential beings, encouraging to their best expression—their life."

"Good Lord, Sir!" Bittacy heard himself saying, "but you're putting my own thoughts into words. D'you know, I've felt something like that for years. As though—" he looked round to make sure his wife was not there, then finished the sentence—"as though the trees were after me!"

"'Amalgamate' seems the best word, perhaps," said Sanderson slowly. "They would draw you to themselves. Good forces, you see, always seek to merge; evil to separate; that's why Good in the end must always win the day—everywhere. The accumulation in the long run becomes overwhelming. Evil tends to separation, dissolution, death. The comradeship of trees, their instinct to run together, is a vital symbol. Trees in a mass are good; alone, you may take it generally, are—well, dangerous. Look at a monkey-puzzler, or better still, a holly. Look at it, watch it, understand it. Did you ever see more plainly an evil thought made visible? They're wicked. Beautiful too, oh yes! There's a strange, miscalculated beauty often in evil—"

"That cedar, then—?"

"Not evil, no; but alien, rather. Cedars grow in forests all together. The poor thing has drifted, that is all."

They were getting rather deep. Sanderson, talking against time, spoke so fast. It was too condensed. Bittacy hardly followed that last bit. His mind floundered among his own less definite, less sorted thoughts, till presently another sentence from the artist startled him into attention again.

"That cedar will protect you here, though, because you both have humanized it by your thinking so lovingly of its presence. The others can't get past it, as it were."

"Protect me!" he exclaimed. "Protect me from their love?"

Sanderson laughed. "We're getting rather mixed," he said; "we're talking of one thing in the terms of another really. But what I mean is—you see—that their love for you, their 'awareness' of your personality and presence involves the idea of winning you—across the border—into themselves—into their world of living. It means, in a way, taking you over."

The ideas the artist started in his mind ran furious wild races to and fro. It was like a maze sprung suddenly into movement. The whirling of the intricate lines bewildered him. They went so fast, leaving but half an explanation of their goal. He followed first one, then another, but a new one always dashed across to intercept before he could get anywhere.

"But India," he said, presently in a lower voice. "India is so far away—from this little English forest. The trees, too, are utterly different for one thing?"

The rustle of skirts warned of Mrs. Bittacy's approach. This was a sentence he could turn round another way in case she came up and pressed for explanation.

"There is communion among trees all the world over," was the strange quick reply. "They always know."

"They always know! You think then—?"

"The winds, you see—the great, swift carriers! They have their ancient rights of way about the world. An easterly wind, for instance, carrying on stage by stage as it were—linking dropped messages and meanings from land to land like the birds—an easterly wind—"

Mrs. Bittacy swept in upon them with the tumbler—

"There, David," she said, "that will ward off any beginnings of attack. Just a spoonful, dear. Oh, oh! Not all!" for he had swallowed half the contents at a single gulp as usual; "another dose before you go to bed, and the balance in the morning, first thing when you wake."

She turned to her guest, who put the tumbler down for her upon a table at his elbow. She had heard them speak of the east wind. She emphasized the warning she had misinterpreted. The private part of the conversation came to an abrupt end.

"It is the one thing that upsets him more than any other—an east wind," she said, "and I am glad, Mr. Sanderson, to hear you think so too."

3

A deep hush followed, in the middle of which an owl was heard calling its muffled note in the forest. A big moth whirred with a soft collision against one of the windows. Mrs. Bittacy started slightly, but no one spoke. Above the trees the stars were faintly visible. From the distance came the barking of a dog.

Bittacy, relighting his cigar, broke the little spell of silence that had caught all three.

"It's rather a comforting thought," he said, throwing the match out of the window, "that life is about us everywhere, and that there is really no dividing line between what we call organic and inorganic."

"The universe, yes," said Sanderson, "is all one, really. We're puzzled by the gaps we cannot see across, but as a fact, I suppose, there are no gaps at all."

Mrs. Bittacy rustled ominously, holding her peace meanwhile. She feared long words she did not understand. Beelzebub lay hid among too many syllables.

"In trees and plants especially, there dreams an exquisite life that no one yet has proved unconscious."

"Or conscious either, Mr. Sanderson," she neatly interjected. "It's only man that was made after His image, not shrubberies and things . . . ."

Her husband interposed without delay.

"It is not necessary," he explained suavely, "to say that they're alive in the sense that we are alive. At the same time," with an eye to his wife, "I see no harm in holding, dear, that all created things contain some measure of His life Who made them. It's only beautiful to hold that He created nothing dead. We are not pantheists for all that!" he added soothingly.

"Oh, no! Not that, I hope!" The word alarmed her. It was worse than pope. Through her puzzled mind stole a stealthy, dangerous thing . . . .like a panther.

"I like to think that even in decay there's life," the painter murmured. "The falling apart of rotten wood breeds sentiency, there's force and motion in the falling of a dying leaf, in the breaking up and crumbling of everything indeed. And take an inert stone: it's crammed with heat and weight and potencies of all sorts. What holds its particles together indeed? We understand it as little as gravity or why a needle always turns to the 'North.' Both things may be a mode of life . . . ."

"You think a compass has a soul, Mr. Sanderson?" exclaimed the lady with a crackling of her silk flounces that conveyed a sense of outrage even more plainly than her tone. The artist smiled to himself in the darkness, but it was Bittacy who hastened to reply.

"Our friend merely suggests that these mysterious agencies," he said quietly, "may be due to some kind of life we cannot understand. Why should water only run downhill? Why should trees grow at right angles to the surface of the ground and towards the sun? Why should the worlds spin for ever on their axes? Why should fire change the form of everything it touches without really destroying them? To say these things, follow the law of their being explains nothing. Mr. Sanderson merely suggests—poetically, my dear, of course—that these may be manifestations of life, though life at a different stage to ours."

"The '*breath* of life,' we read, 'He breathed into them. These things do not breathe." She said it with triumph.

Then Sanderson put in a word. But he spoke rather to himself or to his host than by way of serious rejoinder to the ruffled lady.

"But plants do breathe too, you know," he said. "They breathe, they eat, they digest, they move about, and they adapt themselves to their environment as men and animals do. They have a nervous system too . . . .at least a complex system of nuclei which have some of the qualities of nerve cells. They may have memory too. Certainly, they know definite action in response to stimulus. And though this may be physiological, no one has proved that it is only that, and not—psychological."

He did not notice, apparently, the little gasp that was audible behind the yellow shawl. Bittacy cleared his throat, threw his extinguished cigar upon the lawn, crossed and recrossed his legs.

"And in trees," continued the other, "behind a great forest, for instance," pointing towards the woods, "may stand a rather splendid Entity that manifests through all the thousand individual trees—some huge collective life, quite as minutely and delicately organised as our own. It might merge and blend with ours under certain conditions, so that we could understand it by *being* it, for a time at least. It might even engulf human vitality into the immense whirlpool of its own vast dreaming life. The pull of a big forest on a man can be tremendous and utterly overwhelming."

The mouth of Mrs. Bittacy was heard to close with a snap. Her shawl, and particularly her crackling dress, exhaled the protest that burned within her like a pain. She was too distressed to be overawed, but at the same time too confused 'mid the litter of words and meanings half understood, to find immediate phrases she could use. Whatever the actual meaning of his language might be, however, and whatever subtle dangers lay concealed behind them meanwhile, they certainly wove a kind of gentle spell with the glimmering darkness that held all three delicately enmeshed there by that open window. The odours of dewy lawn, flowers, trees, and earth formed part of it.

"The moods," he continued, "that people waken in us are due to their hidden life affecting our own. Deep calls to sleep. A person, for instance, joins you in an empty room: you both instantly change. The new arrival, though in silence, has caused a change of mood. May not the moods of Nature touch and stir us in virtue of a similar prerogative? The sea, the hills, the desert, wake passion, joy, terror, as the case may be; for a few, perhaps," he glanced significantly at his host so that Mrs. Bittacy again caught the turning of his eyes, "emotions of a curious, flaming splendour that are quite nameless. Well . . . . whence come these powers? Surely from nothing that is . . . . dead! Does not the influence of a forest, its sway and strange ascendancy over certain minds, betray a direct manifestation of life? It lies otherwise beyond all explanation, this mysterious emanation of big woods. Some natures, of course, deliberately invite it. The authority of a host of trees,"—his voice grew almost solemn as he said the words—"is something not to be denied. One feels it here, I think, particularly."

There was considerable tension in the air as he ceased speaking. Mr. Bittacy had not intended that the talk should go so far. They had drifted. He did not wish to see his wife unhappy or afraid, and he was aware—acutely so—that her feelings were stirred to a point he did not care about. Something in her, as he put it, was "working up" towards explosion.

He sought to generalise the conversation, diluting this accumulated emotion by spreading it.

"The sea is His and He made it," he suggested vaguely, hoping Sanderson would take the hint, "and with the trees it is the same . . . ."

"The whole gigantic vegetable kingdom, yes," the artist took him up, "all at the service of man, for food, for shelter and for a thousand purposes of his daily life. Is it not striking what a lot of the globe they cover . . . . exquisitely organised life, yet stationary, always ready to our had when we want them, never running away? But the taking them, for all that, not so easy. One man shrinks from picking flowers, another from cutting down trees. And, it's curious that most of the forest tales and legends are dark, mysterious, and somewhat ill-omened. The forest-beings are rarely gay and harmless. The forest life was felt as terrible. Tree-worship still survives today. Wood-cutters . . . . those who take the life of trees . . . . you see a race of haunted men . . . ."

He stopped abruptly, a singular catch in his voice. Bittacy felt something even before the sentences were over. His wife, he knew, felt it still more strongly. For it was in the middle of the heavy silence following upon these last remarks, that Mrs. Bittacy, rising with a violent abruptness from her chair, drew the attention of the others to something moving towards them across the lawn. It came silently. In outline it was large and curiously spread. It rose high, too, for the sky above the shrubberies, still pale gold from the sunset, was dimmed by its passage. She declared afterwards that it moved in "looping circles," but what she perhaps meant to convey was "spirals."

She screamed faintly. "It's come at last! And it's you that brought it!"

She turned excitedly, half afraid, half angry, to Sanderson. With a breathless sort of gasp, she said it, politeness all forgotten. "I knew it ....if you went on. I knew it. Oh! Oh!" And she cried again, "Your talking has brought it out!" The terror that shook her voice was rather dreadful.

But the confusion of her vehement words passed unnoticed in the first surprise they caused. For a moment nothing happened.

"What is it you think you see, my dear?" asked her husband, startled. Sanderson said nothing. All three leaned forward, the men still sitting, but Mrs. Bittacy had rushed hurriedly to the window, placing herself of a purpose, as it seemed, between her husband and the lawn. She pointed. Her little hand made a silhouette against the sky, the yellow shawl hanging from the arm like a cloud.

"Beyond the cedar—between it and the lilacs." The voice had lost its shrillness; it was thin and hushed. "There ....now you see it going round upon itself again—going back, thank God! ....going back to the forest." It sank to a whisper, shaking. She repeated, with a great dropping sigh of relief—"Thank God! I thought ....at first ....it was coming here ....to us! ....David ....to *you!*"

She stepped back from the window, her movements confused, feeling in the darkness for the support of a chair, and finding her husband's outstretched hand instead. "Hold me, dear, hold me, please . ...tight. Do not let me go." She was in what he called afterwards "a regular state." He drew her firmly down upon her chair again.

"Smoke, Sophie, my dear," he said quickly, trying to make his voice calm and natural. "I see it, yes. It's smoke blowing over from the gardener's cottage ...."

"But, David,"—and there was a new horror in her whisper now—"it made a noise. It makes it still. I hear it swishing." Some such word she used—swishing, sishing, rushing, or something of the kind. "David, I'm very frightened. It's something awful! That man has called it out ....!"

"Hush, hush," whispered her husband. He stroked her trembling hand beside him.

"It is in the wind," said Sanderson, speaking for the first time, very quietly. The expression on his face was not visible in the gloom, but his voice was soft and unafraid. At the sound of it, Mrs. Bittacy started violently again. Bittacy drew his chair a little forward to obstruct her

113

view of him. He felt bewildered himself, a little, hardly knowing quite what to say or do. It was all so very curious and sudden.

But Mrs. Bittacy was badly frightened. It seemed to her that what she saw came from the enveloping forest just beyond their little garden. It emerged in a sort of secret way, moving towards them as with a purpose, stealthily, difficultly. Then something stopped it. It could not advance beyond the cedar. The cedar—this impression remained with her afterwards too—prevented, kept it back. Like a rising sea the forest had surged a moment in their direction through the covering darkness, and this visible movement was its first wave.

Thus, to her mind it seemed . . . .like that mysterious turn of the tide that used to frighten and mystify her in childhood on the sands. The outward surge of some enormous Power was what she felt . . . something to which every instinct in her being rose in opposition because it threatened her and hers. In that moment she realised the Personality of the forest . . . .menacing.

In the stumbling movement that she made away from the window and towards the bell she barely caught the sentence Sanderson—or was it her husband?—murmured to himself: "It came because we talked of it; our thinking made it aware of us and brought it out. But the cedar stops it. It cannot cross the lawn, you see . . . ."

All three were standing now, and her husband's voice broke in with authority while his wife's fingers touched the bell.

"My dear, I should *not* say anything to Thompson." The anxiety he felt was manifest in his voice, but his outward composure had returned. "The gardener can go . . . ."

Then Sanderson cut him short. "Allow me," he said quickly. "I'll see if anything's wrong." And before either of them could answer or object, he was gone, leaping out by the open window. They saw his figure vanish with a run across the lawn into the darkness.

A moment later the maid entered, in answer to the bell, and with her came the loud barking of the terrier from the hall.

"The lamps," said her master shortly, and as she softly closed the door behind her, they heard the wind pass with a mournful sound of singing round the outer walls. A rustle of foliage from the distance passed within it.

"You see, the wind *is* rising. It *was* the wind!" He put a comforting arm about her, distressed to feel that she was trembling. But he knew that he was trembling too, though with a kind of odd elation rather than alarm. "And it *was* smoke that you saw coming from Stride's cottage, or from the rubbish heaps he's been burning in the kitchen garden. The noise we heard was the branches rustling in the wind. Why should you be so nervous?"

A thin whispering voice answered him:

"I was afraid for *you*, dear. Something frightened me for *you*. That man makes me feel so uneasy and uncomfortable for his influence upon you. It's very foolish, I know. I think . . . .I'm tired; I feel so overwrought and restless." The words poured out in a hurried jumble and she kept turning to the window while she spoke.

"The strain of having a visitor," he said soothingly, "has taxed you. We're so unused to having people in the house. He goes tomorrow." He warmed her cold hands between his own, stroking them tenderly. More, for the life of him, he could not say or do. The joy of a strange, internal excitement made his heart beat faster. He knew not what it was. He knew only, perhaps, whence it came.

She peered close into his face through the gloom, and said a curious thing. "I thought, David, for a moment . . . .you seemed . . . .different. My nerves are all on edge tonight." She made no further reference to her husband's visitor.

A sound of footsteps from the lawn warned of Sanderson's return, as he answered quickly in a lowered tone—"There's no need to be afraid on my account, dear girl. There's nothing wrong with me. I assure you; I never felt so well and happy in my life."

Thompson came in with the lamps and brightness, and scarcely had she gone again when Sanderson in turn was seen climbing through the window.

"There's nothing," he said lightly, as he closed it behind him. "Somebody's been burning leaves, and the smoke is drifting a little through the trees. The wind," he added, glancing at his host a moment significantly, but in so discreet a way that Mrs. Bittacy did not observe it, "the wind, too, has begun to roar . . . .in the forest . . . .further out."

But Mrs. Bittacy noticed about him two things which increased her uneasiness. She noticed the shining of his eyes, because a similar light had suddenly come into her husband's; and she noticed, too, the apparent depth of meaning he put into those simple words that "the wind had begun to roar in the forest. . . .further out." Her mind retained the disagreeable impression that he meant more than he said. In his tone lay quite another implication. It was not actually "wind" he spoke of, and it would not remain "further out". . . rather, it was coming in. Another impression she got too—still more unwelcome—was

115

that her husband understood his hidden meaning.

4

"David, dear," she observed gently as soon as they were alone up-stairs, "I have a horrible uneasy feeling about that man. I cannot get rid of it." The tremor in her voice caught all his tenderness.

He turned to look at her. "Of what kind, my dear? You're so im-aginative sometimes, aren't you?"

"I think," she hesitated, stammering a little, confused, still fright-ened, "I mean—isn't he a hypnotist, or full of those theosophical ideas, or something of the sort? You know what I mean—"

He was too accustomed to her little confused alarms to explain them away seriously as a rule, or to correct her verbal inaccuracies, but tonight he felt she needed careful, tender treatment. He soothed her as best he could.

"But there's no harm in that, even if he is," he answered quietly. "Those are only new names for very old ideas, you know, dear." There was no trace of impatience in his voice.

"That's what I mean," she replied, the texts he dreaded rising in an unuttered crowd behind the words. "He's one of those things that we are warned would come—one of those Latter-Day things." For her mind still bristled with the bogeys of the Antichrist and Prophecy, and she had only escaped the Number of the Beast, as it were, by the skin of her teeth. The Pope drew most of her fire usually, because she could understand him; the target was plain and she could shoot. But this tree-and-forest business was so vague and horrible. It terrified her. "He makes me think," she went on, "of Principalities and Powers in high places, and of things that walk in the darkness. I did *not* like the way he spoke of trees getting alive in the night, and all that; it made me think of wolves in sheep's clothing. And when I saw that awful thing in the sky above the lawn—"

But he interrupted her at once, for that was something he had decided it was best to leave unmentioned. Certainly, it was better not discussed.

"He only meant, I think, Sophie," he put in gravely, yet with a little smile, "that trees may have a measure of conscious life—rather a nice idea on the whole, surely—something like that bit we read in the Times the other night, you remember—and that a big forest may possess a sort of Collective Personality. Remember, he's an artist, and poetical."

"It's dangerous," she said emphatically. "I feel it's playing with fire, unwise, unsafe—"

"Yet all to the glory of God," he urged gently. "We must not shut our ears and eyes to knowledge—of any kind, must we?"

"With you, David, the wish is always farther than the thought," she rejoined. For, like the child who thought that "suffered under Pontius Pilate" was "suffered under a bunch of violets," she heard her proverbs phonetically and reproduced them thus. She hoped to convey her warning in the quotation. "And we must always try the spirits whether they be of God," she added tentatively.

"Certainly, dear, we can always do that," he assented, getting into bed.

But, after a little pause, during which she blew the light out, David Bittacy settling down to sleep with an excitement in his blood that was new and bewilderingly delightful, realised that perhaps he had not said quite enough to comfort her. She was lying awake by his side, still frightened. He put his head up in the darkness.

"Sophie," he said softly, "you must remember, too, that in any case between us and—and all that sort of thing—there is a great gulf fixed, a gulf that cannot be crossed—er—while we are still in the body."

And hearing no reply, he satisfied himself that she was already asleep and happy. But Mrs. Bittacy was not asleep. She heard the sentence, only she said nothing because she felt her thought was better unexpressed. She was afraid to hear the words in the darkness. The forest outside was listening and might hear them too—the forest that was "roaring further out."

And the thought was this: That gulf, of course, existed, but Sanderson had somehow bridged it.

★★★★★★★★★★★★★★★★

It was much later than night when she awoke out of troubled, uneasy dreams and heard a sound that twisted her very nerves with fear. It passed immediately with full waking, for, listen as she might, there was nothing audible but the inarticulate murmur of the night. It was in her dreams she heard it, and the dreams had vanished with it. But the sound was recognisable, for it was that rushing noise that had come across the lawn; only this time closer. Just above her face while she slept had passed this murmur as of rustling branches in the very room, a sound of foliage whispering. "A going in the tops of the mulberry trees," ran through her mind. She had dreamed that she lay beneath a spreading tree somewhere, a tree that whispered with ten thousand soft lips of green; and the dream continued for a moment even after waking.

She sat up in bed and stared about her. The window was open at the top; she saw the stars; the door, she remembered, was locked as usual; the room, of course, was empty. The deep hush of the summer night lay over all, broken only by another sound that now issued from the shadows close beside the bed, a human sound, yet unnatural, a sound that seized the fear with which she had waked and instantly increased it. And, although it was one she recognised as familiar, at first she could not name it. Some seconds certainly passed—and, they were very long ones—before she understood that it was her husband talking in his sleep.

The direction of the voice confused and puzzled her, moreover, for it was not, as she first supposed, beside her. There was distance in it. The next minute, by the light of the sinking candle flame, she saw his white figure standing out in the middle of the room, half-way towards the window. The candle-light slowly grew. She saw him move then nearer to the window, with arms outstretched. His speech was low and mumbled, the words running together too much to be distinguishable.

And she shivered. To her, sleep-talking was uncanny to the point of horror; it was like the talking of the dead, mere parody of a living voice, unnatural.

"David!" she whispered, dreading the sound of her own voice, and half afraid to interrupt him and see his face. She could not bear the sight of the wide-opened eyes. "David, you're walking in your sleep. Do—come back to bed, dear, *please!*"

Her whisper seemed so dreadfully loud in the still darkness. At the sound of her voice he paused, then turned slowly round to face her. His widely-opened eyes stared into her own without recognition; they looked through her into something beyond; it was as though he knew the direction of the sound, yet cold not see her. They were shining, she noticed, as the eyes of Sanderson had shone several hours ago; and his face was flushed, distraught. Anxiety was written upon every feature.

And, instantly, recognising that the fever was upon him, she forgot her terror temporarily in practical considerations. He came back to bed without waking. She closed his eyelids. Presently he composed himself quietly to sleep, or rather to deeper sleep. She contrived to make him swallow something from the tumbler beside the bed.

Then she rose very quietly to close the window, feeling the night

118

air blow in too fresh and keen. She put the candle where it could not reach him. The sight of the big Baxter Bible beside it comforted her a little, but all through her under-being ran the warnings of a curious alarm. And it was while in the act of fastening the catch with one hand and pulling the string of the blind with the other, that her husband sat up again in bed and spoke in words this time that were distinctly audible. The eyes had opened wide again. He pointed. She stood stock still and listened, her shadow distorted on the blind. He did not come out towards her as at first, she feared.

The whispering voice was very clear, horrible, too, beyond all she had ever known.

"They are roaring in the forest further out . . . .and I . . . .must go and see." He stared beyond her as he said it, to the woods. "They are needing me. They sent for me . . . ." Then his eyes wandering back again to things within the room, he lay down, his purpose suddenly changed. And that change was horrible as well, more horrible, perhaps, because of its revelation of another detailed world he moved in far away from her.

The singular phrase chilled her blood, for a moment she was utterly terrified. That tone of the somnambulist, differing so slightly yet so distressingly from normal, waking speech, seemed to her somehow wicked. Evil and danger lay waiting thick behind it. She leaned against the window-sill, shaking in every limb. She had an awful feeling for a moment that something was coming in to fetch him.

"Not yet, then," she heard in a much lower voice from the bed, "but later. It will be better so . . . .I shall go later . . . ."

The words expressed some fringe of these alarms that had haunted her so long, and that the arrival and presence of Sanderson seemed to have brought to the very edge of a climax she could not even dare to think about. They gave it form; they brought it closer; they sent her thoughts to her Deity in a wild, deep prayer for help and guidance. For here was a direct, unconscious betrayal of a world of inner purposes and claims her husband recognised while he kept them almost wholly to himself.

By the time she reached his side and knew the comfort of his touch, the eyes had closed again, this time of their own accord, and the head lay calmly back upon the pillows. She gently straightened the bed clothes. She watched him for some minutes, shading the candle carefully with one hand. There was a smile of strangest peace upon the face.

Then, blowing out the candle, she knelt down and prayed before getting back into bed. But no sleep came to her. She lay awake all night thinking, wondering, praying, until at length with the chorus of the birds and the glimmer of the dawn upon the green blind, she fell into a slumber of complete exhaustion.

But while she slept the wind continued roaring in the forest further out. The sound came closer—sometimes very close indeed.

5

With the departure of Sanderson, the significance of the curious incidents waned, because the moods that had produced them passed away. Mrs. Bittacy soon afterwards came to regard them as some growth of disproportion that had been very largely, perhaps, in her own mind. It did not strike her that this change was sudden for it came about quite naturally. For one thing her husband never spoke of the matter, and for another she remembered how many things in life that had seemed inexplicable and singular at the time turned out later to have been quite commonplace.

Most of it, certainly, she put down to the presence of the artist and to his wild, suggestive talk. With his welcome removal, the world turned ordinary again and safe. The fever, though it lasted as usual a short time only, had not allowed of her husband's getting up to say goodbye, and she had conveyed his regrets and *adieux*. In the morning Mr. Sanderson had seemed ordinary enough. In his town hat and gloves, as she saw him go, he seemed tame and unalarming.

"After all," she thought as she watched the pony-cart bear him off, "he's only an artist!" What she had thought he might be otherwise her slim imagination did not venture to disclose. Her change of feeling was wholesome and refreshing. She felt a little ashamed of her behaviour. She gave him a smile—genuine because the relief she felt was genuine—as he bent over her hand and kissed it, but she did not suggest a second visit, and her husband, she noted with satisfaction and relief, had said nothing either.

The little household fell again into the normal and sleepy routine to which it was accustomed. The name of Arthur Sanderson was rarely if ever mentioned. Nor, for her part, did she mention to her husband the incident of his walking in his sleep and the wild words he used. But to forget it was equally impossible. Thus, it lay buried deep within her like a centre of some unknown disease of which it was a mysterious symptom, waiting to spread at the first favourable opportunity.

She prayed against it every night and morning: prayed that she might forget it—that God would keep her husband safe from harm.

For in spite of much surface foolishness that many might have read as weakness, Mrs. Bittacy had balance, sanity, and a fine deep faith. She was greater than she knew. Her love for her husband and her God were somehow one, an achievement only possible to a single-hearted nobility of soul.

There followed a summer of great violence and beauty; of beauty, because the refreshing rains at night prolonged the glory of the spring and spread it all across July, keeping the foliage young and sweet; of violence, because the winds that tore about the south of England brushed the whole country into dancing movement. They swept the woods magnificently, and kept them roaring with a perpetual grand voice. Their deepest notes seemed never to leave the sky. They sang and shouted, and torn leaves raced and fluttered through the air long before their usually appointed time.

Many a tree, after days of roaring and dancing, fell exhausted to the ground. The cedar on the lawn gave up two limbs that fell upon successive days, at the same hour too—just before dusk. The wind often makes its most boisterous effort at that time, before it drops with the sun, and these two huge branches lay in dark ruin covering half the lawn. They spread across it and towards the house. They left an ugly gaping space upon the tree, so that the Lebanon looked unfinished, half destroyed, a monster shorn of its old-time comeliness and splendour. Far more of the forest was now visible than before; it peered through the breach of the broken defences. They could see from the windows of the house now—especially from the drawing-room and bedroom windows—straight out into the glades and depths beyond.

Mrs. Bittacy's niece and nephew, who were staying on a visit at the time, enjoyed themselves immensely helping the gardeners carry off the fragments. It took two days to do this, for Mr. Bittacy insisted on the branches being moved entire. He would not allow them to be chopped; also, he would not consent to their use as firewood. Under his superintendence the unwieldy masses were dragged to the edge of the garden and arranged upon the frontier line between the forest and the lawn.

The children were delighted with the scheme. They entered into it with enthusiasm. At all costs this defence against the inroads of the forest must be made secure. They caught their uncle's earnestness, felt even something of a hidden motive that he had; and the visit, usually rather dreaded, became the visit of their lives instead. It was Aunt Sophia this time who seemed discouraging and dull.

"She's got so old and funny," opined Stephen.

But Alice, who felt in the silent displeasure of her aunt some secret thing that alarmed her, said:

"I think she's afraid of the woods. She never comes into them with us, you see."

"All the more reason then for making this wall impreg—all fat and thick and solid," he concluded, unable to manage the longer word. "Then nothing—simply *nothing*—can get through. Can't it, Uncle David?"

And Mr. Bittacy, jacket discarded and working in his speckled waistcoat, went puffing to their aid, arranging the massive limb of the cedar like a hedge.

"Come on," he said, "whatever happens, you know, we must finish before it's dark. Already the wind is roaring in the forest further out." And Alice caught the phrase and instantly echoed it. "Stevie," she cried below her breath, "look sharp, you lazy lump. Didn't you hear what Uncle David said? It'll come in and catch us before we've done!"

They worked like Trojans, and, sitting beneath the wisteria tree that climbed the southern wall of the cottage, Mrs. Bittacy with her knitting watched them, calling from time to time insignificant messages of counsel and advice. The messages passed, of course, unheeded. Mostly, indeed, they were unheard, for the workers were too absorbed. She warned her husband not to get too hot, Alice not to tear her dress, Stephen not to strain his back with pulling. Her mind hovered between the homeopathic medicine-chest upstairs and her anxiety to see the business finished.

For this breaking up of the cedar had stirred again her slumbering alarms. It revived memories of the visit of Mr. Sanderson that had been sinking into oblivion; she recalled his queer and odious way of talking, and many things she hoped forgotten drew their heads up from that subconscious region to which all forgetting is impossible. They looked at her and nodded. They were full of life; they had no intention of being pushed aside and buried permanently. "Now look!" they whispered, "didn't we tell you so?" They had been merely waiting the right moment to assert their presence. And all her former vague distress crept over her. Anxiety, uneasiness returned. That dreadful sinking of the heart came too.

This incident of the cedar's breaking up was actually so unimportant, and yet her husband's attitude towards it made it so significant. There was nothing that he said in particular, or did, or left undone that frightened, her, but his general air of earnestness seemed so unwarranted. She felt that he deemed the thing important He was so exercised about it. This evidence of sudden concern and interest, buried all the summer from her sight and knowledge, she realised now had been buried purposely, he had kept it intentionally concealed.

Deeply submerged in him there ran this tide of other thoughts, desires, hopes. What were they? Whither did they lead? The accident to the tree betrayed it most unpleasantly, and, doubtless, more than he was aware.

She watched his grave and serious face as he worked there with the children, and as she watched she felt afraid. It vexed her that the children worked so eagerly. They unconsciously supported him. The thing she feared she would not even name. But it was waiting.

Moreover, as far as her puzzled mind could deal with a dread so vague and incoherent, the collapse of the cedar somehow brought it nearer. The fact that, all so ill-explained and formless, the thing yet lay in her consciousness, out of reach but moving and alive, filled her with a kind of puzzled, dreadful wonder. Its presence was so very real, its power so gripping, its partial concealment so abominable. Then, out of the dim confusion, she grasped one thought and saw it stand quite clear before her eyes. She found difficulty in clothing it in words, but its meaning perhaps was this: That cedar stood in their life for something friendly; its downfall meant disaster; a sense of some protective influence about the cottage, and about her husband in particular, was thereby weakened.

"Why do you fear the big winds so?" he had asked her several days before, after a particularly boisterous day; and the answer she gave surprised her while she gave it. One of those heads poked up unconsciously, and let slip the truth.

"Because, David, I feel they—bring the forest with them," she faltered. "They blow something from the trees—into the mind—into the house."

He looked at her keenly for a moment.

"That must be why I love them then," he answered. "They blow the souls of the trees about the sky like clouds."

The conversation dropped. She had never heard him talk in quite that way before.

And another time, when he had coaxed her to go with him down one of the nearer glades, she asked why he took the small hand-axe with him, and what he wanted it for.

"To cut the ivy that clings to the trunks and takes their life away," he said.

"But can't the verdurers do that?" she asked. "That's what they're paid for, isn't it?"

Whereupon he explained that ivy was a parasite the trees knew not how to fight alone, and that the verdurers were careless and did not do it thoroughly. They gave a chop here and there, leaving the tree to do the rest for itself if it could.

"Besides, I like to do it for them. I love to help them and protect," he added, the foliage rustling all about his quiet words as they went.

And these stray remarks, as his attitude towards the broken cedar, betrayed this curious, subtle change that was going forward to his personality. Slowly and surely all the summer it had increased.

It was growing—the thought startled her horribly—just as a tree grows, the outer evidence from day to day so slight as to be unnoticeable, yet the rising tide so deep and irresistible. The alteration spread all through and over him, was in both mind and actions, sometimes almost in his face as well. Occasionally, thus, it stood up straight outside himself and frightened her. His life was somehow becoming linked so intimately with trees, and with all that trees signified. His interests became more and more their interests, his activity combined with theirs, his thoughts and feelings theirs, his purpose, hope, desire, his fate—

His fate! The darkness of some vague, enormous terror dropped its shadow on her when she thought of it. Some instinct in her heart she dreaded infinitely more than death—for death meant sweet translation for his soul—came gradually to associate the thought of him with the thought of trees, in particular with these forest trees. Sometimes, before she could face the thing, argue it away, or pray it into silence, she found the thought of him running swiftly through her mind like a thought of the forest itself, the two most intimately linked and joined together, each a part and complement of the other, one being.

The idea was too dim for her to see it face to face. Its mere possibility dissolved the instant she focused it to get the truth behind it. It was too utterly elusive, made, protean. Under the attack of even a minute's concentration the very meaning of it vanished, melted away. The idea lay really behind any words that she could ever find, beyond the touch of definite thought.

Her mind was unable to grapple with it. But, while it vanished, the trail of its approach and disappearance flickered a moment before her shaking vision. The horror certainly remained.

Reduced to the simple human statement that her temperament sought instinctively, it stood perhaps at this: Her husband loved her, and he loved the trees as well; but the trees came first, claimed parts of him she did not know. *She* loved her God and him. *He* loved the trees and her.

Thus, in guise of some faint, distressing compromise, the matter shaped itself for her perplexed mind in the terms of conflict. A silent, hidden battle raged, but as yet raged far away. The breaking of the cedar was a visible outward fragment of a distant and mysterious encounter that was coming daily closer to them both. The wind, instead of roaring in the forest further out, now cam nearer, booming in fitful gusts about its edge and frontiers.

Meanwhile the summer dimmed. The autumn winds went sighing through the woods, leaves turned to golden red, and the evenings were drawing in with cosy shadows before the first sign of anything seriously untoward made its appearance. It came then with a flat, decided kind of violence that indicated mature preparation beforehand. It was not impulsive nor ill-considered. In a fashion it seemed expected, and indeed inevitable. For within a fortnight of their annual change to the little village of Seillans above St. Raphael—a change so regular for the past ten years that it was not even discussed between them—David Bittacy abruptly refused to go.

Thompson had laid the tea-table, prepared the spirit lamp beneath the urn, pulled down the blinds in that swift and silent way she had, and left the room. The lamps were still unlit. The fire-light shone on the chintz armchairs, and Boxer lay asleep on the black horse-hair rug. Upon the walls the gilt picture frames gleamed faintly, the pictures themselves indistinguishable. Mrs. Bittacy had warmed the teapot and was in the act of pouring the water in to heat the cups when her husband, looking up from his chair across the hearth, made the abrupt announcement:

"My dear," he said, as though following a train of thought of which she only heard this final phrase, "it's really quite impossible for me to go."

And so abrupt, inconsequent, it sounded that she at first misunderstood. She thought he meant to go out into the garden or the woods. But her heart leaped all the same. The tone of his voice was ominous.

"Of course not," she answered, "it would be *most* unwise. Why should you—?" She referred to the mist that always spread on autumn nights upon the lawn, but before she finished the sentence, she knew that *he* referred to something else. And her heart then gave its second horrible leap.

"David! You mean abroad?" she gasped.

"I mean abroad, dear, yes."

It reminded her of the tone he used when saying goodbye years ago, before one of those jungle expeditions she dreaded. His voice then was so serious, so final. It was serious and final now. For several moments she could think of nothing to say. She busied herself with the teapot. She had filled one cup with hot water till it overflowed, and she emptied it slowly into the slop-basin, trying with all her might not to let him see the trembling of her hand. The firelight and the dimness of the room both helped her. But in any case, he would hardly have noticed it. His thoughts were far away . . . .

6

Mrs. Bittacy had never liked their present home. She preferred a flat, more open country that left approaches clear. She liked to see things coming. This cottage on the very edge of the old hunting grounds of William the Conqueror had never satisfied her ideal of a safe and pleasant place to settle down in. The sea-coast, with treeless downs behind and a clear horizon in front, as at Eastbourne, say, was her ideal of a proper home.

It was curious, this instinctive aversion she felt to being shut in—by trees especially; a kind of claustrophobia almost; probably due, as has been said, to the days in India when the trees took her husband off and surrounded him with dangers. In those weeks of solitude, the feeling had matured. She had fought it in her fashion, but never conquered it. Apparently routed, it had a way of creeping back in other forms. In this particular case, yielding to his strong desire, she thought the battle won, but the terror of the trees came back before the first month had passed. They laughed in her face.

She never lost knowledge of the fact that the leagues of forest lay about their cottage like a mighty wall, a crowding, watching, listening presence that shut them in from freedom and escape. Far from morbid naturally, she did her best to deny the thought, and so simple and unartificial was her type of mind that for weeks together she would wholly lose it. Then, suddenly it would return upon her with a rush of bleak reality. It was not only in her mind; it existed apart from any mere mood; a separate fear that walked alone; it came and went, yet when it went—went only to watch her from another point of view. It was in abeyance—hidden round the corner.

The forest never let her go completely. It was ever ready to encroach. All the branches, she sometimes fancied, stretched one way—towards their tiny cottage and garden, as though it sought to draw them in and merge them in itself. Its great, deep-breathing soul resented the mockery, the insolence, the irritation of the prim garden at its very gates. It would absorb and smother them if it could. And every wind that blew its thundering message over the huge sounding-board of the million, shaking trees conveyed the purpose that it had. They had angered its great soul. At its heart was this deep, incessant roaring.

All this she never framed in words, the subtleties of language lay far beyond her reach. But instinctively she felt it; and more besides. It troubled her profoundly. Chiefly, moreover, for her husband. Merely for herself, the nightmare might have left her cold. It was David's peculiar interest in the trees that gave the special invitation. Jealousy, then, in its most subtle aspect came to strengthen this aversion and dislike, for it came in a form that no reasonable wife could possibly object to. Her husband's passion, she reflected, was natural and inborn. It had decided his vocation, fed his ambition, nourished his dreams, desires, hopes.

All his best years of active life had been spent in the care and guardianship of trees. He knew them, understood their secret life and nature, "managed" them intuitively as other men "managed" dogs and horses. He could not live for long away from them without a strange, acute nostalgia that stole his peace of mind and consequently his strength of body. A forest made him happy and at peace; it nursed and fed and soothed his deepest moods. Trees influenced the sources of his life, lowered or raised the very heart-beat in him. Cut off from them he languished as a lover of the sea can droop inland, or a mountaineer may pine in the flat monotony of the plains.

This she could understand, in a fashion at least, and make allowances for. She had yielded gently, even sweetly, to his choice of their English home; for in the little island there is nothing that suggests the woods of wilder countries so nearly as the New forest. It has the genuine air and mystery, the depth and splendour, the loneliness, and there and there the strong, untameable quality of old-time forests as Bittacy of the Department knew them.

In a single detail only had he yielded to her wishes. He consented to a cottage on the edge, instead of in the heart of it. And for a dozen years now they had dwelt in peace and happiness at the lips of this great spreading thing that covered so many leagues with its tangle of swamps and moors and splendid ancient trees.

Only with the last two years or so—with his own increasing age, and physical decline perhaps—had come this marked growth of passionate interest in the welfare of the forest. She had watched it grow, at first had laughed at it, then talked sympathetically so far as sincerity permitted, then had argued mildly, and finally come to realise that its treatment lay altogether beyond her powers, and so had come to fear it with all her heart.

★★★★★★★★★★★★★★★★★

The six weeks they annually spent away from their English home, each regarded very differently, of course. For her husband it meant a painful exile that did his health no good; he yearned for his trees—the sight and sound and smell of them; but for herself it meant release from a haunting dread—escape. To renounce those six weeks by the sea on the sunny, shining coast of France, was almost more than this little woman, even with her unselfishness, could face.

After the first shock of the announcement, she reflected as deeply as her nature permitted, prayed, wept in secret—and made up her mind. Duty, she felt clearly, pointed to renouncement. The discipline would certainly be severe—she did not dream at the moment how severe!—but this fine, consistent little Christian saw it plain; she accepted it, too, without any sighing of the martyr, though the courage she showed was of the martyr order. Her husband should never know the cost.

In all but this one passion his unselfishness was ever as great as her own. The love she had borne him all these years, like the love she bore her anthropomorphic deity, was deep and real. She loved to suffer for them both. Besides, the way her husband had put it to her was singular. It did not take the form of a mere selfish predilection. Something higher than two wills in conflict seeking compromise was in it from the beginning.

"I feel, Sophia, it would be really more than I could manage," he said slowly, gazing into the fire over the tops of his stretched-out muddy boots. "My duty and my happiness lie here with the forest and with you. My life is deeply rooted in this place. Something I can't define connects my inner being with these trees, and separation would make me ill—might even kill me. My hold on life would weaken; here is my source of supply. I cannot explain it better than that." He looked up steadily into her face across the table so that she saw the gravity of his expression and the shining of his steady eyes.

"David, you feel it as strongly as that!" she said, forgetting the tea things altogether.

"Yes," he replied, "I do. And it's not of the body only, I feel it in my soul."

The reality of what he hinted at crept into that shadow-covered room like an actual Presence and stood beside them. It came not by the windows or the door, but it filled the entire space between the walls and ceiling. It took the heat from the fire before her face. She felt suddenly cold, confused a little, frightened. She almost felt the rush of foliage in the wind. It stood between them.

"There are things—some things," she faltered, "we are not intended to know, I think." The words expressed her general attitude to life, not alone to this particular incident.

And after a pause of several minutes, disregarding the criticism as though he had not heard it—"I cannot explain it better than that, you see," his grave voice answered. "There is this deep, tremendous link—some secret power they emanate that keeps me well and happy and—alive. If you cannot understand, I feel at least you may be able to—forgive." His tone grew tender, gentle, soft. "My selfishness, I know, must seem quite unforgivable. I cannot help it somehow; these trees, this ancient forest, both seem knitted into all that makes me live, and if I go—"

There was a little sound of collapse in his voice. He stopped abruptly, and sank back in his chair. And, at that, a distinct lump came up into her throat which she had great difficulty in managing while she went over and put her arms about him.

"My dear," she murmured, "God will direct. We will accept His guidance. He has always shown the way before."

"My selfishness afflicts me—" he began, but she would not let him finish.

"David, He will direct. Nothing shall harm you. You've never once been selfish, and I cannot bear to hear you say such things. The way will open that is best for you—for both of us." She kissed him, she would not let him speak; her heart was in her throat, and she felt for him far more than for herself.

And then he had suggested that she should go alone perhaps for a shorter time, and stay in her brother's villa with the children, Alice and

Stephen. It was always open to her as she well knew.

"You need the change," he said, when the lamps had been lit and the servant had gone out again; "you need it as much as I dread it. I could manage somehow until you returned, and should feel happier that way if you went. I cannot leave this forest that I love so well. I even feel, Sophie dear"—he sat up straight and faced her as he half whispered it—"that I can *never* leave it again. My life and happiness lie here together."

And even while scorning the idea that she could leave him alone with the Influence of the forest all about him to have its unimpeded way, she felt the pangs of that subtle jealousy bite keen and close. He loved the forest better than herself, for he placed it first. Behind the words, moreover, hid the unuttered thought that made her so uneasy. The terror Sanderson had brought revived and shook its wings before her very eyes. For the whole conversation, of which this was a fragment, conveyed the unutterable implication that while he could not spare the trees, they equally could not spare him. The vividness with which he managed to conceal and yet betray the fact brought a profound distress that crossed the border between presentiment and warning into positive alarm.

He clearly felt that the trees would miss him—the trees he tended, guarded, watched over, loved.

"David, I shall stay here with you. I think you need me really—don't you?" Eagerly, with a touch of heart-felt passion, the words poured out.

"Now more than ever, dear. God bless you for your sweet unselfishness. And your sacrifice," he added, "is all the greater because you cannot understand the thing that makes it necessary for me to stay."

"Perhaps in the spring instead—" she said, with a tremor in the voice.

"In the spring—perhaps," he answered gently, almost beneath his breath. "For they will not need me then. All the world can love them in the spring. It's in the winter that they're lonely and neglected. I wish to stay with them particularly then. I even feel I ought to—and I must."

And in this way, without further speech, the decision was made. Mrs. Bittacy, at least, asked no more questions. Yet she could not bring herself to show more sympathy than was necessary. She felt, for one thing, that if she did, it might lead him to speak freely, and to tell her things she could not possibly bear to know. And she dared not take the risk of that.

7

This was at the end of summer, but the autumn followed close. The conversation really marked the threshold between the two seasons, and marked at the same time the line between her husband's negative and aggressive state. She almost felt she had done wrong to yield; he grew so bold, concealment all discarded. He went, that is, quite openly to the woods, forgetting all his duties, all his former occupations. He even sought to coax her to go with him. The hidden thing blazed out without disguise. And, while she trembled at his energy, she admired the virile passion he displayed. Her jealousy had long ago retired before her fear, accepting the second place. Her one desire now was to protect. The wife turned wholly mother.

He said so little, but—he hated to come in. From morning to night, he wandered in the forest; often he went out after dinner; his mind was charged with trees—their foliage, growth, development; their wonder, beauty, strength; their loneliness in isolation, their power in a herded mass. He knew the effect of every wind upon them; the danger from the boisterous north, the glory from the west, the eastern dryness, and the soft, moist tenderness that a south wind left upon their thinning boughs.

He spoke all day of their sensations: how they drank the fading sunshine, dreamed in the moonlight, thrilled to the kiss of stars. The dew could bring them half the passion of the night, but frost sent them plunging beneath the ground to dwell with hopes of a later coming softness in their roots. They nursed the life they carried—insects, larvae, chrysalis—and when the skies above them melted, he spoke of them standing "motionless in an ecstasy of rain," or in the noon of sunshine "self-poised upon their prodigy of shade."

And once in the middle of the night she woke at the sound of his voice, and heard him—wide awake, not talking in his sleep—but talking towards the window where the shadow of the cedar fell at noon:

O art thou sighing for Lebanon
In the long breeze that streams to thy delicious East?
Sighing for Lebanon,
Dark cedar;

. . . and, when, half charmed, half terrified, she turned and called to him by name, he merely said—

"My dear, I felt the loneliness—suddenly realised it—the alien

131

desolation of that tree, set here upon our little lawn in England when all her Eastern brothers call her in sleep." And the answer seemed so queer, so "un-evangelical," that she waited in silence till he slept again. The poetry passed her by. It seemed unnecessary and out of place. It made her ache with suspicion, fear, jealousy.

The fear, however, seemed somehow all lapped up and banished soon afterwards by her unwilling admiration of the rushing splendour of her husband's state. Her anxiety, at any rate, shifted from the religious to the medical. She thought he might be losing his steadiness of mind a little. How often in her prayers she offered thanks for the guidance that had made her stay with him to help and watch is impossible to say. It certainly was twice a day.

She even went so far once, when Mr. Mortimer, the vicar, called, and brought with him a more or less distinguished doctor—as to tell the professional man privately some symptoms of her husband's queerness. And his answer that there was "nothing he could prescribe for" added not a little to her sense of unholy bewilderment. No doubt Sir James had never been "consulted" under such unorthodox conditions before. His sense of what was becoming naturally overrode his acquired instincts as a skilled instrument that might help the race.

"No fever, you think?" she asked insistently with hurry, determined to get something from him.

"Nothing that *I* can deal with, as I told you, Madam," replied the offended allopathic Knight.

Evidently, he did not care about being invited to examine patients in this surreptitious way before a teapot on the lawn, chance of a fee most problematical. He liked to see a tongue and feel a thumping pulse; to know the pedigree and bank account of his questioner as well. It was most unusual, in abominable taste besides. Of course, it was. But the drowning woman seized the only straw she could.

For now, the aggressive attitude of her husband overcame her to the point where she found it difficult even to question him. Yet in the house he was so kind and gentle, doing all he could to make her sacrifice as easy as possible.

"David, you really *are* unwise to go out now. The night is damp and very chilly. The ground is soaked in dew. You'll catch your death of cold."

His face lightened. "Won't you come with me, dear—just for once? I'm only going to the corner of the hollies to see the beech that stands so lonely by itself."

She had been out with him in the short dark afternoon, and they had passed that evil group of hollies where the gypsies camped. Nothing else would grow there, but the hollies thrive upon the stony soil.

"David, the beech is all right and safe." She had learned his phraseology a little, made clever out of due season by her love. "There's no wind tonight."

"But it's rising," he answered, "rising in the east. I heard it in the bare and hungry larches. They need the sun and dew, and always cry out when the wind's upon them from the east."

She sent a short, unspoken prayer most swiftly to her deity as she heard him say it. For every time now, when he spoke in this familiar, intimate way of the life of the trees, she felt a sheet of cold fasten tight against her very skin and flesh. She shivered. How could he possibly know such things?

Yet, in all else, and in the relations of his daily life, he was sane and reasonable, loving, kind and tender. It was only on the subject of the trees he seemed unhinged and queer. Most curiously it seemed that, since the collapse of the cedar they both loved, though in different fashion, his departure from the normal had increased. Why else did he watch them as a man might watch a sickly child? Why did he hunger especially in the dusk to catch their "mood of night" as he called it? Why think so carefully upon them when the frost was threatening or the wind appeared to rise?

As she put it so frequently now herself—How could he possibly *know* such things?

He went. As she closed the front door after him, she heard the distant roaring in the forest.

★★★★★★★★★★★★★★★★★

And then it suddenly struck her: How could she know them too?

It dropped upon her like a blow that she felt at once all over, upon body, heart and mind. The discovery rushed out from its ambush to overwhelm. The truth of it, making all arguing futile, numbed her faculties. But though at first it deadened her, she soon revived, and her being rose into aggressive opposition. A wild yet calculated courage like that which animates the leaders of splendid forlorn hopes flamed in her little person—flamed grandly, and invincible.

While knowing herself insignificant and weak, she knew at the same time that power at her back which moves the worlds. The faith that filled her was the weapon in her hands, and the right by which she claimed it; but the spirit of utter, selfless sacrifice that characterised her life was the means by which she mastered its immediate use. For a kind of white and faultless intuition guided her to the attack. Behind her stood her Bible and her God.

How so magnificent a divination came to her at all may well be a matter for astonishment, though some clue of explanation lies, perhaps, in the very simpleness of her nature. At any rate, she saw quite clearly certain things; saw them in moments only—after prayer, in the still silence of the night, or when left alone those long hours in the house with her knitting and her thoughts—and the guidance which then flashed into her remained, even after the manner of its coming was forgotten.

They came to her, these things she saw, formless, wordless; she could not put them into any kind of language; but by the very fact of being uncaught in sentences they retained their original clear vigour.

Hours of patient waiting brought the first, and the others followed easily afterwards, by degrees, on subsequent days, a little and a little. Her husband had been gone since early morning, and had taken his luncheon with him. She was sitting by the tea things, the cups and teapot warmed, the muffins in the fender keeping hot, all ready for his return, when she realised quite abruptly that this thing which took him off, which kept him out so many hours day after day, this thing that was against her own little will and instincts—was enormous as the sea. It was no mere prettiness of single trees, but something massed and mountainous.

About her rose the wall of its huge opposition to the sky, its scale gigantic, its power utterly prodigious. What she knew of it hitherto as green and delicate forms waving and rustling in the winds was but, as it were the spray of foam that broke into sight upon the nearer edge of viewless depths far, far away. The trees, indeed, were sentinels set visibly about the limits of a camp that itself remained invisible. The awful hum and murmur of the main body in the distance passed into that still room about her with the firelight and hissing kettle. Out yonder—in the forest further out—the thing that was ever roaring at the centre was dreadfully increasing.

The sense of definite battle, too—battle between herself and the forest for his soul—came with it. Its presentiment was as clear as though Thompson had come into the room and quietly told her that the cottage was surrounded. "Please, ma'am, there are trees come up about the house," she might have suddenly announced. And equally might have heard her own answer: "It's all right, Thompson. The main body is still far away."

Immediately upon its heels, then, came another truth, with a close reality that shocked her. She saw that jealousy was not confined to the human and animal world alone, but ran though all creation. The Vegetable Kingdom knew it too. So-called inanimate nature shared it with the rest. Trees felt it. This forest just beyond the window—standing there in the silence of the autumn evening across the little lawn—this forest understood it equally. The remorseless, branching power that sought to keep exclusively for itself the thing it loved and needed, spread like a running desire through all its million leaves and stems and roots.

In humans, of course, it was consciously directed; in animals it acted with frank instinctiveness; but in trees this jealousy rose in some blind tide of impersonal and unconscious wrath that would sweep opposition from its path as the wind sweeps powdered snow from the surface of the ice. Their number was a host with endless reinforcements, and once it realised its passion was returned the power increased . . . . Her husband loved the trees . . . . They had become aware of it . . . . They would take him from her in the end . . . .

Then, while she heard his footsteps in the hall and the closing of the front door, she saw a third thing clearly;—realised the widening of the gap between herself and him. This other love had made it. All these weeks of the summer when she felt so close to him, now especially when she had made the biggest sacrifice of her life to stay by his side and help him, he had been slowly, surely—drawing away. The estrangement was here and now—a fact accomplished. It had been all this time maturing; there yawned this broad deep space between them. Across the empty distance she saw the change in merciless perspective. It revealed his face and figure, dearly-loved, once fondly worshipped, far on the other side in shadowy distance, small, the back turned from her, and moving while she watched—moving away from her.

They had their tea in silence then. She asked no questions, he volunteered no information of his day. The heart was big within her, and the terrible loneliness of age spread through her like a rising icy mist. She watched him, filling all his wants. His hair was untidy and his boots were caked with blackish mud. He moved with a restless, swaying motion that somehow blanched her cheek and sent a miserable shivering down her back. It reminded her of trees. His eyes were very bright.

He brought in with him an odour of the earth and forest that seemed to choke her and make it difficult to breathe; and—what she noticed with a climax of almost uncontrollable alarm—upon his face beneath the lamplight shone traces of a mild, faint glory that made her think of moonlight falling upon a wood through speckled shadows. It was his new-found happiness that shone there, a happiness uncaused by her and in which she had no part.

In his coat was a spray of faded yellow beech leaves. "I brought this from the forest to you," he said, with all the air that belonged to his little acts of devotion long ago. And she took the spray of leaves mechanically with a smile and a murmured "thank you, dear," as though he had unknowingly put into her hands the weapon for her own destruction and she had accepted it.

And when the tea was over and he left the room, he did not go to his study, or to change his clothes. She heard the front door softly shut behind him as he again went out towards the forest.

A moment later she was in her room upstairs, kneeling beside the bed—the side she slept on—and praying wildly through a flood of tears that God would save and keep him to her. Wind brushed the window panes behind her while she knelt.

8

One sunny November morning, when the strain had reached a pitch that made repression almost unmanageable, she came to an impulsive decision, and obeyed it. Her husband had again gone out with luncheon for the day. She took adventure in her hands and followed him. The power of seeing-clear was strong upon her, forcing her up to some unnatural level of understanding. To stay indoors and wait inactive for his return seemed suddenly impossible. She meant to know what he knew, feel what he felt, put herself in his place. She would dare the fascination of the forest—share it with him. It was greatly daring; but it would give her greater understanding how to help and save him and therefore greater Power. She went upstairs a moment first to pray.

In a thick, warm skirt, and wearing heavy boots—those walking boots she used with him upon the mountains about Seillans—she left the cottage by the back way and turned towards the forest. She could not actually follow him, for he had started off an hour before and she knew not exactly his direction. What was so urgent in her was the wish to be with him in the woods, to walk beneath leafless branches just as he did: to be there when he was there, even though not together. For it had come to her that she might thus share with him for once this horrible mighty life and breathing of the trees he loved.

In winter, he had said, they needed him particularly, and winter now was coming. Her love must bring her something of what he felt himself—the huge attraction, the suction and the pull of all the trees. Thus, in some vicarious fashion, she might share, though unknown to himself, this very thing that was taking him away from her. She might thus even lessen its attack upon himself.

The impulse came to her clairvoyantly, and she obeyed without a sign of hesitation. Deeper comprehension would come to her of the whole awful puzzle. And come it did, yet not in the way she imagined and expected.

The air was very still, the sky a cold pale blue, but cloudless. The entire forest stood silent, at attention. It knew perfectly well that she had come. It knew the moment when she entered; watched and followed her; and behind her something dropped without a sound and shut her in. Her feet upon the glades of mossy grass fell silently, as the oaks and beeches shifted past in rows and took up their positions at her back. It was not pleasant, this way they grew so dense behind her the instant she had passed. She realised that they gathered in an ever-growing army, massed, herded, trooped, between her and the cottage, shutting off escape. They let her pass so easily, but to get out again she would know them differently—thick, crowded, branches all drawn and hostile.

Already their increasing numbers bewildered her. In front, they looked so sparse and scattered, with open spaces where the sunshine fell; but when she turned it seemed they stood so close together, a serried army, darkening the sunlight. They blocked the day, collected all the shadows, stood with their leafless and forbidding rampart like the night. They swallowed down into themselves the very glade by which she came. For when she glanced behind her—rarely—the way she had come was shadowy and lost.

Yet the morning sparkled overhead, and a glance of excitement ran quivering through the entire day. It was what she always knew as "children's weather," so clear and harmless, without a sign of danger, nothing ominous to threaten or alarm. Steadfast in her purpose, looking back as little as she dared, Sophia Bittacy marched slowly and deliberately into the heart of the silent woods, deeper, ever deeper.

And then, abruptly, in an open space where the sunshine fell unhindered, she stopped. It was one of the breathing places of the forest.

Dead, withered bracken lay in patches of unsightly grey. There were bits of heather too. All round the trees stood looking on—oak, beech, holly, ash, pine, larch, with here and there small groups of juniper. On the lips of this breathing space of the woods she stopped to rest, disobeying her instinct for the first time. For the other instinct in her was to go on. She did not really want to rest.

This was the little act that brought it to her—the wireless message from a vast Emitter.

"I've been stopped," she thought to herself with a horrid qualm.

She looked about her in this quiet, ancient place. Nothing stirred. There was no life nor sign of life; no birds sang; no rabbits scuttled off at her approach. The stillness was bewildering, and gravity hung down upon it like a heavy curtain. It hushed the heart in her. Could this be part of what her husband felt—this sense of thick entanglement with stems, boughs, roots, and foliage?

"This has always been as it is now," she thought, yet not knowing why she thought it. "Ever since the forest grew it has been still and secret here. It has never changed." The curtain of silence drew closer while she said it, thickening round her. "For a thousand years—I'm here with a thousand years. And behind this place stand all the forests of the world!"

So foreign to her temperament were such thoughts, and so alien to all she had been taught to look for in Nature, that she strove against them. She made an effort to oppose. But they clung and haunted just the same; they refused to be dispersed. The curtain hung dense and heavy as though its texture thickened. The air with difficulty came through.

And then she thought that curtain stirred. There was movement somewhere. That obscure dim thing which ever broods behind the visible appearances of trees came nearer to her. She caught her breath and stared about her, listening intently. The trees, perhaps because she saw them more in detail now, it seemed to her had changed. A vague, faint alteration spread over them, at first so slight she scarcely would admit it, then growing steadily, though still obscurely, outwards. "They tremble and are changed," flashed through her mind the horrid line that Sanderson had quoted. Yet the change was graceful for all the uncouthness attendant upon the size of so vast a movement. They had turned in her direction.

That was it. *They saw her.* In this way the change expressed itself in her groping, terrified thought. Till now it had been otherwise: she had looked at them from her own point of view; now they looked at her from theirs. They stared her in the face and eyes; they stared at her all over. In some unkind, resentful, hostile way, they watched her. Hitherto in life she had watched them variously, in superficial ways, reading into them what her own mind suggested. Now they read into her the things they actually *were*, and not merely another's interpretations of them.

They seemed in their motionless silence there instinct with life, a life, moreover, that breathed about her a species of terrible soft enchantment that bewitched. It branched all through her, climbing to the brain. The forest held her with its huge and giant fascination. In this secluded breathing spot that the centuries had left untouched, she had stepped close against the hidden pulse of the whole collective mass of them. They were aware of her and had turned to gaze with their myriad, vast sight upon the intruder. They shouted at her in the silence. For she wanted to look back at them, but it was like staring at a crowd, and her glance merely shifted from one tree to another, hurriedly, finding in none the one she sought. They saw her so easily, each and all. The rows that stood behind her also stared. But she could not return the gaze. Her husband, she realised, could. And their steady stare shocked her as though in some sense she knew that she was naked. They saw so much of her: she saw of them—so little.

Her efforts to return their gaze were pitiful. The constant shifting increased her bewilderment. Conscious of this awful and enormous sight all over her, she let her eyes first rest upon the ground, and then she closed them altogether. She kept the lids as tight together as ever they would go.

But the sight of the trees came even into that inner darkness behind the fastened lids, for there was no escaping it. Outside, in the light, she still knew that the leaves of the hollies glittered smoothly, that the dead foliage of the oaks hung crisp in the air about her, that the needles of the little junipers were pointing all one way. The spread perception of the forest was focused on herself, and no mere shutting of the eyes could hide its scattered yet concentrated stare—the all-inclusive vision of great woods.

There was no wind, yet here and there a single leaf hanging by its dried-up stalk shook all alone with great rapidity—rattling. It was the sentry drawing attention to her presence. And then, again, as once long weeks before, she felt their Being as a tide about her. The tide had turned. That memory of her childhood sands came back, when the nurse said, "The tide has turned now; we must go in," and she saw the mass of piled-up waters, green and heaped to the horizon, and realised that it was slowly coming in. The gigantic mass of it, too vast for hurry, loaded with massive purpose, she used to feel, was moving towards herself. The fluid body of the sea was creeping along beneath the sky to the very spot upon the yellow sands where she stood and played. The sight and thought of it had always overwhelmed her with a sense of awe—as though her puny self were the object of the whole sea's advance. "The tide has turned; we had better now go in."

This was happening now about her—the same thing was happening in the woods—slow, sure, and steady, and its motion as little discernible as the sea's. The tide had turned. The small human presence that had ventured among its green and mountainous depths, moreover, was its objective.

That all was clear within her while she sat and waited with tight-shut lids. But the next moment she opened her eyes with a sudden realisation of something more. The presence that it sought was after all not hers. It was the presence of someone other than herself. And then she understood. Her eyes had opened with a click, it seemed, but the sound, in reality, was outside herself.

Across the clearing where the sunshine lay so calm and still, she saw the figure of her husband moving among the trees—a man, like a tree, walking.

With hands behind his back, and head uplifted, he moved quite slowly, as though absorbed in his own thoughts. Hardly fifty paces separated them, but he had no inkling of her presence there so near. With mind intent and senses all turned inwards, he marched past her like a figure in a dream, and like a figure in a dream she saw him go. Love, yearning, pity rose in a storm within her, but as in nightmare she found no words or movement possible. She sat and watched him go—go from her—go into the deeper reaches of the green enveloping woods.

Desire to save, to bid him stop and turn, ran in a passion through her being, but there was nothing she could do. She saw him go away from her, go of his own accord and willingly beyond her; she saw the branches drop about his steps and hid him. His figure faded out among the speckled shade and sunlight. The trees covered him. The tide just took him, all unresisting and content to go. Upon the bosom of the green soft sea, he floated away beyond her reach of vision. Her eyes could follow him no longer. He was gone.

And then for the first time she realised, even at that distance, that the look upon his face was one of peace and happiness—rapt, and caught away in joy, a look of youth. That expression now he never showed to her. But she *had* known it. Years ago, in the early days of their married life, she had seen it on his face. Now it no longer obeyed the summons of her presence and her love. The woods alone could call it forth; it answered to the trees; the forest had taken every part of him—from her—his very heart and soul.

Her sight that had plunged inwards to the fields of faded memory now came back to outer things again. She looked about her, and her love, returning empty-handed and unsatisfied, left her open to the invading of the bleakest terror she had ever known. That such things could be real and happen found her helpless utterly. Terror invaded the quietest corners of her heart, that had never yet known quailing. She could not—for moments at any rate—reach either her Bible or her God. Desolate in an empty world of fear she sat with eyes too dry and hot for tears, yet with a coldness as of ice upon her very flesh. She stared, unseeing, about her. That horror which stalks in the stillness of the noonday, when the glare of an artificial sunshine lights up the motionless trees, moved all about her. In front and behind she was aware of it.

Beyond this stealthy silence, just within the edge of it, the things of another world were passing. But she could not know them. Her husband knew them, knew their beauty and their awe, yes, but for her they were out of reach. She might not share with him the very least of them. It seemed that behind and through the glare of this wintry noonday in the heart of the woods there brooded another universe of life and passion, for her all unexpressed. The silence veiled it, the stillness hid it; but he moved with it all and understood. His love interpreted it.

She rose to her feet, tottered feebly, and collapsed again upon the moss. Yet for herself she felt no terror; no little personal fear could touch her whose anguish and deep longing streamed all out to him whom she so bravely loved. In this time of utter self-forgetfulness, when she realised that the battle was hopeless, thinking she had lost even her God, she found Him again quite close beside her like a little Presence in this terrible heart of the hostile forest. But at first, she did not recognise that He was there; she did not know Him in that strangely unacceptable guise. For He stood so very close, so very intimate, so very sweet and comforting, and yet so hard to understand—as Resignation.

★★★★★★★★★★★★★★★★★

Once more she struggled to her feet, and this time turned successfully and slowly made her way along the mossy glade by which she came. And at first, she marvelled, though only for a moment, at the ease with which she found the path. For a moment only, because almost at once she saw the truth. The trees were glad that she should go. They helped her on her way. The forest did not want her.

The tide was coming in, indeed, yet not for her.

And so, in another of those flashes of clear-vision that of late had lifted life above the normal level, she saw and understood the whole terrible thing complete.

Till now, though unexpressed in thought or language, her fear had been that the woods her husband loved would somehow take him from her—to merge his life in theirs—even to kill him on some mysterious way. This time she saw her deep mistake, and so seeing, let in upon herself the fuller agony of horror. For their jealousy was not the petty jealousy of animals or humans. They wanted him because they loved him, but they did *not* want him dead. Full charged with his splendid life and enthusiasm they wanted him. They wanted him—alive.

It was she who stood in their way, and it was she whom they intended to remove.

This was what brought the sense of abject helplessness. She stood upon the sands against an entire ocean slowly rolling in against her. For, as all the forces of a human being combine unconsciously to eject a grain of sand that has crept beneath the skin to cause discomfort, so the entire mass of what Sanderson had called the Collective Consciousness of the forest strove to eject this human atom that stood across the path of its desire. Loving her husband, she had crept beneath its skin.

It was her they would eject and take away; it was her they would destroy, not him. Him, whom they loved and needed, they would keep alive. They meant to take him living. She reached the house in safety, though she never remembered how she found her way. It was made all simple for her. The branches almost urged her out.

But behind her, as she left the shadowed precincts, she felt as though some towering Angel of the Woods let fall across the threshold the flaming sword of a countless multitude of leaves that formed behind her a barrier, green, shimmering, and impassable. Into the forest she never walked again.

★★★★★★★★★★★★★★★★★

And she went about her daily duties with a calm and quietness that was a perpetual astonishment even to herself, for it hardly seemed of this world at all. She talked to her husband when he came in for tea—after dark. Resignation brings a curious large courage—when there is nothing more to lose. The soul takes risks, and dares. Is it a curious short-cut sometimes to the heights?

"David, I went into the forest, too, this morning, soon after you I went. I saw you there."

"Wasn't it wonderful?" he answered simply, inclining his head a little. There was no surprise or annoyance in his look; a mild and gentle *ennui* rather. He asked no real question. She thought of some garden tree the wind attacks too suddenly, bending it over when it does not want to bend—the mild unwillingness with which it yields. She often saw him this way now, in the terms of trees.

"It was very wonderful indeed, dear, yes," she replied low, her voice not faltering though indistinct. "But for me it was too—too strange and big."

The passion of tears lay just below the quiet voice all unbetrayed. Somehow, she kept them back.

There was a pause, and then he added:

"I find it more and more so every day." His voice passed through the lamp-lit room like a murmur of the wind in branches. The look of youth and happiness she had caught upon his face out there had wholly gone, and an expression of weariness was in its place, as of a man distressed vaguely at finding himself in uncongenial surroundings where he is slightly ill at ease. It was the house he hated—coming back to rooms and walls and furniture. The ceilings and closed windows confined him. Yet, in it, no suggestion that he found *her* irksome. Her presence seemed of no account at all; indeed, he hardly noticed her. For whole long periods he lost her, did not know that she was there. He had no need of her. He lived alone. Each lived alone.

The outward signs by which she recognised that the awful battle was against her and the terms of surrender accepted were pathetic. She put the medicine-chest away upon the shelf; she gave the orders for his pocket-luncheon before he asked; she went to bed alone and early, leaving the front door unlocked, with milk and bread and butter in the hall beside the lamp—all concessions that she felt impelled to make. For more and more, unless the weather was too violent, he went out after dinner even, staying for hours in the woods.

But she never slept until she heard the front door close below, and knew soon afterwards his careful step come creeping up the stairs and into the room so softly. Until she heard his regular deep breathing close beside her, she lay awake. All strength or desire to resist had gone for good. The thing against her was too huge and powerful. Capitulation was complete, a fact accomplished. She dated it from the day she followed him to the forest.

Moreover, the time for evacuation—her own evacuation—seemed approaching. It came stealthily ever nearer, surely and slowly as the rising tide she used to dread. At the high-water mark she stood waiting calmly—waiting to be swept away. Across the lawn all those terrible days of early winter the encircling forest watched it come, guiding its silent swell and currents towards her feet. Only she never once gave up her Bible or her praying. This complete resignation, moreover, had somehow brought to her a strange great understanding, and if she could not share her husband's horrible abandonment to powers outside himself, she could, and did, in some half-groping way grasp at shadowy meanings that might make such abandonment—possible, yes, but more than merely possible—in some extraordinary sense not evil.

Hitherto she had divided the beyond-world into two sharp halves—spirits good or spirits evil. But thoughts came to her now, on soft and very tentative feet, like the footsteps of the gods which are on wool, that besides these definite classes, there might be other Powers as well, belonging definitely to neither one nor other. Her thought stopped dead at that. But the big idea found lodgement in her little mind, and, owing to the largeness of her heart, remained there unejected. It even brought a certain solace with it.

The failure—or unwillingness, as she preferred to state it—of her God to interfere and help, that also she came in a measure to understand. For here, she found it more and more possible to imagine, was perhaps no positive evil at work, but only something that usually stands away from humankind, something alien and not commonly recognised. There *was* a gulf fixed between the two, and Mr. Sanderson *had* bridged it, by his talk, his explanations, his attitude of mind. Through these her husband had found the way into it. His temperament and natural passion for the woods had prepared the soul in him, and the moment he saw the way to go he took it—the line of least resistance.

Life was, of course, open to all, and her husband had the right to choose it where he would. He had chosen it—away from her, away from other men, but not necessarily away from God. This was an enormous concession that she skirted, never really faced; it was too revolutionary to face. But its possibility peeped into her bewildered mind. It might delay his progress, or it might advance it. Who could know? And why should God, who ordered all things with such magnificent detail, from the pathway of a sun to the falling of a sparrow, object to his free choice, or interfere to hinder him and stop?

She came to realise resignation, that is, in another aspect. It gave her comfort, if not peace. She fought against all belittling of her God. It was, perhaps, enough that He—knew.

"You are not alone, dear in the trees out there?" she ventured one night, as he crept on tiptoe into the room not far from midnight. "God is with you?"

"Magnificently," was the immediate answer, given with enthusiasm, "for He is everywhere. And I only wish that you—"

But she stuffed the clothes against her ears. That invitation on his lips was more than she could bear to hear. It seemed like asking her to hurry to her own execution. She buried her face among the sheets and blankets, shaking all over like a leaf.

9

And so, the thought that she was the one to go remained and grew. It was, perhaps, first sign of that weakening of the mind which indicated the singular manner of her going. For it was her mental opposition, the trees felt, that stood in their way. Once that was overcome, obliterated, her physical presence did not matter. She would be harmless.

Having accepted defeat, because she had come to feel that his obsession was not actually evil, she accepted at the same time the conditions of an atrocious loneliness. She stood now from her husband farther than from the moon. They had no visitors. Callers were few and far between, and less encouraged than before. The empty dark of winter was before them.

Among the neighbours was none in whom, without disloyalty to her husband, she could confide. Mr. Mortimer, had he been single, might have helped her in this desert of solitude that preyed upon her mind, but his wife was there the obstacle; for Mrs. Mortimer wore sandals, believed that nuts were the complete food of man, and indulged in other idiosyncrasies that classed her inevitably among the "latter signs" which Mrs. Bittacy had been taught to dread as dangerous. She stood most desolately alone.

Solitude, therefore, in which the mind unhindered feeds upon its own delusions, was the assignable cause of her gradual mental disruption and collapse.

With the definite arrival of the colder weather her husband gave up his rambles after dark; evenings were spent together over the fire; he read *The Times*; they even talked about their postponed visit abroad in the coming spring. No restlessness was on him at the change; he seemed content and easy in his mind; spoke little of the trees and woods; enjoyed far better health than if there had been change of scene, and to herself was tender, kind, solicitous over trifles, as in the distant days of their first honeymoon.

But this deep calm could not deceive her; it meant, she fully understood, that he felt sure of himself, sure of her, and sure of the trees as well. It all lay buried in the depths of him, too secure and deep, too intimately established in his central being to permit of those surface fluctuations which betray disharmony within. His life was hid with trees. Even the fever, so dreaded in the damp of winter, left him free. She now knew why: the fever was due to their efforts to obtain him, his efforts to respond and go—physical results of a fierce unrest he had never understood till Sanderson came with his wicked explanations. Now it was otherwise. The bridge was made. And—he had gone.

And she, brave, loyal, and consistent soul, found herself utterly alone, even trying to make his passage easy. It seemed that she stood at the bottom of some huge ravine that opened in her mind, the walls whereof instead of rock were trees that reached enormous to the sky, engulfing her. God alone knew that she was there. He watched, permitted, even perhaps approved. At any rate—He knew.

During those quiet evenings in the house, moreover, while they sat over the fire listening to the roaming winds about the house, her husband knew continual access to the world his alien love had furnished for him. Never for a single instant was he cut off from it. She gazed at the newspaper spread before his face and knees, saw the smoke of his cheroot curl up above the edge, noticed the little hole in his evening socks, and listened to the paragraphs he read aloud as of old. But this was all a veil he spread about himself of purpose.

Behind it—he escaped. It was the conjurer's trick to divert the sight to unimportant details while the essential thing went forward unobserved. He managed wonderfully; she loved him for the pains he took to spare her distress; but all the while she knew that the body lolling in that armchair before her eyes contained the merest fragment of his actual self. It was little better than a corpse. It was an empty shell.

146

The essential soul of him was out yonder with the forest—farther out near that ever-roaring heart of it.

And, with the dark, the forest came up boldly and pressed against the very walls and windows, peering in upon them, joining hands above the slates and chimneys. The winds were always walking on the lawn and gravel paths; steps came and went and came again; some one seemed always talking in the woods, someone was in the building too. She passed them on the stairs, or running soft and muffled, very large and gentle, down the passages and landings after dusk, as though loose fragments of the day had broken off and stayed there caught among the shadows, trying to get out. They blundered silently all about the house. They waited till she passed, then made a run for it.

And her husband always knew. She saw him more than once deliberately avoid them—because *she* was there. More than once, too, she saw him stand and listen when he thought she was not near, then heard herself the long bounding stride of their approach across the silent garden. Already *he* had heard them in the windy distance of the night, far, far away. They sped, she well knew, along that glade of mossy turf by which she last came out; it cushioned their tread exactly as it had cushioned her own.

It seemed to her the trees were always in the house with him, and in their very bedroom. He welcomed them, unaware that she also knew, and trembled.

One night in their bedroom it caught her unawares. She woke out of deep sleep and it came upon her before she could gather her forces for control.

The day had been wildly boisterous, but now the wind had dropped, only its rags went fluttering through the night. The rays of the full moon fell in a shower between the branches. Overhead still raced the scud and wrack, shaped like hurrying monsters; but below the earth was quiet. Still and dripping stood the hosts of trees. Their trunks gleamed wet and sparkling where the moon caught them. There was a strong smell of mould and fallen leaves. The air was sharp—heavy with odour.

And she knew all this the instant that she woke; for it seemed to her that she had been elsewhere—following her husband—as though she had been *out*! There was no dream at all, merely the definite, haunting certainty. It dived away, lost, buried in the night. She sat upright in bed. She had come back.

The room shone pale in the moonlight reflected through the windows, for the blinds were up, and she saw her husband's form beside her, motionless in deep sleep. But what caught her unawares was the horrid thing that by this fact of sudden, unexpected waking she had surprised these other things in the room, beside the very bed, gathered close about him while he slept. It was their dreadful boldness—herself of no account as it were—that terrified her into screaming before she could collect her powers to prevent.

She screamed before she realised what she did—a long, high shriek of terror that filled the room, yet made so little actual sound. For wet and shimmering presences stood grouped all round that bed. She saw their outline underneath the ceiling, the green, spread bulk of them, their vague extension over walls and furniture. They shifted to and fro, massed yet translucent, mild yet thick, moving and turning within themselves to a hushed noise of multitudinous soft rustling. In their sound was something very sweet and sinning that fell into her with a spell of horrible enchantment. They were so mild, each one alone, yet so terrific in their combination. Cold seized her. The sheets against her body had turned to ice.

She screamed a second time, though the sound hardly issued from her throat. The spell sank deeper, reaching to the heart; for it softened all the currents of her blood and took life from her in a stream—towards themselves. Resistance in that moment seemed impossible.

Her husband then stirred in his sleep, and woke. And, instantly, the forms drew up, erect, and gathered themselves in some amazing way together. They lessened in extent—then scattered through the air like an effect of light when shadows seek to smother it. It was tremendous, yet most exquisite. A sheet of pale-green shadow that yet had form and substance filled the room. There was a rush of silent movement, as the Presences drew past her through the air—and they were gone.

But, clearest of all, she saw the manner of their going; for she recognised in their tumult of escape by the window open at the top, the same wide "looping circles"—spirals as it seemed—that she had seen upon the lawn those weeks ago when Sanderson had talked. The room once more was empty.

In the collapse that followed, she heard her husband's voice, as though coming from some great distance. Her own replies she heard as well. Both were so strange and unlike their normal speech, the very words unnatural.

"What is it, dear? Why do you wake me *now*?" And his voice whispered it with a sighing sound, like wind in pine boughs.

"A moment since something went past me through the air of the room. Back to the night outside it went." Her voice, too, held the same note as of wind entangled among too many leaves.

"My dear, I *was* the wind."

"But it called, David. It was calling *you*—by name!"

"The air of the branches, dear, was what you heard. Now, sleep again, I beg you, sleep."

"It had a crowd of eyes all through and over it—before and behind—" Her voice grew louder. But his own in reply sank lower, far away, and oddly hushed.

"The moonlight, dear, upon the sea of twigs and boughs in the rain, was what you saw."

"But it frightened me. I've lost my God—and you—I'm cold as death!"

"My dear, it is the cold of the early morning hours. The whole world sleeps. Now sleep again yourself."

He whispered close to her ear. She felt his hand stroking her. His voice was soft and very soothing. But only a part of him was there; only a part of him was speaking; it was a half-emptied body that lay beside her and uttered these strange sentences, even forcing her own singular choice of words. The horrible, dim enchantment of the trees was close about them in the room—gnarled, ancient, lonely trees of winter, whispering round the human life they loved.

"And let me sleep again," she heard him murmur as he settled down among the clothes, "sleep back into that deep, delicious peace from which you called me."

His dreamy, happy tone, and that look of youth and joy she discerned upon his features even in the filtered moonlight, touched her again as with the spell of those shining, mild green presences. It sank down into her. She felt sleep grope for her. On the threshold of slumber one of those strange vagrant voices that loss of consciousness lets loose cried faintly in her heart—

"There is joy in the forest over one sinner that—"

Then sleep took her before she had time to realise even that she was vilely parodying one of her most precious texts, and that the irreverence was ghastly.

And though she quickly slept again, her sleep was not as usual, dreamless. It was not woods and trees she dreamed of, but a small and curious dream that kept coming again and again upon her; that she stood upon a wee, bare rock in the sea, and that the tide was rising.

The water first came to her feet, then to her knees, then to her waist. Each time the dream returned, the tide seemed higher. Once it rose to her neck, once even to her mouth, covering her lips for a moment so that she could not breathe. She did not wake between the dreams; a period of drab and dreamless slumber intervened. But, finally, the water rose above her eyes and face, completely covering her head.

And then came explanation—the sort of explanation dreams bring. She understood. For, beneath the water, she had seen the world of seaweed rising from the bottom of the sea like a forest of dense green-long, sinuous stems, immense thick branches, millions of feelers spreading through the darkened watery depths the power of their ocean foliage. The Vegetable Kingdom was even in the sea. It was everywhere. Earth, air, and water helped it, way of escape there was none.

And even underneath the sea she heard that terrible sound of roaring—was it surf or wind or voices?—further out, yet coming steadily towards her.

★★★★★★★★★★★★★★★★★

And so, in the loneliness of that drab English winter, the mind of Mrs. Bittacy, preying upon itself, and fed by constant dread, went lost in disproportion. Dreariness filled the weeks with dismal, sunless skies and a clinging moisture that knew no wholesome tonic of keen frosts. Alone with her thoughts, both her husband and her God withdrawn into distance, she counted the days to Spring. She groped her way, stumbling down the long dark tunnel. Through the arch at the far end lay a brilliant picture of the violet sea sparkling on the coast of France. There lay safety and escape for both of them, could she but hold on. Behind her the trees blocked up the other entrance. She never once looked back.

She drooped. Vitality passed from her, drawn out and away as by some steady suction. Immense and incessant was this sensation of her powers draining off. The taps were all turned on. Her personality, as it were, streamed steadily away, coaxed outwards by this Power that never wearied and seemed inexhaustible. It won her as the full moon wins the tide. She waned; she faded; she obeyed.

At first, she watched the process, and recognised exactly what was going on. Her physical life, and that balance of mind which depends on physical well-being, were being slowly undermined. She saw that clearly. Only the soul, dwelling like a star apart from these and independent of them, lay safe somewhere—with her distant God. That she knew—tranquilly. The spiritual love that linked her to her husband was safe from all attack. Later, in His good time, they would merge together again because of it. But meanwhile, all of her that had kinship with the earth was slowly going. This separation was being remorselessly accomplished. Every part of her the trees could touch was being steadily drained from her. She was being—removed.

After a time, however, even this power of realisation went, so that she no longer "watched the process" or knew exactly what was going on. The one satisfaction she had known—the feeling that it was sweet to suffer for his sake—went with it. She stood utterly alone with this terror of the trees . . . .mid the ruins of her broken and disordered mind.

She slept badly; woke in the morning with hot and tired eyes; her head ached dully; she grew confused in thought and lost the clues of daily life in the most feeble fashion. At the same time, she lost sight, too, of that brilliant picture at the exist of the tunnel; it faded away into a tiny semicircle of pale light, the violet sea and the sunshine the merest point of white, remote as a star and equally inaccessible. She knew now that she could never reach it. And through the darkness that stretched behind, the power of the trees came close and caught her, twining about her feet and arms, climbing to her very lips.

She woke at night, finding it difficult to breathe. There seemed wet leaves pressing against her mouth, and soft green tendrils clinging to her neck. Her feet were heavy, half rooted, as it were, in deep, thick earth. Huge creepers stretched along the whole of that black tunnel, feeling about her person for points where they might fasten well, as ivy or the giant parasites of the Vegetable Kingdom settle down on the trees themselves to sap their life and kill them.

Slowly and surely the morbid growth possessed her life and held her. She feared those very winds that ran about the wintry forest. They were in league with it. They helped it everywhere.

"Why don't you sleep, dear?" It was her husband now who played the *rôle* of nurse, tending her little wants with an honest care that at least aped the services of love. He was so utterly unconscious of the raging battle he had caused. "What is it keeps you so wide awake and restless?"

"The winds," she whispered in the dark. For hours she had been watching the tossing of the trees through the blindless windows. "They go walking and talking everywhere tonight, keeping me awake. And all the time they call so loudly to you."

And his strange whispered answer appalled her for a moment until

151

the meaning of it faded and left her in a dark confusion of the mind that was now becoming almost permanent.

"The trees excite them in the night. The winds are the great swift carriers. Go with them, dear—and not against. You'll find sleep that way if you do."

"The storm is rising," she began, hardly knowing what she said.

"All the more then—go with them. Don't resist. They'll take you to the trees, that's all."

Resist! The word touched on the button of some text that once had helped her.

"Resist the devil and he will flee from you," she heard her whispered answer, and the same second had buried her face beneath the clothes in a flood of hysterical weeping.

But her husband did not seem disturbed. Perhaps he did not hear it, for the wind ran just then against the windows with a booming shout, and the roaring of the forest farther out came behind the blow, surging into the room. Perhaps, too, he was already asleep again. She slowly regained a sort of dull composure. Her face emerged from the tangle of sheets and blankets. With a growing terror over her—she listened. The storm was rising. It came with a sudden and impetuous rush that made all further sleep for her impossible.

Alone in a shaking world, it seemed, she lay and listened. That storm interpreted for her mind the climax. The forest bellowed out its victory to the winds; the winds in turn proclaimed it to the Night. The whole world knew of her complete defeat, her loss, her little human pain. This was the roar and shout of victory that she listened to.

For, unmistakably, the trees were shouting in the dark. These were sounds, too, like the flapping of great sails, a thousand at a time, and sometimes reports that resembled more than anything else the distant booming of enormous drums. The trees stood up—the whole beleaguering host of them stood up—and with the uproar of their million branches drummed the thundering message out across the night.

It seemed as if they had all broken loose. Their roots swept trailing over field and hedge and roof. They tossed their bushy heads beneath the clouds with a wild, delighted shuffling of great boughs. With trunks upright they raced leaping through the sky. There was upheaval and adventure in the awful sound they made, and their cry was like the cry of a sea that has broken through its gates and poured loose upon the world . . . .

Through it all her husband slept peacefully as though he heard it not. It was, as she well knew, the sleep of the semi-dead. For he was out with all that clamouring turmoil. The part of him that she had lost was there. The form that slept so calmly at her side was but the shell, half emptied.

And when the winter's morning stole upon the scene at length, with a pale, washed sunshine that followed the departing tempest, the first thing she saw, as she crept to the window and looked out, was the ruined cedar lying on the lawn. Only the gaunt and crippled trunk of it remained. The single giant bough that had been left to it lay dark upon the grass, sucked endways towards the forest by a great wind eddy. It lay there like a mass of drift-wood from a wreck, left by the ebbing of a high spring-tide upon the sands—remnant of some friendly, splendid vessel that once sheltered men.

And in the distance, she heard the roaring of the forest further out. Her husband's voice was in it.

The Regeneration of Lord Ernie

1

John Hendricks was bear-leading at the time. He had originally studied for Holy Orders, but had abandoned the Church later for private reasons connected with his faith, and had taken to teaching and tutoring instead. He was an honest, upstanding fellow of five-and-thirty, incorruptible, intelligent in a simple, straightforward way. He played games with his head, more than most Englishmen do, but he went through life without much calculation. He had qualities that made boys like and respect him; he won their confidence. Poor, proud, ambitious, he realised that fate offered him a chance when the Secretary of State for Scotland asked him if he would give up his other pupils for a year and take his son, Lord Ernie, round the world upon an educational trip that might make a man of him.

For Lord Ernie was the only son, and the marquess's influence was naturally great. To have deposited a regenerated Lord Ernie at the castle gates might have guaranteed Hendricks' future. After leaving Eton prematurely the lad had come under Hendricks' charge for a time, and with such excellent results—'I'd simply swear by that chap, you know,' the boy used to say—that his father, considerably impressed, and rather as a last resort, had made this proposition. And Hendricks, without much calculation, had accepted it. He liked 'Bindy' for himself. It was in his heart to 'make a man of him,' if possible. They had now been round the world together and had come up from Brindisi to the Italian Lakes, and so into Switzerland. It was middle October. With a week or two to spare they were making leisurely for the ancestral halls in Aberdeenshire.

The nine months' travel, Hendricks realised with keen disappointment, had accomplished, however, very little. The job had been exhausting, and he had conscientiously done his best. Lord Ernie liked him thoroughly, admiring his vigour with a smile of tolerant good-nature through his ceaseless cigarette smoke. They were almost like two boys together. 'You *are* a chap and a half, Mr. Hendricks. You really ought to be in the Cabinet with my father.' Hendricks would deliver up his useless parcel at the castle gates, pocket the thanks and the hard-earned fee, and go back to his arduous life of teaching and writing in dingy lodgings.

It was a pity, even on the lowest grounds. The tutor, truth to tell, felt undeniably depressed. Hopeful by nature, optimistic, too, as men of action usually are, he cast about him, even at the last hour, for something that might stir the boy to life, wake him up, put zest and energy into him. But there was only Paris now between them and the end; and Paris certainly could not be relied upon for help. Bindy's desire for Paris even was not strong enough to count. No desire in him was ever strong. There lay the crux of the problem in a word—Lord Ernie was without desire which is life.

Tall, well-built, handsome, he was yet such a feeble creature, without the energy to be either wild or vicious. Languid, yet certainly not decadent, life ran slowly, flabbily in him. He took to nothing. The first impression he made was fine—then nothing. His only tastes, if tastes they could be called, were out-of-door tastes: he was vaguely interested in flying, yet not enough to master the mechanism of it; he liked motoring at high speed, being driven, not driving himself; and he loved to wander about in woods, making fires like a Red Indian, provided they lit easily, yet even this, not for the poetry of the thing nor for any love of adventure, but just 'because.' 'I like fire, you know; like to watch it burn.'

Heat seemed to give him curious satisfaction, perhaps because the heat of life, he realised, was deficient in his six-foot body. It was significant, this love of fire in him, though no one could discover why. As a child he had a dangerous delight in fireworks—anything to do with fire. He would watch a candle flame as though he were a fire-worshipper, but had never been known to make a single remark of interest about it. In a wood, as mentioned, the first thing he did was to gather sticks—though the resulting fire was never part of any purpose. He had no purpose. There was no wind or fire of life in the lad at all. The fine body was inert.

Hendricks did wrong, of course, in going where he did—to this little desolate village in the Jura Mountains—though it was the first time all these trying months he had allowed himself a personal desire. But from Domo Dossola the Simplon Express would pass Lausanne, and from Lausanne to the Jura was but a step—all on the way home, moreover. And what prompted him was merely a sentimental desire to revisit the place where ten years before he had fallen violently in love with the pretty daughter of the *pasteur*, M. Leysin, in whose house he lodged. He had gone there to learn French. The very slight detour seemed pardonable.

His spiritless charge was easily persuaded.

'We might go home by Pontarlier instead of Bâle, and get a glimpse of the Jura,' he suggested. 'The line slides along its frontiers a bit, and then goes bang across it. We might even stop off a night on the way—if you cared about it. I know a curious old village—Villaret—where I went at your age to pick up French.'

'Top-hole,' replied Lord Ernie listlessly. 'All on the way to Paris, ain't it?'

'Of course. You see there's a fortnight before we need get home.'

'So, there is, yes. Let's go.' He felt it was almost his own idea, and that he decided it.

'If you'd *really* like it.'

'Oh, yes. Why not? I'm sick of cities.' He flicked some dust off his coat sleeve with an immaculate silk handkerchief, then lit a cigarette. 'Just as you like,' he added with a drawl and a smile. 'I'm ready for anything.' There was no keenness, no personal desire, no choice in reality at all; flabby good-nature merely.

A suggestion was invariably enough, as though the boy had no will of his own, his opposition rarely more than negative sulking that soon flattened out because it was forgotten. Indeed, no sign of positive life lay in him anywhere—no vitality, aggression, coherence of desire and will; vacuous rather than imbecile; unable to go forward upon any definite line of his own, as though all wheels had slipped their cogs; a pasty soul that took good enough impressions, yet never mastered them for permanent use. Nothing stuck. He would never make a politician, much less a statesman. The family title would be borne by a nincompoop. Yet all the machinery was there, one felt—if only it could be driven, made to go.

It was sad. Lord Ernie was heir to great estates, with a name and position that might influence thousands.

And Hendricks had been a good selection, with his virility and gentle, understanding firmness. He understood the problem. 'You'll do what no one else could,' the anxious father told him, 'for he worships you, and you can sting without hurting him. You'll put life and interest into him if anybody in this world can. I have great hopes of this tour. I shall always be in your debt, Mr. Hendricks.' And Hendricks had accepted the onerous duty in his big, high-minded way. He was conscientious to the backbone. This little side-trip was his sole deflection, if such it can be called even. 'Life, light and cheerful influences,' had been his instructions, 'nothing dull or melancholy; an occasional fling, if he wants it—I'd welcome a fling as a good sign—and as much intercourse with decent people, and stimulating sight-seeing as you can manage—or can stand,' the marquess added with a smile. 'Only you won't overtax the lad, will you? Above all, let him think *he* chooses and decides, when possible.'

Villaret, however, hardly complied with these conditions; there was melancholy in it; Hendricks' mind—whose reflexes the spongy nature of the empty lad absorbed too easily—would be in a minor key. Yet a night could work no harm. Whence came, he wondered, the fleeting notion that it might do good? Was it, perhaps, that Leysin, the vigorous old *pasteur*, might contribute something? Leysin had been a considerable force in his own development, he remembered; they had corresponded a little since; Leysin was out of the common, certainly, restless energy in him as of the sea. Hendricks found difficulty in sorting out his thoughts and motives, but Leysin was in them somewhere—this idea that his energetic personality might help. His vitalising effect, at least, would counteract the melancholy.

For Villaret lay huddled upon unstimulating slopes, the robe of gloomy pine-woods sweeping down towards its poverty from bleak heights and desolate gorges. The peasants were morose, ill-living folk. It was a dark untaught corner in a range of otherwise fairy mountains, a backwater the sun had neglected to clean out. Superstitions, Hendricks remembered, of incredible kind still lingered there; a touch of the sinister hovered about the composite mind of its inhabitants. The *pasteur* fought strenuously this blackness in their lives and thoughts; in the village itself with more or less success—though even there the drinking and habits of living were utterly unsweetened—but on the heights, among the somewhat arid pastures, the mountain men remained untamed, turbulent, even menacing.

Hendricks knew this of old, though he had never understood too well. But he remembered how the English boys at *la cure* were forbidden to climb in certain directions, because the life in these scattered *châlets* was somehow loose and violent. There was danger there, the danger, however, never definitely stated. Those lonely ridges lay cursed beneath dark skies. He remembered, too, the savage dogs, the difficulty of approach, the aggressive attitude towards the plucky *pasteur's* visits to these remote upland *pâturages*. They did not lie in his parish: Leysin made his occasional visits as man and missionary; for extraordinary rumours, Hendricks recalled, were rife, of some queer worship of their own these lawless peasants kept alive in their distant, windy territory, planted there first, the story had it, by some renegade priest whose name was now forgotten.

Hendricks himself had no personal experiences. He had been too deeply in love to trouble about outside things, however strange. But Marston's case had never quite left his memory—Marston, who climbed up by unlawful ways, stayed away two whole days and nights, and came back suddenly with his air of being broken, shattered, appallingly used up, his face so lined and strained it seemed aged by twenty years, and yet with a singular new life in him, so vehement, loud, and reckless, it was like a kind of sober intoxication. He was packed off to England before he could relate anything. But he had suffered shocks. His white, passionate face, his boisterous new vigour, the way M. Leysin screened his view of the heights as he put him personally into the Paris train—almost as though he feared the boy would see the hills and make another dash for them!—made up an unforgettable picture in the mind.

Moreover, between the sodden village and that string of evil *châlets* that lay in their dark line upon the heights there had been links. Exactly of what nature he never knew, for love made all else uninteresting; only, he remembered swarthy, dark-faced messengers descending into the sleepy hamlet from time to time, big. mountain-limbed fellows with wind in their hair and fire in their eyes; that their visits produced commotion and excitement of difficult kinds; that wild orgies invariably followed in their wake; and that, when the messengers went back, they did not go alone. There was life up there, whereas the village was moribund. And none who went ever cared to return.

Cudrefin, the young giant *vigneron*, taken in this way, from the very side of his sweetheart too, came back two years later as a messenger himself. He did not even ask for the girl, who had meanwhile married another. 'There's life up there with us,' he told the drunken loafers in the 'Guillaume Tell,' 'wind and fire to make you spin to the devil—or to heaven!' He was enthusiasm personified. In the village he had been merely drinking himself stupidly to death. Vaguely, too, Hendricks remembered visits of police from the neighbouring town, some of them on horseback, all armed, and that once even soldiers accompanied them, and on another occasion a bishop, or whatever the church dignitary was called, had arrived suddenly and promised radical assistance of a spiritual kind that had never materialised—oh, and many other details that now trooped back with suggestions time had certainly not made smaller. For the love had passed along its way and gone, and he was free now to the invasion of other memories, dwarfed at the time by that dominating, sweet passion.

Yet all the tutor wanted now, this chance week in late October, was to see again the corner of the mossy forest where he had known that marvellous thing, first love; renew his link with Leysin who had taught him much; and see if, perchance, this man's stalwart, virile energy might possibly overflow with benefit into his listless charge. The expenses he meant to pay out of his own pocket. Those wild pagans on the heights—even if they still existed—there was no need to mention. Lord Ernie knew little French, and certainly no word of *patois*. For one night, or even two, the risk was negligible.

Was there, indeed, risk at all of any sort? Was not this vague uneasiness he felt merely conscience faintly pricking? He could not feel that he was doing wrong. At worst, the youth might feel depression for a few hours—speedily curable by taking the train.

Something, nevertheless, did gnaw at him in subconscious fashion, producing a sense of apprehension; and he came to the conclusion that this memory of the mountain tribe was the cause of it—a revival of forgotten boyhood's awe. He glanced across at the figure of Bindy lounging upon the hotel lawn in an easy-chair, full in the sunshine, a newspaper at his feet. Reclining there, he looked so big and strong and handsome, yet in reality was but a painted lath without resistance, much less attack, in all his many inches.

And suddenly the tutor recalled another thing, the link, however, undiscoverable, and it was this: that the boy's mother, a Canadian, had suffered once severely from a winter in Quebec, where the marquess had first made her acquaintance. Frost had robbed her, if he remembered rightly, of a foot—with the result, at any rate, that she had a wholesome terror of the cold. She sought heat and sun instinctively—fire. Also, that asthma had been her sore affliction—sheer inability to take a full, deep breath. This deficiency of heat and air, therefore, were in her mind. And he knew that Bindy's birth had been an anxious time, the anxiety justified, moreover, since she had yielded up her life for him.

And so, the singular thought flashed through him suddenly as he watched the reclining, languid boy, Cudrefin's descriptive phrase oddly singing in his head—

'Heat and fire, fire and wind—why, it's the very thing he lacks! And he's always after them. I wonder——!'

2

The lumbering yellow diligence brought them up from the Lake shore, a long two hours, deposited them at the opening of the village street, and went its grinding, toiling way towards the frontier. They arrived in a blur of rain. It was evening. Lowering clouds drew night before her time upon the world, obscuring the distant summits of the Oberland, but lights twinkled here and there in the nearer landscape, mapping the gloom with signals. The village was very still. Above and below it, however, two big winds were at work, with curious results. For a lower wind from the east in gusty draughts drove the body of the lake into quick white horses which shone like wings against the deep *asses Alpes*, while a westerly current swept the heights immediately above the village.

There was this odd division of two weathers, presaging a change. A narrow line of clear bright sky showed up the Jura outline finely towards the north, stars peeping sharply through the pale moist spaces. Hurrying vapours, driven by the upper westerly wind, concealed them thinly. They flashed and vanished. The entire ridge, five thousand feet in the air, had an appearance of moving through the sky. Between these opposing winds at different levels the village itself lay motionless, while the world slid past, as it were, in two directions.

'The earth seems turning round,' remarked Lord Ernie. He had been reading a novel all day in train and steamer, and smoking endless cigarettes in the diligence, his companion and himself its only occupants. He seemed suddenly to have waked up. 'What is it?' he asked with interest.

Hendricks explained the queer effect of the two contrary winds. Columns of peat smoke rose in thin straight lines from the blur of houses, untouched by the careering currents above and below. The winds whirled round them.

Lord Ernie listened attentively to the explanation.

'I feel as if I were spinning with it—like a top,' he observed, putting his hand to his head a moment. 'And what are those lights up there?'

He pointed to the distant ridge, where fires were blazing as though stars had fallen and set fire to the trees. Several were visible, at regular intervals. The sharp summits of the limestone mountains cut hard into the clear spaces of northern sky thousands of feet above.

'Oh, the peasants burning wood and stuff, I suppose,' the tutor told him.

The youth turned an instant, standing still to examine them with a shading hand.

'People live up there?' he asked. There was surprise in his voice, and his body stiffened oddly as he spoke.

'In mountain *châlets*, yes,' replied the other a trifle impatiently, noticing his attitude. 'Come along now,' he added, 'let's get to our rooms in the carpenter's house before the rain comes down. You can see the windows twinkling over there,' and he pointed to a building near the church. 'The storm will catch us.' They moved quickly down the deserted street together in the deepening gloom, passing little gardens, doors of open barns, straggling manure heaps, and courtyards of cobbled stones where the occasional figure of a man was seen. But Lord Ernie lingered behind, half loitering. Once or twice, to the other's increasing annoyance, he paused, standing still to watch the heights through openings between the tumble-down old houses. Half a dozen big drops of rain splashed heavily on the road.

'Hurry up!' cried Hendricks, looking back, 'or we shall be caught. It's the mountain wind—the *coup de joran*. You can hear it coming!' For the lad was peering across a low wall in an attitude of fixed attention. He made a gesture with one hand, as though he signalled towards the ridges where the fires blazed. Hendricks called pretty sharply to him then. It was possible, of course, that he misinterpreted the movement; it *may* merely have been that he passed his fingers through his hair, across his eyes, or used the palm to focus sight, for his hat was off and the light was quite uncertain. Only Hendricks did not like the lingering or the gesture. He put authority into his tone at once. 'Come along, will you; come along, Bindy!' he called.

The answer filled him with amazement.

'All right, all right. I'll follow in a moment. I like this.'

The tutor went back a few steps towards him. The tone startled him.

'Like what?' he asked.

And Lord Ernie turned towards him with another face. There was fighting in it. There was resolution.

'This, of course,' the boy answered steadily, but with excitement

162

shut down behind, as he waved one arm towards the mountains. 'I've dreamed this sort of thing; I've known it somewhere. We've seen nothing like it all our stupid trip.' The flash in his brown eyes passed then, as he added more quietly, but with firmness: 'Don't wait for me; I'll follow.'

Hendricks stood still in his tracks. There was a decision in the voice and manner that arrested him. The confidence, the positive statement, the eager desire, the hint of energy—all this was new. He had never encouraged the boy's habit of vivid dreaming, deeming the narration unwise. It flashed across him suddenly now that the 'deficiency' might be only on the surface. Energy and life hid, perhaps, subconsciously in him. Did the dreams betray an activity he knew not how to carry through and correlate with his everyday, external world? And were these dreams evidence of deep, hidden desire—a clue, possibly, to the energy he sought and needed, the exact kind of energy that might set the inert machinery in motion and drive it?

He hesitated an instant, waiting in the road. He was on the verge of understanding something that yet just evaded him. Bindy's childish, instinctive love of fire, his passion for air, for rushing wind, for oceans of limitless——

There came at that moment a deep roaring in the mountains. Far away, but rapidly approaching, the ominous booming of it filled the air. The westerly wind descended by the deep gorges, shaking the forests, shouting as it came. Clouds of white dust spiralled into the sky off the upper roads, spread into sheets like snow, and swept downwards with incredible velocity. The air turned suddenly cooler. More big drops of rain splashed and thudded on the roofs and road. There was a feeling of something violent and instantaneous about to happen, a sense almost of attack. The *joran* tore headlong down into the valley.

'Come on, man,' he cried at the top of his voice. 'That's the *joran*! I know it of old! It's terrific. Run!' And he caught the lad, still lingering, by the arm.

But Lord Ernie shook himself free with an excitement almost violent.

'I've been up there with those great fires,' he shouted. 'I know the whole blessed thing. But where was it? Where?' His face was white, eyes shining, manner strangely agitated. 'Big, naked fellows who dance like wind, and rushing women of fire, and——'

Two things happened then, interrupting the boy's wild language. The *joran* reached the village and struck it; the houses shook, the trees bent double, and the cloud of limestone dust, painting the darkness white, swept on between Hendricks and the boy with extraordinary force, even separating them. There was a clatter of falling tiles, of banging doors and windows, and then a burst of icy rain that fell like iron shot on everything, raising actual spray. The air was in an instant thick. Everything drove past, roared, trembled. And, secondly—just in that brief instant when man and boy were separated—there shot between them with shadowy swiftness the figure of a man, hatless, with flying hair, who vanished with running strides into the darkness of the village street beyond—all so rapidly that sight could focus the manner neither of his coming nor of his going.

Hendricks caught a glimpse of a swarthy, elemental type of face, the swing of great shoulders, the leap of big loose limbs—something rushing and elastic in the whole appearance—but nothing he could claim for definite detail. The figure swept through the dust and wind like an animal—and was gone. It was, indeed, only the contrast of Lord Ernie's whitened skin, of his graceful, half-elegant outline, that enabled him to recall the details that he did. The weather-beaten visage seemed to storm away. Bindy's delicate aristocratic face shone so pale and eager. But that a real man had passed was indubitable, for the boy made a flurried movement as though to follow. Hendricks caught his arm with a determined grip and pulled him back.

'Who was that? Who was it?' Lord Ernie cried breathlessly, resisting with all his strength, but vainly.

'Some mountain fellow, of course. Nothing to do with us.' And he dragged the boy after him down the road. For a second both seemed to have lost their heads. Hendricks certainly felt a gust of something strike him into momentary consternation that was half alarm.

'From up there, where the fires are?' asked the boy, shouting above the wind and rain.

'Yes, yes, I suppose so. Come along. We shall be soused. Are you mad?' For Bindy still held back with all his weight, trying to turn round and see. Hendricks used more force. There was almost a scuffle in the road.

'All right, I'm coming. I only wanted to look a second. You needn't drag my arm out.' He ceased resistance, and they lurched forward together. 'But what a chap he was! He went like the wind. Did you see the light streaming out of him—like fire?'

'Like what?' shouted Hendricks, as they dashed now through the driving tempest.

'Fire!' bawled the boy. 'It lit me up as he passed—fire that lights but does not burn, and wind that blows the world along——'

'Button your coat and run!' interrupted the other, hurrying his pace, and pulling the lad forcibly after him.

'Don't twist! You're hurting! I can run as well as you!' came back, with an energy Bindy had never shown before in his life. He was breathless, panting, charged with excitement still. 'It touched me as he passed—fire that lights but doesn't burn, and wind that blows the heart to flame—let me go, will you? Let go my hand.'

He dashed free and away. The torrential rain came down in sheets now from a windless sky, for the *joran* was already miles beyond them, tearing across the angry lake. They reached the carpenter's house, where their lodging was, soaked to the skin. They dried themselves, and ate the light supper of soup and omelette prepared for them—ate it in their dressing-gowns. Lord Ernie went to bed with a hot-water bottle of rough stone. He declared with decision that he felt no chill. His excitement had somewhat passed.

'But, I say, Mr. Hendricks,' he remarked, as he settled down with his novel and a cigarette, calmed and normal again, 'this *is* a place and a half, isn't it? It stirs me all up. I suppose it's the storm. What do *you* think?'

'Electrical state of the air, yes,' replied the tutor briefly.

Soon afterwards he closed the shutters on the weather side, said goodnight, and went into his own room to unpack. The singular phrase Bindy had used kept singing through his head: 'Fire that lights but doesn't burn, and wind that blows the heart to flame'—the first time he had said 'blows the world along.' Where on earth had the boy got hold of such queer words? He still saw the figure of that wild mountain fellow who had passed between them with the dust and wind and rain. There was confusion in the picture, or rather in his memory of it, perhaps. But it seemed to him, looking back now, that the man in passing had paused a second—the briefest second merely—and had spoken, or, at any rate, had stared closely a moment into Bindy's face, and that some communication had been between them in that moment of elemental violence.

3

Pasteur Leysin Hendricks remembered very well. Even now in his old age he was a vigorous personality, but in his youth he had been almost revolutionary; wild enough, too, it was rumoured, until he had turned to God of his own accord as offering a larger field for his strenuous vitality. The little man was possessed of tireless life, a born leader of forlorn hopes, attack his *métier*, and heavy odds the conditions that he loved. Before settling down in this isolated spot— *pasteur de l'église indépendente* in a protestant Canton—he had been a missionary in remote pagan lands. His horizon was a big one, he had seen strange things. An uncouth being, with a large head upon a thin and wiry body supported by steely bowed legs, he had that courage which makes itself known in advance of any proof.

Hendricks slipped over to *la curé* about nine o'clock and found him in his study. Lord Ernie was asleep; at least his light was out, no sound or movement audible from his room. The *joran* had swept the heavens of clouds. Stars shone brilliantly. The fires still blazed faintly upon the heights.

The visit was not unexpected, for Hendricks had already sent a message to announce himself, and the moment he sat down, met the *pasteur's* eye, heard his voice, and observed his slight imperious gestures, he passed under the influence of a personality stronger than his own. Something in Leysin's atmosphere stretched him, lifting his horizon. He had come chiefly—he now realised it—to borrow help and explanation with regard to Lord Ernie; the events of two hours before had impressed him more than he quite cared to own, and he wished to talk about it. But, somehow, he found it difficult to state his case; no opening presented itself; or, rather, the *pasteur's* mind, intent upon something of his own, was too preoccupied.

In reply to a question presently, the tutor gave a brief outline of his present duties, but omitted the scene of excitement in the village street, for as he watched the furrowed face in the light of the study lamp, he realised both anxiety and spiritual high pressure at work below the surface there. He hesitated to intrude his own affairs at first. They discussed, nevertheless, the psychology of the boy, and the unfavourable chances of regeneration, while the old man's face lit up and flashed from time to time, until at length the truth came out, and Hendricks understood his friend's preoccupation.

'What you're attempting with an individual,' Leysin exclaimed with ardour, 'is precisely what I'm attempting with a crowd. And it's difficult. For poor sinners make poor saints, and the lukewarm I will spue out of my mouth.' He made an abrupt, resentful gesture to signify his disgust and weariness, perhaps his contempt as well. 'Cut it down! Why cumbereth it the ground?'

'A hard, uncharitable doctrine,' began the tutor, realising that he must discuss the Parish before he could introduce Bindy's case effectively. 'You mean, of course, that there's no material to work on?'

'No energy to direct,' was the emphatic reply. 'My sheep here are—real sheep; mere negative, drink-sodden loafers without desire. Hospital cases! I could work with tigers and wild beasts, but who ever trained a slug?'

'Your proper place is on the heights,' suggested Hendricks, interrupting at a venture. 'There's scope enough up there, or used to be. Have they died out, those wild men of the mountains?' And hit by chance the target in the bull's-eye.

The old man's face turned younger as he answered quickly.

'Men like that,' he exclaimed, 'do not die off. They breed and multiply.' He leaned forward across the table, his manner eager, fervent, almost impetuous with suppressed desire for action. 'There's evil thinking up there,' he said suggestively, 'but, by heaven, it's alive; it's positive, ambitious, constructive. With violent feeling and strong desire to work on, there's hope of some result. Upon vehement impulses like that, pagan or anything else, a man can work with a will. Those are the tigers; down here I have the slugs!'

He shrugged his shoulders and leaned back into his chair. Hendricks watched him, thinking of the stories told about his missionary days among savage and barbarian tribes.

'Born of the vital landscape, I suppose?' he asked. 'Wind and frost and blazing sun. Their wild energy, I mean, is due to——'

A gesture from the old man stopped him. 'You know who started them upon their wild performances,' he said gravely in a lower voice; 'you know how that ambitious renegade priest from the Valais chose them for his nucleus, then died before he could lead them out, trained and competent, upon his strange campaign? You heard the story when you were with me as a boy——?'

'I remember Marston,' put in the other, uncommonly interested, 'Marston—the boy who——' He stopped because he hardly knew how to continue. There was a minute's silence. But it was not an empty silence, though no word broke it. Leysin's face was a study.

'Ah, Marston, yes,' he said slowly, without looking up; 'you remember him. But that is at my door, too, I suppose. His father was ignorant and obstinate; I might have saved him otherwise.' He seemed talking to himself rather than to his listener. Pain showed in the lines about the rugged mouth. 'There was no one, you see, who knew how to di-

167

rect the great life that woke in the lad. He took it back with him, and turned it loose into all manner of useless enterprises, and the doctors mistook his abrupt and fierce ambitions for—for the hysteria which they called the vestibule of lunacy....Yet small characters may have big ideas. . . . They didn't understand, of course.... It was sad, sad, sad.' He hid his face in his hands a moment.

'Marston went wrong, then, in the end?' for the other's manner suggested disaster of some kind. Hendricks asked it in a whisper. Leysin uncovered his face, looped his neck with one finger, and pointed to the ceiling.

'Hanged himself!' murmured Hendricks, shocked.

The *pasteur* nodded, but there was impatience, half anger in his tone.

'They checked it, kept it in. Of course, it tore him!'

The two men looked into each other's eyes for a moment, and something in the younger of them shrank. This was all beyond his ken a little. An odd hint of bleak and cruel reality was in the air, making him shiver along nerves that were normally inactive. The uneasiness he felt about Lord Ernie became alarm. His conscience pricked him.

'More than he could assimilate,' continued Leysin. 'It broke him. Yet, had outlets been provided, had he been taught how to use it, this elemental energy drawn direct from Nature——' He broke off abruptly, struck perhaps by the expression in his listener's eyes. 'It seems incredible, doesn't it, in the twentieth century? I know.'

'Evil?' asked Hendricks, stammering rather.

'Why evil?' was the impatient reply. 'How can any force be evil? That's merely a question of direction.'

'And the priest who discovered these forces and taught their use, then——?'

'Was genuinely spiritual and followed the truth in his own way. He was not necessarily evil.' The little *pasteur* spoke with vehemence. 'You talk like the religion-primers in the kindergarten,' he went on. 'Listen. This man, sick and weary of his lukewarm flock, sought vital, stalwart systems who might be clean enough to use the elemental powers he had discovered how to attract. Only the bias of the users could make it "evil" by wrong use. His idea was big and even holy—to train a corps that might regenerate the world. And he chose unreasoning, unintellectual types with a purpose—primitive, giant men who could assimilate the force without risk of being shattered. Under his direction he intended they should prove as effective as the twelve disciples of old who were fisher-folk. And, had he gone on——'

'He, too, failed then?' asked the other, whose tangled thoughts struggled with incredulity and belief as he heard this strange new thing. 'He died, you mean?'

'*Maison de santé*,' was the laconic reply, 'strait-waistcoats, padded cells, and the rest; but still alive, I'm told. It was more than he could manage.'

It was a startling story, even in this brief outline, deep suggestion in it. The tutor's sense of being out of his depth increased. After nine months with a lifeless, devitalised human being, this was—well, he seemed to have fallen in his sleep from a comfortable bed into a raging mountain torrent. Strong currents rushed through and over him. The lonely, peaceful village outside, sleeping beneath the stars, heightened the contrast.

'Suppressed or misdirected energy again, I suppose,' he said in a low tone, respecting his companion's emotion. 'And these mountain men,' he asked abruptly, 'do they still keep up their—practices?'

'Their ceremonies, yes,' corrected the other, master of himself again. 'Turbulent moments of nature, storms and the like, stir them to clumsy rehearsals of once vital rituals—not entirely ineffective, even in their incompleteness, but dangerous for that very reason. This *joran*, for instance, invariably communicates something of its atmospherical energy to themselves. They light their fires as of old. They blunder through what they remember of *his* ceremonies. With the glasses you may see them in their dozens, men and women, leaping and dancing. It's an amazing sight, great beauty in it, impossible to witness even from a distance without feeling the desire to take part in it. Even my people feel it—the only time they ever get alive,'—he jerked his big head contemptuously towards the street—'or feel desire to act. And someone from the heights—a messenger perhaps—will be down later, this very evening probably, on the hunt——'

'On the hunt?' Hendricks asked it half below his breath. He felt a touch of awe as he heard this experienced, genuinely religious man speak with conviction of such curious things. 'On the hunt?' he repeated more eagerly.

'Messengers do come down,' was the reply. 'A living belief always seeks to increase, to grow, to add to itself. Where there's conviction there's always propaganda.'

'Ah, converts——?'

Leysin shrugged his big black shoulders. 'Desire to add to their number—desire to *save*,' he said. 'The energy they absorb overflows, that's all.'

The Englishman debated several questions vaguely in his mind; only his mind, being disturbed, could not hold the balance exactly true. Leysin's influence, as of old, was upon him. A possibility, remote, seductive, dangerous, began to beckon to him, but from somewhere just outside his reasoning mind.

'And they always know when one of their kind is near,' the voice slipped in between his tumbling thoughts, 'as though they get it instinctively from these universal elements they worship. They select their recruits with marvellous judgment and precision. No messenger ever goes back alone; nor has a recruit ever been known to return to the lazy squalor of the conditions whence he escaped.'

The younger man sat upright in his chair, suddenly alert, and the gesture that he made unconsciously might have been read by a keen psychiatrist as evidence of mental self-defence. He felt the forbidden impulse in him gathering force, and tried to call a halt. At any rate, he called upon the other man to be explicit. He enquired point-blank what this religion of the heights might be. What were these elements these people worshipped? In what did their wild ceremonies consist?

And Leysin, breaking bounds, let his speech burst forth in a stream of explanation, learned of actual knowledge, as he claimed, and uttered with a vehement conviction that produced an undeniable effect upon his astonished listener. Told by no dreamer, but by a righteous man who lived, not merely preached his certain faith, Hendricks, before the half was heard, forgot what age and land he dwelt in. Whole blocks of conventional belief crumbled and fell away. Brick walls erected by routine to mark narrow paths of proper conduct—safe, moral, advisable conduct—thawed and vanished.

Through the ruins, scrambling at him from huge horizons never recognised before, came all manner of marvellous possibilities. The little confinement of modern thought appalled him suddenly. Leysin spoke slowly, said little, was not even speculative. It was no mere magic of words that made the dim-lit study swim these deep waters beyond the ripple of pert creeds, but rather the overwhelming sense of sure conviction driving behind the statements. The little man had witnessed curious things, yes, in his missionary days, and that he had found truth in them in place of ignorant nonsense was remarkable enough.

That silly superstitions prevalent among older nations could be signs really of their former greatness, linked mightily close to natural forces, was a startling notion, but it paved the way in Hendricks' receptive mind just then for the belief that certain so-called elements might be worshipped—known intimately, that is—to the uplifting advantage of the worshippers. And what elements more suitable for adoring imitation than wind and fire? For in a human body the first signs of what men term life are heat which is combustion, and breath which is a measure of wind. Life means fire, drawn first from the sun, and breathing, borrowed from the omnipresent air; there might credibly be ways of assaulting these elements and taking heaven by storm; of seizing from their inexhaustible stores an abnormal measure, of straining this huge raw supply into effective energy for human use—vitality.

Living with fire and wind in their most active moments; closely imitating their movements, following in their footsteps, understanding their 'laws of being,' going *identically* with them—there lay a hint of the method. It was once, when men were primitively close to Nature, instinctual knowledge. The ceremony was the teaching. The Powers of fire, the Principalities of air, existed; and humanity *could* know their qualities by the ritual of imitation, could actually absorb the fierce enthusiasm of flame and the tireless energy of wind. Such transference was conceivable.

Leysin, at any rate, somehow made it so. His description of what he had personally witnessed, both in wilder lands and here in this little mountain range of middle Europe, had a reality in it that was upsetting to the last degree. 'There is nothing more difficult to believe,' he said, 'yet more certainly true, than the effect of these singular elemental rites.' He laughed a short dry laugh. 'The mediaeval superstition that a witch could raise a storm is but a remnant of a once completely efficacious system,' he concluded, 'though how that strange being, the *Valais* priest, rediscovered the process and introduced it here, I have never been able to ascertain. That he did so results have proved. At any rate, it lets in life, life moreover in astonishing abundance; though, whether for destruction or regeneration, depends, obviously, upon the use the recipient puts it to. That's where direction comes in.'

The beckoning impulse in the tutor's bewildered thoughts drew closer. The moment for communicating it had come at last. Without more ado he took the opening. He told his companion the incident in the village street, the boy's abrupt excitement, his new-found energy, the curious words he used, the independence and vitality of his attitude. He told also of his parentage, of his mother's disabilities, his craving for rushing air in abundance, his love of fire for its own sake, of his magnificent physical machinery, yet of his uselessness.

And Leysin, as he listened, seemed built on wires.

Searching questions shot forth like blows into the other's mind. The *pasteur's* sudden increase of enthusiasm was infectious. He leaped intuitively to the thing in Hendricks' thought. He understood the beckoning.

The tutor answered the questions as best he could, aware of the end in view with trepidation and a kind of mental breathlessness. Yes, unquestionably, Bindy *had* exchanged communication of some sort with the man, though his excitement had been evident even sooner.

'And you saw this man yourself?' Leysin pressed him.

'Indubitably—a tall and hurrying figure in the dusk.'

'He brought energy with him? The boy felt it and responded?'

Hendricks nodded. 'Became quite unmanageable for some minutes,' he replied.

'He assimilated it though? There was no distress exactly?' Leysin asked sharply.

'None—that I could see. Pleasurable excitement, something aggressive, a rather wild enthusiasm. His will began to act. He used that curious phrase about wind and fire. He turned alive. He wanted to follow the man——'

'And the face—how would you describe it? Did it bring terror, I mean, or confidence?'

'Dark and splendid,' answered the other as truthfully as he could. 'In a certain sense, rushing, tempestuous, yet stern rather.'

'A face like the heights,' suggested Leysin impatiently, 'a windy, fiery aspect in it, eh?'

'The man swept past like the spirit of a storm in imaginative poetry——' began the tutor, hunting through his thoughts for adequate description, then stopped as he saw that his companion had risen from his chair and begun to pace the floor.

The *pasteur* paused a moment beside him, hands thrust deep into his pockets, head bent down, and shoulders forward. For twenty seconds he stared into his visitor's face intently, as though he would force into him the thought in his own mind. His features seemed working visibly, yet behind a mask of strong control.

'Don't you see what it is? Don't you see?' he said in a lower, deeper tone. '*They knew.* Even from a distance they were aware of his coming. He is one of themselves.' And he straightened up again. 'He belongs to them.'

'One of them? One of the wind-and-fire lot?' the tutor stammered.

The restless little man returned to his chair opposite, full of suppressed and vigorous movement, as though he were strung on springs.

'He's *of* them,' he continued, 'but in a peculiar and particular sense. More than merely a possible recruit, his empty organism would provide the very link they need, the perfect conduit.' He watched his companion's face with careful keenness. 'In the country where I first experienced this marvellous thing,' he added significantly, 'he would have been set apart as the offering, the sacrifice, as they call it there. The tribe would have chosen him with honour. He would have been the special bait to attract.'

'Death?' whispered the other.

But Leysin shook his head. 'In the end, perhaps,' he replied darkly, 'for the vessel might be torn and shattered. But at first charged to the brim and crammed with energy—with transformed vitality they could draw into themselves through him. A monster, if you will, but to them a deity; and superhuman, in our little sense, most certainly.'

Then Hendricks faltered inwardly and turned away. No words came to him at the moment. In silence the minds of the two men, one a religious, the other a secular teacher, and each with a burden of responsibility to the race, kept pace together without speech. The religious, however, outstripped the pedagogue. What he next said seemed a little disconnected with what had preceded it, although Hendricks caught the drift easily enough—and shuddered.

'An organism needing heat,' observed Leysin calmly, 'can absorb without danger what would destroy a normal person. Alcohol, again, neither injures nor intoxicates—up to a given point—the system that really requires it.'

The tutor, perplexed and sorely tempted, felt that he drifted with a tide he found it difficult to stem.

'Up to a point,' he repeated. 'That's true, of course.'

'Up to a given point,' echoed the other, with significance that made his voice sound solemn. 'Then rescue—in the nick of time.'

He waited two full minutes and more for an answer; then, as none was audible, he said another thing. His eyes were so intent upon the tutor's that the latter raised his own unwillingly, and understood thus all that lay behind the pregnant little sentence.

'With a number it would not be possible, but with an individual it could be done. Brim the empty vessel first. Then rescue—in the nick of time! Regeneration!'

4

In the Englishman's mind there came a crash, as though something fell. There was dust, confusion, noise. Moral platitudes shouted at conventional admonitions. Warnings laughed and copy-book maxims shrivelled up. Above the lot, rising with a touch of grandeur, stood the pulpit figure of the little *pasteur*, his big face shining clear through all the turmoil, strength and vision in the flaming eyes—a commanding outline with spiritual audacity in his heart. And Hendricks saw then that the man himself was standing erect in the centre of the room, one finger raised to command attention—listening. Some considerable interval must have passed while he struggled with his inner confusion.

Leysin stood, intently listening, his big head throwing a grotesque shadow on wall and ceiling.

'Hark!' he exclaimed, half whispering. 'Do you hear that? Listen.'

A deep sound, confused and roaring, passed across the night, far away, and slightly booming. It entered the little room so that the air seemed to tremble a moment. To Hendricks it held something ominous.

'The wind,' he whispered, as the noise died off into the distance; 'yet a moment ago the night was still enough. The stars were shining.' There was tense excitement in the room just then. It showed in Leysin's face, which had gone white as a cloth. Hendricks himself felt extraordinarily stirred.

'Not wind, but human voices,' the older man said quickly. 'It's shouting. Listen!' and his eyes ran round the room, coming to rest finally in a corner where his hat and cloak hung from a nail. A gesture accompanied the look. He wanted to be out. The tutor half rose to take his leave. 'You have duties tonight elsewhere,' he stammered. 'I'm forgetting.' His own instinct was to get away himself with Bindy by the first early diligence. He was afraid of yielding.

'Hush!' whispered Leysin peremptorily. 'Listen!'

He opened the window at the top, and through the crack, where the stars peeped brightly, there came, louder than before, the uproar of human voices floating through the night from far away. The air of the great pine forests came in with it. Hendricks listened intently a moment. He positively jumped to feel a hand upon his arm. Leysin's big head was thrust close up into his face.

'That's the commotion in the village,' he whispered. 'A messenger

174

has come and gone; someone has gone back with him. Tonight I shall be needed—down here, but tomorrow night when the great ritual takes place—up there———!'

Hendricks tried to push him away so as not to hear the words; but the little man seemed immovable as a rock. The impulse remained probably in the mind without making the muscles work. For the tutor, sorely tempted, longed to dare, yet faltered in his will.

'———if you felt like taking the risk,' the words continued seductively, 'we might place the empty vessel near enough to let it fill, then rescue it, charged with energy, in the nick of time.' And the *pasteur's* eyes were aglow with enthusiasm, his voice even trembling at the thought of high adventure to save another's soul.

'Watch merely?' Hendricks heard his own voice whisper, hardly aware that he was saying it, 'without taking part?' He said it thickly, stupidly, a man wavering and unsure of himself. 'It would be an experience,' he stammered. 'I've never———'

'Merely watch, yes; look on; let him see,' interrupted the other with eagerness. 'We must be very careful. It's worth trying—a last resort.'

They still stood close together. Hendricks felt the little man's breath on his face as he peered up at him.

'I admit the chance,' he began weakly.

'There is no chance,' was the vigorous reply, 'there is only Providence. You have been guided.'

'But as to risk and failure, what of them? What's involved?' he asked, recklessness increasing in him.

'New wine in old bottles,' was the answer. 'But here, you tell me, the vessel is not damaged, but merely empty. The machinery is all right. If he merely watches, as from a little distance———'

'Yes, yes, the machinery *is* there, I agree. The boy has breeding, health, and all the physical qualities—good blood and nerves and muscles. It's only that life refuses to stay and drive them.' His heart beat with violence even as he said it; he felt the energy and zeal from the older man pour into him. He was realising in himself on a smaller scale what might take place with the boy in large. But still he shrank. Leysin for the moment said no more. His spiritual discernment was equal to his boldness. Having planted the seed, he left it to grow or die. The decision was not for him.

In the light of the single lamp the two men sat facing each other, listening, waiting, while Leysin talked occasionally, but in the main kept silence. Some time passed, though how long the tutor could not say. In his mind was wild confusion. How could he justify such a mad proposal? Yet how could he refuse the opening, preposterous though it seemed? The enticement was very great; temptation rushed upon him. Striving to recall his normal world, he found it difficult. The face of the old marquess seemed a mere lifeless picture on a wall—it watched but could not interfere. Here was an opportunity to take or leave. He fought the battle in terms of naked souls, while the ordinary four-cornered morality hid its face awhile. He heard himself explaining, delaying, hedging, half-toying with the problem.

But the redemption of a soul was at stake, and he tried to forget the environment and conditions of modern thought and belief. Sentences flashed at him out of the battle: 'I must take him back worse than when I started, or—what? A violent being like Marston, or a redeemed, converted system with new energy? It's a chance, and my last.' Moreover, odd, half-comic detail—there was the support of the Church, of a protestant clergyman whose fundamental beliefs were similar to the evangelical persuasions of the boy's family. Conversion, as demoniacal possession, were both traditions of the blood. After all, the old marquess might understand and approve. 'You took the opening God set in your way in His wisdom. You showed faith and courage. Far be it from me to condemn you.' The picture on the wall looked down at him and spoke the words.

The wild hypothesis of the intrepid little missionary-pasteur swept him with an effect like hypnotism. Then, suddenly, something in him seemed to decide finally for itself. He flung himself, morality and all, upon this vigorous other personality. He leaned across the table, his face close to the lamp. His voice shook as he spoke.

'Would *you*?' he asked—then knew the question foolish, and that such a man would shrink from nothing where the redemption of a soul was at stake; knew also that the question was proof that his own decision was already made.

There was something grotesque almost in the torrent of colloquial French Leysin proceeded to pour forth, while the other sat listening in amazement, half ashamed and half exhilarated. He looked at the stalwart figure, the wiry bowed legs as he paced the floor, the shortness of the coat-sleeves and the absence of shirt-cuffs round the powerful lean wrists. It was a great fighting man he watched, a man afraid of nothing in heaven or earth, prepared to lead a forlorn hope into a hostile unknown land. And the sight, combined with what he heard, set the seal upon his half-hearted decision. He would take the risk and go.

'Pfui!' exclaimed the little *pasteur* as though it might have been an oath, his loud whisper breaking through into a guttural sound, 'pfui! Bah! Would that *my* people had machinery like that so that I could use it! I've no material to work on, no force to direct, nothing but heavy, sodden clay. Jelly!' he cried, 'negative, useless, lukewarm stuff at best.' He lowered his voice suddenly, so as to listen at the same time. 'I might as well be a baker kneading dough,' he continued. 'They drink and yield and drink again; they never attack and drive; they're not worth labouring to save.' He struck the wooden table with his fist, making the lamp rattle, while his listener started and drew back. 'What good can weak souls, though spotless, be to God? The best have long ago gone up to them,' and he jerked his leonine old head towards the mountains. 'Where there's *life* there's hope,' he stamped his foot as he said it, 'but the lukewarm—pfui!—I will spue them out of my mouth!'

He paused by the window a moment, listened attentively, then resumed his pacing to and fro. Clearly, he longed for action. Indifference, half-heartedness had no place in his composition. And Hendricks felt his own slower blood take fire as he listened.

'Ah!' cried Leysin louder, 'what a battle I could fight up there for God, could I but live among them, stem the flow of their dark strong vitality, then twist it round and up, up, up!' And he jerked his finger skywards. 'It's the great sinners we want, not the meek-faced saints. There's energy enough among those devils to bring a whole Canton to the great Footstool, could I but direct it.' He paused a moment, standing over his astonished visitor. 'Bring the boy up with you, and let him drink his fill. And pray, pray, I say, that he become a violent sinner first in order that later there shall be something worth offering to God. Over one *sinner* that repenteth——'

A rapid, nervous knocking interrupted the flow of words, and the figure of a woman stood upon the threshold. With the opening of the door came also again the roaring from the night outside. Hendricks saw the tall, somewhat dishevelled outline of the wife—he remembered her vaguely, though she could hardly see him now in his darker corner—and recalled the fact that she had been sent out to Leysin in his missionary days, a worthy, illiterate, but adoring woman. She wore a shawl, her hair was untidy, her eyes fixed and staring. Her husband's sturdy little figure, as he rose, stood level with her chin.

'You hear it, Jules?' she whispered thickly. 'The *joran* has brought them down. You'll be needed in the village.' She said it anxiously, though Hendricks understood the *patois* with difficulty. They talked excitedly together a moment in the doorway, their outlines blocked against the corridor where a single oil lamp flickered. She warned, urging something; he expostulated. Fragments reached Hendricks in his corner. Clearly the woman worshipped her husband like a king, yet feared for his safety. He, for his part, comforted her, scolded a little, argued, told her to 'believe in God and go back to bed.'

'They'll take you too, and you'll never return. It's not your parish anyhow . . . .' a touch of anguish in her tone.

But Leysin was impatient to be off. He led her down the passage. 'My parish is wherever I can help. I belong to God. Nothing can harm me but to leave undone the work He gives me.' The steps went farther away as he guided her to the stairs. Outside the roar of voices rose and fell. Wind brought the drifting sound, wind carried it away. It was like the thunder of the sea.

And the Englishman, using the little scene as a flashlight upon his own attitude, saw it for an instant as God might have seen it. Leysin's point of view was high, scanning a very wide horizon. His eye being single, the whole body was full of light. The risk, it suddenly seemed, was—nothing; to shirk it, indeed, the merest cowardice.

He went up and seized the *pasteur's* hand.

'To-morrow,' he said, a trifle shakily perhaps, yet looking straight into his eyes. 'If we stay over—I'll bring the lad with me—provided he comes willingly.'

'You will stay over,' interrupted the other with decision. 'Come to supper at seven. Come in mountain boots. Use persuasion, but not force. He shall see it from a distance—without taking part.'

'From a distance—yes,' the tutor repeated, 'but without taking part.'

'I know the signs,' the *pasteur* broke in significantly. 'We can rescue him in the nick of time—charged with energy and life, yet before the danger gets——'

A sudden clangour of bells drowned the whispering voice, cutting the sentence in the middle. It was like an alarm of fire. Leysin sprang sharply round.

'The signal!' he cried; 'the signal from the church. Some one's been taken. I must go at once—I shall be needed.' He had his hat and cloak on in a moment, was through the passage and into the street, Hendricks following at his heels. The whole place seemed alive. Yet the roadway was deserted, and no lights showed at the windows of the houses. Only from the farther end of the village, where stood the cabaret, came a roar of voices, shouting, crying, singing. The impression was that the population was centred there. Far in the starry sky a line of fires blazed upon the heights, throwing a lurid reflection above the deep black valley. Excitement filled the night.

'But how extraordinary!' exclaimed Hendricks, hurrying to overtake his alert companion; 'what life there is about! Everything's on the rush.' They went faster, almost running. 'I feel the waves of it beating even here.' He followed breathlessly.

'A messenger has come—and gone,' replied Leysin in a sharp, decided voice. 'What you feel here is but the overflow. This is the aftermath. I must work down here with my people——'

'I'll work with you,' began the other. But Leysin stopped him.

'Keep yourself for tomorrow night—up there,' he said with grave authority, pointing to the fiery line upon the heights, and at the same time quickening his pace along the street. 'At the moment,' he cried, looking back, 'your place is yonder.' He jerked his head towards the carpenter's house among the vineyards. The next minute he was gone.

5

And Hendricks, accredited tutor to a sprig of nobility in the twentieth century, asked himself suddenly how such things could possibly be. The adventure took on abruptly a touch of nightmare. Only the light in the sky above the cabaret windows, and the roar of voices where men drank and sang, brought home the reality of it all. With a shudder of apprehension he glanced at the lurid glare upon the mountains. He was committed now; not because he had merely promised, but because he had definitely made up his mind.

Lighting a match, he saw by his watch that the visit had lasted over two hours. It was after eleven. He hurried, letting himself in with the big house-key, and going on tiptoe up the granite stairs. In his mind rose a picture of the boy as he had known him all these weary, sight-seeing months—the mild brown eyes, the facile indolence, the pliant, watery emotions of the listless creature, but behind him now, like storm clouds, the hopes, desires, fears the *pasteur's* talk had conjured up. The yearning to save stirred strongly in his heart, and more and more of the little man's reckless spiritual audacity came with it.

His own affection for the lad was genuine, but impatience and adventure pushed eagerly through the tenderness. If only, oh, if only he could put life into that great six-foot, big-boned frame! Some energy as of fire and wind into that inert machinery of mind and body! The idea was utterly incredible, but surely no harm could come

179

of trying the experiment. There *were* the huge and elemental forces, of course, in Nature, and if . . . A sound in the bedroom, as he crept softly past the door, caught his attention, and he paused a moment to listen. Lord Ernie was not asleep, then, after all. He wondered why the sound got somehow at his heart. There was shuffling behind the door; there was a voice, too—or was it voices? He knocked.

'Who is it?' came at once, in a tone he hardly recognised. And, as he answered, 'It's I, Mr. Hendricks; let me in,' there followed a renewal of the shuffling, but without the sound of voices, and the door flew open—it was not even locked. Lord Ernie stood before him, dressed to go out. In the faint starlight the tall ungainly figure filled the doorway, erect and huge, the shoulders squared, the trunk no longer drooping. The listlessness was gone. He stood upright, limbs straight and alert; the sagging limp had vanished from the knees. He looked, in this semi-darkness, like another person, almost monstrous. And the tutor drew back instinctively, catching an instant at his breath.

'But, my dear boy! why aren't you asleep?' he stammered. He glanced half nervously about him. 'I heard you talking, surely?' He fumbled for a match; but, before he found it, the other had turned on the electric switch. The light flared out. There was no one else in the room. 'Is anything wrong with you? What's the matter?'

But the boy answered quietly, though in a deeper voice than Hendricks had ever known in him before:

'I'm all right; only I couldn't sleep. I've been watching those fires on the mountains. I—I wanted to go out and see.'

He still held the field-glasses in his hand, swinging them vigorously by the strap. The room was littered with clothes, just unpacked, the heavy shooting boots in the middle of the floor; and Hendricks, noticing these signs, felt a wave of excitement sweep through him, caught somehow from the presence of the boy. There was a sense of vitality in the room—as though a rush of active movement had just passed through it. Both windows stood wide open, and the roar of voices was clearly audible. Lord Ernie turned his head to listen.

'That's only the village people drinking and shouting,' said Hendricks, closely watching each movement that he made. 'It's perfectly natural, Bindy, that you feel too excited to sleep. We're in the mountains. The air stimulates tremendously—it makes the heart beat faster.' He decided not to press the lad with questions.

'But I never felt like this in the Rockies or the Himalayas,' came the swift rejoinder, as he moved to the window and looked out. 'There

180

was nothing in India or Japan like *that!*' He swept his hand towards the wooded heights that towered above the village so close. He talked volubly. 'All those things we saw out there were sham—done on purpose for tourists. Up there it's real. I've been watching through the glasses till—I felt I simply must go out and join it. You can see men dancing round the fires, and big, rushing women. Oh, Mr. Hendricks, isn't it all glorious—all too glorious and ripping for words!' And his brown eyes shone like lamps.

'You mean that it's spontaneous, natural?' the other guided him, welcoming the new enthusiasm, yet still bewildered by the startling change. It was not mere nerves he saw. There was nothing morbid in it.

'They're doing it, I mean, because they have to,' came the decided answer, 'and because they feel it. They're not just copying the world.' He put his hand upon the other's arm. There was dry heat in it that Hendricks felt even through his clothes. 'And that's what *I* want,' the boy went on, raising his voice; 'what I've always wanted without knowing it—real things that can make me alive. I've often had it in my dreams, you know, but now I've found it.'

'But I didn't know. You never told me of those dreams.'

The boy's cheeks flushed, so that the colour and the fire in his eyes made him positively splendid. He answered slowly, as out of some part he had hitherto kept deliberately concealed.

'Because I never could get hold of it in words. It sounded so silly even to myself, and I thought Father would train it all away and laugh at it. It's awfully far down in me, but it's so real I knew it must come out one day, and that I should find it. Oh, I say, Mr. Hendricks,' and he lowered his voice, leaning out across the window-sill suddenly, '*that* fills me up and feeds me'—he pointed to the heights—'and gives me life. The life I've seen till now was only a kind of show. It starved me. I want to go up there and feel it pouring through my blood.' He filled his lungs with the strong mountain air, and paused while he exhaled it slowly, as though tasting it with delight and understanding. Then he burst out again, 'I vote we go. Will you come with me? What d'you say. Eh?'

They stared at each other hard a moment. Something as primitive and irresistible as love passed through the air between them. With a great effort the older man kept the balance true.

'Not tonight, not now,' he said firmly. 'It's too late. Tomorrow, if you like—with pleasure.'

181

'But tomorrow *night*,' cried the boy with a rush, 'when the fires are blazing and the wind is loose. Not in the stupid daylight.'

'All right. Tomorrow night. And my old friend, Monsieur Leysin, shall be our guide. He knows the way, and he knows the people too.'

Lord Ernie seized his hands with enthusiasm. His vigour was so disconcerting that it seemed to affect his physical appearance. The body grew almost visibly; his very clothes hung on him differently; he was no longer a nonentity yawning beneath an ancient pedigree and title; he was an aggressive personality. The boy in him rushed into manhood, as it were, while still retaining boyish speech and gesture. It was uncanny. 'We'll go more than once, I vote; go again and again. This *is* a place and a half. It's *my* place with a vengeance——!'

'Not exactly the kind of place your father would wish you to linger in,' his tutor interrupted. 'But we might stay a day or two—especially as you like it so.'

'It's far better than the towns and the rotten embassies; better than fifty Simlas and Bombays and filthy Cairos,' cried the other eagerly. 'It's just the thing I need, and when I get home I'll show 'em something. I'll prove it. Why, they simply won't know me!' He laughed, and his face shone with a kind of vivid radiance in the glare of the electric light. The transformation was more than curious. Waiting a moment to see if more would follow, Hendricks moved slowly then towards the door, with the remark that it was advisable now to go to bed since they would be up late the following night—when he noticed for the first time that the pillow and sheets were crumpled and that the bed had already been lain in. The first suspicion flashed back upon him with new certainty.

Lord Ernie was already taking off his heavy coat, preparatory to undressing. He looked up quickly at the altered tone of voice.

'Bindy,' the tutor said with a touch of gravity, 'you *were* alone just now—weren't you—of course?'

The other sat up from stooping over his boots. With his hands resting on the bed behind him, he looked straight into his companion's eyes. Lying was not among his faults. He answered slowly after a decided interval.

'I—I was asleep,' he whispered, evidently trying to be accurate, yet hesitating how to describe the thing he had to say, 'and had a dream—one of my real, vivid dreams when something happens. Only, this time, it was more real than ever before. It was'—he paused, searching for words, then added—'sweet and awful.'

And Hendricks repeated the surprising sentence. 'Sweet and awful, Bindy! What in the world do you mean, boy?'

Lord Ernie seemed puzzled himself by the choice of words he used.

'I don't know exactly,' he went on honestly, 'only I mean that it was awfully real and splendid, a bit of my own life somewhere—somewhere else—where it lies hidden away behind a lot of days and months that choke it up. I can never get at it except in woods and places, quite alone, hearing the wind or making fires, or—in sleep.' He hid his face in his hands a moment, then looked up with a hint of censure in his eyes. 'Why didn't you tell me that such things *were* done? You never told me,' he repeated.

'I didn't know it myself until this evening. Leysin——'

'I thought you knew everything,' Lord Ernie broke in in that same half-chiding tone.

'Monsieur Leysin told me to-night for the first time,' said Hendricks firmly, 'that such people and such practices existed. Till now I had never dreamed that such superstitions survived anywhere in the world at all.' He resented the reproach. But he was also aware that the boy resented his authority. For the first time his ascendency seemed in question; his voice, his eye, his manner did not quell as formerly. 'So you mean, when you say "sweet and awful," that it was very real to you?' he asked. He insisted now with purpose. 'Is that it, Bindy?'

The other replied eagerly enough. 'Yes, that's it, I think—partly. This time it was more than dreaming. It was real. I got there. I remembered. That's what I meant. And after I woke up the thing still went on. The man seemed still in the room beside the bed, calling me to get up and go with him——'

'Man! What man?' The tutor leant upon the back of a chair to steady himself. The wind just then went past the open windows with a singing rush.

'The dark man who passed us in the village, and who pointed to the fires on the heights. He came with the wind, you remember. He pulled my coat.'

The boy stood up as he said it. He came across the naked boarding, his step light and dancing. 'Fire that heats but does not burn, and wind that blows the heart alight, or something—I forget now exactly. *You* heard it too.' He whispered the words with excitement, raising his arms and knees as in the opening movements of a dance.

Hendricks kept his own excitement down, but with a distinctly

183

conscious effort.

'I heard nothing of the kind,' he said calmly. 'I was only thinking of getting home dry. You say,' he asked with decision, 'that you *heard* those words?'

Lord Ernie stood back a little. It was not that he wished to conceal, but that he felt uncertain how to express himself. 'In the street,' he said, 'I heard nothing; the words rose up in my own head, as it were. But in the dream, and afterwards too, when I was wide awake, I heard them out loud, clearly: Fire that heats but does not burn, and wind that blows the heart to flame—that's how it was.'

'In French, Bindy? You heard it in French?'

'Oh, it was no language at all. The eyes said it—both times.' He spoke as naturally as though it was the Durbah he described again. Only this new aggressive certainty was in his voice and manner. 'Mr. Hendricks,' he went on eagerly, '*you* understand what I mean, don't you? When certain people look at one, words start up in the mind as though one heard them spoken. I heard the words in my head, I suppose; only they seemed so familiar, as though I'd known them before—always——'

'Of course, Bindy, I understand. But this man—tell me—did he stay on after you woke up? And how did he go?' He looked round at the barely furnished room for hiding-places. 'It was really the dream you carried on after waking, wasn't it?'

Then Bindy laughed, but inwardly, as to himself. There was the faintest possible hint of derision in his voice. 'No doubt,' he said; 'only it was one of my big, real dreams. And how he went I can't explain at all, for I didn't see. You knocked at the door; I turned, and found myself standing in the room, dressed to go out. There was a rush of wind outside the window—and when I looked he was no longer there. The same minute you came in. It was all as quick as that. I suppose I dressed—in my sleep.'

They stood for several minutes, staring at each other without speaking. The tutor hesitated between several courses of action, unable, for the life of him, to decide upon any particular one. His instinct on the whole was to stop nothing, but to encourage all possible expression, while keeping rigorous watch and guard. Repression, it seemed to him just then, was the least desirable line to take. Somewhere there was truth in the affair. He felt out of his depth, his authority impaired, and under these temporary disadvantages he might so easily make a grave mistake, injuring instead of helping. While Lord Ernie finished

184

his undressing he leaned out of the window, taking great draughts of the keen night air, watching the blazing fires and listening to the roar of voices, now dying down into the distance.

And the voice of his thinking whispered to him, 'Let it all come out. Repress nothing. Let him have the entire adventure. If it's nonsense it can't injure, and if it's true it's inevitable.' He drew his head in and moved towards the door. 'Then it's settled,' he said quietly, as though nothing unusual had happened; 'we'll go up there tomorrow night—with Monsieur Leysin to show us the way. And you'll go to sleep now, won't you? For tomorrow we may be up very late. Promise me, Bindy.'

'I'm dead tired,' came the answer from the sheets. 'I certainly shan't dream any more, if that's what you mean. I promise.'

Hendricks turned the light out and went softly from the room. He could always trust the boy.

'Goodnight, Bindy,' he said.

'Goodnight,' came the drowsy reply.

Upstairs he lingered a long time over his own undressing, listening, waiting, watching for the least sound below. But nothing happened. Once, for his own peace of mind, he stole stealthily downstairs to the boy's door; then, reassured by the heavy breathing that was distinctly audible, he went up finally and got into bed himself. The night was very still now. It was cool, and the stars were brilliant over lake and forest and mountain. No voices broke the silence. He only heard the tinkle of the little streams beyond the vineyards. And by midnight he was sound asleep.

6

And next day broke as soft and brilliant as though October had stolen it from June; the Alps gleamed through an almost summery haze across the lake; the air held no hint of coming winter; and the Jura mountains wore the true blue of memory in Hendricks' mind. Patches of red and yellow splashed the great pine-woods here and there where beech and ash put autumn in the vast dark carpet.

The tutor woke clear-headed and refreshed. All that had happened the night before seemed out of proportion and unreasonable. There had been exaggerated emotion in it: in himself, because he returned to a place still charged with potent memories of youth; and in Lord Ernie, because the lad was overwrought by the electrical disturbance of the atmosphere. The nearness of the ancestral halls, which they both

185

disliked, had emphasised it; the ominous, wild weather had favoured it; and the coincidence of these pagan rites of superstitious peasants had focused it all into a melodramatic form with an added touch of the supernatural that was highly picturesque and—dangerously suggestive. Hendricks recovered his common sense; judgment asserted itself again.

Yet, for all that, certain things remained authentic. The effect upon the boy was not illusion, nor his words about fire and wind mere meaningless invention. There hid some undivined and significant correspondence between the gaps in his deficient nature and these two turbulent elements. The talk with Leysin, as the conduct of his wife, remained authentic; those facts were too steady to be dismissed, the *pasteur* too genuinely in earnest to be catalogued in dream. Neither daylight nor common sense could dissipate their actuality. Truth lay somewhere in it all.

Thus the day, for the tutor, was a battle that shifted with varying fortune between doubt and certainty. In the morning his mind was decided: the wild experiment was unjustifiable; in the afternoon, as the sunshine grew faint and melancholy, it became 'interesting, for what harm could come of it?' but towards evening, when shadows lengthened across the purple forests and the trees stood motionless in the calm and windless air, the adventure seemed, as it had seemed the night before, not only justifiable, but right and necessary.

It only became inevitable, however, when, after tea together on the balcony, Lord Ernie, mentioning the subject for the first time that day, asked pointedly what time the *pasteur* expected them to supper; then, noticing the flash of hesitancy in his companion's eyes, added in his strange deep voice, 'You promised we should go.' Withdrawal after that was out of the question. To retract would have meant, for one thing, final loss of the boy's confidence—a possibility not to be contemplated for a moment.

Until this moment no word of the preceding night had passed the lips of either. Lord Ernie had been quiet and preoccupied, silent rather, but never listless. He was peaceful, perhaps subdued a little, yet with a suppressed energy in his bearing that Hendricks watched with secret satisfaction. The tutor, closely observant, detected nothing out of gear; life stirred strongly in him; there was purpose, interest, will; there was desire; but there was nothing to cause alarm.

Availing himself then of the lad's absorption in his own affairs, he wandered forth alone upon his sentimental tour of inspection. No ghost of emotion rose to stalk beside him. That early tragedy, he now saw clearly, had been no more than youthful explosion of mere physical passion, wholesome and natural, but due chiefly to propinquity. His thoughts ran idly on; and he was even congratulating himself upon escape and freedom when, abruptly, he remembered a phrase Bindy had used the night before, and stumbled suddenly upon a clue when least expecting it.

He came to a sudden halt. The significance of it crashed through his mind and startled him. 'There are big rushing women . . .' It was the first reference to the other sex, as evidence of their attraction for him, Hendricks had ever known to pass his lips. Hitherto, though twenty years of age, the lad had never spoken of women as though he was aware of their terrible magic. He had not discovered them as females, necessary to every healthy male. It was not purity, of course, but ignorance: he had felt nothing.

Something had now awakened sex in him, so that he knew himself a man, and naked. And it had revolutionised the world for him. This new life came from the roots, transforming listless indifference into positive desire; the will woke out of sleep, and all the currents of his system took aggressive form. For all energy, intellectual, emotional, or spiritual, is fundamentally one: it is primarily sexual.

Hendricks paused in his sentimental walk, marvelling that he had not realised sooner this simple truth. It brought a certain logical meaning even into the pagan rites upon the mountains, these ancient rites which symbolised the marriage of the two tremendous elements of wind and fire, heat and air. And the lad's quiet, busy mood that morning confirmed his simple discovery. It involved restraint and purpose. Lord Ernie was alive. Hendricks would take home with him to those ancestral halls a vessel bursting with energy—creative energy. It was admirable that he should witness—from a safe distance—this primitive ceremony of crude pagan origin. It was the very thing. And the tutor hurried back to the house among the vineyards, aware that his responsibility had increased, but persuaded more than ever that his course was justified.

The sky held calm and cloudless through the day, the forests brooding beneath the hazy autumn sunshine. Indications that the second hurricane lay brewing among the heights were not wanting, however, to experienced eyes. Almost a preternatural silence reigned; there was a warm heaviness in the placid atmosphere; the surface of the lake was patched and streaky; the extreme clarity of the air an ominous omen. Distant objects were too close. Towards sunset, moreover, the streaks and patches vanished as though sucked below, while thin strips of tenuous cloud appeared from nowhere above the northern cliffs. They moved with great rapidity at an enormous height, touched with a lurid brilliance as the sun sank out of sight; and when Hendricks strolled over with Lord Ernie to *la curé* for supper there came a sudden rush of heated wind that set the branches sharply rattling, then died away as abruptly as it rose.

They seemed reflected, too, these disturbances, in the human atmospheres about the supper table—there was suppression of various emotions, emotions presaging violence. Lord Ernie was exhilarated, Hendricks uneasy and preoccupied, the *pasteur* grave and thoughtful. In Hendricks was another feeling as well—that he had lightly summoned a storm which might carry him off his feet. The boy's excitement increased it, as wind-puffs fan a starting fire. His own judgment had somewhere played him false, betraying him into this incredible adventure. And yet he could not stop it. The *pasteur's* influence was over him perhaps. He was ashamed to turn back. He was committed. The unusual circumstances found the weakness in his character.

For somewhere in the preposterous superstition there lay a big forgotten truth. He could not believe it, and yet he did believe it. The world had forgotten how to live truly close to Nature.

A desultory conversation was carried on, chiefly between the two men, while the boy ate hungrily, and Mme. Leysin watched her husband with anxiety as she served the simple meal.

'So you are coming with us, and you like to come?' the *pasteur* observed quietly, Hendricks translating.

Lord Ernie replied with a gesture of unmistakable enthusiasm.

'A wild lot of men and women,' Leysin went on, keeping his eye hard upon him, 'with an interesting worship of their own copied from very ancient times. They live on the heights, and mix little with us valley folk. You shall see their ceremonies tonight.'

'They get the wind and fire into themselves, don't they?' asked the boy keenly, and somewhat to the distress of the translator who rendered it, 'They get into wind and fire.'

'They worship wind and fire,' Leysin replied, 'and they do it by means of a wonderful dance that somehow imitates the leap of flame and the headlong rush of wind. If you copy the movements and gestures of a person you discover the emotion that causes them. You share it. Their idea is, apparently, that by imitating the movements they invite or attract the force—draw these elemental powers into their systems, so that in the end——'

He stopped suddenly, catching the tutor's eye. Lord Ernie seemed to understand without translation; he had laid down his knife and fork, and was leaning forward across the table, listening with deep absorption. His expression was alert with a new intelligence that was almost cunning. An acute sensibility seemed to have awakened in him.

'As with laughing, I suppose?' he said in an undertone to Hendricks quickly. 'If you imitate a laugher, you laugh yourself in the end and feel all the jolly excitement of laughter Is that what he means?'

The tutor nodded with assumed indifference. 'Imitation is always infectious,' he said lightly; 'but, of course, you will not imitate these wild people yourself, Bindy. We'll just look on from a distance.'

'From a distance!' repeated the boy, obviously disappointed. 'What's the good of that?' A look of obstinacy passed across his altered face.

Hendricks met his eyes squarely. 'At a circus,' he said firmly, 'you just watch. You don't imitate the clown, do you?'

'If you look on long enough, you do,' was the rather dogged reply.

'Well, take the Russian dancers we saw in Moscow,' the other insisted patiently; 'you felt the power and beauty without jumping up and whirling in your stall?'

Bindy half glared at him. There was almost contempt in his quiet answer: 'But your mind whirled with them. And later your body would too; otherwise it's given you nothing.' He paused a second. 'I can only get the fun of riding by being on a horse's back and doing his movements exactly with him—not by watching him.'

Hendricks smiled and shrugged his shoulders. He did not wish to discourage the enthusiasm lying behind this analysis. The uneasiness in him grew apace. He said something rapidly in French, using an undertone and laughter to confuse the actual words.

'Of course we must not interfere with their ceremonies,' put in the *pasteur* with decision. 'It's sacred to them. We can hide among the trees and watch. You would not leave your seat in church to imitate the priest, would you?' He glanced smilingly at the eager youth before him.

'If he did something real, I would.' It was said with a bright flash in the eyes. 'Anything real I'd copy like a shot. Only, I never find it.'

The reply was disconcerting rather: and Hendricks, as he hurriedly translated, made a clatter with his knife and fork, for something in him rose to meet the truth behind the curious words. From that moment, as though catching a little of the boy's exhilaration, he passed under a kind of spell perhaps. It was, in spite of the exaggeration, oddly stimulating. This dull little meal at the village *curé* masked an accumulating vehemence, eager to break loose. He heard the old father's voice: 'Well done, Hendricks! You have accomplished wonders!' He would take back the boy—alive. . . .

Yet all the time there were streaks and patches on his soul as upon the surface of the lake that afternoon. There were signs of terror. He felt himself letting go, an increasing recklessness, a yielding up more and more of his own authority to that of this triumphant boy. Bindy understood the meaning of it all and felt secure; Hendricks faltered, hesitated, stood on the defensive. Yet, ever less and less. Already he accepted the other's guidance. Already Lord Ernie's leadership was in the ascendant. Conviction invariably holds dominion over doubt.

They ate little. It was near the end of the meal when the wind, falling from a clear and starlit sky, struck its first violent blow, dropping with the force of an explosion that shook the wooden house, and passing with a roar towards the distant lake. The oil lamp, suspended from the ceiling, trembled; the *pasteur* looked apprehensively at the shuttered windows; and Lord Ernie, with startling abruptness, stood up. His eyes were shining. His voice was brisk, alert, and deep.

'The wind, the wind!' he cried. 'Think what it'll be up there! We shall feel it on our bodies!' His enthusiasm was like a rush of air across the table. 'And the fire!' he went on. 'The flames will lick all over, and tear about the sky. I feel wild and full of them already! How splendid!' And the flame of the little lamp leaped higher in the chimney as he said it.

'The violence of the *coup de joran* is extraordinary,' explained Leysin as he got up to turn down the wick, 'and the second outburst——' The rest of his sentence was drowned by the noise of Hendricks' voice telling the boy to sit down and finish his supper. And at the same moment the *pasteur's* wife came in as though a stroke of wind drove behind her down the passage. The door slammed in the draught. There was a momentary confusion in the room above which her voice rose shrill and frightened.

'The fires are alight, Jules,' she whispered in her half-intelligible *patois*, 'the forest is burning all along the upper ridge.' Her face was pale and her speech came stumbling. She lowered her lips to her husband's ear. 'They'll be looking out for recruits tonight. Is it necessary, is it right for you to go?' She glanced uneasily at the English visitors. 'You know the danger——'

He stopped her with a gesture. 'Those who look on at life accomplish nothing,' he answered impatiently. 'One must act, always act. Chances are sent to be taken, not stared at.' He rose, pushing past her into the passage, and as he did so she gave him one swift comprehensive look of tenderness and admiration, then hurried after him to find his hat and cloak. Willingly she would have kept him at home that night, yet gladly, in another sense, she saw him go. She fumbled in her movements, ready to laugh or cry or pray. Hendricks saw her pain and understood. It was singular how the woman's attitude intensified his own misgivings; her behaviour, the mere expression of her face alone, made the adventure so absolutely real.

Three minutes later they were in the village street. Hendricks and Lord Ernie, the latter impatient in the road beyond, saw her tall figure stoop to embrace him. 'I shall pray all night: I shall watch from my window for your return. God, who speaks from the whirlwind, and whose pathway is the fire, will go with you. Remember the younger men; it is ever the younger men that they seek to take. . .!' Her words were half hysterical. The kiss was given and taken; the open doorway framed her outline a moment; then the buttress of the church blotted her out, and they were off.

7

And at once the curious confusion of strong wind was upon them. Gusts howled about the corners of the shuttered houses and tore noisily across the open yards. Dust whirled with the rapidity as of some spectral white machinery. A tile came clattering down about their feet, while overhead the roofs had an air of shifting, toppling, bending. The entire village seemed scooped up and shaken, then dropped upon the earth again in tottering fashion.

'This way,' gasped the little *pasteur*, blown sideways like a sail; 'follow me closely.' Almost arm-in-arm at first they hurried down the deserted street, past lampless windows and tight-fastened doors, and soon were beyond the cabaret in that open stretch between the village and the forest where the wind had unobstructed way. Far above them ran the fiery mountain ridge. They saw the glare reflected in the sky as the tempest first swept them all three together, then separated them in the same moment. They seemed to spin or whirl. 'It's far worse than I expected,' shouted their guide; 'here! Give me your hand!' then found, once disentangled from his flapping cloak, that no one stood beside him. For each of them it was a single fight to reach the shelter of the woods, where the actual ascent began.

An instant the *pasteur* seemed to hesitate. He glanced back at the lighted window of *la curé* across the fields, at the line of fire in the sky, at the figure disappearing in the blackness immediately ahead. 'Where's the boy?' he shouted. 'Don't let him get too far in front. Keep close. Wait till I come!' They staggered back against each other. 'Look how easily he's slipped ahead already!'

'This howling wind——' Hendricks shouted, as they advanced side by side, pushing their shoulders against the storm.

The rest of the sentence vanished into space. Leysin shoved him forward, pointing to where, some twenty yards in front, the figure of Lord Ernie, head down, was battling eagerly with the hurricane. Already he stood near to the shelter of the trees waving his arms with energy towards the summits where the fire blazed. He was calling something at the top of his voice, urging them to hurry. His voice rushed down upon them with a pelt of wind.

'Don't let him get away from us,' bawled Leysin, holding his hands cup-wise to his mouth. 'Keep him in reach. He may see, but must not take part. . . .' A blow full in the face that smote him like the flat of a great sword clapped the sentence short. 'That's *your* part. He won't obey me!' Hendricks heard it as they plunged across the windswept reach, panting, struggling, forcing their bodies sideways like two-legged crabs against the terrific force of the descending *joran*. They reached the protection of the forest wall without further attempt at speech. Here there was sudden peace and silence, for the tall, dense trees received the tempest's impact like a cushion, stopping it. They paused a moment to recover breath.

But although the first exhaustion speedily passed, that original confusion of strong wind remained—in Hendricks' mind at least,—for wind violent enough to be battled with has a scattering effect on thought and blows the very blood about. Something in him snapped its cables and blew out to sea. His breath drew in an impetuous quality from the tempest each time he filled his lungs. There was agitation in him that caused an odd exaggeration of the emotions. The boy, as they came up, leaped down from a boulder he had climbed. He opened his arms, making of his cloak a kind of sail that filled and flapped.

'At last!' he cried, impatient, almost vexed. 'I thought you were never coming. The wind blew me along. We shall be late——'

The tutor caught his arm with vigour. 'You keep by us, Ernest; d'you hear now? No rushing ahead like that. Leysin's the guide, not you.' He even shook him. But as he did so he was aware that he him-self resisted something that he did not really want to resist, something that urged him forcibly; a little more and he would yield to it with pleasure, with abandon, finally with recklessness. A reaction of panic fear ran over him.

'It was the wind, I tell you,' cried the boy, flinging himself free with a hint of insolence in his voice, 'for it's alive. I mean to see everything. The wind's our leader and the fire's our guide.' He made a movement to start on again.

'You'll obey me,' thundered Hendricks, 'or else you'll go home. D'you understand?'

With exasperation, yet with uneasy delight, he noted the words Bindy made use of. It was in him that he might almost have uttered them himself. He stepped already into an entirely new world. Exhila-ration caught him even now. Putting the brake on was mere pretence. He seized the lad by both shoulders and pushed him to the rear, then placed himself next, so that Leysin moved in front and led the way. The procession started, diving into the comparative shelter of the forest. 'Don't let him pass you,' he heard in rapid French; 'guide him, that's all. The power's already in his blood. Keep yourself in hand as well, and follow me closely.' The roar of the storm above them carried the words clean off the world.

Here in the forest they moved, it seemed, along the floor of an ocean whose surface raged with dreadful violence; any moment one or other of them might be caught up to that surface and whirled off to destruction. For the procession was not one with itself. The dark-ness, the difficulty of hearing what each said, the feeling, too, that each climbed for himself, made everything seem at sixes and sevens. And the tutor, this secret exultation growing in his heart, denied the anxiety that kept it pace, and battled with his turbulent emotions, a divided personality. His power over the boy, he realised, had gravely weakened.

A little time ago they had seemed somehow equal. Now, however, a complete reversal of their relative positions had taken place. The boy was sure of himself. While Leysin led at a steady mountaineer's pace on his wiry, short, bowed legs, Hendricks, a yard or two behind him, stumbled a good deal in the darkness, Lord Ernie forever on his heels, eager to push past. But Bindy never stumbled. There was no flagging in his muscles. He moved so lightly and with so sure a tread that he almost seemed to dance, and often he stopped aside to leap a boulder or to run along a fallen trunk. Path there was none. Occasional gusts of wind rushed gustily down into these depths of forest where they moved, and now, from time to time, as they rose nearer to the line of fire on the ridge, an increasing glare lit up the knuckled roots or glimmered on the bramble thickets and heavy beds of moss.

It was astonishing how the little *pasteur* never missed his way. Periods of thick silence alternated with moments when the storm swept down through gullies among the trees, reverberating like thunder in the hollows.

Slowly they advanced, buffeted, driven, pushed, the wildness of some *Walpurgis* night growing upon all three. In the tutor's mind was this strange lift of increasing recklessness, the old proportion gone, the spiritual aspect of it troubling him to the point of sheer distress. He followed Leysin as blindly with his body as he followed this new Bindy eagerly with his mind. For this languid boy, now dancing to the tune of flooding life at his very heels, seemed magical in the true sense: energy created as by a wizard out of nothing. From lips that ordinarily sighed in listless boredom poured now a ceaseless stream of questions and ejaculations, ringing with enthusiasm.

How long would it take to reach the fiery ridge? Why did they go so slowly? Would they arrive too late? Would their intrusion be welcomed or understood? Already one great change was effected— accepted by Hendricks, too—that the role of mere spectator was impossible. The answers Hendricks gave, indeed, grew more and more encouraging and sympathetic. He, too, was impatient with their leader's crawling pace. Some elemental spell of wind and fire urged him towards the open ridge. The pull became irresistible. He despised the *pasteur's* caution, denied his wisdom, wholly rejected now the spirit of compromise and prudence.

And once, as the hurricane brought down a flying burst of voices, he caught himself leaping upon a big grey boulder in their path. He leaped at the very moment that the boy behind him leaped, yet hardly realised that he did so; his feet danced without a conscious order from his brain. They met together on the rounded top, stumbled, clutched one another frantically, then slid with waving arms and flying cloaks down the slippery surface of damp moss—laughing wildly.

'Fool!' cried Hendricks, saving himself. 'What in the world——?'

'*You* called,' laughed Bindy, picking himself up and dropping back to his place in the rear again. 'It's the wind, not me; it's in our feet. Half the time you're shouting and jumping yourself!'

And it was a few minutes after this that Lord Ernie suddenly forged ahead. He slipped in front as silently as a shadow before a moving candle in a room. Passing the tutor at a moment when his feet were entangled among roots and stones, he easily overtook the *pasteur* and found himself in the lead. He never stumbled; there seemed steel springs in his legs.

From Leysin, too breathless to interfere, came a cry of warning. 'Stop him! Take his hand!' his tired voice instantly smothered by the roaring skies. He turned to catch Hendricks by the cloak. 'You see *that*!' he shouted in alarm. 'For the love of God, don't lose sight of him! He must see, but not take part—remember——!'

And Hendricks yelled after the vanishing figure, 'Bindy, go slow, go slow! Keep in touch with us.' But he quickened his pace instantly, as though to overtake the boy. He passed his companion the same minute, and was out of sight. 'I'll wait for you,' came back the boy's shrill answer through the thinning trees. And a flare of light fell with it from the sky, for the final climb of a steep five hundred feet had now begun, and overhead the naked ridge ran east and west with its line of blazing fires. Boulders and rocky ground replaced the pines and spruces.

'But you'll never find the way,' shouted Leysin, while a deep trumpeting roar of the storm beyond muffled the remainder of the sentence.

Hendricks heard the next words close beside him from a clump of shadows. He was in touching distance of the excited boy.

'The fires and the singing guide me. Only a fool could miss the way.'

'But you *are* a——'

He swallowed the unuttered word. A new, extraordinary respect was suddenly in him. That tall, virile figure, instinct with life, springing so cleverly through the choking darkness, guiding with decision and intelligence, almost infallible—it was no fool that led them thus. He hurried after till his very sinews ached. His eyes, troubled and confused, strained through the trees to find him. But these same trees now fled past him in a torrent.

'Bindy, Bindy!' he cried, at the top of his voice, yet not with the imperious tone the situation called for. The sentence dropped into a lull of wind. Instead of command there was entreaty, almost supplication, in it. 'Wait for me, I'm coming. We'll see the glorious thing together!'

And then suddenly the forest lay behind him, with a belt of open pasture-land in front below the actual ridge. He felt the first great draught of heat, as a line of furnaces burst their doors with a mighty roar and turned the sky into a blaze of golden daylight. There was a crackling as of musketry. The flare shot up and burned the air about him, and the voices of a multitude, as yet invisible, drove through it like projectiles on the wind. This was the first impression, wholesale and terrific, that met him as he paused an instant on the edge of the sheltering forest and looked forward.

Leysin and Lord Ernie seemed to leave his mind, forgotten in this first attack of splendour, but forgotten, as it were, the first with contempt, the latter with an overwhelming regret. For the *pasteur's* mistake in that instant seemed obvious. In half measures lay the fatal error, and in compromise the danger. Bindy all along had known the better way and followed it. The lukewarm was the worthless.

'Bindy, boy, where are you? I'm coming . . .' and stepping on to the grassy strip of ground, soft to his feet, he met a wind that fell upon his body with a shower of blows from all directions at once and beat him to his knees. He dropped, it seemed, into the cover of a sheltering rock, for there followed then a moment of sudden and delicious still-ness in which the weary muscles recovered themselves and thought grew slightly steadier. Crouched thus close to the earth he no longer offered a target to the hurricane's attack. He peered upwards, making a screen of his hands.

The ridge, some fifty feet above him, he saw, ran in a generous platform along the mountain crest; it was wide and flat; between the enormous fires of piled-up wood that stretched for half a mile coiled a medley of dense smoke and tearing sparks. No human beings were visible, and yet he was aware of crowding life quite near. On hands and knees, crawling painfully, he then slowly retreated again into the shelter of the forest he had sought to leave. He stood up. The awful blaze was veiled by the roof of branches once more But, as he rose, seizing a sapling to steady himself by, two hands caught him with violence from behind, and a familiar voice came shouting against his ear. Leysin, panting, dishevelled and half broken with the speed, stood beside him.

'The boy! Where is he? We're just in time!' He roared the words to make them carry above the din. 'Hurry, hurry! I'll follow. . . . My older

196

legs.... See, for the love of God, that he is not taken.... I warned you!'

And for a second, as he heard, Hendricks caught at the vanished sense of responsibility again. He saw the face of the old marquess watching him among the tree trunks. He heard his voice, amazed, reproachful, furious: 'It was criminal of you, criminal——!'

'Where is the boy—*your* boy?' again broke in the shout of the *pasteur* with a slap of hurricane, as he staggered against the tutor, half collapsing, and trying to point the direction. 'Watch him, find him for the love of heaven before it is too late—before they see him...!'

The tutor's normal and responsible self dived out of sight again as he heard the cry of weakness and alarm. It seemed the wind got under him, lifting him bodily from his feet. He did not pause to think. Like a man midway in a whirling prize-fight, he felt dazed but confident, only conscious of one thing—that he must hold out to the end, take part in all the splendid fighting—*win*.

The lust of the arena, the pride of youth and battle, the impetuous recklessness of the charge in primitive war caught at his heart, brimming it with headlong courage. To play the game for all it might be worth seemed shouted everywhere about him, as the abandon of wind and fire rushed through him like a storm. He felt lifted above all possibility of little failure. The marquess with his conventional traditions, the *pasteur* with his considerations of half-way safety, both vanished utterly; safety, indeed, both for himself and for the boy in his charge lay in unconditional surrender. This was no time for little thought-out actions. It was all or nothing!

'God bless the whirlwind and the fire!' he shouted, opening wide his arms.

But his voice was inaudible amid the uproar, and the forward movement of his body remained at first only in the brain. He turned to push the old man aside, even to strike him down if necessary. 'Lukewarm yourself and a coward!' rose in his throat, yet found no utterance, for in that moment a tall, slim figure, swift as a shadow, steady as a hawk, shot hard across the open space between the forest and the ridge. In the direction of the blazing platform it disappeared against a curtain of thick smoke, emerged for one second in a storm of light, then vanished finally behind a ruin of loose rocks.

And Hendricks, his eyes wounded by heat and wind, his muscles paralysed, understood that the boy deliberately invited capture. The multitude that hid behind the smoke and fire, feeding the blazing heaps with eager hands, had become aware of him, and presently would appear to claim him. They would take him to themselves. Already answering flares ran east and west along the desolate ridge.

'I'll join you! I'm coming! Wait for me!' he tried to cry. The uproar smothered it.

8

And this uproar, he now perceived, was composed entirely of wind and fire. Here, on the roof of the hills beneath a starry sky, these two great elements expressed their nature with unhampered freedom, for there was neither rain to modify the one, nor solid obstacle to check the other. Their voices merged in a single sound—the hollow boom of wind and the deep, resounding clap of flame. The splitting crackle of burning branches imitated the high, shrill whistle of the tearing gusts that, javelin-like, flew to and fro in darts of swifter sound. But one shout rose from the summit, no human cry distinguishable in it, nor amid the thousand lines of skeleton wood that pierced the golden background was any human outline visible. Fire and wind encouraged one another to madness, manifesting in prodigious splendour by themselves.

Then, suddenly, before a gigantic canter of the wind, the driving smoke rolled upwards like a curtain, and the flames, ceasing their wild flapping, soared steadily in gothic windows of living gold towards the stars. In towering rows between columns of black night they transformed the empty space between them into a colossal temple aisle. They tapered aloft symmetrically into vanishing crests. And Hendricks stood upright. Rising so that his shoulders topped the edge of the boulder, and utterly contemptuous of Leysin's hand that sought with violence to drag him into shelter, he gazed as one who sees a vision.

For at first he could only stand and stare, aware of sensation but not of thought. An enormous, overpowering conviction blew his whole being to white heat. Here was a supply of elemental power that human beings—empty, needy, starved, deficient human beings—could use. His love for the boy leaped headlong at the skirts of this terrific salvation. A majestic possibility stormed through him.

Yet it was no nightmare wonder that met his staring and half-shielded eyes, although some touch of awful dream seemed in it, set, moreover, to a scale that scantier minds might deem distortion. The heat from some thirty fires, placed at regular intervals, made midnight quiver with immense vibrations. Of varying, yet calculated size, these towering heaps emitted notes of measured and alternating depth, until the roar along the entire line produced a definite scale almost of melody, the near ones shrilly singing, those more distant booming with mountainous pedal notes. The consonance was monstrous, yet conformed to some magnificent diapason. This chord of fire-music paced the starlit sky, directed, but never overmastered, by the wind that measured it somehow into meaning. Repeated in quick succession, the notes now crashing in a mass, now singing alone in solitary beauty, the effect suggested an idea of ordered sequence, of gigantic rhythm.

It seemed, indeed, as though some controlling agency, mastering excess, coerced both raging elements to express through this stupendous dance some definite idea. Here, as it were, was the alphabet of some natural, undifferentiated language, a language of sight and sound, predating speech, symbolical in the ultimate, deific sense. Some Lord of Fire and some Lord of Air were in command. Harnessed and regulated, these formless cohorts of energy that men call stupidly mere flame and wind, obeyed a higher power that had invoked them, yet a power that, by understanding their laws of being, held them most admirably in control.

This, at least, seems a hint of the explanation that flashed into Hendricks as he stared in amazed bewilderment from the shelter of the nearest boulder. He read a sentence in some natural, forgotten script. He watched a primitive ritual that once invoked the gods. He was aware of rhythm, and he was aware of system, though as yet he did not see the hand that wrote this marvellous sentence on the night. For still the human element remained invisible. He only realised—in dim, blundering fashion—that he witnessed a revelation of those two powers which, in large, lie at the foundations of the Universe, and, in little, are the basic essentials of human existence—the powers behind heat and air.

Fragments of that talk with Leysin stammered back across his mind, like letters in some stupendous word he dared not reconstruct entire. He shuddered and grew wise. Realms of forgotten being opened their doors before his dazzled sight. Vision fluttered into far, piercing vistas of ancient wonder, haunting and half-remembered, then lost its way in blindness that was pain. For a moment, it seemed, he was aware of majestic Presences behind the turmoil, shadowy but mighty, charged with a vague potentiality as of immense algebraical formulae, symbolical and beyond full comprehension, yet willing and able to be used for practical results.

He *felt* the elements as nerves of a living Universe. . . . Yet thinking was not really in him anywhere; feeling was all he knew. The world he moved in, as the script he read, belonged to conditions too utterly remote for reason to recover a single clue to their intelligible reconstruction. Glory, clean and strong as of primitive star-worship, passed between what he saw and all that he had ever known before. The curtain of conventional belief was rent in twain. The terrific thing was true....

For an unmeasured interval the tutor, oblivious of time and actual place, stood on the brink of this majestic pageant, staring with breathless awe, while the swaying of the entire scenery increased, like the sway of an ocean lifted to the sky by many winds. Then, suddenly, in one of those temporary lulls that passed between the beat of the great notes, his searching eyes discovered a new thing. The focus of his sight was altered, and he realised at last the source of the directing and the controlling power. Behind the fires and beyond the smoke he recognised the disc-like, shining ovals that upon this little earth stand in the image of the one, eternal Likeness.

He saw the human faces, symbols of spiritual dominion over all lesser orders, each one possessed of belief, intelligence and will. Singly so feeble, together so invincible, this assemblage, unscorched by the fire and by the wind unmoved, seemed to him impressive beyond all possible words. And a further inkling of the truth flashed on him as he stared: that a group of humans, a crowd, combining upon a given object with concentrated purpose, possessed of that terrific power, certain faith, may know in themselves the energy to move great mountains, and therefore that lesser energy to guide the fluid forces of the elements.

And a sense of cosmic exultation leaped into his being. For a moment he knew a touch of almost frenzy. Proud joy rose in him like a splendour of omnipotence. Humanity, it seemed to him, here came into a grand but long neglected corner of its kingdom as originally planned by Heaven. Into the hands of a weakling and deficient boy the guidance had been given.

Motionless beneath the stars, lit by the glare till they shone like idols of yellow stone, and magnified by the sheets of flying, intolerable light the wind chased to and fro, these rows of faces appeared at first as a single line of undifferentiated fire against the background of the night. The eyes were all cast down in prayer, each mind focused steadily upon one clear idea—the control and assimilation of two elemental powers. The crowd was one; feeling was one; desire, command and certain faith were one. The controlling power that resulted was irresistible.

Then came a remarkable, concerted movement. With one accord the eyes all opened, blazing with reflected fire. A hundred human countenances rose in a single shining line. The men stood upright. Swarthy faces, tanned by sun and wind, heads uncovered, hair and beards tossing in the air, turned all one way. Mouths opened too. There came a roar that even the hurricane could not drown—a word of command, it seemed, that sprang into the pulses of the dancing elements and reduced their turmoil to a wave of steadier movement. And at the same moment a hundred bodies, naked above the waist, arms outstretched and hands with the palms held upwards, swayed forwards through the smoke and fire. They came towards the spot where, half concealed from view, the tutor crouched and watched.

And Hendricks, thinking himself discovered, first quailed, then rose to meet them. No power to resist was in him. It was, rather, willing response that he experienced. He stepped out from the shelter of the boulder and entered the brilliant glare. Hatless himself, shoulders squared, cloak, flying in the wind, he took three strides towards the advancing battalion—then, undecided, paused. For the line, he saw, disregarded him as though he were not there at all. It was not *him* the worshippers sought. The entire troop swept past to a point some fifty feet below where the end of the ridge broke out of the thinning trees.

Beautiful as a curving wave of flame, the figures streamed across the narrow, open space with a drilled precision as of some battle line, and Hendricks, with a sense of wild, secret triumph, saw them pause at the brink of the platformed ridge, form up their serried ranks yet closer, then open two hundred arms to welcome some one whom the darkness should immediately deliver. Simultaneously, from the covering trees, the tall, slim shadow of Lord Ernie darted out into the light.

'Magnificent!' cried Hendricks, but his voice was smothered instantly in a mightier sound, and his movement forward seemed ineffective stumbling. The hundred voices thundered out a single note. Like a deer the boy leaped; like a tongue of flame he flew to join his own; and instantly was surrounded, borne shoulder-high upon those upturned palms, swept back in triumph towards the procession of enormous fires. Wrapped by smoke and sparks, lifted by wind, he became part of the monstrous rhythm that turned that mountain ridge alive.

He stood upright upon the platform of interlacing arms; he swayed with their movements as a thing of wind and fire that flew. The shining faces vanished then, turned all towards the blazing piles so that the boy had the appearance of standing on a wall of living black. His outline was visible a moment against the sky, firelight between his wide-stretched legs, streaming from his hair and horizontal arms, issuing almost, as it seemed, from his very body. The next second he leaped to the ground, ran forward—appallingly close—between two heaped-up fires, flung both hands heavenwards, and—knelt.

And Hendricks, sympathetically following the boy's performance as though his own mind and body took part in it, experienced then a singular result: it seemed the heart in him began to roar. This was no rustle of excited blood that the little cavern of his skull increased, but a deeper sound that proclaimed the kinship of his entire being with the ritual. His own nature had begun to answer. From that moment he perceived the spectacle, not with the senses of sight and hearing, separately, but with his entire body—synthetically. He became a part of this assembly that was itself one single instrument: a cosmic sounding-board for the rhythmical expression of impersonal Nature Powers.

Leysin, he dimly realised, fixed in his churchy tenets, remained outside, apart, and compromising; Hendricks accepted and went with. All little customary feelings dipped utterly away, lost, false, denied, even as a unit in a crowd loses its normal characteristics in the greater mood that sways the whole. The fire no longer burned him, for he was the fire; nor did he stagger against the furious wind, because the wind was in his heart. He moved all over, alive in every point and corner. With his skin he breathed, his bones and tissue ran with glorious heat.

He cried aloud. He praised. 'I am the whirlwind and I am the fire! Fire that lights but does not burn, and wind that blows the heart to flame!' His body sang it, or rather the elements sang it through his body; for the sound of his voice was not audible, and it was wind and fire that thundered forth his feeling in their crashing rhythm.

9

And so it was that he no longer saw this thing pictorially, nor in the little detached reports the individual senses brought, but knew it in himself complete, as a man knows love and passion. Memory afterwards translated these vast central feelings into pictures, but the pictures touched reality without containing it. Like a vision it happened all at once, as a room or landscape happens, and what happens all at once, coming through a synthesis of the senses, is not properly describable later. To instantaneous knowledge mere sequence is a falsehood. The sequence first comes in with the telling afterwards. That kneeling form, he understood, was the empty vessel to which conventional life had hitherto denied the heat and air it craved. The breath of life now poured at full tide into it, the fire of deity lit its heart of touchwood, wind blew into desire; and later flame would burst forth in action, consuming opposition. He must let it fill to the brim. It was not salvation, but creation. Then thought went out, extinguished by a puff of something greater. . . . . .

For beyond the smoke and sparks, beyond the space the men had occupied, a new and gentler movement, lyrical with bird-like beauty, ran suddenly along the ridge. What Hendricks had taken for branches heaped in rows for the burning, stirred marvellously throughout their whole collective mass, stirred sweetly, too, and with an exquisite loveliness. The entire line rose gracefully into the air with a whirr as of sweeping birds. There was a soft and undulating motion as though a draught of flowing wind turned faintly visible, yet with an increasing brilliance, like shining lilies of flame that now flocked forward in a troop, bending deliciously all one way.

And in the same second these tall lilies of fire revealed themselves as figures, naked above the waist, hair streaming on the wind, eyes alight and bare arms waving. Above the men's deep pedal bass their voices rose with clear, shrill sweetness on the storm. The band swept forwards swift as wind towards the kneeling boy. The long line curved about him foldingly. The women took him as the south wind takes a bird.

There may have been—indeed, there was—an interval, for Hendricks caught, again and again repeated, the boy's great cry of passionate delight above the tumult. Ringing and virile it rose to heaven, clear as a fine-wrought bell. And instantaneously the knitted figures of flame disentangled themselves again, the mass unfolded like an opening flower, and, as by a military word of command, dissolved itself once more into a long thin line of running fire. The women advanced, and the waiting men flowed forward in a stream to meet them.

This interweaving of the figures was as easily accomplished as the mingling of light and heavy threads upon some living loom. Hands joining hands, all singing, these naked worshippers of fire and wind passed in and out among the blazing piles with a headlong precision that was torrential and yet orderly. The speed increased; the faces

flashed and vanished, then flashed and passed again; each woman between two men, each man between two women, and Lord Ernie,
radiantly alive, between two girls of rich, o'erflowing beauty. Their
movements were undulating, like the undulations of fire, yet with
sudden, unexpected upward leaps as when fire is partnered abruptly
by a cantering wind. For the women were fire, and the men were
wind. The imitative dance was in full swing. The marvellous wind and
fire ritual unrolled its old-world magic.

It was awe-inspiring certainly, but for Hendricks, as he watched,
the terror of big conflagrations was wholly absent: rather, he felt the
sense of deep security that rhythmic movement causes. Bathed in a
sea of elemental power, he burned to share the pagan splendour and
the rush of primitive delight. It seemed he had a cosmic body in
which new centres stirred to life, linking him on to this source of
natural forces. Through these centres he drew the chaotic energy into
nerves and blood and muscle, into the very substance of his thought,
indeed, transmuting them into the magic of the will. Abundant and
inexhaustible vigour filled the air, pouring freely into whatever empty
receptacle lay at hand.

Sheets of flame, whole separate fragments of it, torn at the edges,
raced, loudly, hungrily flapping on vehement gusts of wind; curved as
they flew; leaped, twisted, flashed and vanished. And the figures closely
copied them. The women tossed their bodies aloft, then dipped suddenly to the earth, invisible, till the rushing men urged them into view
again with wild impetuous swing, so that the entire line stretched and
contracted like an immense elastic band of life, now knotted, now
dissolved.

Yet, while of raging and terrific beauty, there was never that mad
abandon which is disorder; but rather a kind of sacred natural revel that
prohibited mere licence. There was even a singular austerity in it that
betrayed a definite ritual and not mere reckless pageantry. No walls
could possibly have contained it. In cathedral, temple, or measured
space, however grand, it could only have seemed exaggerated and
apostate; here, beneath the open sky, it was beautiful and true. For
overhead the stars burned clear and steady, the constellations watching
it from their immovable towers—a representation of their own
leisured and hierarchic dance in swifter miniature.

And indeed this relationship it bore to a universal rhythm was
the key, it seemed, to its deep significance; for the close imitation
of natural movements seduced the colossal powers of fire and wind

to swell human emotions till they became mould and vessel for this elemental manifestation in men and women. Golden yellow in the blaze, the limbs of the women flashed and passed; their hair flew dark a moment across gleaming breasts; and their waving arms tossed in ever-shifting patterns through the driving smoke. The fires boiled and roared, scattering torrents of showering sparks like stars; and amid it all the slim, white shoulders of the boy, his clothes torn from him, his eyes ablaze, and his lips opened to the singing as though he had known it always, drove to and fro on the crest of the ritual like some flying figure of wind and fire incarnate.

All of which, instantaneously yet in sequence, Hendricks witnessed, painted upon the wild night sky. A volcanic energy poured through him too. He knew a golden enthusiasm of immeasurable strength, of unconquerable hope, of irresistible delight. Wind set his feet to dancing, and fire swept across his face without a trace of burning.

Nature was part of him. He had stepped inside. No obstacle existed that could withstand for a single second the torrential energy that fired his heart and blood. There was lightning in his veins. He could sweep aside life's difficult barriers with the ease of a tornado, and shake the rubbish of doubt and care from the years with earthquake shocks. Empires he could mould, and play with nations, drive men and women before him like a flock of sheep, shatter convention, and dislocate the machinery time has foisted upon natural energies. He knew in himself the omnipotence of the lesser elemental deities. Yet, as sympathetic observer, he can but have felt a tithe of what Lord Ernie felt.

'We are the whirlwind and we are the fire!' he cried aloud with the rushing worshippers. 'We are unconquerable and immense! We destroy the lukewarm and absorb the weak! For we can make evil into good by bending it all one way!....'

The roar swept thunderingly past him, catching at his voice and body. He felt himself snatched forward by the wind. The fire licked sweetly at him. It was the final abandonment. He plunged recklessly towards the surge of dancers....

10

What stopped him he did not know. Some hard and steely thing pricked sharply into him. An opposing power, fierce as a sword, stabbed at his heart—and he heard a little sound quite close beside him, a sound that pierced the babel, reaching his consciousness as from far away.

'Keep still! Cling tight to this old rock! Hold yourself in, or else they'll have you too!'

It was as if some insect scratched within his ear. His arm, that same instant, was violently seized. He came down with a crash. He had been half in the air. He had been dancing.

'Turn your eyes away, away! Take hold of this big tree!' The voice cried furiously, but with a petty human passion in it that marred the world. There was an intolerable revulsion in him as he heard it. He felt himself dragged forcibly backwards. He lost his balance, stumbling among loose stones.

'Loose me! Let me go!' he shouted, struggling like a wild animal, yet vainly, against the inflexible grip that held him. 'I am one with the fire that lights but does not burn. I am the wind that blows the worlds along! Damnation take you. . .. Let me free! . . .'

Confusion caught him, smothering speech and blinding sight. He fell backwards, away from the heat and wind. He was furious, but furious with he knew not whom or what. The interference had destroyed the rhythm, broken it into fragments. Violent impulses clashed through him without the will to choose or guide them. For power had deserted him and flowed elsewhere. He stood no longer in the stream of energy. He was emptied.

And at first he could not tell whether his instinct was to return himself, to rescue his precious boy, or—to crush the interfering object out of existence with what was left to him of raging anger. He turned, stood up, and flung the *pasteur* aside with violence. He raised his feet to stamp and kill . . . when a phrase with meaning darted suddenly across his wild confusion and recalled him to some fragment of truer responsibility and life.

'. . . There'll be only violence in him—reckless violence instead of strength—destructive. Save him before it is too late!'

'It *is* too late,' he roared in answer. 'What devil hinders me?'

But his roar was feeble, and his ironed boots refused the stamping. Power slipped wholly out of him. The rhythm poured past, instead of through him. Interference had destroyed the circuit. More glimmerings of responsibility came back. He stooped like a drunken man and helped the other to his feet. The rapidity of the change was curious, proving that the spell had been put upon him from without. It was not, as with the boy, mere development of pre-existing tendencies.

'Help me,' he implored suddenly instead, 'help me! There has been

206

madness in me. For God's sake, help me to get him out!' It seemed the face of the old marquess, stern and terrible, broke an instant through the smoky air, black with reproach and anger. And, with a violent effort of the will, Hendricks turned round to face the elemental orgy, bent on rescue. But this time the heat was intolerable and drove him back. The hair, hitherto untouched, now singed upon his head. Fire licked his very breath away. He bent double, covering his face with arms and cloak.

'Pray!' shouted Leysin, dropping to his knees. 'It is the only way. My God is higher than this. Pray, pray!'

And, automatically, Hendricks fell upon his knees beside him, though to pray he knew not how. For no real faith was in him as in the other, and his eye was far from single. The fast fading grandeur of what he had experienced still left its pagan tumult in his blood. The pretence of prayer could only have been blasphemy. He watched instead, letting the other invoke his mighty Deity alone, that Deity he had served unflinchingly all his life with faith and fasting, and with belief beyond assault.

It was an impressive picture, fraught with passionate drama. On his knees behind a sheltering boulder, a blackened pine-tree tossing scorched branches above his head, this righteous man prayed to his God, sure of his triumphant answer. Hendricks watched with an admiration that made him realise his own insignificance. The eyes were closed, the leonine big head set firm upon the diminutive body, the face now lit by flame, now veiled by smoke, the strong hands clasped together and upraised. He envied him. He recognised, too, that the elements themselves, with all their chaos of might and terror, were after all but servants of the Vastness which dips the butterflies in colour and puts down upon the breasts of little robins.

And, because the *pasteur's* life had been always prayer in action, his little human will invoked the Will of Greatness, merged with it, used it, and directed it steadily against the commotion of these unleashed elements. Certain of himself and of his God, the *pasteur* never doubted. His prayer set instantly in action those forces which balance suns and keep the stars afloat.

Thus, trembling with terror that made him wholly ineffective, Hendricks watched, and, as he watched, became aware of the amazing change. For it seemed as if a stream of power, steady and in opposition to the tumult, now poured audaciously against the elemental rhythm, altering its direction, modifying gradually its stupendous impetus.

There were pauses in the huge vibrations: they wavered, broke, and fled. They knew confusion, as when the prow of a steel-nosed vessel drives against the tide. The tide is vaster, but the steel is—different. The whole sky shivered, as this new entering force, so small, so soft, yet of such incalculable energy, began at once its overmastering effect. Signs of violence or rout, or of anything disordered, had no part in it; excess before it slipped into willing harness; there was light that sponged away all glare, as when morning sunshine cleans a forest of its shadows. Some little whispering power sang marvellously as of old across the desolate big mountains, 'Peace! Be still!' turning the monstrous turbulence into obedient sweetness. And upon his face and hands Hendricks felt faint, delicate touches of some refreshing softness that he could not understand.

Yet not instantly was this harmony restored; at first there was the stress of vehement opposition. The night of wind and fire drove roaring through the sky. There were bursts of triumphant tumult, but convulsion in them and no true steadiness as before. The human figures hitherto had danced with that fluid appearance which belongs to fire, and with that instantaneous rush which is of wind, the men increasing the women, and the women answering with joy; limbs and faces had melted into each other till the circular ritual looked like a glowing wheel of flame rotating audibly. But slowly now the speed of the wheel decreased; the single utterance was marred by the crying of many voices, all at different pitch, discordant, inharmonious, dismayed.

The fires somehow dwindled; there came pauses in the wind; and Hendricks became aware of a curious hissing noise, as more and more of these odd soft touches found his face and hands. Here and there, he saw, a figure stumbled, fell, then gathered itself clumsily together again with a frightened shout, breaking violently out of the circle. More and more these figures blundered and dropped out; and although they returned again, so that the dance apparently increased, these were but moments in the final violence of the dispersing hurricane.

The rejected ones dashed back wildly into the wrong places; men and women no longer stood alternate, but in groups together, falsely related. The entire movement was dislocated; the ceremony grew rapidly incoherent; meaning forsook it. The composite instrument that had transmuted the elemental forces into human, emotional storage was imperfect, broken, out of tune. The disarray turned rout.

And then it was, while Leysin continued without ceasing his burning and successful prayer, that his companion, conscious of returning harmony, rose to his feet, aware suddenly that he could also help. A portion of the powers he had absorbed still worked in him, but in a new direction. He felt confident and unafraid. He did not stumble. With unerring tread he advanced towards the lessening fires, feeling as he did so the cold soft touches multiply with a rush upon his skin. From all sides they came by hundreds, like messengers of help.

'Ernest!' he cried aloud, and his voice, though little raised, carried resonantly above the dying turmoil; 'Ernest! Come back to us. Your father calls you!'

And from threescore faces hurrying in confusion through the smoke, one paused and turned. It stood apart, hovering as though in air, while the mob of disordered figures rushed in a body along the ridge. Plunging like frightened cattle below the farther edge, then vanishing into thick darkness, they left behind them this one solitary face. A final dying flame licked out at it; a rush of smoke drove past to hide it; there was a high, wild scream—and the figure shot forward with a headlong leap and fell with a crash at Hendricks' feet. Lord Ernie, blackened by smoke and scorched by fire, lay safe outside the danger zone.

And Hendricks knelt beside him. Remorse and shame made him powerless to do more as he pulled the torn clothing over the neck and chest and heard his own heart begging for forgiveness. He realised his own weakness and faithlessness. A great temptation had found him wanting. . . .

It was owing to Leysin that the rescue was complete. The *pasteur* was instantly by his side.

'Saved as by water,' he cried, as he folded his cloak about the prostrate body, and then raised the head and shoulders; 'saved by His ministers of rain. For His miracles are love, and work through natural laws.'

He made a sign to Hendricks. Carrying the boy between them, they scrambled down the slope into the shelter of the trees below. The cold, soft touches were then explained. The *joran* had dropped as suddenly as it rose, and the torrential rain that invariably follows now poured in rivers from the sky. Water, drenching the fires and padding the savage wind, had stopped the dancers midway in their frenzied ritual. It was the element they dreaded, for it was hostile.

Rain soused the mountain ridge, extinguishing the last embers of the numerous fires. It rushed in rivulets between their feet. The heated earth gave out a hissing steam, and the only sound in the spaces where wind and fire had boomed and thundered a little while before was now the splash of water and the drip of quenching drops.

In the cover of the sheltering trees the body stirred, lifted its head, and sat up slowly. The eyes opened.

'I'm cold. I'm frightened,' whispered a shivering voice. 'Where am I?'

Only the pelt and thud of the rain sounded behind the quavering words.

'Where are the others? Have I been away? Hendricks—Mr. Hendricks—is that you——?'

He stared about him, his face now a mere luminous disc in the thick darkness. No breath of wind was loose. They spoke to him till he answered with assurance, groping to find their hands with his own, his words confused and strange with hidden meaning for a time. 'I'm all right now,' he kept repeating. 'I know exactly. It was one of my big dreams . . . I suppose I fell asleep . . . and the rain woke me. Great heavens! What a night to be out.' And then he clambered vigorously to his feet with a sudden movement of great energy again, saying that hunger was in him and he must eat. There was no complaint of heat or cold, of burning or of bruises.

The boy recovered marvellously. In ten minutes, breaking away from all support, he led, as they descended through the dripping forest in the gloom and chill of very early morning. It was the others who called to him for guidance in the tangled woods. Lord Ernie was in the lead. Throughout the difficult woods he was ever in front, and singing:

'Fire that lights but does not burn! And wind that blows the heart to flame! They both are in me now for ever and ever! Oh, praise the Lord of Fire and the Lord of Wind. . . !'

And this voice, now near, now distant, sounding through the dripping forest on their homeward journey, was an experience weird and unforgettable for those other two. Leysin, it seemed, had one sentence only which he kept repeating to himself—'Heaven grant he may direct it all for good. For they have filled him to the brim, and he is become an instrument of power.'

But Hendricks, though he understood the risk, felt only confidence. Lord Ernie's regeneration had begun.

Soaked and bedraggled, all three, they reached the village about two o'clock. The boy, utterly unmanageable, said an emphatic No to spirits, soup, or medical appliances. His skin, indeed, showed no signs of burning, nor was there the smallest symptom of cold or fever in him. 'I'm a perfect furnace,' he laughed; 'I feel health and strength personified.' And the brightness of his eyes, his radiant colour, the vigour of his voice and manner—both in some way astonishing—made all pretence of assistance unnecessary and absurd. 'It's like a new birth,' he cried to Hendricks, as he almost cantered beside him down the road to their house, 'and, by Jove, I'll wake 'em up at home and make the world go round. I know a hundred schemes. I tell you, sir, I'm simply bursting! For the first time I'm alive!'

And an hour later, when the tutor peeped in upon him, the boy was calmly sleeping. The candle-light, shaded carefully with one hand, fell upon the face. There were new lines and a new expression in it. Will and purpose showed in the stern set of the lips and jaw. It was the face of a man, and of a man one would not lightly trifle with. Purpose, will, and power were established on their thrones. To such a man the entire world might one day bow the head.

'If only it will last,' thought Hendricks, as, shaken, bewildered, and more than a little awed, he tiptoed out of the room again and went to bed. But through his dreams, sheeted in flame and veiled in angry smoke, the face of the old marquess glowered upon him from a heavy sky above ancestral towers.

11

From the obituary notices of the 9th Marquess of Oakham the following selections have their interest: He succeeded to his father, then in the Cabinet as Minister for Foreign Affairs, at the age of twenty-one. His career was brief but singular, the early magnificence of the younger Pitt offering a standard of comparison, though by no means a parallel, to his short record of astonishing achievement. His effect upon the world, first as Chief of the Government Labour Department and subsequently as Home Secretary, and Minister of War, is described as shattering, even cataclysmic. His public life lasted five years. He died at the age of twenty-nine. His personality was revolutionary and overwhelming.

For, judging by these extracts, he was a 'Napoleonic figure whose personal influence combined the impetus of Mirabeau and the dominance of Alexander. His authority held an incalculable element, precisely described as uncanny. His spirit was puissant, elemental, his activity irresistible.' Yet, according to another journal, 'he was, properly speaking, neither intellectual, astute, nor diplomatic, and possessed as little subtlety as might be expected of a miner whose psychology was called upon to explain the Trinity. In no sense was he Statesman, and even less strategist, yet his name swept Europe, changed the map of the Nearer East, its mere whisper among the Chancelleries convulsing men's counsels with an influence almost menacing.'

His enthusiasm appears to have been amazing. 'Some stupendous and untiring energy drove through him, paralysing attack, and rendering the bitterest and most skilful opposition nugatory. His hand was imperious, upsetting with a touch the chessboards set by the most able statecraft, and his voice was heard with a kind of reverence in every capital.'

The brevity of his astonishing career.called for universal comment, as did the hypnotising effect of his singular ascendency. 'In five short years of power he achieved his sway. He rushed upon the world, he shook it, he retired,' as one journal picturesquely phrased it. 'The manner of his ending, moreover—a stroke of lightning,—seemed in keeping with his life. There was neither lingering, delay, nor warning. Of distinguished stock, noble, yet ordinary enough in all but name, his power is unexplained by heredity; his family furnished no approach to greatness, as history supplied no parallel to his dynamic intensity. Nor, we are informed, among his near of kin, does any inherit his volcanic energy.'

The world, however, was apparently well relieved of his tumultuous presence, for his influence was generally surveyed as 'destructive rather than constructive.' He was unmarried, and the title went to a nephew.

The cheaper journals abounded, of course, in details of his personal and private life that were freely copied into the foreign press, and supply curious material for the student of human nature and the psychologist. The amazing revelations no doubt were picturesquely exaggerated, yet the sub-stratum of truth in them all was generally admitted. No contradictions, at any rate, appeared. They read like the story of some primitive, wild giant let loose upon the world— primitive, because his specific brain power was admittedly of no high order; wild, because he was in favour of fierce, spontaneous action, and his mere presence, on occasions, could stir a nation, not alone a crowd, to vehement, terrific methods. His energy seemed inexhaustible, his fire inextinguishable.

Legends were rife, even before he died, among the peasantry of his Scotch estates, that he was in league with the devil. His habit of keeping enormous fires in his private rooms, fires that burned day and night from January to December, and in open hearths widened to thrice their natural size, stimulated the growth of this particular myth among those of his personal environment. All manner of stories raged. But it was his strange custom out-of-doors that provided the diabolical suggestion. For, 'behind a specially walled-in space on an open ridge, denuded of pines, in a distant part of the estate, a series of gigantic heaps of wood, all ready to ignite, were—it was said—kept in a state of constant preparedness.

And on stormy nights, especially when winds were high, and invariably at the period of the equinoctial tempests, his lordship would himself light these tremendous bonfires, and spend the nocturnal hours in their blazing presence, communing, the stories variously relate, with the witches at their Sabbath, or with hordes of fire-spirits, who emerged from the Bottomless Pit in order to feed his soul with their unquenchable supplies. From these nightly orgies, it seems clear, at any rate, he returned at dawn with a splendour of energy that no one could resist, and with a mien whose grandeur invited worship rather than inspired alarm.'

His biography, it was further stated, would be written by Sir John Hendricks, Bt., who began life as Private Secretary to his father, the 8th Marquess, but whose rapid rise to position was due to his intimate association as trusted friend and adviser to the subject of these obituary notices. The biography, however, had not appeared, within five years of Lord Oakham's sudden death, and curiosity is only further stimulated by the suggestive whisper that it never will, and never can appear.

The Wendigo

1

A considerable number of hunting parties were out that year without finding so much as a fresh trail; for the moose were uncommonly shy, and the various Nimrods returned to the bosoms of their respective families with the best excuses the facts of their imaginations could suggest. Dr. Cathcart, among others, came back without a trophy; but he brought instead the memory of an experience which he declares was worth all the bull moose that had ever been shot. But then Cathcart, of Aberdeen, was interested in other things besides moose—amongst them the vagaries of the human mind. This particular story, however, found no mention in his book on *Collective Hallucination* for the simple reason (so he confided once to a fellow colleague) that he himself played too intimate a part in it to form a competent judgment of the affair as a whole. . . .

Besides himself and his guide, Hank Davis, there was young Simpson, his nephew, a divinity student destined for the "Wee Kirk" (then on his first visit to Canadian backwoods), and the latter's guide, Défago. Joseph Défago was a French "Canuck," who had strayed from his native Province of Quebec years before, and had got caught in Rat Portage when the Canadian Pacific Railway was a-building; a man who, in addition to his unparalleled knowledge of wood-craft and bush-lore, could also sing the old *voyageur* songs and tell a capital hunting yarn into the bargain. He was deeply susceptible, moreover, to that singular spell which the wilderness lays upon certain lonely natures, and he loved the wild solitudes with a kind of romantic passion that amounted almost to an obsession. The life of the backwoods fascinated him—whence, doubtless, his surpassing efficiency in dealing with their mysteries.

On this particular expedition he was Hank's choice. Hank knew him and swore by him. He also swore at him, "jest as a pal might," and since he had a vocabulary of picturesque, if utterly meaningless, oaths, the conversation between the two stalwart and hardy woodsmen was often of a rather lively description. This river of expletives, however, Hank agreed to dam a little out of respect for his old "hunting boss," Dr. Cathcart, whom of course he addressed after the fashion of the country as "Doc," and also because he understood that young Simpson was already a "bit of a parson."

He had, however, one objection to Défago, and one only—which was, that the French Canadian sometimes exhibited what Hank described as "the output of a cursed and dismal mind," meaning apparently that he sometimes was true to type, Latin type, and suffered fits of a kind of silent moroseness when nothing could induce him to utter speech. Défago, that is to say, was imaginative and melancholy. And, as a rule, it was too long a spell of "civilization" that induced the attacks, for a few days of the wilderness invariably cured them.

This, then, was the party of four that found themselves in camp the last week in October of that "shy moose year" 'way up in the wilderness north of Rat Portage—a forsaken and desolate country. There was also Punk, an Indian, who had accompanied Dr. Cathcart and Hank on their hunting trips in previous years, and who acted as cook. His duty was merely to stay in camp, catch fish, and prepare venison steaks and coffee at a few minutes' notice. He dressed in the worn-out clothes bequeathed to him by former patrons, and, except for his coarse black hair and dark skin, he looked in these city garments no more like a real redskin than a stage Negro looks like a real African. For all that, however, Punk had in him still the instincts of his dying race; his taciturn silence and his endurance survived; also, his superstition.

The party round the blazing fire that night were despondent, for a week had passed without a single sign of recent moose discovering itself. Défago had sung his song and plunged into a story, but Hank, in bad humour, reminded him so often that "he kep' mussing-up the fac's so, that it was 'most all nothin' but a petered-out lie," that the Frenchman had finally subsided into a sulky silence which nothing seemed likely to break. Dr. Cathcart and his nephew were fairly done after an exhausting day. Punk was washing up the dishes, grunting to himself under the lean-to of branches, where he later also slept. No one troubled to stir the slowly dying fire. Overhead the stars were brilliant in a sky quite wintry, and there was so little wind that ice was already forming stealthily along the shores of the still lake behind them. The

216

silence of the vast listening forest stole forward and enveloped them.

Hank broke in suddenly with his nasal voice.

"I'm in favour of breaking new ground tomorrow, Doc," he observed with energy, looking across at his employer. "We don't stand a dead *Dago's* chance around here."

"Agreed," said Cathcart, always a man of few words. "Think the idea's good."

"Sure pop, it's good," Hank resumed with confidence. "S'pose, now, you and I strike west, up Garden Lake way for a change! None of us ain't touched that quiet bit o' land yet—"

"I'm with you."

"And you, Défago, take Mr. Simpson along in the small canoe, skip across the lake, portage over into Fifty Island Water, and take a good squint down that thar southern shore. The moose 'yarded' there like hell last year, and for all we know they may be doin' it agin this year jest to spite us."

Défago, keeping his eyes on the fire, said nothing by way of reply. He was still offended, possibly, about his interrupted story.

"No one's been up that way this year, an' I'll lay my bottom dollar on *that!*" Hank added with emphasis, as though he had a reason for knowing. He looked over at his partner sharply. "Better take the little silk tent and stay away a couple o' nights," he concluded, as though the matter were definitely settled. For Hank was recognised as general organiser of the hunt, and in charge of the party.

It was obvious to anyone that Défago did not jump at the plan, but his silence seemed to convey something more than ordinary disapproval, and across his sensitive dark face there passed a curious expression like a flash of firelight—not so quickly, however, that the three men had not time to catch it.

"He funked for some reason, *I* thought," Simpson said afterwards in the tent he shared with his uncle. Dr. Cathcart made no immediate reply, although the look had interested him enough at the time for him to make a mental note of it. The expression had caused him a passing uneasiness he could not quite account for at the moment.

But Hank, of course, had been the first to notice it, and the odd thing was that instead of becoming explosive or angry over the other's reluctance, he at once began to humour him a bit.

"But there ain't no *speshul* reason why no one's been up there this year," he said with a perceptible hush in his tone; "not the reason you mean, anyway! Las' year it was the fires that kep' folks out, and this year

I guess—I guess it jest happened so, that's all!" His manner was clearly meant to be encouraging.

Joseph Défago raised his eyes a moment, then dropped them again. A breath of wind stole out of the forest and stirred the embers into a passing blaze. Dr. Cathcart again noticed the expression in the guide's face, and again he did not like it. But this time the nature of the look betrayed itself. In those eyes, for an instant, he caught the gleam of a man scared in his very soul. It disquieted him more than he cared to admit.

"Bad Indians up that way?" he asked, with a laugh to ease matters a little, while Simpson, too sleepy to notice this subtle by-play, moved off to bed with a prodigious yawn; "or—or anything wrong with the country?" he added, when his nephew was out of hearing.

Hank met his eye with something less than his usual frankness.

"He's jest skeered," he replied good-humouredly. "Skeered stiff about some ole feery tale! That's all, ain't it, ole pard?" And he gave Défago a friendly kick on the *moccasined* foot that lay nearest the fire.

Défago looked up quickly, as from an interrupted reverie, a reverie, however, that had not prevented his seeing all that went on about him.

"Skeered—*nuthin'!*" he answered, with a flush of defiance. "There's nuthin' in the Bush that can skeer Joseph Défago, and don't you forget it!" And the natural energy with which he spoke made it impossible to know whether he told the whole truth or only a part of it.

Hank turned towards the doctor. He was just going to add something when he stopped abruptly and looked round. A sound close behind them in the darkness made all three start. It was old Punk, who had moved up from his lean-to while they talked and now stood there just beyond the circle of firelight—listening.

"'Nother time, Doc!" Hank whispered, with a wink, "when the gallery ain't stepped down into the stalls!" And, springing to his feet, he slapped the Indian on the back and cried noisily, "Come up t' the fire an' warm yer skin a bit." He dragged him towards the blaze and threw more wood on. "That was a mighty good feed you give us an hour or two back," he continued heartily, as though to set the man's thoughts on another scent, "and it ain't Christian to let you stand out there freezin' yer ole soul to hell while we're gettin' all good an' toasted!" Punk moved in and warmed his feet, smiling darkly at the other's volubility which he only half understood, but saying nothing. And presently Dr. Cathcart, seeing that further conversation was impossible, followed his nephew's example and moved off to the tent, leaving the three men smoking over the now blazing fire.

It is not easy to undress in a small tent without waking one's companion, and Cathcart, hardened and warm-blooded as he was in spite of his fifty odd years, did what Hank would have described as "considerable of his twilight" in the open. He noticed, during the process, that Punk had meanwhile gone back to his lean-to, and that Hank and Défago were at it hammer and tongs, or, rather, hammer and anvil, the little French Canadian being the anvil. It was all very like the conventional stage picture of Western melodrama: the fire lighting up their faces with patches of alternate red and black; Défago, in slouch hat and *moccasins* in the part of the "badlands" villain; Hank, open-faced and hatless, with that reckless fling of his shoulders, the honest and deceived hero; and old Punk, eavesdropping in the background, supplying the atmosphere of mystery.

The doctor smiled as he noticed the details; but at the same time something deep within him—he hardly knew what—shrank a little, as though an almost imperceptible breath of warning had touched the surface of his soul and was gone again before he could seize it. Probably it was traceable to that "scared expression" he had seen in the eyes of Défago; "probably"—for this hint of fugitive emotion otherwise escaped his usually so keen analysis. Défago, he was vaguely aware, might cause trouble somehow. . . .He was not as steady a guide as Hank, for instance. . . .Further than that he could not get. . . .

He watched the men a moment longer before diving into the stuffy tent where Simpson already slept soundly. Hank, he saw, was swearing like a mad man in a New York saloon; but it was the swearing of "affection." The ridiculous oaths flew freely now that the cause of their obstruction was asleep. Presently he put his arm almost tenderly upon his comrade's shoulder, and they moved off together into the shadows where their tent stood faintly glimmering. Punk, too, a moment later followed their example and disappeared between his blankets in the opposite direction.

Dr. Cathcart then likewise turned in, weariness and sleep still fighting in his mind with an obscure curiosity to know what it was that had scared Défago about the country up Fifty Island Water way—wondering, too, why Punk's presence had prevented the completion of what Hank had to say. Then sleep overtook him. He would know tomorrow. Hank would tell him the story while they trudged after the elusive moose.

Deep silence fell about the little camp, planted there so audaciously in the jaws of the wilderness. The lake gleamed like a sheet of black glass beneath the stars. The cold air pricked. In the draughts of night that poured their silent tide from the depths of the forest, with messages from distant ridges and from lakes just beginning to freeze, there lay already the faint, bleak odours of coming winter. White men, with their dull scent, might never have divined them; the fragrance of the wood fire would have concealed from them these almost electrical hints of moss and bark and hardening swamp a hundred miles away. Even Hank and Défago, subtly in league with the soul of the woods as they were, would probably have spread their delicate nostrils in vain. . . .

But an hour later, when all slept like the dead, old Punk crept from his blankets and went down to the shore of the lake like a shadow— silently, as only Indian blood can move. He raised his head and looked about him. The thick darkness rendered sight of small avail, but, like the animals, he possessed other senses that darkness could not mute. He listened—then sniffed the air. Motionless as a hemlock stem, he stood there. After five minutes again he lifted his head and sniffed, and yet once again. A tingling of the wonderful nerves that betrayed itself by no outer sign, ran through him as he tasted the keen air. Then, merging his figure into the surrounding blackness in a way that only wild men and animals understand, he turned, still moving like a shadow, and went stealthily back to his lean-to and his bed.

And soon after he slept, the change of wind he had divined stirred gently the reflection of the stars within the lake. Rising among the far ridges of the country beyond Fifty Island Water, it came from the direction in which he had stared, and it passed over the sleeping camp with a faint and sighing murmur through the tops of the big trees that was almost too delicate to be audible. With it, down the desert paths of night, though too faint, too high even for the Indian's hair-like nerves, there passed a curious, thin odour, strangely disquieting, an odour of something that seemed unfamiliar—utterly unknown.

The French Canadian and the man of Indian blood each stirred uneasily in his sleep just about this time, though neither of them woke. Then the ghost of that unforgettably strange odour passed away and was lost among the leagues of tenantless forest beyond.

2

In the morning the camp was astir before the sun. There had been a light fall of snow during the night and the air was sharp. Punk had done his duty betimes, for the odours of coffee and fried bacon reached every tent. All were in good spirits.

"Wind's shifted!" cried Hank vigorously, watching Simpson and his guide already loading the small canoe. "It's across the lake—dead right for you fellers. And the snow'll make bully trails! If there's any moose mussing around up thar, they'll not get so much as a tail-end scent of you with the wind as it is. Good luck, Monsieur Défago!" he added, facetiously giving the name its French pronunciation for once, "*bonne chance!*"

Défago returned the good wishes, apparently in the best of spirits, the silent mood gone. Before eight o'clock old Punk had the camp to himself, Cathcart and Hank were far along the trail that led westwards, while the canoe that carried Défago and Simpson, with silk tent and grub for two days, was already a dark speck bobbing on the bosom of the lake, going due east.

The wintry sharpness of the air was tempered now by a sun that topped the wooded ridges and blazed with a luxurious warmth upon the world of lake and forest below; loons flew skimming through the sparkling spray that the wind lifted; divers shook their dripping heads to the sun and popped smartly out of sight again; and as far as eye could reach rose the leagues of endless, crowding Bush, desolate in its lonely sweep and grandeur, untrodden by foot of man, and stretching its mighty and unbroken carpet right up to the frozen shores of Hudson Bay.

Simpson, who saw it all for the first time as he paddled hard in the bows of the dancing canoe, was enchanted by its austere beauty. His heart drank in the sense of freedom and great spaces just as his lungs drank in the cool and perfumed wind. Behind him in the stern seat, singing fragments of his native chanties, Défago steered the craft of birch bark like a thing of life, answering cheerfully all his companion's questions. Both were gay and light-hearted. On such occasions, men lose the superficial, worldly distinctions; they become human beings working together for a common end. Simpson, the employer, and Défago the employed, among these primitive forces, were simply—two men, the "guider" and the "guided."

Superior knowledge, of course, assumed control, and the younger man fell without a second thought into the quasi-subordinate position. He never dreamed of objecting when Défago dropped the "Mr.," and addressed him as "Say, Simpson," or "Simpson, boss," which was invariably the case before they reached the farther shore after a stiff paddle of twelve miles against a head wind. He only laughed, and liked it; then ceased to notice it at all.

For this "divinity student" was a young man of parts and character, though as yet, of course, untraveled; and on this trip—the first time he had seen any country but his own and little Switzerland—the huge scale of things somewhat bewildered him. It was one thing, he realised, to hear about primeval forests, but quite another to see them. While to dwell in them and seek acquaintance with their wild life was, again, an initiation that no intelligent man could undergo without a certain shifting of personal values hitherto held for permanent and sacred.

Simpson knew the first faint indication of this emotion when he held the new .303 rifle in his hands and looked along its pair of fault-less, gleaming barrels. The three days' journey to their headquarters, by lake and portage, had carried the process a stage farther. And now that he was about to plunge beyond even the fringe of wilderness where they were camped into the virgin heart of uninhabited regions as vast as Europe itself, the true nature of the situation stole upon him with an effect of delight and awe that his imagination was fully capable of appreciating. It was himself and Défago against a multitude—at least, against a Titan!

The bleak splendours of these remote and lonely forests rather overwhelmed him with the sense of his own littleness. That stern quality of the tangled backwoods which can only be described as merciless and terrible, rose out of these far blue woods swimming upon the horizon, and revealed itself. He understood the silent warn-ing. He realised his own utter helplessness. Only Défago, as a symbol of a distant civilization where man was master, stood between him and a pitiless death by exhaustion and starvation.

It was thrilling to him, therefore, to watch Défago turn over the canoe upon the shore, pack the paddles carefully underneath, and then proceed to "blaze" the spruce stems for some distance on either side of an almost invisible trail, with the careless remark thrown in, "Say, Simpson, if anything happens to me, you'll find the canoe all correc' by these marks;—then strike doo west into the sun to hit the home camp agin, see?"

It was the most natural thing in the world to say, and he said it without any noticeable inflexion of the voice, only it happened to express the youth's emotions at the moment with an utterance that was symbolic of the situation and of his own helplessness as a factor in it. He was alone with Défago in a primitive world: that was all. The canoe, another symbol of man's ascendancy, was now to be left behind.

Those small yellow patches, made on the trees by the axe, were the only indications of its hiding place.

Meanwhile, shouldering the packs between them, each man carrying his own rifle, they followed the slender trail over rocks and fallen trunks and across half-frozen swamps; skirting numerous lakes that fairly gemmed the forest, their borders fringed with mist; and towards five o'clock found themselves suddenly on the edge of the woods, looking out across a large sheet of water in front of them, dotted with pine-clad islands of all describable shapes and sizes.

"Fifty Island Water," announced Défago wearily, "and the sun jest goin' to dip his bald old head into it!" he added, with unconscious poetry; and immediately they set about pitching camp for the night.

In a very few minutes, under those skilful hands that never made a movement too much or a movement too little, the silk tent stood taut and cosy, the beds of balsam boughs ready laid, and a brisk cooking fire burned with the minimum of smoke. While the young Scotchman cleaned the fish, they had caught trolling behind the canoe, Défago "guessed" he would "jest as soon" take a turn through the Bush for indications of moose. "*May* come across a trunk where they bin and rubbed horns," he said, as he moved off, "or feedin' on the last of the maple leaves"—and he was gone.

His small figure melted away like a shadow in the dusk, while Simpson noted with a kind of admiration how easily the forest absorbed him into herself. A few steps, it seemed, and he was no longer visible.

Yet there was little underbrush hereabouts; the trees stood somewhat apart, well-spaced; and in the clearings grew silver birch and maple, spearlike and slender, against the immense stems of spruce and hemlock. But for occasional prostrate monsters, and the boulders of grey rock that thrust uncouth shoulders here and there out of the ground, it might well have been a bit of park in the Old Country. Almost, one might have seen in it the hand of man. A little to the right, however, began the great burnt section, miles in extent, proclaiming its real character—*brulé*, as it is called, where the fires of the previous year had raged for weeks, and the blackened stumps now rose gaunt and ugly, bereft of branches, like gigantic match heads stuck into the ground, savage and desolate beyond words. The perfume of charcoal and rain-soaked ashes still hung faintly about it.

The dusk rapidly deepened; the glades grew dark; the crackling of the fire and the wash of little waves along the rocky lake shore were the only sounds audible. The wind had dropped with the sun, and in all that vast world of branches nothing stirred. Any moment, it seemed, the woodland gods, who are to be worshipped in silence and loneliness, might stretch their mighty and terrific outlines among the trees. In front, through doorways pillared by huge straight stems, lay the stretch of Fifty Island Water, a crescent-shaped lake some fifteen miles from tip to tip, and perhaps five miles across where they were camped.

A sky of rose and saffron, more clear than any atmosphere Simpson had ever known, still dropped its pale streaming fires across the waves, where the islands—a hundred, surely, rather than fifty—floated like the fairy barques of some enchanted fleet. Fringed with pines, whose crests fingered most delicately the sky, they almost seemed to move upwards as the light faded—about to weigh anchor and navigate the pathways of the heavens instead of the currents of their native and desolate lake.

And strips of coloured cloud, like flaunting pennons, signalled their departure to the stars. . . .

The beauty of the scene was strangely uplifting. Simpson smoked the fish and burnt his fingers into the bargain in his efforts to enjoy it and at the same time tend the frying pan and the fire. Yet, ever at the back of his thoughts, lay that other aspect of the wilderness: the indifference to human life, the merciless spirit of desolation which took no note of man. The sense of his utter loneliness, now that even Défago had gone, came close as he looked about him and listened for the sound of his companion's returning footsteps.

There was pleasure in the sensation, yet with it a perfectly comprehensible alarm. And instinctively the thought stirred in him: "What should I—*could* I, do—if anything happened and he did not come back—?"

They enjoyed their well-earned supper, eating untold quantities of fish, and drinking unmilked tea strong enough to kill men who had not covered thirty miles of hard "going," eating little on the way. And when it was over, they smoked and told stories round the blazing fire, laughing, stretching weary limbs, and discussing plans for the morrow. Défago was in excellent spirits, though disappointed at having no signs of moose to report. But it was dark and he had not gone far. The *brulé*, too, was bad. His clothes and hands were smeared with charcoal. Simpson, watching him, realised with renewed vividness their position—alone together in the wilderness.

"Défago," he said presently, "these woods, you know, are a bit too big to feel quite at home in—to feel comfortable in, I mean! . . . .Eh?" He merely gave expression to the mood of the moment; he was hardly prepared for the earnestness, the solemnity even, with which the guide took him up.

"You've hit it right, Simpson, boss," he replied, fixing his searching brown eyes on his face, "and that's the truth, sure. There's no end to 'em—no end at all." Then he added in a lowered tone as if to himself, "There's lots found out *that*, and gone plumb to pieces!"

But the man's gravity of manner was not quite to the other's liking; it was a little too suggestive for this scenery and setting; he was sorry he had broached the subject. He remembered suddenly how his uncle had told him that men were sometimes stricken with a strange fever of the wilderness, when the seduction of the uninhabited wastes caught them so fiercely that they went forth, half fascinated, half deluded, to their death. And he had a shrewd idea that his companion held something in sympathy with that queer type. He led the conversation on to other topics, on to Hank and the doctor, for instance, and the natural rivalry as to who should get the first sight of moose.

"If they went doo west," observed Défago carelessly, "there's sixty miles between us now—with ole Punk at halfway house eatin' himself full to bustin' with fish and coffee." They laughed together over the picture. But the casual mention of those sixty miles again made Simpson realise the prodigious scale of this land where they hunted; sixty miles was a mere step; two hundred little more than a step. Stories of lost hunters rose persistently before his memory. The passion and mystery of homeless and wandering men, seduced by the beauty of great forests, swept his soul in a way too vivid to be quite pleasant. He wondered vaguely whether it was the mood of his companion that invited the unwelcome suggestion with such persistence.

"Sing us a song, Défago, if you're not too tired," he asked; "one of those old *voyageur* songs you sang the other night." He handed his tobacco pouch to the guide and then filled his own pipe, while the Canadian, nothing loth, sent his light voice across the lake in one of those plaintive, almost melancholy chanties with which lumbermen and trappers lessen the burden of their labour. There was an appealing and romantic flavour about it, something that recalled the atmosphere of the old pioneer days when Indians and wilderness were leagued together, battles frequent, and the Old Country farther off than it is today. The sound travelled pleasantly over the water, but the forest at their backs seemed to swallow it down with a single gulp that permitted neither echo nor resonance.

It was in the middle of the third verse that Simpson noticed something unusual—something that brought his thoughts back with a rush from faraway scenes. A curious change had come into the man's voice. Even before he knew what it was, uneasiness caught him, and looking up quickly, he saw that Défago, though still singing, was peering about him into the Bush, as though he heard or saw something. His voice grew fainter—dropped to a hush—then ceased altogether. The same instant, with a movement amazingly alert, he started to his feet and stood upright—*sniffing the air*. Like a dog scenting game, he drew the air into his nostrils in short, sharp breaths, turning quickly as he did so in all directions, and finally "pointing" down the lake shore, eastwards. It was a performance unpleasantly suggestive and at the same time singularly dramatic. Simpson's heart fluttered disagreeably as he watched it.

"Lord, man! How you made me jump!" he exclaimed, on his feet beside him the same instant, and peering over his shoulder into the sea of darkness. "What's up? Are you frightened—?"

Even before the question was out of his mouth, he knew it was foolish, for any man with a pair of eyes in his head could see that the Canadian had turned white down to his very gills. Not even sunburn and the glare of the fire could hide that.

The student felt himself trembling a little, weakish in the knees. "What's up?" he repeated quickly. "D'you smell moose? Or anything queer, anything—wrong?" He lowered his voice instinctively.

The forest pressed round them with its encircling wall; the nearer tree stems gleamed like bronze in the firelight; beyond that—blackness, and, so far as he could tell, a silence of death. Just behind them a passing puff of wind lifted a single leaf, looked at it, then laid it softly down again without disturbing the rest of the covey. It seemed as if a million invisible causes had combined just to produce that single visible effect. *Other* life pulsed about them—and was gone.

Défago turned abruptly; the livid hue of his face had turned to a dirty grey.

"I never said I heered—or smelt—nuthin'," he said slowly and emphatically, in an oddly altered voice that conveyed somehow a touch of defiance. "I was only—takin' a look round—so to speak. It's always a mistake to be too previous with yer questions." Then he added suddenly with obvious effort, in his more natural voice, "Have you got the matches, Boss Simpson?" and proceeded to light the pipe he had half-filled just before he began to sing.

Without speaking another word, they sat down again by the fire. Défago changing his side so that he could face the direction the wind came from. For even a tenderfoot could tell that. Défago changed his position in order to hear and smell—all there was to be heard and smelt. And, since he now faced the lake with his back to the trees it was evidently nothing in the forest that had sent so strange and sudden a warning to his marvellously trained nerves.

"Guess now I don't feel like singing any," he explained presently of his own accord. "That song kinder brings back memories that's troublesome to me; I never oughter've begun it. It sets me on t' imagining things, see?"

Clearly the man was still fighting with some profoundly moving emotion. He wished to excuse himself in the eyes of the other. But the explanation, in that it was only a part of the truth, was a lie, and he knew perfectly well that Simpson was not deceived by it. For nothing could explain away the livid terror that had dropped over his face while he stood there sniffing the air. And nothing—no amount of blazing fire, or chatting on ordinary subjects—could make that camp exactly as it had been before.

The shadow of an unknown horror, naked if unguessed, that had flashed for an instant in the face and gestures of the guide, had also communicated itself, vaguely and therefore more potently, to his companion. The guide's visible efforts to dissemble the truth only made things worse. Moreover, to add to the younger man's uneasiness, was the difficulty, nay, the impossibility he felt of asking questions, and also his complete ignorance as to the . . . .Indians, wild animals, forest fires—all these, he knew, were wholly out of the question. His imagination searched vigorously, but in vain. . . .

★★★★★★★★★★★★★★★★★

Yet, somehow or other, after another long spell of smoking, talking and roasting themselves before the great fire, the shadow that had so suddenly invaded their peaceful camp began to shift. Perhaps Défago's efforts, or the return of his quiet and normal attitude accomplished this; perhaps Simpson himself had exaggerated the affair out of all proportion to the truth; or possibly the vigorous air of the wilderness brought its own powers of healing. Whatever the cause, the feeling of immediate horror seemed to have passed away as mysteriously as it had come, for nothing occurred to feed it. Simpson began to feel that

227

he had permitted himself the unreasoning terror of a child. He put it down partly to a certain subconscious excitement that this wild and immense scenery generated in his blood, partly to the spell of solitude, and partly to overfatigue. That pallor in the guide's face was, of course, uncommonly hard to explain, yet it *might* have been due in some way to an effect of firelight, or his own imagination. . . . He gave it the benefit of the doubt; he was Scotch.

When a somewhat unordinary emotion has disappeared, the mind always finds a dozen ways of explaining away its causes. . . . Simpson lit a last pipe and tried to laugh to himself. On getting home to Scotland, it would make quite a good story. He did not realise that this laughter was a sign that terror still lurked in the recesses of his soul—that, in fact, it was merely one of the conventional signs by which a man, seriously alarmed, tries to persuade himself that he is *not* so.

Défago, however, heard that low laughter and looked up with surprise on his face. The two men stood, side by side, kicking the embers about before going to bed. It was ten o'clock—a late hour for hunters to be still awake.

"What's ticklin' yer?" he asked in his ordinary tone, yet gravely.

"I—I was thinking of our little toy woods at home, just at that moment," stammered Simpson, coming back to what really dominated his mind, and startled by the question, "and comparing them to—to all this," and he swept his arm round to indicate the Bush.

A pause followed in which neither of them said anything.

"All the same I wouldn't laugh about it, if I was you," Défago added, looking over Simpson's shoulder into the shadows. "There's places in there nobody won't never see into—nobody knows what lives in there either."

"Too big—too far off?" The suggestion in the guide's manner was immense and horrible.

Défago nodded. The expression on his face was dark. He, too, felt uneasy. The younger man understood that in a *hinterland* of this size there might well be depths of wood that would never in the life of the world be known or trodden. The thought was not exactly the sort he welcomed. In a loud voice, cheerfully, he suggested that it was time for bed. But the guide lingered, tinkering with the fire, arranging the stones needlessly, doing a dozen things that did not really need doing. Evidently there was something he wanted to say, yet found it difficult to "get at."

"Say, you, Boss Simpson," he began suddenly, as the last shower of sparks went up into the air, "you don't—smell nothing, do you—nothing pertickler, I mean?" The commonplace question, Simpson realised, veiled a dreadfully serious thought in his mind. A shiver ran down his back.

"Nothing but burning wood," he replied firmly, kicking again at the embers. The sound of his own foot made him start.

"And all the evenin' you ain't smelt—nothing?" persisted the guide, peering at him through the gloom; "nothing extrordiny, and different to anything else you ever smelt before?"

"No, no, man; nothing at all!" he replied aggressively, half angrily.

Défago's face cleared. "That's good!" he exclaimed with evident relief. "That's good to hear."

"Have *you?*" asked Simpson sharply, and the same instant regretted the question.

The Canadian came closer in the darkness. He shook his head. "I guess not," he said, though without overwhelming conviction. "It must've been just that song of mine that did it. It's the song they sing in lumber camps and godforsaken places like that, when they're skeered the Wendigo's somewhere around, doin' a bit of swift traveling.—"

"And what's the Wendigo, pray?" Simpson asked quickly, irritated because again he could not prevent that sudden shiver of the nerves. He knew that he was close upon the man's terror and the cause of it. Yet a rushing passionate curiosity overcame his better judgment, and his fear.

Défago turned swiftly and looked at him as though he were suddenly about to shriek. His eyes shone, but his mouth was wide open. Yet all he said, or whispered rather, for his voice sank very low, was: "It's nuthin'—nuthin' but what those lousy fellers believe when they've bin hittin' the bottle too long—a sort of great animal that lives up yonder," he jerked his head northwards, "quick as lightning in its tracks, an' bigger'n anything else in the Bush, an' ain't supposed to be very good to look at—that's all!"

"A backwoods superstition—" began Simpson, moving hastily toward the tent in order to shake off the hand of the guide that clutched his arm. "Come, come, hurry up for God's sake, and get the lantern going! It's time we were in bed and asleep if we're going to be up with the sun tomorrow. . . ."

The guide was close on his heels. "I'm coming," he answered out of the darkness, "I'm coming." And after a slight delay he appeared with the lantern and hung it from a nail in the front pole of the tent.

The shadows of a hundred trees shifted their places quickly as he did so, and when he stumbled over the rope, diving swiftly inside, the whole tent trembled as though a gust of wind struck it.

The two men lay down, without undressing, upon their beds of soft balsam boughs, cunningly arranged. Inside, all was warm and cosy, but outside the world of crowding trees pressed close about them, marshalling their million shadows, and smothering the little tent that stood there like a wee white shell facing the ocean of tremendous forest.

Between the two lonely figures within, however, there pressed another shadow that was *not* a shadow from the night. It was the Shadow cast by the strange Fear, never wholly exorcised, that had leaped suddenly upon Défago in the middle of his singing. And Simpson, as he lay there, watching the darkness through the open flap of the tent, ready to plunge into the fragrant abyss of sleep, knew first that unique and profound stillness of a primeval forest when no wind stirs. . . .and when the night has weight and substance that enters into the soul to bind a veil about it. . . . .Then sleep took him. . . .

3

Thus, it seemed to him, at least. Yet it was true that the lap of the water, just beyond the tent door, still beat time with his lessening pulses when he realised that he was lying with his eyes open and that another sound had recently introduced itself with cunning softness between the splash and murmur of the little waves.

And, long before he understood what this sound was, it had stirred in him the centres of pity and alarm. He listened intently, though at first in vain, for the running blood beat all its drums too noisily in his ears. Did it come, he wondered, from the lake, or from the woods? . . . .

Then, suddenly, with a rush and a flutter of the heart, he knew that it was close beside him in the tent; and, when he turned over for a better hearing, it focused itself unmistakably not two feet away. It was a sound of weeping; Défago upon his bed of branches was sobbing in the darkness as though his heart would break, the blankets evidently stuffed against his mouth to stifle it.

And his first feeling, before he could think or reflect, was the rush of a poignant and searching tenderness. This intimate, human sound, heard amid the desolation about them, woke pity. It was so incongruous, so pitifully incongruous—and so vain! Tears—in this vast and cruel wilderness: of what avail? He thought of a little child crying in mid-Atlantic. . . .Then, of course, with fuller realisation, and the memory of what had gone before, came the descent of the terror upon him, and his blood ran cold.

"Défago," he whispered quickly, "what's the matter?" He tried to make his voice very gentle. "Are you in pain—unhappy—?" There was no reply, but the sounds ceased abruptly. He stretched his hand out and touched him. The body did not stir.

"Are you awake?" for it occurred to him that the man was crying in his sleep. "Are you cold?" He noticed that his feet, which were un-covered, projected beyond the mouth of the tent. He spread an extra fold of his own blankets over them. The guide had slipped down in his bed, and the branches seemed to have been dragged with him. He was afraid to pull the body back again, for fear of waking him.

One or two tentative questions he ventured softly, but though he waited for several minutes there came no reply, nor any sign of move-ment. Presently he heard his regular and quiet breathing, and putting his hand again gently on the breast, felt the steady rise and fall beneath.

"Let me know if anything's wrong," he whispered, "or if I can do anything. Wake me at once if you feel—queer."

He hardly knew what to say. He lay down again, thinking and wondering what it all meant. Défago, of course, had been crying in his sleep. Some dream or other had afflicted him. Yet never in his life would he forget that pitiful sound of sobbing, and the feeling that the whole awful wilderness of woods listened. . . .

His own mind busied itself for a long time with the recent events, of which *this* took its mysterious place as one, and though his rea-son successfully argued away all unwelcome suggestions, a sensation of uneasiness remained, resisting ejection, very deep-seated—peculiar beyond ordinary.

4

But sleep, in the long run, proves greater than all emotions. His thoughts soon wandered again; he lay there, warm as toast, exceed-ingly weary; the night soothed and comforted, blunting the edges of memory and alarm. Half an hour later he was oblivious of everything in the outer world about him.

Yet sleep, in this case, was his great enemy, concealing all approach-es, smothering the warning of his nerves.

As, sometimes, in a nightmare events crowd upon each other's heels with a conviction of dreadfulest reality, yet some inconsistent detail accuses the whole display of incompleteness and disguise, so the events that now followed, though they actually happened, persuaded the mind somehow that the detail which could explain them had been overlooked in the confusion, and that therefore they were but partly true, the rest delusion. At the back of the sleeper's mind something remains awake, ready to let slip the judgment. "All this is not *quite* real; when you wake up, you'll understand."

And thus, in a way, it was with Simpson. The events, not wholly inexplicable or incredible in themselves, yet remain for the man who saw and heard them a sequence of separate facts of cold horror, because the little piece that might have made the puzzle clear lay concealed or overlooked.

So far as he can recall, it was a violent movement, running downwards through the tent towards the door, that first woke him and made him aware that his companion was sitting bolt upright beside him—quivering. Hours must have passed, for it was the pale gleam of the dawn that revealed his outline against the canvas. This time the man was not crying; he was quaking like a leaf; the trembling he felt plainly through the blankets down the entire length of his own body. Défago had huddled down against him for protection, shrinking away from something that apparently concealed itself near the door flaps of the little tent.

Simpson thereupon called out in a loud voice some question or other—in the first bewilderment of waking he does not remember exactly what—and the man made no reply. The atmosphere and feeling of true nightmare lay horribly about him, making movement and speech both difficult. At first, indeed, he was not sure where he was—whether in one of the earlier camps, or at home in his bed at Aberdeen. The sense of confusion was very troubling.

And next—almost simultaneous with his waking, it seemed—the profound stillness of the dawn outside was shattered by a most uncommon sound. It came without warning, or audible approach; and it was unspeakably dreadful. It was a voice, Simpson declares, possibly a human voice; hoarse yet plaintive—a soft, roaring voice close outside the tent, overhead rather than upon the ground, of immense volume, while in some strange way most penetratingly and seductively sweet. It rang out, too, in three separate and distinct notes, or cries, that bore in some odd fashion a resemblance, farfetched yet recognisable, to the name of the guide: "*Dé-fa-go!*"

The student admits he is unable to describe it quite intelligently, for it was unlike any sound he had ever heard in his life, and combined a blending of such contrary qualities. "A sort of windy, crying voice," he calls it, "as of something lonely and untamed, wild and of abominable power. . . ."

And, even before it ceased, dropping back into the great gulfs of silence, the guide beside him had sprung to his feet with an answering though unintelligible cry. He blundered against the tent pole with violence, shaking the whole structure, spreading his arms out frantically for more room, and kicking his legs impetuously free of the clinging blankets. For a second, perhaps two, he stood upright by the door, his outline dark against the pallor of the dawn; then, with a furious, rushing speed, before his companion could move a hand to stop him, he shot with a plunge through the flaps of canvas—and was gone. And as he went—so astonishingly fast that the voice could actually be heard dying in the distance—he called aloud in tones of anguished terror that at the same time held something strangely like the frenzied exultation of delight—

"Oh! oh! My feet of fire! My burning feet of fire! Oh! oh! This height and fiery speed!"

And then the distance quickly buried it, and the deep silence of very early morning descended upon the forest as before.

It had all come about with such rapidity that, but for the evidence of the empty bed beside him, Simpson could almost have believed it to have been the memory of a nightmare carried over from sleep. He still felt the warm pressure of that vanished body against his side; there lay the twisted blankets in a heap; the very tent yet trembled with the vehemence of the impetuous departure. The strange words rang in his ears, as though he still heard them in the distance—wild language of a suddenly stricken mind.

Moreover, it was not only the senses of sight and hearing that reported uncommon things to his brain, for even while the man cried and ran, he had become aware that a strange perfume, faint yet pungent, pervaded the interior of the tent. And it was at this point, it seems, brought to himself by the consciousness that his nostrils were taking this distressing odour down into his throat, that he found his courage, sprang quickly to his feet—and went out.

The grey light of dawn that dropped, cold and glimmering, between the trees revealed the scene tolerably well. There stood the tent behind him, soaked with dew; the dark ashes of the fire, still warm; the lake, white beneath a coating of mist, the islands rising darkly out of it like objects packed in wool; and patches of snow beyond among the clearer spaces of the Bush—everything cold, still, waiting for the sun. But nowhere a sign of the vanished guide—still, doubtless, flying at frantic speed through the frozen woods. There was not even the sound of disappearing footsteps, nor the echoes of the dying voice. He had gone—utterly.

There was nothing; nothing but the sense of his recent presence, so strongly left behind about the camp; *and*—this penetrating, all-pervading odour.

And even this was now rapidly disappearing in its turn. In spite of his exceeding mental perturbation, Simpson struggled hard to detect its nature, and define it, but the ascertaining of an elusive scent, not recognised subconsciously and at once, is a very subtle operation of the mind. And he failed. It was gone before he could properly seize or name it. Approximate description, even, seems to have been difficult, for it was unlike any smell he knew. Acrid rather, not unlike the odour of a lion, he thinks, yet softer and not wholly unpleasing, with something almost sweet in it that reminded him of the scent of decaying garden leaves, earth, and the myriad, nameless perfumes that make up the odour of a big forest. Yet the "odour of lions" is the phrase with which he usually sums it all up.

Then—it was wholly gone, and he found himself standing by the ashes of the fire in a state of amazement and stupid terror that left him the helpless prey of anything that chose to happen. Had a muskrat poked its pointed muzzle over a rock, or a squirrel scuttled in that instant down the bark of a tree, he would most likely have collapsed without more ado and fainted. For he felt about the whole affair the touch somewhere of a great Outer Horror. . . .and his scattered powers had not as yet had time to collect themselves into a definite attitude of fighting self-control.

Nothing did happen, however. A great kiss of wind ran softly through the awakening forest, and a few maple leaves here and there rustled tremblingly to earth. The sky seemed to grow suddenly much lighter. Simpson felt the cool air upon his cheek and uncovered head; realised that he was shivering with the cold; and, making a great effort, realised next that he was alone in the Bush—*and* that he was called upon to take immediate steps to find and succour his vanished companion.

Make an effort, accordingly, he did, though an ill-calculated and futile one. With that wilderness of trees about him, the sheet of water cutting him off behind, and the horror of that wild cry in his blood, he did what any other inexperienced man would have done in similar bewilderment: he ran about, without any sense of direction, like a frantic child, and called loudly without ceasing the name of the guide:

"Défago! Défago! Défago!" he yelled, and the trees gave him back the name as often as he shouted, only a little softened—"Défago! Défago! Défago!"

He followed the trail that lay a short distance across the patches of snow, and then lost it again where the trees grew too thickly for snow to lie. He shouted till he was hoarse, and till the sound of his own voice in all that unanswering and listening world began to frighten him. His confusion increased in direct ratio to the violence of his efforts. His distress became formidably acute, till at length his exertions defeated their own object, and from sheer exhaustion he headed back to the camp again. It remains a wonder that he ever found his way. It was with great difficulty, and only after numberless false clues, that he at last saw the white tent between the trees, and so reached safety.

Exhaustion then applied its own remedy, and he grew calmer. He made the fire and breakfasted. Hot coffee and bacon put a little sense and judgment into him again, and he realised that he had been behaving like a boy. He now made another, and more successful attempt to face the situation collectedly, and, a nature naturally plucky coming to his assistance, he decided that he must first make as thorough a search as possible, failing success in which, he must find his way into the home camp as best he could and bring help.

And this was what he did. Taking food, matches and rifle with him, and a small axe to blaze the trees against his return journey, he set forth. It was eight o'clock when he started, the sun shining over the tops of the trees in a sky without clouds. Pinned to a stake by the fire he left a note in case Défago returned while he was away.

This time, according to a careful plan, he took a new direction, intending to make a wide sweep that must sooner or later cut into indications of the guide's trail; and, before he had gone a quarter of a mile, he came across the tracks of a large animal in the snow, and beside it the light and smaller tracks of what were beyond question human feet—the feet of Défago. The relief he at once experienced was natural, though brief; for at first sight, he saw in these tracks a simple explanation of the whole matter: these big marks had surely been left by a bull moose that, wind against it, had blundered upon the camp, and uttered its singular cry of warning and alarm the moment its mistake was apparent. Défago, in whom the hunting instinct was developed to the point of uncanny perfection, had scented the brute coming down the wind hours before. His excitement and disappearance were due, of course, to—to his—

Then the impossible explanation at which he grasped faded, as common sense showed him mercilessly that none of this was true. No guide, much less a guide like Défago, could have acted in so irrational a way, going off even without his rifle . . . . The whole affair demanded a far more complicated elucidation, when he remembered the details of it all—the cry of terror, the amazing language, the grey face of horror when his nostrils first caught the new odour; that muffled sobbing in the darkness, and—for this, too, now came back to him dimly—the man's original aversion for this particular bit of country . . . .

Besides, now that he examined them closer, these were not the tracks of a bull moose at all! Hank had explained to him the outline of a bull's hoofs, of a cow's or calf's, too, for that matter; he had drawn them clearly on a strip of birch bark. And these were wholly different. They were big, round, ample, and with no pointed outline as of sharp hoofs. He wondered for a moment whether bear tracks were like that. There was no other animal he could think of, for caribou did not come so far south at this season, and, even if they did, would leave hoof marks.

They were ominous signs—these mysterious writings left in the snow by the unknown creature that had lured a human being away from safety—and when he coupled them in his imagination with that haunting sound that broke the stillness of the dawn, a momentary dizziness shook his mind, distressing him again beyond belief. He felt the *threatening* aspect of it all. And, stooping down to examine the marks more closely, he caught a faint whiff of that sweet yet pungent odour that made him instantly straighten up again, fighting a sensation almost of nausea.

Then his memory played him another evil trick. He suddenly recalled those uncovered feet projecting beyond the edge of the tent, and the body's appearance of having been dragged towards the opening; the man's shrinking from something by the door when he woke later. The details now beat against his trembling mind with concerted attack. They seemed to gather in those deep spaces of the silent forest about him, where the host of trees stood waiting, listening, watching to see what he would do. The woods were closing round him.

With the persistence of true pluck, however, Simpson went forward, following the tracks as best he could, smothering these ugly emotions that sought to weaken his will. He blazed innumerable trees as he went, ever fearful of being unable to find the way back, and calling aloud at intervals of a few seconds the name of the guide. The dull tapping of the axe upon the massive trunks, and the unnatural accents of his own voice became at length sounds that he even dreaded to make, dreaded to hear. For they drew attention without ceasing to his presence and exact whereabouts, and if it were really the case that something was hunting himself down in the same way that he was hunting down another—

With a strong effort, he crushed the thought out the instant it rose. It was the beginning, he realised, of a bewilderment utterly diabolical in kind that would speedily destroy him.

★★★★★★★★★★★★★★★★★

Although the snow was not continuous, lying merely in shallow flurries over the more open spaces, he found no difficulty in following the tracks for the first few miles. They went straight as a ruled line wherever the trees permitted. The stride soon began to increase in length, till it finally assumed proportions that seemed absolutely impossible for any ordinary animal to have made. Like huge flying leaps they became. One of these he measured, and though he knew that "stretch" of eighteen feet must be somehow wrong, he was at a complete loss to understand why he found no signs on the snow between the extreme points. But what perplexed him even more, making him feel his vision had gone utterly awry, was that Défago's stride increased in the same manner, and finally covered the same incredible distances. It looked as if the great beast had lifted him with it and carried him across these astonishing intervals. Simpson, who was much longer in the limb, found that he could not compass even half the stretch by taking a running jump.

And the sight of these huge tracks, running side by side, silent evidence of a dreadful journey in which terror or madness had urged to impossible results, was profoundly moving. It shocked him in the secret depths of his soul. It was the most horrible thing his eyes had ever looked upon. He began to follow them mechanically, absentmindedly almost, ever peering over his shoulder to see if he, too, were being followed by something with a gigantic tread. . . . And soon it came about that he no longer quite realised what it was they signified—these impressions left upon the snow by something nameless and untamed, always accompanied by the footmarks of the little French Canadian, his guide, his comrade, the man who had shared his tent a few hours before, chatting, laughing, even singing by his side . . . .

5

For a man of his years and inexperience, only a canny Scot, perhaps, grounded in common sense and established in logic, could have preserved even that measure of balance that this youth somehow or other did manage to preserve through the whole adventure. Otherwise, two things he presently noticed, while forging pluckily ahead, must have sent him headlong back to the comparative safety of his tent, instead of only making his hands close more tightly upon the rifle stock, while his heart, trained for the Wee Kirk, sent a wordless prayer winging its way to heaven. Both tracks, he saw, had undergone a change, and this change, so far as it concerned the footsteps of the man, was in some undecipherable manner—appalling.

It was in the bigger tracks he first noticed this, and for a long time he could not quite believe his eyes. Was it the blown leaves that produced odd effects of light and shade, or that the dry snow, drifting like finely ground rice about the edges, cast shadows and high lights? Or was it actually the fact that the great marks had become faintly coloured? For round about the deep, plunging holes of the animal there now appeared a mysterious, reddish tinge that was more like an effect of light than of anything that dyed the substance of the snow itself. Every mark had it, and had it increasingly—this indistinct fiery tinge that painted a new touch of ghastliness into the picture.

But when, wholly unable to explain or to credit it, he turned his attention to the other tracks to discover if they, too, bore similar witness, he noticed that these had meanwhile undergone a change that was infinitely worse, and charged with far more horrible suggestion. For, in the last hundred yards or so, he saw that they had grown gradually into the semblance of the parent tread. Imperceptibly the change had come about, yet unmistakably. It was hard to see where the change first began. The result, however, was beyond question. Smaller, neater, more cleanly modelled, they formed now an exact and careful duplicate of the larger tracks beside them. The feet that produced them had, therefore, also changed. And something in his mind reared up with loathing and with terror as he saw it.

Simpson, for the first time, hesitated; then, ashamed of his alarm and indecision, took a few hurried steps ahead; the next instant stopped dead in his tracks. Immediately in front of him all signs of the trail ceased; both tracks came to an abrupt end. On all sides, for a hundred yards and more, he searched in vain for the least indication of their continuance. There was—nothing.

The trees were very thick just there, big trees all of them, spruce, cedar, hemlock; there was no underbrush. He stood, looking about him, all distraught; bereft of any power of judgment. Then he set to work to search again, and again, and yet again, but always with the same result: *nothing*. The feet that printed the surface of the snow thus far had now, apparently, left the ground!

And it was in that moment of distress and confusion that the whip of terror laid its most nicely calculated lash about his heart. It dropped with deadly effect upon the sorest spot of all, completely unnerving him. He had been secretly dreading all the time that it would come—and come it did.

Far overhead, muted by great height and distance, strangely thinned and wailing, he heard the crying voice of Défago, the guide.

The sound dropped upon him out of that still, wintry sky with an effect of dismay and terror unsurpassed. The rifle fell to his feet. He stood motionless an instant, listening as it were with his whole body, then staggered back against the nearest tree for support, disorganized hopelessly in mind and spirit. To him, in that moment, it seemed the most shattering and dislocating experience he had ever known, so that his heart emptied itself of all feeling whatsoever as by a sudden draught.

"Oh! oh! This fiery height! Oh, my feet of fire! My burning feet of fire ....!" ran in far, beseeching accents of indescribable appeal this voice of anguish down the sky. Once it called—then silence through all the listening wilderness of trees.

And Simpson, scarcely knowing what he did, presently found himself running wildly to and fro, searching, calling, tripping over roots and boulders, and flinging himself in a frenzy of undirected pursuit after the Caller. Behind the screen of memory and emotion with which experience veils events, he plunged, distracted and half-deranged, picking up false lights like a ship at sea, terror in his eyes and heart and soul. For the Panic of the Wilderness had called to him in that far voice—the Power of untamed Distance—the Enticement of the Desolation that destroys. He knew in that moment all the pains of someone hopelessly and irretrievably lost, suffering the lust and travail of a soul in the final Loneliness. A vision of Défago, eternally hunted, driven and pursued across the skiey vastness of those ancient forests fled like a flame across the dark ruin of his thoughts . . . .

It seemed ages before he could find anything in the chaos of his disorganised sensations to which he could anchor himself steady for a moment, and think . . . .

The cry was not repeated; his own hoarse calling brought no response; the inscrutable forces of the Wild had summoned their victim beyond recall—and held him fast.

★★★★★★★★★★★★★★★★

Yet he searched and called, it seems, for hours afterwards, for it was late in the afternoon when at length he decided to abandon a useless pursuit and return to his camp on the shores of Fifty Island Water. Even then he went with reluctance, that crying voice still echoing in his ears. With difficulty he found his rifle and the homeward trail. The concentration necessary to follow the badly blazed trees, and a biting hunger that gnawed, helped to keep his mind steady. Otherwise, he admits, the temporary aberration he had suffered might have been prolonged to the point of positive disaster. Gradually the ballast shifted back again, and he regained something that approached his normal equilibrium.

But for all that the journey through the gathering dusk was miserably haunted. He heard innumerable following footsteps; voices that laughed and whispered; and saw figures crouching behind trees and boulders, making signs to one another for a concerted attack the moment he had passed. The creeping murmur of the wind made him start and listen. He went stealthily, trying to hide where possible, and making as little sound as he could. The shadows of the woods, hitherto protective or covering merely, had now become menacing, challenging; and the pageantry in his frightened mind masked a host of possibilities that were all the more ominous for being obscure. The presentiment of a nameless doom lurked ill-concealed behind every detail of what had happened.

It was really admirable how he emerged victor in the end; men of riper powers and experience might have come through the ordeal with less success. He had himself tolerably well in hand, all things considered, and his plan of action proves it. Sleep being absolutely out of the question and traveling an unknown trail in the darkness equally impracticable, he sat up the whole of that night, rifle in hand, before a fire he never for a single moment allowed to die down. The severity of the haunted vigil marked his soul for life; but it was successfully accomplished; and with the very first signs of dawn, he set forth upon the long return journey to the home camp to get help. As before, he left a written note to explain his absence, and to indicate where he had left a plentiful *cache* of food and matches—though he had no expectation that any human hands would find them!

How Simpson found his way alone by the lake and forest might well make a story in itself, for to hear him tell it is to *know* the passionate loneliness of soul that a man can feel when the Wilderness holds him in the hollow of its illimitable hand—and laughs. It is also to admire his indomitable pluck.

He claims no skill, declaring that he followed the almost invisible trail mechanically, and without thinking. And this, doubtless, is the truth. He relied upon the guiding of the unconscious mind, which is instinct. Perhaps, too, some sense of orientation, known to animals and primitive men, may have helped as well, for through all that tangled region he succeeded in reaching the exact spot where Défago had hidden the canoe nearly three days before with the remark, "Strike doo west across the lake into the sun to find the camp."

There was not much sun left to guide him, but he used his compass to the best of his ability, embarking in the frail craft for the last twelve miles of his journey with a sensation of immense relief that the forest was at last behind him. And, fortunately, the water was calm; he took his line across the centre of the lake instead of coasting round the shores for another twenty miles. Fortunately, too, the other hunters were back. The light of their fires furnished a steering point without which he might have searched all night long for the actual position of the camp.

It was close upon midnight all the same when his canoe grated on the sandy cove, and Hank, Punk and his uncle, disturbed in their sleep by his cries, ran quickly down and helped a very exhausted and broken specimen of Scotch humanity over the rocks toward a dying fire.

6

The sudden entrance of his prosaic uncle into this world of wizardry and horror that had haunted him without interruption now for two days and two nights, had the immediate effect of giving to the affair an entirely new aspect. The sound of that crisp "Hulloa, my boy! And what's up *now*?" and the grasp of that dry and vigorous hand introduced another standard of judgment. A revulsion of feeling washed through him. He realised that he had let himself "go" rather badly. He even felt vaguely ashamed of himself. The native hard-headedness of his race reclaimed him.

And this doubtless explains why he found it so hard to tell that group round the fire—everything. He told enough, however, for the immediate decision to be arrived at that a relief party must start at the earliest possible moment, and that Simpson, in order to guide it capably, must first have food and, above all, sleep. Dr. Cathcart observing the lad's condition more shrewdly than his patient knew, gave him a very slight injection of morphine. For six hours he slept like the dead.

From the description carefully written out afterwards by this student of divinity, it appears that the account he gave to the astonished group omitted sundry vital and important details. He declares that, with his uncle's wholesome, matter-of-fact countenance staring him in the face, he simply had not the courage to mention them. Thus, all the search party gathered, it would seem, was that Défago had suffered in the night an acute and inexplicable attack of mania, had imagined himself "called" by someone or something, and had plunged into the bush after it without food or rifle, where he must die a horrible and lingering death by cold and starvation unless he could be found and rescued in time. "In time," moreover, meant *at once*.

In the course of the following day, however—they were off by seven, leaving Punk in charge with instructions to have food and fire always ready—Simpson found it possible to tell his uncle a good deal more of the story's true inwardness, without divining that it was drawn out of him as a matter of fact by a very subtle form of cross examination. By the time they reached the beginning of the trail, where the canoe was laid up against the return journey, he had mentioned how Défago spoke vaguely of "something he called a 'Wendigo'"; how he cried in his sleep; how he imagined an unusual scent about the camp; and had betrayed other symptoms of mental excitement. He also admitted the bewildering effect of "that extraordinary odour" upon himself, "pungent and acrid like the odour of lions."

And by the time they were within an easy hour of Fifty Island Water he had let slip the further fact—a foolish avowal of his own hysterical condition, as he felt afterwards—that he had heard the vanished guide call "for help." He omitted the singular phrases used, for he simply could not bring himself to repeat the preposterous language. Also, while describing how the man's footsteps in the snow had gradually assumed an exact miniature likeness of the animal's plunging tracks, he left out the fact that they measured a *wholly* incredible distance. It seemed a question, nicely balanced between individual pride and honesty, what he should reveal and what suppress. He mentioned the fiery tinge in the snow, for instance, yet shrank from telling that body and bed had been partly dragged out of the tent . . . .

With the net result that Dr. Cathcart, adroit psychologist that he fancied himself to be, had assured him clearly enough exactly where his mind, influenced by loneliness, bewilderment and terror, had yielded to the strain and invited delusion. While praising his conduct, he managed at the same time to point out where, when, and how his mind had gone astray. He made his nephew think himself finer than he was by judicious praise, yet more foolish than he was by minimizing the value of the evidence. Like many another materialist, that is, he lied cleverly on the basis of insufficient knowledge, *because* the knowledge supplied seemed to his own particular intelligence inadmissible.

"The spell of these terrible solitudes," he said, "cannot leave any mind untouched, any mind, that is, possessed of the higher imaginative qualities. It has worked upon yours exactly as it worked upon my own when I was your age. The animal that haunted your little camp was undoubtedly a moose, for the 'belling' of a moose may have, sometimes, a very peculiar quality of sound. The coloured appearance of the big tracks was obviously a defect of vision in your own eyes produced by excitement. The size and stretch of the tracks we shall prove when we come to them.

"But the hallucination of an audible voice, of course, is one of the commonest forms of delusion due to mental excitement—an excitement, my dear boy, perfectly excusable, and, let me add, wonderfully controlled by you under the circumstances. For the rest, I am bound to say, you have acted with a splendid courage, for the terror of feeling oneself lost in this wilderness is nothing short of awful, and, had I been in your place, I don't for a moment believe I could have behaved with one quarter of your wisdom and decision. The only thing I find it uncommonly difficult to explain is—that—damned odour."

"It made me feel sick, I assure you," declared his nephew, "positively dizzy!" His uncle's attitude of calm omniscience, merely because he knew more psychological formulae, made him slightly defiant. It was so easy to be wise in the explanation of an experience one has not personally witnessed. "A kind of desolate and terrible odour is the only way I can describe it," he concluded, glancing at the features of the quiet, unemotional man beside him.

"I can only marvel," was the reply, "that under the circumstances it did not seem to you even worse." The dry words, Simpson knew, hov-

ered between the truth, and his uncle's interpretation of "the truth."
★★★★★★★★★★★★★★★★★

And so, at last they came to the little camp and found the tent still standing, the remains of the fire, and the piece of paper pinned to a stake beside it—untouched. The *cache*, poorly contrived by inexperienced hands, however, had been discovered and opened—by musk rats, mink and squirrel. The matches lay scattered about the opening, but the food had been taken to the last crumb.

"Well, fellers, he ain't here," exclaimed Hank loudly after his fashion. "And that's as sartain as the coal supply down below! But whar he's got to by this time is 'bout as unsartain as the trade in crowns in t'other place." The presence of a divinity student was no barrier to his language at such a time, though for the reader's sake it may be severely edited. "I propose," he added, "that we start out at once an' hunt for'm like hell!"

The gloom of Défago's probable fate oppressed the whole party with a sense of dreadful gravity the moment they saw the familiar signs of recent occupancy. Especially the tent, with the bed of balsam branches still smoothed and flattened by the pressure of his body, seemed to bring his presence near to them. Simpson, feeling vaguely as if his world were somehow at stake, went about explaining particulars in a hushed tone. He was much calmer now, though overwearied with the strain of his many journeys. His uncle's method of explaining—"explaining away," rather—the details still fresh in his haunted memory helped, too, to put ice upon his emotions.

"And that's the direction he ran off in," he said to his two companions, pointing in the direction where the guide had vanished that morning in the grey dawn. "Straight down there he ran like a deer, in between the birch and the hemlock...."

Hank and Dr. Cathcart exchanged glances.

"And it was about two miles down there, in a straight line," continued the other, speaking with something of the former terror in his voice, "that I followed his trail to the place where—it stopped—dead!"

"And where you heered him callin' an' caught the stench, an' all the rest of the wicked entertainment," cried Hank, with a volubility that betrayed his keen distress.

"And where your excitement overcame you to the point of producing illusions," added Dr. Cathcart under his breath, yet not so low that his nephew did not hear it.
★★★★★★★★★★★★★★★★★

It was early in the afternoon, for they had travelled quickly, and there were still a good two hours of daylight left. Dr. Cathcart and Hank lost no time in beginning the search, but Simpson was too exhausted to accompany them. They would follow the blazed marks on the trees, and where possible, his footsteps. Meanwhile the best thing he could do was to keep a good fire going, and rest.

But after something like three hours' search, the darkness already down, the two men returned to camp with nothing to report. Fresh snow had covered all signs, and though they had followed the blazed trees to the spot where Simpson had turned back, they had not discovered the smallest indication of a human being—or for that matter, of an animal. There were no fresh tracks of any kind; the snow lay undisturbed.

It was difficult to know what was best to do, though in reality there was nothing more they *could* do. They might stay and search for weeks without much chance of success. The fresh snow destroyed their only hope, and they gathered round the fire for supper, a gloomy and despondent party. The facts, indeed, were sad enough, for Défago had a wife at Rat Portage, and his earnings were the family's sole means of support.

Now that the whole truth in all its ugliness was out, it seemed useless to deal in further disguise or pretence. They talked openly of the facts and probabilities. It was not the first time, even in the experience of Dr. Cathcart, that a man had yielded to the singular seduction of the Solitudes and gone out of his mind; Défago, moreover, was predisposed to something of the sort, for he already had a touch of melancholia in his blood, and his fibre was weakened by bouts of drinking that often lasted for weeks at a time. Something on this trip—one might never know precisely what—had sufficed to push him over the line, that was all. And he had gone, gone off into the great wilderness of trees and lakes to die by starvation and exhaustion.

The chances against his finding camp again were overwhelming; the delirium that was upon him would also doubtless have increased, and it was quite likely he might do violence to himself and so hasten his cruel fate. Even while they talked, indeed, the end had probably come. On the suggestion of Hank, his old pal, however, they proposed to wait a little longer and devote the whole of the following day, from dawn to darkness, to the most systematic search they could devise. They would divide the territory between them. They discussed their plan in great detail. All that men could do they would do. And, meanwhile, they talked about the particular form in which the singular Panic of the Wilderness had made its attack upon the mind of the unfortunate guide.

Hank, though familiar with the legend in its general outline, obviously did not welcome the turn the conversation had taken. He contributed little, though that little was illuminating. For he admitted that a story ran over all this section of country to the effect that several Indians had "seen the Wendigo" along the shores of Fifty Island Water in the "fall" of last year, and that this was the true reason of Défago's disinclination to hunt there. Hank doubtless felt that he had in a sense helped his old pal to death by overpersuading him. "When an Indian goes crazy," he explained, talking to himself more than to the others, it seemed, "it's always put that he's 'seen the Wendigo.' An' pore old Défaygo was superstitious down to his very . . . .!"

And then Simpson, feeling the atmosphere more sympathetic, told over again the full story of his astonishing tale; he left out no details this time; he mentioned his own sensations and gripping fears. He only omitted the strange language used.

"But Défago surely had already told you all these details of the Wendigo legend, my dear fellow," insisted the doctor. "I mean, he had talked about it, and thus put into your mind the ideas which your own excitement afterwards developed?"

Whereupon Simpson again repeated the facts. Défago, he declared, had barely mentioned the beast. He, Simpson, knew nothing of the story, and, so far as he remembered, had never even read about it. Even the word was unfamiliar.

Of course, he was telling the truth, and Dr. Cathcart was reluctantly compelled to admit the singular character of the whole affair. He did not do this in words so much as in manner, however. He kept his back against a good, stout tree; he poked the fire into a blaze the moment it showed signs of dying down; he was quicker than any of them to notice the least sound in the night about them—a fish jumping in the lake, a twig snapping in the bush, the dropping of occasional fragments of frozen snow from the branches overhead where the heat loosened them. His voice, too, changed a little in quality, becoming a shade less confident, lower also in tone.

Fear, to put it plainly, hovered close about that little camp, and though all three would have been glad to speak of other matters, the only thing they seemed able to discuss was this—the source of their fear. They tried other subjects in vain; there was nothing to say about them. Hank was the most honest of the group; he said next to nothing. He never once, however, turned his back to the darkness. His face was always to the forest, and when wood was needed, he didn't go farther than was necessary to get it.

7

A wall of silence wrapped them in, for the snow, though not thick, was sufficient to deaden any noise, and the frost held things pretty tight besides. No sound but their voices and the soft roar of the flames made itself heard. Only, from time to time, something soft as the flutter of a pine moth's wings went past them through the air. No one seemed anxious to go to bed. The hours slipped towards midnight.

"The legend is picturesque enough," observed the doctor after one of the longer pauses, speaking to break it rather than because he had anything to say, "for the Wendigo is simply the Call of the Wild personified, which some natures hear to their own destruction."

"That's about it," Hank said presently. "An' there's no misunderstandin' when you hear it. It calls you by name right 'nough."

Another pause followed. Then Dr. Cathcart came back to the forbidden subject with a rush that made the others jump.

"The allegory *is* significant," he remarked, looking about him into the darkness, "for the Voice, they say, resembles all the minor sounds of the Bush—wind, falling water, cries of the animals, and so forth. And, once the victim hears *that*—he's off for good, of course! His most vulnerable points, moreover, are said to be the feet and the eyes; the feet, you see, for the lust of wandering, and the eyes for the lust of beauty. The poor beggar goes at such a dreadful speed that he bleeds beneath the eyes, and his feet burn."

Dr. Cathcart, as he spoke, continued to peer uneasily into the surrounding gloom. His voice sank to a hushed tone.

"The Wendigo," he added, "is said to burn his feet—owing to the friction, apparently caused by its tremendous velocity—till they drop off, and new ones form exactly like its own."

Simpson listened in horrified amazement; but it was the pallor on Hank's face that fascinated him most. He would willingly have stopped his ears and closed his eyes, had he dared.

"It don't always keep to the ground neither," came in Hank's slow, heavy drawl, "for it goes so high that he thinks the stars have set him all a-fire. An' it'll take great thumpin' jumps sometimes, an' run along the tops of the trees, carrying its partner with it, an' then droppin' him

247

jest as a fish hawk'll drop a pickerel to kill it before eatin'. An' its food, of all the muck in the whole Bush is—moss!" And he laughed a short, unnatural laugh. "It's a moss-eater, is the Wendigo," he added, looking up excitedly into the faces of his companions. "Moss-eater," he repeated, with a string of the most outlandish oaths he could invent.

But Simpson now understood the true purpose of all this talk. What these two men, each strong and "experienced" in his own way, dreaded more than anything else was—silence. They were talking against time. They were also talking against darkness, against the invasion of panic, against the admission reflection might bring that they were in an enemy's country—against anything, in fact, rather than allow their inmost thoughts to assume control. He himself, already initiated by the awful vigil with terror, was beyond both of them in this respect. He had reached the stage where he was immune. But these two, the scoffing, analytical doctor, and the honest, dogged backwoodsman, each sat trembling in the depths of his being.

Thus, the hours passed; and thus, with lowered voices and a kind of taut inner resistance of spirit, this little group of humanity sat in the jaws of the wilderness and talked foolishly of the terrible and haunting legend. It was an unequal contest, all things considered, for the wilderness had already the advantage of first attack—and of a hostage. The fate of their comrade hung over them with a steadily increasing weight of oppression that finally became insupportable.

It was Hank, after a pause longer than the preceding ones that no one seemed able to break, who first let loose all this pent-up emotion in very unexpected fashion, by springing suddenly to his feet and letting out the most ear-shattering yell imaginable into the night. He could not contain himself any longer, it seemed. To make it carry even beyond an ordinary cry he interrupted its rhythm by shaking the palm of his hand before his mouth.

"That's for Défago," he said, looking down at the other two with a queer, defiant laugh, "for it's my belief"—the sandwiched oaths may be omitted—"that my ole partner's not far from us at this very minute."

There was a vehemence and recklessness about his performance that made Simpson, too, start to his feet in amazement, and betrayed even the doctor into letting the pipe slip from between his lips. Hank's face was ghastly, but Cathcart's showed a sudden weakness—a loosening of all his faculties, as it were. Then a momentary anger blazed into his eyes, and he too, though with deliberation born of habitual self-control, got upon his feet and faced the excited guide. For this was unpermissible, foolish, dangerous, and he meant to stop it in the bud.

What might have happened in the next minute or two one may speculate about, yet never definitely know, for in the instant of profound silence that followed Hank's roaring voice, and as though in answer to it, something went past through the darkness of the sky overhead at terrific speed—something of necessity very large, for it displaced much air, while down between the trees there fell a faint and windy cry of a human voice, calling in tones of indescribable anguish and appeal—

"Oh, oh! This fiery height! Oh, oh! My feet of fire! My burning feet of fire!"

White to the very edge of his shirt, Hank looked stupidly about him like a child. Dr. Cathcart uttered some kind of unintelligible cry, turning as he did so with an instinctive movement of blind terror towards the protection of the tent, then halting in the act as though frozen. Simpson, alone of the three, retained his presence of mind a little. His own horror was too deep to allow of any immediate reaction. He had heard that cry before.

Turning to his stricken companions, he said almost calmly—

"That's exactly the cry I heard—the very words he used!"

Then, lifting his face to the sky, he cried aloud, "Défago, Défago! Come down here to us! Come down—!"

And before there was time for anybody to take definite action one way or another, there came the sound of something dropping heavily between the trees, striking the branches on the way down, and landing with a dreadful thud upon the frozen earth below. The crash and thunder of it was really terrific.

"That's him, s'help me the good Gawd!" came from Hank in a whispering cry half choked, his hand going automatically toward the hunting knife in his belt. "And he's coming! He's coming!" he added, with an irrational laugh of horror, as the sounds of heavy footsteps crunching over the snow became distinctly audible, approaching through the blackness towards the circle of light.

And while the steps, with their stumbling motion, moved nearer and nearer upon them, the three men stood round that fire, motionless and dumb. Dr. Cathcart had the appearance of a man suddenly withered; even his eyes did not move. Hank, suffering shockingly, seemed on the verge again of violent action; yet did nothing. He, too, was hewn of stone. Like stricken children they seemed. The picture was hideous. And, meanwhile, their owner still invisible, the footsteps came closer, crunching the frozen snow. It was endless—too prolonged to be quite real—this measured and pitiless approach. It was accursed.

8

Then at length the darkness, having thus laboriously conceived, brought forth—a figure. It drew forward into the zone of uncertain light where fire and shadows mingled, not ten feet away; then halted, staring at them fixedly. The same instant it started forward again with the spasmodic motion as of a thing moved by wires, and coming up closer to them, full into the glare of the fire, they perceived then that—it was a man; and apparently that this man was—Défago.

Something like a skin of horror almost perceptibly drew down in that moment over every face, and three pairs of eyes shone through it as though they saw across the frontiers of normal vision into the Unknown.

Défago advanced, his tread faltering and uncertain; he made his way straight up to them as a group first, then turned sharply and peered close into the face of Simpson. The sound of a voice issued from his lips—

"Here I am, Boss Simpson. I heered someone calling me." It was a faint, dried up voice, made wheezy and breathless as by immense exertion. "I'm havin' a reg'lar hellfire kind of a trip, I am." And he laughed, thrusting his head forward into the other's face.

But that laugh started the machinery of the group of waxwork figures with the wax-white skins. Hank immediately sprang forward with a stream of oaths so farfetched that Simpson did not recognise them as English at all, but thought he had lapsed into Indian or some other lingo. He only realised that Hank's presence, thrust thus between them, was welcome—uncommonly welcome. Dr. Cathcart, though more calmly and leisurely, advanced behind him, heavily stumbling.

Simpson seems hazy as to what was actually said and done in those next few seconds, for the eyes of that detestable and blasted visage peering at such close quarters into his own utterly bewildered his senses at first. He merely stood still. He said nothing. He had not the trained will of the older men that forced them into action in defiance of all emotional stress.

He watched them moving as behind a glass that half destroyed their reality; it was dreamlike; perverted. Yet, through the torrent of Hank's meaningless phrases, he remembers hearing his uncle's tone of authority—hard and forced—saying several things about food and warmth, blankets, whisky and the rest very . . . .and, further, that whiffs of that penetrating, unaccustomed odour, vile yet sweetly bewildering, assailed his nostrils during all that followed.

It was no less a person than himself, however—less experienced and adroit than the others though he was—who gave instinctive utterance to the sentence that brought a measure of relief into the ghastly situation by expressing the doubt and thought in each one's heart.

"It *is*—YOU, isn't it, Défago?" he asked under his breath, horror breaking his speech.

And at once Cathcart burst out with the loud answer before the other had time to move his lips. "Of course, it is! Of course, it is! Only—can't you see—he's nearly dead with exhaustion, cold and terror! Isn't *that* enough to change a man beyond all recognition?" It was said in order to convince himself as much as to convince the others. The overemphasis alone proved that. And continually, while he spoke and acted, he held a handkerchief to his nose. That odour pervaded the whole camp.

For the "Défago" who sat huddled by the big fire, wrapped in blankets, drinking hot whisky and holding food in wasted hands, was no more like the guide they had last seen alive than the picture of a man of sixty is like a daguerreotype of his early youth in the costume of another generation. Nothing really can describe that ghastly caricature, that parody, masquerading there in the firelight as Défago. From the ruins of the dark and awful memories he still retains, Simpson declares that the face was more animal than human, the features drawn about into wrong proportions, the skin loose and hanging, as though he had been subjected to extraordinary pressures and tensions.

It made him think vaguely of those bladder faces blown up by the hawkers on Ludgate Hill, that change their expression as they swell, and as they collapse emit a faint and wailing imitation of a voice. Both face and voice suggested some such abominable resemblance. But Cathcart long afterwards, seeking to describe the indescribable, asserts that thus might have looked a face and body that had been in air so rarefied that, the weight of atmosphere being removed, the entire structure threatened to fly asunder and become—*incoherent* very . . . .

It was Hank, though all distraught and shaking with a tearing volume of emotion he could neither handle nor understand, who brought things to a head without much ado. He went off to a little distance from the fire, apparently so that the light should not dazzle him too much, and shading his eyes for a moment with both hands, shouted in a loud voice that held anger and affection dreadfully mingled:

"You ain't Défaygo! You ain't Défaygo at all! I don't give a—damn, but that ain't you, my ole pal of twenty years!" He glared upon the huddled figure as though he would destroy him with his eyes. "An' if it is, I'll swab the floor of hell with a wad of cotton wool on a toothpick, s'help me the good Gawd!" he added, with a violent fling of horror and disgust.

It was impossible to silence him. He stood there shouting like one possessed, horrible to see, horrible to hear—*because it was the truth*. He repeated himself in fifty different ways, each more outlandish than the last. The woods rang with echoes. At one time it looked as if he meant to fling himself upon "the intruder," for his hand continually jerked towards the long hunting knife in his belt.

But in the end, he did nothing, and the whole tempest completed itself very shortly with tears. Hank's voice suddenly broke, he collapsed on the ground, and Cathcart somehow or other persuaded him at last to go into the tent and lie quiet. The remainder of the affair, indeed, was witnessed by him from behind the canvas, his white and terrified face peeping through the crack of the tent door flap.

Then Dr. Cathcart, closely followed by his nephew who so far had kept his courage better than all of them, went up with a determined air and stood opposite to the figure of Défago huddled over the fire. He looked him squarely in the face and spoke. At first his voice was firm.

"Défago, tell us what's happened—just a little, so that we can know how best to help you?" he asked in a tone of authority, almost of command. And at that point, it *was* command. At once afterwards, however, it changed in quality, for the figure turned up to him a face so piteous, so terrible and so little like humanity, that the doctor shrank back from him as from something spiritually unclean. Simpson, watching close behind him, says he got the impression of a mask that was on the verge of dropping off, and that underneath they would discover something black and diabolical, revealed in utter nakedness. "Out with it, man, out with it!" Cathcart cried, terror running neck and neck with entreaty. "None of us can stand this much longer very . . . .!" It was the cry of instinct over reason.

And then "Défago," smiling *whitely*, answered in that thin and fading voice that already seemed passing over into a sound of quite another character—

252

"I seen that great Wendigo thing," he whispered, sniffing the air about him exactly like an animal. "I been with it too—"

Whether the poor devil would have said more, or whether Dr. Cathcart would have continued the impossible cross examination cannot be known, for at that moment the voice of Hank was heard yelling at the top of his voice from behind the canvas that concealed all but his terrified eyes. Such a howling was never heard.

"His feet! Oh, Gawd, his feet! Look at his great changed—feet!"

Défago, shuffling where he sat, had moved in such a way that for the first time his legs were in full light and his feet were visible. Yet Simpson had no time, himself, to see properly what Hank had seen. And Hank has never seen fit to tell. That same instant, with a leap like that of a frightened tiger, Cathcart was upon him, bundling the folds of blanket about his legs with such speed that the young student caught little more than a passing glimpse of something dark and oddly massed where *moccasined* feet ought to have been, and saw even that but with uncertain vision.

Then, before the doctor had time to do more, or Simpson time to even think a question, much less ask it, Défago was standing upright in front of them, balancing with pain and difficulty, and upon his shapeless and twisted visage an expression so dark and so malicious that it was, in the true sense, monstrous.

"Now *you* seen it too," he wheezed, "you seen my fiery, burning feet! And now—that is, unless you kin save me an' prevent—it's 'bout time for—"

His piteous and beseeching voice was interrupted by a sound that was like the roar of wind coming across the lake. The trees overhead shook their tangled branches. The blazing fire bent its flames as before a blast. And something swept with a terrific, rushing noise about the little camp and seemed to surround it entirely in a single moment of time. Défago shook the clinging blankets from his body, turned towards the woods behind, and with the same stumbling motion that had brought him—was gone: gone, before anyone could move muscle to prevent him, gone with an amazing, blundering swiftness that left no time to act.

The darkness positively swallowed him; and less than a dozen seconds later, above the roar of the swaying trees and the shout of the sudden wind, all three men, watching and listening with stricken hearts, heard a cry that seemed to drop down upon them from a great height of sky and distance—

"Oh, oh! This fiery height! Oh, oh! My feet of fire! My burning feet of fire very . . . .!" then died away, into untold space and silence.

Dr. Cathcart—suddenly master of himself, and therefore of the others—was just able to seize Hank violently by the arm as he tried to dash headlong into the Bush.

"But I want ter know,—you!" shrieked the guide. "I want ter see! That ain't him at all, but some—devil that's shunted into his place very . . . .!"

Somehow or other—he admits he never quite knew how he accomplished it—he managed to keep him in the tent and pacify him. The doctor, apparently, had reached the stage where reaction had set in and allowed his own innate force to conquer. Certainly he "managed" Hank admirably. It was his nephew, however, hitherto so wonderfully controlled, who gave him most cause for anxiety, for the cumulative strain had now produced a condition of *lachrymose* hysteria which made it necessary to isolate him upon a bed of boughs and blankets as far removed from Hank as was possible under the circumstances.

And there he lay, as the watches of that haunted night passed over the lonely camp, crying startled sentences, and fragments of sentences, into the folds of his blanket. A quantity of gibberish about speed and height and fire mingled oddly with biblical memories of the classroom. "People with broken faces all on fire are coming at a most awful, awful, pace towards the camp!" he would moan one minute; and the next would sit up and stare into the woods, intently listening, and whisper, "How terrible in the wilderness are—are the feet of them that—" until his uncle came across to change the direction of his thoughts and comfort him.

The hysteria, fortunately, proved but temporary. Sleep cured him, just as it cured Hank.

Till the first signs of daylight came, soon after five o'clock, Dr. Cathcart kept his vigil. His face was the colour of chalk, and there were strange flushes beneath the eyes. An appalling terror of the soul battled with his will all through those silent hours. These were some of the outer signs very . . . .

At dawn he lit the fire himself, made breakfast, and woke the others, and by seven they were well on their way back to the home camp—three perplexed and afflicted men, but each in his own way having reduced his inner turmoil to a condition of more or less systematised order again.

They talked little, and then only of the most wholesome and common things, for their minds were charged with painful thoughts that clamoured for explanation, though no one dared refer to them. Hank, being nearest to primitive conditions, was the first to find himself, for he was also less complex. In Dr. Cathcart "civilization" championed his forces against an attack singular enough. To this day, perhaps, he is not *quite* sure of certain things. Anyhow, he took longer to "find himself."

Simpson, the student of divinity, it was who arranged his conclusions probably with the best, though not most scientific, appearance of order. Out there, in the heart of unreclaimed wilderness, they had surely witnessed something crudely and essentially primitive. Something that had survived somehow the advance of humanity had emerged terrifically, betraying a scale of life still monstrous and immature.

He envisaged it rather as a glimpse into prehistoric ages, when superstitions, gigantic and uncouth, still oppressed the hearts of men; when the forces of nature were still untamed, the Powers that may have haunted a primeval universe not yet withdrawn. To this day he thinks of what he termed years later in a sermon "savage and formidable Potencies lurking behind the souls of men, not evil perhaps in themselves, yet instinctively hostile to humanity as it exists."

With his uncle he never discussed the matter in detail, for the barrier between the two types of mind made it difficult. Only once, years later, something led them to the frontier of the subject—of a single detail of the subject, rather—

"Can't you even tell me what—*they* were like?" he asked; and the reply, though conceived in wisdom, was not encouraging, "It is far better you should not try to know, or to find out."

"Well—that odour very ....?" persisted the nephew. "What do you make of that?"

Dr. Cathcart looked at him and raised his eyebrows.

"Odours," he replied, "are not so easy as sounds and sights of telepathic communication. I make as much, or as little, probably, as you do yourself."

He was not quite so glib as usual with his explanations. That was all.

★★★★★★★★★★★★★★★★

At the fall of day, cold, exhausted, famished, the party came to the end of the long portage and dragged themselves into a camp that at first glimpse seemed empty. Fire there was none, and no Punk came forward to welcome them. The emotional capacity of all three was too over-spent to recognise either surprise or annoyance; but the cry of spontaneous affection that burst from the lips of Hank, as he rushed ahead of them towards the fireplace, came probably as a warning that the end of the amazing affair was not quite yet. And both Cathcart and his nephew confessed afterwards that when they saw him kneel down in his excitement and embrace something that reclined, gently moving, beside the extinguished ashes, they felt in their very bones that this "something" would prove to be Défago—the true Défago, returned.

And so, indeed, it was.

It is soon told. Exhausted to the point of emaciation, the French Canadian—what was left of him, that is—fumbled among the ashes, trying to make a fire. His body crouched there, the weak fingers obeying feebly the instinctive habit of a lifetime with twigs and matches. But there was no longer any mind to direct the simple operation. The mind had fled beyond recall. And with it, too, had fled memory. Not only recent events, but all previous life was a blank.

This time it was the real man, though incredibly and horribly shrunken. On his face was no expression of any kind whatever—fear, welcome, or recognition. He did not seem to know who it was that embraced him, or who it was that fed, warmed and spoke to him the words of comfort and relief. Forlorn and broken beyond all reach of human aid, the little man did meekly as he was bidden. The "something" that had constituted him "individual" had vanished for ever.

In some ways it was more terribly moving than anything they had yet seen—that idiot smile as he drew wads of coarse moss from his swollen cheeks and told them that he was "a damned moss-eater"; the continued vomiting of even the simplest food; and, worst of all, the piteous and childish voice of complaint in which he told them that his feet pained him—"burn like fire"—which was natural enough when Dr. Cathcart examined them and found that both were dreadfully frozen. Beneath the eyes there were faint indications of recent bleeding.

The details of how he survived the prolonged exposure, of where he had been, or of how he covered the great distance from one camp to the other, including an immense detour of the lake on foot since he had no canoe—all this remains unknown. His memory had vanished completely. And before the end of the winter whose beginning witnessed this strange occurrence, Défago, bereft of mind, memory and soul, had gone with it. He lingered only a few weeks.

And what Punk was able to contribute to the story throws no further light upon it. He was cleaning fish by the lake shore about five o'clock in the evening—an hour, that is, before the search party returned—when he saw this shadow of the guide picking its way weakly into camp. In advance of him, he declares, came the faint whiff of a certain singular odour.

That same instant old Punk started for home. He covered the entire journey of three days as only Indian blood could have covered it. The terror of a whole race drove him. He knew what it all meant. Défago had "seen the Wendigo."

LEONAUR

ALSO FROM LEONAUR
AVAILABLE IN SOFTCOVER OR HARDCOVER WITH DUST JACKET

MR MUKERJI'S GHOSTS *by S. Mukerji*—Supernatural tales from the British Raj period by India's Ghost story collector.

KIPLINGS GHOSTS *by Rudyard Kipling*—Twelve stories of Ghosts, Hauntings, Curses, Werewolves & Magic.

THE COLLECTED SUPERNATURAL AND WEIRD FICTION OF WASHINGTON IRVING: VOLUME 1 *by Washington Irving*—Including one novel 'A History of New York', and nine short stories of the Strange and Unusual.

THE COLLECTED SUPERNATURAL AND WEIRD FICTION OF WASHINGTON IRVING: VOLUME 2 *by Washington Irving*—Including three novelettes 'The Legend of the Sleepy Hollow', 'Dolph Heyliger', 'The Adventure of the Black Fisherman' and thirty-two short stories of the Strange and Unusual.

THE COLLECTED SUPERNATURAL AND WEIRD FICTION OF JOHN KENDRICK BANGS: VOLUME 1 *by John Kendrick Bangs*—Including one novel 'Toppleton's Client or A Spirit in Exile', and ten short stories of the Strange and Unusual.

THE COLLECTED SUPERNATURAL AND WEIRD FICTION OF JOHN KENDRICK BANGS: VOLUME 2 *by John Kendrick Bangs*—Including four novellas 'A House-Boat on the Styx', 'The Pursuit of the House-Boat', 'The Enchanted Typewriter' and 'Mr. Munchausen' of the Strange and Unusual.

THE COLLECTED SUPERNATURAL AND WEIRD FICTION OF JOHN KENDRICK BANGS: VOLUME 3 *by John Kendrick Bangs*—Including twor novellas 'Olympian Nights', 'Roger Camerden: A Strange Story', and ten short stories of the Strange and Unusual.

THE COLLECTED SUPERNATURAL AND WEIRD FICTION OF MARY SHELLEY: VOLUME 1 *by Mary Shelley*—Including one novel 'Frankenstein or the Modern Prometheus', and fourteen short stories of the Strange and Unusual.

THE COLLECTED SUPERNATURAL AND WEIRD FICTION OF MARY SHELLEY: VOLUME 2 *by Mary Shelley*—Including one novel 'The Last Man', and three short stories of the Strange and Unusual.

THE COLLECTED SUPERNATURAL AND WEIRD FICTION OF AMELIA B. EDWARDS *by Amelia B. Edwards*—Contains two novelettes 'Monsieur Maurice', and 'The Discovery of the Treasure Isles', one ballad 'A Legend of Boisguilbert'and seventeen short stories to cill the blood.